Thursday's Child

Thursday's
Child

Jeanne Whitmee

LONDON NEW YORK SYDNEY TORONTO

This edition published 1996
by BCA
by arrangement with Judy Piatkus (Publishers) Ltd

First Reprint 1997
Second Reprint 1998
Third Reprint 1998

CN 3917

Set in 11/12 pt Times by Intype London Ltd
Printed & bound in Great Britain by
Antony Rowe Ltd, Chippenham, Wiltshire

Chapter 1

Hackney, London, June 1989

'Yes, but where are we going?'

Fleur's voice was tinged with impatience as her friend Bobby held on to her arm and hurried her along the street.

'Not much further. You'll see.'

Fleur shook off the other girl's hand and stopped walking. 'Look, Bobby. I've still got some packing to do. I want to catch an early train in the morning, 'cause I've got to find a place to stay when I get there. I've got no time for pratting about.'

Bobby looked hurt. 'Sounds like you can't wait to get away from us all,' she said.

'It's not that.' Fleur relented. 'Oh – all right then.' She sighed indulgently. 'Let's get it over with. But just one drink – right?'

'Right.' They'd stopped outside the Royal Albert and Bobby's big brown eyes danced with excitement. 'Okay. Now, close your eyes.'

'Oh, come *on!*'

'No, close them. You've got to.'

Fleur sighed and did as she was told, allowing Bobby to lead her by the arm. She was aware of being taken inside the pub and led down a corridor. A door was opened and she was pushed inside. When she opened her eyes the sight that met them took her breath away.

The function room of the Royal Albert had been decorated with balloons and streamers and there, assembled in front of her were all the friends and neighbours she had grown up with. Many of her schoolfriends were there; neighbours from Brightman Lane and the flats, including Bobby's brothers and sisters and her mum, Ada. The Wallaces from the fish bar were there; the Smiths from the shop;

1

Hosein and Melini Patel and many others. At her entrance into the room they all clapped and cheered, making her blush with embarrassment. Hands reached out for her and led her into the room as Bobby's elder brother, who was in charge of the disco, put on Fleur's current favourite record, *Lady In Red.*

'Now you know why I made you wear your red dress,' Bobby said delightedly.

'And why *you're* all dressed up. I thought it was a bit over the top for a quick drink at The Royal.'

'Yeah. Great, eh?' Bobby was already dancing to the music. She never could resist a rhythmic beat.

Fleur looked affectionately at her vivacious friend in the tiny skin-tight black lycra mini skirt. Her crinkly black hair was drawn tightly back into tiny plaits and the bright yellow cropped top she wore exposed six inches of golden brown midriff. 'Oh Bobby. Did you really do all this for me?'

'It was my idea. Mine and Mum's,' Bobby admitted with a grin. 'But we had plenty of help. We couldn't let you go without doing something and once they knew everyone offered to pitch in,' she said. 'A lot of people round here are fond of you, you know. They wanted the chance to say goodbye properly.'

'Including me. Come and dance. Fleur.' Gary Johnson reached out to take Fleur's hand and led her into the throng of dancers. 'So – you're really going then?' he said as they danced. 'Tell you the truth I thought you might bottle out when it came to the crunch. Seems I underestimated you!'

Fleur smiled. She and Gary had gone out together for a while earlier that year. They'd known each other since schooldays. He worked for a computer firm, a nice, hard working guy, just the kind that Dolly, her grandmother, would have approved of. Good looking too. Fleur knew that some of their friends had seen them as an item. But she didn't intend to get into a serious relationship with anyone. Not yet. Too many girls she knew were already saddled with babies and debt. There were things she needed to do before that day came and she'd always made that clear to Gary. She smiled at him.

'I need to get away from Hackney,' she said. 'It's what Grandma wanted. Me too. I think I always have.'

'I think so too,' he said perceptively. He smiled down at her. 'Going to find yourself – that the idea?'

She glanced up quickly to see if he was laughing at her. He wasn't. The smile in his eyes was wistful as if he sensed that there was more to her leaving than she'd ever tell him.

2

'There's no need, you know. It's like Bobby said. Folks round here like you. They take you at face value. Just look around you. All the proof you need is right here.'

'I know.' Fleur shrugged. 'I can't explain, Gary. It's more to do with never knowing my parents than with colour.'

He shrugged. 'Okay – whatever you want. It's your life. But I'll miss you,' he said softly.

'I'll miss you too – all of you. Maybe I'll come back someday. Who knows? Everything changes though, Gary. Grandma's gone. Bobby will be off to college soon. Nothing stays the same.'

'Some things do.' He smiled, shrugging resignedly. 'S'pose you're right though.'

It was a happy evening, ending at midnight with Bobby making a short speech and presenting Fleur with a present they'd all clubbed together to buy. The main gift was a leather writing case complete with stationery and pens. 'To make sure you don't forget to write,' Bobby said with an impish grin. In another tiny box wrapped in gold paper Fleur found a little amber heart pendant on a silver chain from Bobby and Ada. Everyone hugged Fleur and wished her well before they left, then Gary and Bobby walked her home.

When they had gone she stood in the almost empty flat and tried to imagine what it would be like not to live here any more, not to see her friends each day.

It was a warm night and from the street below the accustomed roar of traffic from Hackney Road and the familiar smells floated up to Fleur through the open window. There were just a few last chores to be done. Most of her belongings were packed in two suitcases, the last few sticks of furniture would be collected tomorrow. In the morning she would leave here for ever. She tried hard to view her future positively, swallowing the chill of uncertainty she had felt ever since her grandmother died, strengthened by this evening's touching farewell party. *It will be a challenge, an adventure*, she told herself. But the uncertain child that still lingered somewhere deep inside her, wept for the loss of comfort and love and security.

It seemed such a very short time since she and Bobby had played down there in those streets, taking it in turn to ride Bobby's brother's ancient rusting bike, begging the boys to let them join in their games of street football, swinging on the lamp posts and swapping the treasures that children love to collect. This street in the East End was the only playground Fleur had ever known. It had been her home for all of her nineteen years.

It was here in the cramped little flat two floors above the Smiths' grocer's shop that she had shared her life with her grandparents, London-born Dolly Sylvester and her West Indian husband, Maurice. Like so many other East End families, the Sylvesters had been poor, but Fleur's childhood had been a happy one. What she had lacked in luxuries had been more than made up for by the love Dolly and Maurice had lavished on her. Now both her grandparents were gone and life must change. Tomorrow she would say goodbye to the East End and all her friends and leave her childhood behind for ever.

Fleur had been three years old before she had realised that children were supposed to have a mother and father as well as grandparents. When she had asked Grandma where hers were she had been told that they were away working hard and that she would see them some day soon when they came home. She knew that her father's name was Dean and that he was the Sylvesters' only child. She also knew that he earned his living by playing the guitar and had left home shortly before her birth in 1966 to make his name in the world of pop music.

When his talent had first begun to show itself Dolly and Maurice had been immensely proud of their handsome son. They were convinced that he had inherited his talent for music from his Jamaican father, to whom rhythm came as naturally as breathing. Maurice would tap a rhythm out instinctively with anything that came to hand, and although he had never had a lesson in his life, could coax a tune out of anything from a comb and paper to a trombone.

Eager to encourage his son's gift for music, Maurice had put in as much overtime as he could get on his job as a labourer for British Rail in order to give him the best possible chance of success. Dolly had done her share too, putting in extra shifts at the Royal Albert where she worked in the kitchen, and using her culinary skills catering for local weddings and other informal festivities.

By the time Dean was eighteen he had formed his own group, playing first in the pubs and at small local gigs. Two years later, full of the brash confidence of youth, he had left home and set out to make his fortune.

It had been big, gentle Grandpa Maurice who had told Fleur all this, taking his small granddaughter onto his knee, his molasses-dark eyes smiling and the deep voice, that still held the warmth of the Caribbean sun, throbbing with pride.

'Your daddy will be famous one day, sugarplum,' he told her confidently. 'Then he'll take us all back to Jamaica for a holiday and you can meet *aa-all* your cousins and aunts and uncles. So

4

many of them. What a party we'll all have then!' He would throw back his big head with its tight mass of greying curls and chuckle with delighted anticipation. 'Oh you're going to *love* it there, sugar. The sun always shines and the sea is so blue and warm.' His brown eyes would grow soft with reminiscence. 'Maybe we'll even stay – make our home there when your daddy comes home.'

Dolly, although equally proud of her son, listened to it all with silent scepticism as she went about her work in the kitchen. She did not share her husband's optimism or his illusions about their son. Maurice had always spoiled Dean. She knew why. He had wanted a better life for the boy than he had had as the eldest of a family of nine hungry, barefoot children growing up in his native Jamaica. He wanted his son to be given the chance to foster his talent and he thought, naively, that one day Dean would share his good fortune with the parents who had sacrificed so much to give him that chance, in the same way that he still scraped together what little money he could afford to send home to his aged mother.

But so far all Dean had given them was Fleur, his illegitimate daughter. Another mouth to feed out of their meagre earnings while he went on his self-seeking way without a qualm. As for Fleur's mother, it had been left to Dolly to fill in the details and answer the endless questions fired at her by her increasingly curious grand-daughter.

'What's my mum like, Grandma?'

'Well – I haven't seen her for a long time. She was very young when you were born,' Dolly said as she rolled out pastry at the kitchen table.

'What's her name?' Standing on a stool on the other side of the kitchen table, Fleur rolled out her own ball of pastry till it was grey and leathery. She had asked all these questions before, but she never seemed to tire of hearing the answers, and she always knew at once if her grandmother dared to vary them in the smallest detail.

'Her name is Julia, lovie. You already know that.' Dolly looked at the child. The little triangular face with its intelligent brown eyes and the unruly mop of black curls reminded her sharply of Dean at the same age. He'd been such a beautiful little boy, so loving and sweet. The man he'd grown into seemed like quite another person. But at least he had given them Fleur to make up for the disappointment.

The little girl did not resemble her mother at all. Julia had been blonde and delicately built, whilst her daughter, already sturdy and tall for her age, showed signs of growing into a tall, statuesque

5

woman. Fleur was bright and clever too, missing nothing with her sharp ears and those huge dark, enquiring eyes. The hurtful truth could not be kept from her for ever, but Dolly vowed she would protect her for as long as she could.

'I like that name.' Fleur said, her head on one side. 'Why am I called Fleur, Grandma? No one in my class is called Fleur and Bobby says it's a funny name.'

''Course it's not funny,' Dolly said indignantly. 'It's different and it's special. It's French, see? It means flower.'

'Bobby's name sounds funny, doesn't it, Grandma? It's like a boy's name.'

Fleur's best friend, Bobby was Dolly's oldest friend's youngest child. 'Bobby's real name is Roberta,' Dolly explained. 'She was named after her daddy. None of us can help our names. We have to have what our mums and dads give us.'

'So why did I get called Fleur, Grandma?'

'Your mum chose the name because it reminded her of the Flower Children.'

'Who are the Flower Children?'

Dolly sighed. Fleur's questions seemed endless. Satisfying her curiosity was like trying to fill a bottomless pit. She always tried to answer the child's questions as best she could, assuming that she was too young to understand what had really happened, but she was acutely aware that with each year that passed the time was rapidly approaching when Fleur would no longer be satisfied with half-truths. She was unsure herself what it was that the strangely garbed people with flowers in their unkempt hair and beards had really stood for. In her view the philosophy of the free-living hippies seemed to be to take what they wanted from life regardless of who it upset. They had certainly played a big part in leading Dean astray, of that she was convinced.

'*Grandma!* Who are the Flower Children?'

Dolly looked up and saw that Fleur's bright eyes were still upon her, waiting for an answer; she went on: 'Oh yes, the Flower Children. Well, they were all the rage at the time when you were born,' she explained. 'They dressed up in long frocks, liked bright colours and wore flowers in their hair, and they liked to gather together and listen to the kind of music your daddy played. Your mum and daddy met at one of their festivals. And that's why your mum gave you the name of Fleur.'

'I think they sound nice.' Fleur looked up at her grandmother and startled her by asking, 'Is my mum white, like you, Grandma? Or black, like Grandpa?'

6

'She's white – like me.' Dolly avoided the child's eyes, busying herself with her baking.

'So – when will she come and see me, Grandma – soon?'

Dolly avoided the bright enquiring eyes. 'Maybe, lovie, maybe,' she said.

'Why doesn't she write to me, Grandma?'

Dolly shook her head. 'I expect she leaves that to your dad, lovie.'

From time to time postcards arrived from Dean. They all had brightly coloured pictures of exotic places, the names of which meant little to Fleur. She would study the gaudy pictures carefully, then turn the cards over and touch the spidery writing on the reverse side with her fingertips as though by so doing she could somehow communicate with her unknown father. Dolly would pin all the postcards up on the dresser shelves in the kitchen so that everyone could see them and Fleur knew that her grandma would have liked to write back. Later, when she had mastered her letters sufficiently she longed to send him a letter herself. But there never seemed to be an address to which they could write on any of his cards. The brief messages Dean scrawled on the backs of the cards would read, *'Appearing here for two nights.'* or *'Played a one night stand at this theatre.'* So even if they had tried to write he would have left long before the letters could have reached him. Dolly kept hoping that he would eventually get back to London and come and see them, but he never did. Neither, to her fury, did he ever remember the chid's birthday or send her a Christmas present.

There was just the one photograph of Dean. It stood on the living room mantelpiece in a frame decorated with flowers. In it he carried his electric guitar and wore his thick black curly hair very long. He had on flared jeans embroidered with silver thread and a brightly coloured shirt with full sleeves. Fleur knew the photograph so well that she could picture every detail of it when she closed her eyes. He wasn't black like Grandpa. His skin was brown as though he'd spent a long time in the sun. It was several shades darker than her own. Once she had asked why there were no photographs of her mum. Grandma had explained that Julie had gone away before any could be taken.

Fleur had been twelve when Grandpa Maurice was killed in a tragic accident on the railway. She was stunned and deeply saddened by her grandfather's death, but Dolly was totally devastated. Her first instinct had been to send for Dean, but she had no way of contacting him. The last they had heard of him was a postcard to say that he had split from the group and was going to California to look for work in the clubs there. She made endless enquiries of all his old friends but none of them knew where he was. No one had heard from him. It was almost as though he had vanished into thin air. Then one evening about six months later Dolly answered a knock on the door to find the local parish priest standing outside. He was closeted with Dolly in the living room for almost an hour and when he had gone Fleur learned that he had come to tell her that Dean had died.

Apparently it had been almost two months ago that he had been found dying in the room he had rented in a cheap lodging house in a run-down area of Los Angeles. It had taken all this time to trace his original home address.

The priest had told Dolly as gently as he could that Dean had been out of work and living rough for some months and that his death was attributed to malnutrition coupled with drug abuse. Later Dolly broke the news to Fleur, though she could not bring herself to tell the child the full sordid facts.

Fleur felt sad for Grandma's sake. She knew that it was terrible for Grandma to lose her son, and it should be equally bad for her to lose her father. Yet how could she mourn a man she had never known?

Apart from Fleur, Dolly's only comfort during this time of grief was her friend Ada. The two women, both now widows, would sit at the kitchen table in the Sylvesters' flat, drinking endless cups of tea and talking about happier times, while the two girls played quietly in the living room. Ada Morris had six other children, the youngest of whom was already fourteen when Bobby was born. Bobby's older brothers and sisters alternately spoiled and bullied her and she loved to escape to the comparative peace and quiet of the Sylvesters' flat to play with Fleur.

Fleur grew up very quickly after the news of Dean's death. She worried about her grandmother. The shock about Dean coming so close on the heels of Grandpa's death seemed to have turned her into an old woman overnight. Dolly had always enjoyed her job at the Royal Albert Hotel where she was a cook, but with Maurice gone money was short and she took all the extra work she could. Luckily her party catering was popular and, guided by her grandmother, Fleur helped out with the work as much as she could as she grew older. But during the four years that followed she watched her grandmother's health failing inch by inch. The catering being spasmodic, Dolly was obliged to take on extra work. She took on a regular office cleaning job, and rose at the crack of dawn, leaving the flat before Fleur was awake each morning.

Fleur watched helplessly as Dolly grew increasingly tired and frail from grief and hard work. Once, when she collapsed downstairs in the shop, Ethel Smith sent for the doctor. He told Dolly she must ease up. Fleur had overheard him when he had finished examining her upstairs in the flat.

'That old ticker of yours isn't what it was, Dolly,' he said gently. 'Your blood pressure is higher than I'd like it to be too. Take as a warning. Ease up now, my dear before it's too late.'

The words, *before it's too late*, made Fleur's blood run cold as she stood outside the half open door of Dolly's bedroom. Losing Grandpa had been terrible. It would be unbearable to lose Grandma as well. She made up her mind there and then. She and Bobby had taken their 'O' levels that summer. They'd both done well and planned to go on to 'A' levels and then, if they were lucky enough, perhaps to university. But at sixteen Fleur knew that she could legally leave school and get a job. Her decision to do so horrified Bobby.

'What'll you do though?' she asked.

Fleur shrugged. 'I could take over Grandma's job at the pub,' she said. 'I think I can cook almost as well as her now. I could probably do the catering work too.'

Bobby looked crestfallen. 'If you want to do something in that line you could go in for hotel management,' she said. 'Take a proper college course. You can't throw away everything you've worked for. We've both worked so hard. It'll be awful if you leave now. It won't be the same without you, Fleur.'

Fleur shook her head sadly. 'I know. I'll miss you too – and school. But I can't let Grandma struggle on when I could be helping her, can I? You still have your mum to help you. Now that all your brothers and sisters have left home they'll help you too. I don't think Grandma could ever have managed to keep me there anyway.' The girls hugged each other and cried a little in their disappointment.

'But we'll always be friends, won't we?' Bobby said earnestly. 'We'll always keep in touch no matter what happens.'

'Course we will,' Fleur promised.

But if Bobby was upset by Fleur's decision to leave school, Dolly was devastated. She enlisted the help of Fleur's teacher to try to get her to change her mind. There was so much to be gained by staying on, at least for two more years. But the girl would not be deterred.

9

'What's the good of a lot of bits of paper if I lose you, Grandma,' she said. 'Mrs Wallace at the fish bar on Hackney Road has offered me a job. It isn't very good pay but if you keep teaching me all you know about cooking I might be able to take over your job in the kitchen at The Royal Albert when I'm eighteen. I could help out behind the bar too. The girls there get tips as well as wages.'

Dolly was mortified. She felt she was letting the girl down. Fleur had grown into such a lovely girl. Although still in her early teens she had fulfilled her promise of statuesque womanhood. She was tall and well built, stunningly attractive with her honey warm complexion and glossy black hair. She and Maurice had pinned such hopes on the granddaughter who had already more than made up for her father's shortcomings. They'd wanted something better for her than a job in a fish and chip shop.

'No, love – no,' she said weakly, shaking her head and rubbing Fleur's hand between both of hers. 'Your Grandpa would be so disappointed if he knew I'd let you leave school, 'specially to go an' serve in a pub.'

'It's not for ever,' Fleur assured her. 'I'll get something better as soon as I can and I can always take my 'A' levels at night school. In the meantime you can at least give up that awful cleaning job and have a lie in of a morning.'

Dolly was sad, but proud of the girl at the same time. She might look like Dean but at least she hadn't inherited her father's selfishness. Maybe there was something in what she said; if she had a rest she would get her strength back, then, as soon as she felt herself again she would see to it that Fleur went back and completed her education.

For a while after Maurice's death and the news of her father's demise, Fleur had moved in to share her grandmother's room so that she wouldn't feel lonely at night and it was after the light w out at night that Dolly began little by little to tell her the story of how she came to be born. Her conscience pricked her. The girl . had sacrificed a lot. The least she was entitled to was the truth. She should know the full story about her parents while there was still time. Somehow Dolly found it easier to tell in the dark.

'Your Grandpa and I didn't even know Dean had a girlfriend till he brought her home that time,' she said. 'He told us they'd met the previous summer at a pop festival on the Isle of Wight. By the time we met her she'd been on the road with the group for four months. They came for a weekend. At least that's what Dean said it would be. Then when he got me on my own he broke the news that Julia was expecting and he wanted to leave her with us for a while.'

Fleur turned her head on the pillow to look at her grandmother's dim profile. 'I see – so they weren't married then?'

Dolly reached for her hand and gave it a squeeze. 'No love. Dean had promised that they would be – after his tour was over. I expect he meant it too – at the time. He was always making promises he couldn't keep. Somehow other, more important things always came along and got in the way. He told me that Julia had got tired of touring round in that ropey old van they used. She used to get very sick and the smell of the petrol and the bumping around was making her ill. He said it would only be for a little while. To begin with he used to write to her and even sent a bit of money now and again. He came home a couple of times. Just flying visits. Then he stopped coming home and gradually the letters and the money stopped.'

Fleur bit her lip, trying to imagine what it must have been like. 'That must have made her very unhappy.'

'Oh yes, it did. We used to feel so helpless, your grandpa and me, lying awake at nights hearing the poor gel crying herself to sleep through the wall. We felt guilty too, after all, it was our boy who was the cause of it. But we never had an address for him what with the group bein' on the move all the time, so we couldn't even write and tell him to come home.'

'So – what happened?' Fleur whispered.

'Well, eventually you were born. We took Julia along to the London Hospital down at Whitechapel late on Wednesday night and I stayed there with her till you were born early next morning.' Fleur felt her hand squeezed tightly. 'Such a dear little baby you were. Just like my Dean when he was born. Tight black curls and big dark eyes. Brought it all back, it did. Thursday's child, I told Julia. Remember the old rhyme? "Thursday's child has far to go." '

'And what about Julia – my mum? Was she pleased when I was born?'

Dolly paused. 'She was only a kid,' she sighed. 'No older than you are now and she was already unhappy. I thought she might settle down once she'd had you – be happier with a little baby of her own to look after.' Again she sighed. 'She wasn't though – just got even more miserable and restless. I think she was homesick. She started to talk a lot about her mum and dad – told me all about this lovely house they had at the place where she come from. Elvemere, it was called. 'Course, I always knew she was used to something a lot better than what we had,' Dolly said without resentment. 'You could tell she'd 'ad a good education. I reckon she was

11

hardly out of school when she met Dean, I don't know why she wanted to leave a nice home like she had and go rattlin' round the country in an old beat-up van. But then my Dean could turn any gel's head with his looks and his music.' Dolly sighed. 'I think she regretted it soon enough though. Life in the East End must've been a real eye-opener after what she was used to.'

'Didn't Dean – my dad ever come back?'

Dolly nodded. 'Just the once!'

'To see me?'

'It was just after you were born. I don't know exactly what he and Julia said to each other but he told me before he left that he'd tried to get Julia to go home to her own folks. He said it had all been a mistake and that he wasn't ready to be a father. I tried to talk to him – make him see sense and face up to his responsibilities, but he was so obsessed with his career – couldn't see no further than the next gig as he called it. He was so sure he was going to make the big time – fame and fortune.' Dolly sighed. 'Well, he gave Julia what money he had and told her he wasn't coming back any more.'

'What did she do?'

'What could she do, love? She couldn't work. I don't think she'd ever done a hand's turn. All she knew was what she'd learned at the posh school she'd been to. So it all fell to your grandpa and me to provide. Oh, we didn't mind. We loved you and we got quite fond of poor little Julia too. But I won't pretend it wasn't hard. Your grandpa was always makin' excuses for Dean; sayin' he'd change his mind when he'd had time to think straight. Couldn't believe his precious son could've done anything wrong. But I knew what he was up to all right. Off with some new girl, more like. Drinkin' and livin' it up with his showbiz mates. Julia knew it too, though she never said nothin'.' Dolly shook her head, muttering to herself under her breath. 'Always had a selfish streak, that boy. I don't know where he got it from. Not me, and certainly not your grandpa.' She took a deep breath and continued, 'Anyway, in the end even your granddad got the message. Dean had dumped Julia and you and cleared off, knowing that we'd see no harm'd come to her. He knew we was both a soft touch when it came to kids.'

'What happened to Julia then?'

'Ah, well . . .' Dolly fell silent for a moment. 'I should've seen it coming, I suppose. In the end she couldn't take no more. She'd always hated it here in the East End and after Dean told her he wasn't coming back I s'pose she just got to the end of her tether. One morning – you were about three months old at the time – we

12

got up and found you in your cot, alone in the room. Julia's bed was empty; neatly made with a note pinned to the pillow. She'd gone off home to her parents, she said. Thanked us for all we'd done and asked us to forgive her. Begged us to take care of you and not let you go to strangers.'

'You mean she – she didn't want me?' Fleur swallowed hard at the lump that had suddenly risen in her throat. 'Wasn't she going to come back for me – not ever?'

'She never made any false promises,' Dolly said noncommittally.

'But – how could she do that?' Fleur asked angrily. 'If I had a baby I'd never just walk away and leave it. I *couldn't*!' She sat up in bed. 'You're saying she abandoned me, aren't you, Grandma? All those years when I kept on hoping she'd come and see me and all the time she couldn't care less. She never wanted me – she'd probably even forgotten she ever had me, hadn't she? She didn't give a damn! That's it, isn't it?'

Dolly squeezed her hand. 'Now, now. Don't take on love. None of us knows what we might do if we was really desperate. It won't do no good gettin' angry about it either.'

'But didn't it make *you* angry? Didn't you want to go and bring her back?'

'It don't do to judge folks, Fleur. You'll learn that as you get older.' Dolly's eyes glistened moistly in the dimness. 'I'd watched that poor gel going downhill for eight months. She was fretting her heart out over Dean and the mistake she'd made. She was heart-broken, homesick an' scared stiff of the future. I reckon she got to the stage where she couldn't see no other way out. I couldn't find it in my heart to blame her for leaving. It was Dean I was angry with, but he wasn't coming back to face up to his responsibilities, was he?'

'But she – Julia could have taken me home with her, couldn't she?'

'Think about it, love. How could she turn up on her mum and dad's doorstep with a baby? It would've been a terrible shock for them – a disgrace too.' Dolly sat up and switched on the bedside light. 'See, Julia 'ad let on to her mum an' dad that she had a good job in London and was sharin' a flat with two other girls, you see.' She shook her head. 'I expect she hoped she'd be married by the time she had to face them and it would have been too late then to do anything about it.'

'So – she hadn't told them about Dean then – or me?' Very slowly the truth was dawning on Fleur. Dolly was trying to let her down lightly. 'It wasn't just that she had a baby and no husband, was it?' she said. 'What you're really saying is that she'd have been ashamed of – of my colour.'

Dolly winced. She'd racked her mind to think of a way to put it that wouldn't hurt. 'Not ashamed, love – not of *you*. But it's like I said. It would have shocked her parents – made life difficult for them all,' she said awkwardly. 'People who live in them little places are narrow-minded. Up here in London it might have been different.'

'No it wouldn't,' Fleur said quietly. 'There's prejudice everywhere. You know that as well as I do. It hasn't changed much since you married Grandpa, has it?'

Dolly sighed. It was true of course. Her own family had turned their backs on her when she refused to give Maurice up. That had been one of the main reasons she'd understood and sympathised with Julia. 'Your mum was very young,' she said. 'She loved Dean – trusted him and he'd let her down, left her high and dry with a baby on her hands. It was very different with your grandpa and me. No one could've had a better, truer man. I never regretted marryin' 'im for a minute. Everything he ever did was for us – his family and I loved him till the day he died. I still do and I always will.' She sighed, lapsing again into audible thoughts. 'Why Dean couldn't have been more like his dad I don't know,' she muttered. 'Maybe it was our fault for lovin' him too much. For spoiling him.'

Becoming acquainted with the fact that Dean had never cared enough to want to be a father to her, and her mother was too ashamed to acknowledge her existence affected Fleur deeply. Her grandparents had been wonderful. But neither her mother nor father could have known for sure that they would keep and bring her up. For all they knew she could have ended up in care, or been shunted round a series of indifferent foster homes. Her confidence suffered. Just what and who was she? Neither black nor white; despised and rejected by her own parents. Where and to whom did she really belong?

It was only as Fleur grew older that she became increasingly aware of racial prejudice. There were certain people who made a point of creating situations where fights would erupt. Racist elements among their society who got their pleasure out of seeing someone weaker than themselves suffer. But Fleur had always seen these for what they were: dangerously inadequate people, needing someone to victimise because brutality was their one twisted claim to dominance.

Not that she had ever suffered this kind of prejudice herself. Her honey-coloured skin, black curly hair and brown eyes had a look more of the Mediterranean than the Caribbean and, as she grew up, her cheerful nature and strong personality had always made her popular. But after she had learned the truth about her parents betrayal she became subdued. She grew defensive and quick to sense criticism. She had always hated any kind of bullying, but now she was fiercely protective. Any kind of injustice infuriated her, a trait that was brought to the fore one Friday evening when she was serving behind the counter at Wallace's Fish Bar.

From her place at the end of the counter she saw a young Asian boy being bullied in the street outside. Four skinheads with brawny tattooed arms were jeering and pushing him around, clearly trying to make him retaliate with their racist jibes and threatening behaviour. Fleur knew the boy. Hosein was a quiet studious boy in his late teens. He lived with his Pakistani family in Brightman Lane and Fleur had been in the same class as his younger sister Melini. She knew that he was studying law and worked hard at a part time job as a waiter to help his parents.

Serving the queue that snaked around the shop she kept an eye on the group outside the steamy window until suddenly she heard one of the thugs shout a racist obscenity and land a blow that sent the boy sprawling into the gutter. Blazing with anger she abruptly abandoned the woman she was serving and ran round the counter, pushing her way through the startled customers and out into the street.

'What the bloody hell do you think you're doing?' she demanded, her dark eyes flashing as she brandished the fish slice still in her hand. 'What kind of lousy wimps are you? Four of you and one of him – and he's smaller than you too!'

The thugs turned to stare at her in shocked surprise, momentarily speechless. Then one of them took a step forward, leering at her. 'Who're you callin' wimps?' He looked her up and down and turned to the others. 'What d'ya reckon – is she another Paki slag or what?'

The others closed in on her menacingly. 'Wimps, are we? So whatcher gonna do about it then?' the ringleader challenged. 'Make men of us all?'

The others laughed raucously and, encouraged, he stepped right up to stand in front of her. 'Come on then, get 'em off and give us a treat. Bet you could take us all on, couldn't ya?' He spread his arms and thrust his pelvis forward suggestively. 'Me first! Comin' round the back with me then, eh? Gonna show us what you c'n do! Never know, maybe we c'n teach you a trick or two. I bet you been gang-banged loads a times!'

15

As the other three cat-called and whistled, Fleur felt a prickle of fear down her spine, but she stood her ground, calling to Hosein to make himself scarce. Her challenger's leering face was thrust close to hers now and his appearance repelled her. His small, pale eyes glinted sadistically and there was a swastika tattooed on one unshaven, spotty cheek. She saw that there was a hoop through one nostril as well as the one through his left earlobe. Adrenalin surged through her veins like fire, fuelling her anger.

'Yeah? Teach me a trick or two, could you?' she said, throwing caution to the winds. 'Well, s'pose I teach *you* one first?' Stepping aside to avoid his clutching hands, she lashed out at him with the fish slice. The implement was made of sturdy stainless steel and Fleur swung it with considerable force catching him a clanging blow on the side of his shaven head. The mean eyes watered with pain and he let out a piercing yell, clasping one hand to his head and shooting her a look of purest hatred.

'*Shit!* You bloody little *cow*! I'll . . .' He broke off to finger his ear gingerly, muttering under his breath.

Fleur's instinct for self-preservation urged her to turn and run, but she stood her ground, knowing that it would be fatal to show any sign of weakness now. She wondered briefly if any of the chip shop customers would intervene to help her should the rest of the gang decided to set about her. She'd noticed with relief that young Hosein had taken her advice and vanished into the night. Then she saw to her surprise that her victim's three companions also seemed to have faded away. A moment later the reason presented itself in the form of a dark uniformed figure who loomed up behind the wounded skinhead, who was tenderly prodding his ear and muttering dark threats.

'Having a spot of bother, miss?' The policeman was clearly trying not to grin, which replaced her relief at seeing him with annoyance.

'Oh, *there* you are then, *officer*!' she said, her eyes flashing. 'Good at turning up when the trouble's all over, you lot, aren't you? Maybe you should go and see if you can find the poor young kid these creeps were thumping! Four of 'em onto one.'

The chip shop queue, their appetites temporarily forgotten, had spilled out onto the pavement by now and one or two of them spoke up on Fleur's behalf.

'Real guts that gel's got.'

'Wants a medal if you ask me!'

The injured skinhead, burning with indignity, spoke up. 'I want her nicked!' He pointed an accusing finger at Fleur. 'She's a bleedin' maniac! Just attacked me, she 'as – for nuthin! If I got caught with an offensive weapon I'd get banged to rights. No danger!' He held out a grubby finger. 'Look, I'm bleedin'. Reckon I need an ambulance.'

The policeman turned sternly to Fleur, sucking in his breath sharply. 'Attack with an offensive weapon is it? That's serious. Let's have a look then. Come on, hand it over.' He took the fish slice from Fleur's hand and examined it carefully. 'Well now, that's some weapon!' He turned to the skinhead. 'Nearly brain you with it, did she sonny?' He shook his head, tutting in mock sympathy. 'Clipped round the ear by a young gel with a fish slice. Oh yeah, I reckon you've got a good case there.' He pulled out his mobile phone. 'Still want an ambulance do we?'

His support gone, the skinhead slunk away, muttering obscenities under his breath as he elbowed his way through the jeering crowd. The policeman looked at Fleur as the crowd began to disperse, his eyes concerned.

'You all right, love?'

Fleur tossed her head, trying to ignore the reaction that was beginning to set in. She found she was trembling, visualising for the first time what might have happened had it not been for the policeman's intervention. 'I'm fine, thanks. Can't stand to see them ganging up like that.'

'No? Well, just the same, I wouldn't recommend tangling with the likes of that lot,' he said. 'You're lucky they didn't pull a knife on you.'

'Like to see 'em try!' she said with a bravado she didn't feel.

'*I* wouldn't. Seen too many knifings for my liking. I know we can't be everywhere at once as you've already pointed out,' he said with a wry smile. 'But next time try dialling 999 instead, eh?' He paused as he moved away. 'And I'd watch my back for a day or two now if I were you.'

Back inside the shop Harry Wallace eyed Fleur wryly. 'I 'ope you ain't gonna make a habit of that kinda thing,' he said. 'Half o'them customers never come back after your little frac-arse out there. Some of 'em conveniently forgot to pay for what they'd 'ad an' all.'

His wife, Marj was more sympathetic. 'Leave the kid alone, 'Arry. It was brave, what she done.' She peered into Fleur's face. 'Wanna go 'ome, luv? You look a bit green round the gills.'

'I'm all right, thanks,' Fleur told her. 'I'd rather stay till closing time. Grandma'll think something's wrong if I go home early.'

But if Harry Wallace was worrying about a lack of trade he had no need. The word had spread like wildfire and for the rest of the evening the shop was crowded with people curious for a glimpse of the heroine who had stood up to four skinheads armed only with a fish slice. Wallace's Fish Bar had never done such good business. Urged by his wife to make amends, Harry pushed a parcel into Fleur's hands as she was putting on her coat.

'For your gran an' you,' he said with a wink. 'I know Dolly likes a fish supper. Tell 'er this one's on me.'

The policeman's warning to Fleur was not made merely to frighten her. He'd seen the sadistic retribution doled out by these thugs too many times to speak lightly. Fleur remembered his warning when she became aware of being followed on her way home from work. Often there were scufflings and footsteps behind her as she walked, sometimes a muted whistle or half-heard call. She guessed that it was the gang of skinheads and although their unseen presence unnerved her she tried to tell herself that scaring her was all they meant to do. If she stuck it out and showed no fear they'd eventually get bored and turn their attention to someone else.

Fleur said nothing to her grandmother about the incident with the skinheads and Dolly might never have known about it had it not been for Hosein's conscience. A few days later, feeling bad about leaving her to face the skinheads alone, he came round to the Sylvesters' flat to apologise and to thank her. Fleur had already left for work and it was Dolly who answered the door to him and heard the story of his attack from his own lips. When Fleur arrived home late that evening her grandmother was waiting for her.

'Don't you ever do nothing like that again!' she said. 'Okay, I know you wanted to help the lad. I saw the nasty bruise where those thugs hit him. He come round 'cause he felt bad about leggin' it and leavin' you, otherwise I might never 'ave 'eard. Why didn't you tell me?'

'It wasn't important, Grandma,' Fleur said lightly, taking off her coat. 'I'd forgotten by the time I got home.'

'Don't you lie to me, gel!' Dolly's face was pink with anguish. 'You've always been too quick to stick your neck out for other people. It was all right when you was a kid at school, but this is something else. It ain't for the likes o' you to go fightin' other folks's battles for 'em, putting yourself in that kind of danger!'

Fleur hung up her coat and turned to her grandmother. 'Who else then, Grandma? There were at least eight men in the chip shop when it happened, and they weren't doing anything. Someone had to.'

'Not you though. Not any more. Promise me!' Dolly demanded. 'Promise me you won't do nothing like that *ever* again!'

'All *right*, Grandma. I'm big enough to look after myself. No need to go on about it.'

'Yes there is!' Dolly drew a long shuddering breath and lowered herself into a chair. 'Life round 'ere ain't what it was when I was a gel. Them days we looked after one another. Nobody never locked their street doors and you knew who you could trust. Now there's never a week goes by without we 'ears about a muggin' or a knifin'. It's like livin' in the jungle – every man for 'imself and the sooner you faces that fact my gel, the better.'

'I can't *be* like that, Grandma. If more people stood up for what's right things'd have to get better.'

'I wish I believed that.' Dolly drew in her breath sharply and clasped one hand to her side. 'Listen love, I want you to promise me something. It's been on my mind for a long time now.'

Alarmed at her grandmother's sudden pallor, Fleur sat down beside her and took her hand. 'What is it, Grandma? I didn't mean to upset you. I wasn't even going to tell you about it. I won't do anything like it again if you say so. It was just that . . .'

But Dolly was shaking her head. 'It ain't that . . .' She took a deep breath and squeezed Fleur's hand. 'Look, I want to you promise that if anything 'appens to me you won't stay on round 'ere.'

Fleur frowned. 'But – where else would I go? Anyway, nothing's going to happen to you.'

'It will love – bound to sooner or later. You're a grown woman now and it's time to face facts. My heart's not strong – angina, the doctor says. I've known it for a long time. I could go any time an' I don't want to have to worry about what's going to happen to you.' She shook her head at Fleur's worried frown. 'Don't look at me like that. It don't bother me – not that part. What does worry me is the thought of you bein' left 'ere on your own.'

'But there's always Bobby and her family. I know they'd help me.'

Dolly shook her head. 'You know as well as I do that Bobby will be goin' off to college soon. Ada deserves some time to herself after bringin' up all them kids.'

'So, what's the alternative?'

'I want to you promise me you'll go and find your mum.'

'Go and *what*?' Fleur stared at her incredulously. 'You're *joking*!'

Dolly shook her head. 'No. She left her address in the note she left. I know she never wanted you adopted or to go to a foster home. I reckon if you was in trouble – an' you was to go and see

19

her she'd help you. Maybe she's even been *hoping* you'd go all these years.'

'I bet she hasn't!' Fleur said. 'It was *years* ago she said that, when I was a baby. I expect she felt guilty, going off and leaving me with you like that. Who was she to say what should happen? She didn't want me, did she?'

'It don't matter how long ago it was,' Dolly insisted, her blue eyes dark with anxiety behind the spectacles. 'You're still 'er daughter and nothing can't change that. Julia come from a good family. There's no shortage of money there. She'll see you right. She owes you that much.'

'I don't *need* help, specially not from *her*!' Fleur said indignantly. 'I'm strong and healthy. I can work for myself. I . . .' She caught sight of her grandmother's anguished face and stopped, bending forward to stroke the white hair. 'Oh, look, Grandma, nothing's going to happen to you for years and years.'

'All the same, I'd rest easy if I knew you were going to be all right.'

'I *will* be,' Fleur said firmly. 'Maybe one of these days I'll even go and look Julia up too, just out of curiosity. Who knows?'

'That ain't good enough gel. I want you to promise me faithfully.' Dolly squeezed Fleur's hand imploringly till the girl nodded.

'Okay, Grandma. If you say so. I promise.'

Sighing with relief, Dolly heaved herself to her feet and went to the bedroom, returning a few minutes later with a scrap of paper. 'Here's the address. I've looked after it all these years so mind you keep it somewhere safe.' She pressed it into Fleur's hand. 'And don't forget your promise now, will you, gel? Don't stay round 'ere. It's no place for a young gel on 'er own.'

Fleur kissed her cheek. 'Okay, I promise. Now let's stop being morbid and forget all about it, shall we?' Later she pushed the paper into the back of her underwear drawer, reflecting that Julia had most probably forgotten by now that she had ever had an illegitimate daughter.

It was just four weeks later that Fleur arrived home late one evening to find the flat strangely silent. She called out as she always did, 'Grandma! I'm home! What's for supper?'

As she hung up her outdoor clothes she sniffed. There was no welcoming smell of cooking. Normally at this time of the evening Dolly could be heard singing along to one of Grandpa's records. He had a collection of big band numbers from the fifties and Dolly loved them. She always left the kitchen door open so that she could hear the music above the sizzling of the chip pan. Tonight the kitchen door was firmly shut and the old-fashioned radiogram that Grandpa Maurice had been so proud of stood silent in its corner, the lid closed and Dolly's prized potted fern standing on the top.

Fleur stood for a moment, prevented from moving by the sudden icy dread that froze her muscles. Slowly, with feet of lead, she crossed the hall to the bedroom and stood fearfully in the half open doorway. Without entering she could see Dolly's reflection in the mirror of the dressing table on the opposite side of the room. The old lady half sat, half lay on the bed, supported by the headboard. She was still fully dressed, the print overall she always wore in the kitchen covering her skirt and blouse. Her glasses were slightly awry and on her face was an expression of gentle surprise, as though someone had just given her a piece of unexpected news.

'Grandma . . .?' Fleur took a step into the room and turned to look down at the old woman slumped across the bed. Then her hand flew to her mouth to stifle her cry of anguish. '*Grandma* – oh, no – *no*!' The moment she had dreaded – that she had refused to accept would ever happen, had come. She knew even without touching her that Dolly was dead.

It was two days after the funeral that Ethel Smith came up to the flat to speak to Fleur.

'Are you all right, love?'

'Yes, thanks, Mrs Smith.'

'Managin' okay?'

'Fine.'

Ethel sighed. What she had to say wasn't going to be easy, especially under the circumstances. 'I – er – wondered if you had any plans?' she asked tentatively.

Fleur frowned. 'What kind of plans?'

'Well – this flat for a start. It's a bit big for one and I wondered if you might find the rent hard to find now there's only you.' She cleared her throat. 'Had you thought of applyin' for one of them council flats down Tower Hamlets?'

'Well, no. I hadn't.'

Ethel bit her lip. There was nothing for it but to come out with it straight. 'Fact is love, Alf and me are retirin'. We're goin' down to Kent – bought a little place near Maidstone. Well, Alf's never been keen on the business as you know.'

'I see. So you've sold the shop?' Fleur tried not to think of the implications.

'Well – not exactly.' Ethel licked her lips. 'My daughter's husband lost his job a few months ago. He worked at Ford's and he got made redundant. He can't seem to find nothing else, so they're going to sell their house at Dagenham and come and run the business for us. Trouble is, they'll be needin' these rooms up 'ere as well as our flat. With the kids there's five of 'em altogether, see?'

'Oh.' Fleur swallowed hard. The flat wasn't exactly a palace but it was the only home she had ever known. Grandpa Maurice, Dolly and she had been happy here. Now she would have to find somewhere else to live. Somewhere she could afford. The prospect was daunting to say the least.

'I feel terrible askin' you to leave,' Ethel was saying. 'Specially with you just havin' lost your gran and everything, but I can't see no other way round it. Kath and Jim have got three kiddies to think of, see? They've been havin' a real struggle and it'll mean a lot to them to have a job and a secure roof over their heads.'

'Yes, of course.' Fleur took a deep breath. 'When do you want me to leave, Mrs Smith?'

'Oh, no mad rush,' Ethel said, trying to hide her relief. 'Shall we say the beginnin' of next month?'

Fleur gasped. That gave her only three weeks and she knew that her prospect of getting a council flat in that time, especially as a single teenaged girl was practically nil. Forcing a smile, she nodded. 'I'll start looking round for something else right away.'

Ethel looked around her. 'If you're not takin' the furniture p'raps I could buy some of it off you? The place we've bought is bigger than our flat downstairs and we'll be needin' a few more things. Would that help you?'

Fleur brightened. Dolly had some good pieces of furniture. It was old-fashioned, but solid and well made. There was no way she could manage to keep any of it herself. 'Well, yes, it might,' she said. 'Providing you're willing to pay me what it's worth.' Some of the light came back into her eyes. If Ethel thought she could rip her off she had another think coming! She'd go down the market and check out the price of second hand furniture. It wouldn't do to let the woman think she was a push-over. 'After all, Mrs Smith,' she went on, 'I'll need to get the best price I can, seeing as you're chucking me out!'

That night Fleur lay awake into the small hours trying to make some kind of plan. Even if she'd been able to stay on at the flat her job at Wallace's Fish Bar would not be enough to pay the rent, feed and clothe her. Yet jobs for someone with her lack of experience were few and far between. It was expensive, living in London, even in the East End. Dolly had left her everything she owned, but the little money there was in her Post Office account plus what Fleur could get for the furniture would not last long.

Sometimes she wondered about her father. Had the daily grind of life in the East End been his reason for his leaving? Had he used his gift for music as a passport to a better life? And did he ever achieve success? Had he ever spared a thought for the girl he had abandoned or the child he had seen only once?

Every day of the following week Fleur raked the papers for a flat to let, but they were all too expensive, even the bed-sits. She looked for jobs too and even went after one or two, but either she had no experience or she was dismissed sight-unseen as 'over-qualified' because of her eight O levels. At last in desperation she asked Harry Wallace if he could give her some extra hours. He shook his head.

'Matter of fact love we were about to ask you if we could put you on short time,' he said. 'Business has fallen off something chronic these past few months. Marj had to stand off the cleaner last week. We just can't afford to pay her no more.'

The stab of insecurity Fleur had felt when Ethel Smith had asked her to vacate the flat grew into a feeling of near panic. 'Only I've lost my flat,' she said bleakly. 'And everything else I've looked at is so expensive.'

Marj had come into the shop. She'd been listening to the conversation as she buttoned her overall and now she joined in. 'If I was your age I'd get out of London love,' she said. 'A young gel like you with no ties could go anywhere. What have you got to lose?'

But Fleur lifted her shoulders uncertainly. 'I'd rather stay here,' she said. 'I was born here. It's all I know. I expect I'll find something if I keep looking.'

That night on her way home there were no footsteps following Fleur as she walked home. As she turned the corner into Brightman Lane everything was quiet, just a few residents returning from a night out at the pub and the endless muted roar of the traffic on Hackney Road. Before entering the narrow alleyway between the buildings that led to the flat's entrance, she paused under the street lamp, fumbling in her bag for her key and the torch she always carried. It was pitch dark in the passage and it wasn't until she had stopped in front of the door and inserted the key in the lock that she was chillingly aware that she was not alone. Instinct told her that someone had stepped out of the shadows and now stood close behind her. When he spoke quietly behind her she felt his breath, hot on the back of her neck and her blood ran cold.

'Ullo darlin'. You an' me've got a little business to settle. Remember me, do ya?'

Fleur would have recognised the voice anywhere. Her heart beating fast, she wrestled with the key in a vain attempt at forestalling him, but before she could get the door open he grasped her by the shoulders and turned her round, pinning her against the wall.

'Oh no you don't!' He laughed hoarsely and thrust his face close to hers, breathing beer fumes into her face. 'Thought you could make a prat outa me, didn't you?' he hissed. 'Well I'm gonna show you what happens to gels who try an' get clever with me.'

'My grandmother's expecting me. She'll ring the police.'

He laughed in her face. 'Who're you tryin' to kid? The old cow's dead. You buried 'er more'n a month ago. 'Sides, you aint even got a phone. Whatcher take me for – stupid or somethin'?' He spat the words at her and she felt her face spattered with moisture. Pinning her body against the wall with his own he forced his mouth on hers, prizing her lips apart with his hard tongue and thrusting it into her mouth. Fleur struggled, feeling her stomach heave as his teeth ground against hers. The nauseating taste of him made her gag. She pushed frantically against his shoulders as his hands clawed at her buttons, tearing her blouse open. Then she felt one rough hand painfully squeezing her breast as he pressed himself even closer. 'Come on.' He forced his knee between her legs and his breath rasped in her ear. 'I've been lookin' forward to this for weeks.'

Fleur wrestled with every ounce of strength that was in her and when he thrust his tongue into her mouth a second time she clamped her teeth down on it hard till she tasted blood.

'Ooow! Vicious *bitch*!' One big hard hand around her throat, he jerked her towards him, then propelled her backwards to the end of the passage where the dustbins stood. 'Wanna play rough, do you?' Forcing her off balance, her back against one of the bins he squeezed her throat so tightly that she could scarcely breathe, let alone scream, and with his other hand he ripped her jeans undone. To her horror she felt his fingers snake inside her panties and heard his breath rasp with lust as they made contact with her naked skin.

She struggled frantically, dislodging the dustbin lid so that they both staggered sideways, but the hand around her throat tightened its strangling grip on her till she felt herself beginning to pass out.

She gulped in air through her open mouth in a desperate attempt to gain strength and suddenly she realised that the torch she had taken from her bag was still clutched in her hand. It was a large nightwatchman's torch that had belonged to Grandpa. Dolly had always insisted on her carrying it when she had to walk home alone

24

at night. She managed to get her arm free and brought the torch down hard against the side of her attacker's neck. He gave a surprised grunt, then as he moved back slightly she brought her knee up between his legs with as much force as she could. At once the hand around her throat relaxed its hold. He let out a scream of pain and doubled up. Pushing him to one side with a deafening clatter of overturned dustbins, she scrambled as fast as she could to the door, clutching her torn jeans around her. Finding the key still in the lock almost made her weep with gratitude. Already she could hear the cries of pain turning to roars of reprisal and she knew she had only seconds.

She turned the key, pushed the door open and slipped inside, shooting the bolts at top and bottom and leaning against it breathlessly, weak with relief. Outside the skinhead's bellowed obscenities and violent poundings reverberated through her body and she stepped backwards to sink onto the bottom stair, one hand over her mouth and her eyes fixed on the vibrating door, praying that the hinges would hold. Then there was a pause.

The letter box rattled, making her start with fright. 'You're for it now, you snotty tart!' he yelled through the aperture. 'Better watch your back from now on, 'cause I'm gonna get you. You can bet on it! Next time I'll slice that face o' yours – cut you so bad no one won't never wanna *look* at you again, you *bitch*!'

For what felt like an eternity she sat there in the dark, numb with shock. She remembered with dismay that her handbag still lay out there in the alleyway. It contained a week's wages, paid to her this evening. She owed that money to Ethel Smith for the rent, but she guessed that by now even if the bag was still there it would have been emptied of everything of any value.

Finally she found the strength to climb the stairs. Once inside the flat she went to the window and peered down into the street. To her relief it was empty. She drew the curtains and switched on the light. It was then that her stomach began to churn. A moment later, one hand over her mouth, she made a dash for the lavatory where she threw up violently.

In the kitchen as she filled the kettle with shaking hands and set it on the gas stove, tears began to trickle down her cheeks. For the first time in her life she felt vulnerable and utterly alone. She wept for her grandparents and even for the father she had never known, knowing that she would never be able to tell anyone what had happened this evening. It was all too shameful – too sordid and dirty.

At last the tears stopped and she made herself a promise. '*I won't*

25

let them win,' she vowed between clenched teeth. 'I *won't* be beaten!' But she also knew that in a way they already had won. Dolly had been right. She must leave Brightman Lane and the East End if she was to make a worthwhile life for herself.

In the end Fleur put most of her grandparents' furniture into a saleroom. She was pleasantly surprised at the figure it fetched. The auctioneer told her that some of it was Edwardian and coming into vogue again.

Grandpa's radiogram and records she sold to Ethel Smith who had taken a fancy to them. And the chest of drawers from the bedroom she gave to Ada Morris as a keepsake. It was only when she was removing the last of her own things from the chest of drawers that Fleur came across the piece of paper with her mother's address written on it. She smoothed it out and glanced at it. The notepaper was discoloured and dog-eared, the ink faded, but the writing was still clear enough.

> *Miss Julia Philips,*
> *Gresham House,*
> *St Paul's Green,*
> *Elvemere,*
> *Cambridgeshire.*

Her first impulse was to tear it into bits and throw it into the bin, then she changed her mind and put it into the box along with Dean's photograph and the postcards he had sent. These few scraps of yellowing card and paper were her only proof that she had ever had two parents. For a moment she stood pondering. Her mother – Julia Philips would be pushing forty by now. She would more than likely have married and left this Elvemere place in Cambridgeshire long ago.

Out of curiosity she looked up Elvemere on the map and found that it was only an hour's train journey from London. Why shouldn't she go there? she asked herself. Dolly had said it was a nice place and it was as good as anywhere to start a new life. If Julia Philips was still there it might even be interesting to see what she was like and what she had made of her life. From a distance of course. She had no intention of contacting her. Who needed a mother like her?

'I don't need anyone's help to survive,' she told herself. 'I've lost my family, my home and my job and I've survived an attempted rape attack. Nothing worse than that can happen to me. I'll make it in the end and when I do I'll have no one to thank but myself.'

Fleur shivered slightly as she stood there at the window. There was little time left for sleep now. It was almost morning, and now that the time had come to leave she didn't feel quite so brave. These streets might be dirty, noisy and sometimes dangerous, but they were all she had ever known. They were where her friends were. Was she mad to go to a strange town where no one knew her? Crazy even to think of looking for the mother who had wanted to be rid of her? Yet she knew that if she didn't go she would always wonder what she might have found – might have achieved. This was her watershed – her turning point. Now there was no going back.

Chapter 2

Vernon Grant nosed his silver BMW in through the double gates of his parents' house and glanced at his wife. As always she looked immaculate, her blonde hair expertly dressed and her make-up flawless. The dress she wore was her usual style, a dark blue thing, classily plain and obviously expensive. No man could have had a more attractive wife or a better hostess to entertain his business associates. He certainly couldn't fault her on appearance. The trouble with Julia was, she couldn't take criticism. She just wouldn't be told. He drew the car to a smooth halt under the huge flowering cherry tree that was the centre-piece of the Grant's front garden and turned to her.

'Try not to make an atmosphere tonight of all nights, Ju. Remember it's Mother's and Dad's anniversary.'

'In that case, why choose tonight to pick a quarrel?' she returned without looking at him.

He sighed. 'All I said was that you should have asked me first before going ahead with this hare-brained idea.'

She turned to look at him. 'Why should I need your permission to put up for the council? It's hardly going to affect you, is it? You're hardly ever at home. Charlotte doesn't need me around any more. And everyone else seems to think I'd be an asset.' Her eyes were bright with something he hadn't seen in them before: defiance. It irritated him intensely.

'Not permission – *advice*. Christ, Julia, are you really so naive that you can't see that they're taking advantage of you? And by *everyone*, I suppose you mean the Maitland woman?'

'Councillor Eleanor Maitland? Among others, yes.'

Vernon sighed again. 'Look, Julia, this is a crucial by-election. If they don't get another Conservative in this time they'll lose their majority and no one else has come forward. Added to that the

28

Labour bloke is popular. You're there to make up the numbers, can't you see that? God! It infuriates me to think you can be taken in like this. If you don't get in – and you won't – think of the laugh they'll have. At my expense too! What kind of an idiot do you think it'll make me look in front of my business associates?'

'I don't believe they're taking advantage of me,' she said stubbornly. 'Surely if they thought I wouldn't get in, they wouldn't have asked me? And why should it do you any harm? It could even do you some good.'

'Oh, I see. I suppose you're going to get on the planning committee and see that GPC gets all the plum contracts? Do me a favour! Why don't you just stick to your Townswomen's Guild and your committees and leave the serious stuff to those who are capable of handling it?'

She rounded on him indignantly. 'I'm not the complete moron you seem to take me for, Vernon. I do know enough to declare an interest should anything concerning GPC come up.'

He shrugged. 'If you take my advice, you'll stand down before you make a fool of yourself. You won't get elected anyway.'

Julia bit back an angry retort. Maybe Vernon was in for a few surprises. Eleanor Maitland had convinced her that she was capable of being a good councillor. She'd persuaded Julia to stand and she intended to do justice to the older woman's confidence in her. She smiled at her husband. 'In that case, you have nothing to worry about then, do you? Shall we go in?'

His hand shot out and grasped her wrist. 'In a minute. I want to talk to you about Charlotte first. You know Mother's going to be very disappointed that she isn't with us this evening. Why on earth did you say she could go out with her friends when you knew Mother would be expecting her to this family dinner?'

Julia sighed. Once Vernon got the bit between his teeth there was no stopping him. He'd bring up every grievance he could think of. 'It was arranged ages ago,' she said patiently. 'Her friends from school agreed last winter that they'd have a meal out to celebrate the exam results – whatever they were. And as it happens they've all got good reason to celebrate.'

'But you *knew* Mother was planning this anniversary dinner.'

'Charlotte's growing up, Vernon. She's not a child any more, to be told what to do and where to go.'

'She's sixteen, for God's sake. In my book that's still a kid!'

'This is a once in a lifetime thing. She's worked hard and done well. She's already agreed to come into the business with you.'

Vernon snorted indignantly. 'She's *agreed*, has she? That's good of her. Most teenagers would give their eye teeth for a job like that with a secure future assured.'

'I know, but she'd have hated us for making her come with us tonight when all her friends were off enjoying themselves.'

'Ah, now we're coming to it, aren't we?' he sneered. 'Anything to be your daughter's best chum. You'll regret the way you let that girl wind you round her little finger, Ju. You really will have to try to develop some backbone!'

Perhaps I already have, she said inwardly. Maybe putting up for this by-election is just what I need. Aloud she said, 'We're here for your mother's and father's party, so shall we try to forget my shortcomings for once?'

He got out of the car and slammed the door.

Julia picked up her beaded evening bag from the dashboard. Getting out of the car, she smoothed down the skirt of her dress and followed her husband to the front door of her in-laws' house. It had always been like this. Vernon would have his say and then shut her up on some pretext or other before she had a chance to put her side of the argument. Well, things were going to change. She'd made her mind up to that and he was going to have to get used to it.

Queen's Lodge, Vernon's parents' house, was an imposing mock-Tudor villa which Charlie Grant had built himself in the early-sixties when his building firm had first begun to prosper. Charlie had started out as a humble bricklayer and had met his Lancashire-born wife Louise one summer when he was spending a working holiday on her father's farm. Twelve years later when his wealthy father-in-law died he had started his own building firm with the help of his wife's inheritance.

Queen's Lodge had been built to show the public in general that Charlie Grant, the scruffy kid with the backside hanging out of his pants, had made it. It had five bedrooms, two bathrooms and three reception rooms, and its black beams and sparkling latticed windows cocked a snook at the world, Charlie's defiant proof of his rise to success. Inside, the furnishings leant heavily towards Gothic Baronial. The decor favoured flocked wallpapers in reds and blues and most of the furniture was heavily carved, custom-made reproduction Jabobean.

Julia usually found the place intensely depressing. But this evening it had a festive, almost cheerful atmosphere. The windows were thrown open to the warm summer evening sunshine and Louise Grant, her mother-in-law, had obviously done her best. Bowls of flowers were everywhere, scenting the air with their fragrance, and there was an appetising aroma of food coming from the kitchen.

Louise came out on to the porch to greet them, her heavy figure swathed in rose pink lace. Pink was one of her favourite colours, though it did nothing for her rather florid colouring. Her blue-rinsed hair was fluffed out in a girlish halo and she wore a five-strand pearl necklace and earrings to match – her anniversary present from Charlie. She greeted Vernon warmly.

'Lovely to see you, Vernie, chuck.' She'd never quite managed to lose her northern accent or to cure herself of the habit of calling her son 'Vernie chuck' even though she knew it made him wince with embarrassment. She kissed him before turning her attention to Julia.

'What a pretty little frock,' she said, eyes glinting as they swept up and down her daughter-in-law's Versace original. 'That will have cost Vernie a penny or two, I know.' She slipped an arm round her daughter-in-law and gave a little shudder. 'Julia, love, you're nothing but skin and bone. You could do with putting on a bit of weight.' She regarded her thoughtfully. 'Have you ever considered getting yourself a padded bra, lovie?' As they went in through the front door, Vernon ahead of them, she said, 'Our Vernie looks right worn out. Are you sure he's eating properly?'

In the lounge Charlie was over by the cocktail cabinet, dispensing the drinks. In late middle age he looked every inch the prosperous businessman with his florid complexion and thick white hair. His thickening middle was carefully disguised by the expensively tailored dark grey suit he wore. He looked up as they appeared in the doorway.

'There you are then! Late as usual!' He beckoned to them impatiently. 'Well, come on then. Come in, dammit! Don't stand in the doorway like a set of jugs. I've already poured you each a G and T.' As he put Julia's glass into her hand he bent towards her. 'Looking lovely, m'dear. If I were only twenty years younger, eh?' He winked and nudged her so hard she almost spilled her drink. It was his usual joke, and although she was used to it, it never failed to set her teeth on edge.

It was a small family gathering. Julia's parents, May and Harry Philips, were already there, sitting uneasily on opposite sides of the room. May Philips was an older, faded version of her daughter. Slightly built and still slim, she was a complete contrast to plump, overblown Louise. She wore a plain black dress, its only adornment a small diamond clip that had belonged to her mother. Convent-educated May, whose late father had been the local doctor, had caused quite a stir some forty years previously when she had married Harry Philips, a poorly paid young electrician from the wrong side of town.

Harry, a small, balding man with glasses and a placid, genial expression, was Charlie's business partner in Grant Philips Construction Ltd. The two families had been drawn together by Vernon's and Julia's marriage seventeen years ago, and the business partnership had been established soon after.

Harry went to work for a small firm of electrical engineers when he left school at fourteen. He rose to the position of manager and finally bought his employer out on his retirement. Later, with the aid of a bank loan, he expanded into plumbing and heating. Then, after the marriage of their respective children, Philips Electrics and Grant and Son Builders had joined forces to form Grant Philips Construction, with Vernon, newly out of business college, as the new firm's business manager.

They couldn't have chosen a better time to amalgamate. Once an agricultural area, Elvemere was turning to industry and, foreseeing the need for housing estates to accommodate the influx of workers, GPC had invested heavily in the large parcels of local agricultural land made redundant by EEC regulations. They had tendered for all of the new industrial buildings on the massive new trading park and, thanks to Vernon's negotiating skills, had been contracted to build eighty percent of them. Their latest and most adventurous venture was the building of upmarket luxury homes in the town's leafier suburbs, to attract the rising class of young executives. In seventeen years Grant Philips Construction had grown to become the largest building contractor in the county.

On the window seat sat Vernon's divorced sister, Kathleen, a tall, spiky woman who ran a stud farm on the outskirts of town. Her long hair, normally tied back with an elastic band, hung over one shoulder in a loose plait, schoolgirl fashion, and her angular figure, normally clad in jodhpurs and flannel shirts, looked slightly incongruous in a black skirt and frilly white blouse. As Julia took a seat next to her, May Philips looked at her daughter over the rim of her glass and knew at once by the expression in Julia's eyes that something was wrong. She and Vernon must have had another row. She could always tell. She smiled – she hoped reassuringly.

'Such a pity that Charlotte couldn't be with us,' Louise said, sitting down heavily on the other side of Julia. 'Our only granddaughter. I did hope she'd be with us.'

'She asked me to say how sorry she was to miss it,' Julia said diplomatically. 'But she and her friends had arranged this meal out

32

together months ago. It will be the last time they'll all be together, you see. Some of them will be moving on to college next term.'

'Charlotte did so well, didn't she?' May said placatingly, beaming at Louise with a nervous little laugh. 'Ten GCSEs and most of them As and Bs. And isn't it exciting that she'll be joining the family business? It seems only yesterday that she was a tiny . . .'

'Paper qualifications don't cut any ice with me,' Charlie said bluntly. 'I never had any and I don't think I've done so badly. I'd have taken my own granddaughter into the business whether she had any or not. She'll be nothing but a nuisance to start with, with or without GCSEs!' He threw a reproachful glance at his daughter-in-law. 'I had hoped the two of you would produce a lad to take over the business when we're gone, but there, you didn't, and it's too late now, I suppose.'

He sloshed a generous measure of whisky into his glass as though to reinforce his point. 'And another thing: when *we* were kids we'd have been made to put our grandparents first! Youngsters nowadays don't seem to be brought up to have respect for their elders and betters. Still . . .' He tossed back his treble whisky and burped softly. 'That's progress for you, more's the pity.' He looked at his watch, then at his wife. 'What about some food then, Mother? Isn't it time you ran along to the kitchen and got that lass to put on her cap and apron?' He rubbed his hands and looked round at them. 'Don't know about you lot but my stomach's rumbling fit to wake the dead.'

Louise had put on a sumptuous meal and hired a woman to serve it. Prawn cocktails to start, roast turkey with all the trimmings, followed by sherry trifle, and cheese and biscuits. Charlie dispensed the wine with the air of a connoisseur, a light Chablis with the starter, a rosé with the main course and a sweet Sauternes with the desert. When May Philips protested at his refilling her glass for the fourth time, Charlie insisted.

'Come on, woman, it's our anniversary. We don't want any wet blankets here tonight.' He filled her glass to the brim. 'I've got no time for gentility meself,' he announced, reinforcing the statement with a barely stifled burp. 'An occasion like this deserves a slap-up blow-out with plenty of good quality booze. And this stuff . . .' he held the bottle aloft . . . 'is the business. Twenty quid a bottle.'

He sat down, smiling benignly round at them. 'Well, what do you think of Mother's present from me then?' He waved his fork in the direction of his wife's necklace. 'You've not said, any of you. A couple of grand that little lot set me back. And that was at cost too! Got a mate in the jewellery trade. Nothing but the best for my

Lou. Wouldn't be where I am today but for her.' He raised his glass to his wife, sitting at the other end of the table. 'To Lou,' he said. 'To Mother, God bless her.'

The others reiterated the toast while Louise, blushing, waved a plump, heavily ringed hand at them. 'Get away with you all,' she said. 'I told Gladys to serve coffee in the lounge so let's go and get it, shall we?'

As they filed out of the dining room Julia looked surreptitiously at her watch. It was almost ten o'clock. How long before she could decently suggest leaving? she wondered as she made her excuses and went upstairs.

In Louise's bedroom with its half tester bed draped in pink flounces she applied lipstick at the dressing table. The door opened and her mother slipped into the room and leaned against it exhaustedly.

'Oh, dear, that meal,' she said. 'So rich, and so much *of* it. I'm so full I can hardly move, but one daren't refuse anything. They get so offended.' She hiccuped gently. 'Oh, excuse me. I'm afraid I'm a little tipsy too. All that wine that Charles kept insisting on pouring. I never could drink more than half a glass, as you know, and I must have had at least four.'

Julia smiled at her. The fact that she doggedly persisted in calling Charlie Grant 'Charles' irritated him intensely and was the main reason why he always tried so hard to make her feel uncomfortable.

May sat down on the end of Lousie's bed and peered at her daughter's reflection in the mirror. 'Are you all right, dear? You look pale and I thought you looked strained when you first arrived.'

'I'm fine. I suppose it's worrying about Charlotte's exam results but that's all over now.'

May examined her nails. 'Er – you and Vernon – you're – all right?'

'We're fine.'

'You do know, don't you, darling,' May said earnestly, 'that Daddy and I are always there if you're in need of – you know, someone to talk to?'

Julia got up from the dressing table and bent to kiss her mother's cheek. 'I do know and I'm grateful.'

'I know that things are sometimes – well, difficult for you. I do so want to see you happy.'

'I know. And I am.' Julia offered an arm to her mother. 'Shall we go down now?'

In the lounge Charlie was passing round liqueurs. He pounced on May the moment she entered the room. 'Ah, there you are.

34

Come on, sit down and make yourself comfy. I know what *you* like – cherry brandy, eh? Just suits you, May. I've always said you were like a little cherry blossom, so small and dainty.' He pinched her cheek playfully. His face was glowing and red from the wine he'd drunk and he was becoming more outspoken by the minute. 'Mind you,' he went on with a deep-throated chuckle, 'I never went much for *little* women myself. Always liked plenty to get hold of, haven't I, Mother?'

Louise bridled. 'Behave yourself, Charlie. You're making poor May blush.'

But he swept aside her protest. 'Rubbish! May knows it's only my fun. We're all family and friends here.'

Kathleen, who'd hardly spoken all evening, lit a cigarette. As she exhaled the smoke she said casually, 'I hear you're going in for local politics, Julia?'

Everyone turned to stare at Julia who blushed hotly. Charlie's benign smile vanished and he glowered across the room at her.

'*Never*! Well?' he demanded. 'Is it true? Are you?'

'Well, *yes*.' Julia cleared her throat, resenting the embarrassment and the sudden inexplicable guilt she felt. 'As a matter of fact, I'm standing at the by-election in October.'

'You mean you're hoping to take Jack Martin's place?' Charlie stared at her. 'Old Jack was on the Town Council for more than forty years. If he hadn't dropped dead he'd have been on it still.'

'He'd been ailing for a good few years, I believe,' Julia said coolly. 'I understand he hadn't been at a council meeting at all for the past year and he'd been absent from a good many before that.'

Charlie's colour deepened. 'Are you criticising Jack Martin?' he challenged. 'Jack was one of my oldest friends. He was on that council when you were no more'n a glint in your father's eye. Well, I'll tell you this, lass, you'll go a long way to better him. Chairman of the planning committee for years, Jack was. We've got him to thank for a lot of our successes and . . .'

'Never mind that now, Dad,' Vernon put in. 'It's only something Julia's been *thinking* of. Chances are she'll change her mind once she learns of all the hard work that's involved. Anyway, it's unlikely she'd ever get elected.'

'I should just think not!' Charlie said, pouring himself another brandy. 'And I'm surprised at you for allowing it, Vernon. Won't get my vote, I'll tell you that now, Julia. Women in politics! I've never held with it.'

'We do happen to have a woman Prime Minister, Father,' Kathleen put in with a wry smile.

35

'Maggie Thatcher's a one off,' Charlie waved his glass at his daughter. 'She's got a man's mind. Once she's finished you'll not see another like her in many a long year. And a good thing too if you ask me. Women are on this earth for three things. To be good wives, bring up children and to give a man a good . . .'

'That'll *do*, Charlie,' Louise interrupted, her cheeks pink. 'I think we've heard enough on the subject for one night.' She glared reproachfully at Julia, as though Charlie's outburst had been her fault. 'I'm sure Julia has far too much to do at home to want to get herself mixed up with the council anyway. If you take my advice, Julia, you'll leave all the argy-bargying to the menfolk and get on with your own job. I saw the way Vernie tucked in to his dinner tonight. Maybe now that Charlotte's off hand, you'll have more time to cook nice meals for the two of you.'

Seeing her sister-in-law's rising colour, Kathleen got to her feet. 'I'll have to be off,' she said abruptly in an attempt to defuse the situation. 'I've got a mare due to drop a foal at any time and I don't like to be away too long.' In the hall as they saw her off Kathleen bent towards Julia and said in an undertone, 'Sorry if I dropped you in it, but I daresay criticism is something you're going to have to get used to if you're serious about standing for the council. Good luck with it if you do. You'll get my vote, for what it's worth. Time someone got in among all those old fogies and started stirring things up a bit.'

Julia smiled at her. 'Thanks, Kath. I'll remember that.'

'And tell Charlotte to come round and see the new foal whenever she likes.'

'I will. She'll be thrilled.'

The party broke up soon after that. May, glad of the excuse to get away, pleaded a headache, and soon after that Julia and Vernon said their goodnights too.

In the car as they fastened their seat belts, Vernon looked at Julia. 'Satisfied, are you?'

'I don't know what you mean.'

'No? You only managed to ruin the evening with your radical views.'

Julia laughed. 'Radical? Just because I happen to think that councillors are supposed to attend meetings? And might I remind you that it was Kath who brought the subject up, not me? She happens to be on my side.'

'Your side!' Vernon sneered as he started the car. 'My sister would be on the side of anyone about to cause trouble,' he said bitterly. 'She thinks people are there to be schooled, like those horses of hers. Now she hasn't got a husband of her own to push around she's doing her best to disrupt other people's lives. No doubt she saw it as trying to liven the evening up.'

Julia smiled ruefully into the darkness. 'And what's wrong with that?' she muttered under her breath.

As Harry Philips drove his Rover in through the gates of Gresham House he turned to look at his wife in concern. 'All right, dear? Head still bad, is it?'

'I haven't really got a headache at all,' May confessed. 'But I would have if we'd stayed much longer. Charles really is the limit. He's so vulgar. And we really must take a dose of liver salts when we get in, if we want to get a wink of sleep tonight. That meal was enough to give anyone indigestion for a month!'

Harry chuckled. 'I know what you mean. Hardly what you'd call health food, was it? Still, Lou's a good sort at heart. I'm sure she did her best. I suppose it's what they're used to.'

May sighed. Lou could be a real bitch with her snide remarks, but Harry always saw the best in everyone. Sometimes she thought he was too mild, especially where the business was concerned. Charles and Vernon always seemed to be the ones making the important decisions. Harry just did the donkey work and smoothed the men down when Charles upset them. He'd averted industrial action more than once after Charles's abrasive manner had upset things, but he never took any credit for his diplomacy. She laid a hand on his arm. 'They say it's a pity you can't choose your relatives,' she said. 'It seems to me that the same applies to business partners.'

In the hall as she took off her coat she asked, 'Harry – did you think Julia seemed upset?'

He shook his head. 'Can't say I noticed. I thought she was looking especially nice this evening.'

'And what was all that about her standing for the council?' May said, a frown creasing her brow. 'I'd have thought she had enough on her plate with that large house and all her committees.'

Harry patted her shoulder and smiled benignly. 'I shouldn't worry about her if I were you, dear. You know Julia. She'll do what she wants to do in the end whatever we say. She always has. And you've always worried about her unnecessarily, haven't you? Remember that time she left home and worked in London for over a year? I told you then she'd come home when she was ready and she did, didn't she?'

'I daresay you're right, dear.' But May was remembering the girl who came home to them, so changed and withdrawn. She'd never told Harry about the times she had got up in the night and heard Julia sobbing into her pillow. He hadn't seen the girl undressed as she had and noticed the way her ribs showed through her flesh and how pitifully thin she'd grown. She took off her coat, patting her hair thoughtfully in the hall mirror. 'Do you think she and Vernon are happy?' she asked. 'You know, sometimes I wonder if we threw them together all those years ago. We were so anxious to get her safely married to someone suitable at the time, weren't we?'

'And who could be more suitable than Vernon?' Harry's eyes looked startled behind his spectacles. 'I must say it's never struck me that we threw them together. I've always thought how lucky it was that they met and fell in love just at the right time.'

'Well – yes.' May was remembering the dinner parties and barbecues she had thrown, making sure that the Grants and their good-looking son were invited; how much she had hoped and prayed to see her wayward daughter comfortably settled.

'They were an ideal couple and very much in love. I'm sure they still are,' Harry went on. 'After all, look at what they've got; a lovely daughter and a beautiful home. A prosperous business and no money worries. Oh, no, I'm sure they're happy.'

May sighed. 'I expect you're right, dear. You usually are.'

In the pink bedroom at Queen's Lodge Charlie and Louise were getting ready for bed. Louise sat at the dressing table in her pink lace négligée, creaming her face. 'Was it really all right?' she asked. 'People don't seem to eat like they used to. May just picked at everything like a bird. I remember when I was at home on the farm we'd have great joints and piles of vegetables and it'd all get eaten. Nowadays all they seem to want to do is nibble at lettuce leaves and a bit of tomato.'

Charlie, resplendent in purple striped pyjamas, climbed into bed and thumped his pillow into submission. 'Stop whittling, Lou. It was a grand meal. Anyway, May and Harry always look as if a damn good meal would kill them, and as for our Vernon . . .'

Louise swung round. 'You noticed it too, did you? I told Julia straight. Our Vernie's looking right poorly, I said. Are you sure he's eating properly? But I don't think she took the hint. Sometimes I think she's a bit thick. All that rubbish about cholesterol and cardia vasica – what d'you call it! If you ask me it's just an excuse not to cook properly.' She wiped off the last of the cleansing cream and picked up her hair brush. 'What did you make of that business about her standing for the council?'

Charlie grunted. 'Nothing but a bloody fad! I blame Vernon,' he said. 'He should put his foot down; give her a thick ear if needs be.' He began to chuckle as his wife removed her négligée to reveal the filmy nightdress beneath. 'Failing that, a good seeing to. That'd keep her happy. She looks frigid if you ask me!'

'*Charlie!*'

He reached out to pull her on to the bed. 'Come off it, Lou. You're not frigid, I'm happy to say. Come on, you know you love it, and it *is* our anniversary, so how about it?'

Fleur turned over in the narrow bed, closed her eyes tightly and tried hard to sleep. It felt so odd, lying in this bed in an unfamiliar room, knowing that tomorrow morning when she woke and looked out of the window everything outside would be new and strange. Before she slept she'd written a quick letter to Bobby, giving her her new address. The act of writing to her friend had somehow made things feel more settled and less unreal. The train journey from London to Elvemere had taken less than an hour, yet she might as well have been on another planet and already she felt disorientated and homesick.

Her first priority had been finding somewhere to sleep. Outside the station she spotted a policeman and asked him if he knew of any cheap lodgings.

'You could try Mrs Franks at number thirteen Victoria Gardens. She'll put you up, love,' he said kindly. 'I happen to know she's got a room vacant at the moment. It's not posh, mind, but it's clean and cheap. Tell her PC Roberts sent you.'

'Can you tell me how to get there?' Fleur asked.

He pointed across the road. 'If you get on a number four bus over there, it'll drop you off at the park gates. Ask again when you get there. It isn't far.'

Victoria Gardens consisted of a crescent of three-storey terraced houses with a green in the centre encircled by iron railings. It had been built by local tradesmen and merchants in the middle of the nineteenth century at the height of the town's prosperity and had once been a fashionable residential area. But with the advent of the motor car it had fallen out of vogue in favour of the suburbs and now the place had a sad, neglected air. The front doors that once gleamed with immaculate black paintwork and shining brasses were scuffed and peeling. The central green, once meticulously manicured and planted with flowering shrubs, was now a tangle of weeds and rough grass, a hunting ground for the local cats and a dump for empty bottles and used fish and chip wrappings.

Fleur found number thirteen and stood looking up at it before mounting the front steps. The windows were dulled by grease from decades of passing traffic and she could see very little through the greying net curtains. She knocked hopefully on the front door and after a short interval a door below in the area opened and a woman in a blue nylon overall stuck her head out and peered up.

'Can you come down here, love?' she said without removing the cigarette from her mouth. 'Save my legs, eh?' As Fleur descended the area steps the woman looked her over critically, guessing that she'd be after the room. They never stayed vacant for long, but Ivy Franks generally preferred male lodgers, they weren't so much trouble. In her experience young women were always wanting to come down to the kitchen to wash their smalls or cook fussy meals. They left long hairs in the bathroom plughole and spent far too long in the bath. Then there were the boyfriends . . . She could write a book about the love life of some of her female ex-lodgers. You had to be careful of all that. It soon got the place a bad name.

'Yes? What can I do for you then?'

'I've just arrived from London,' Fleur explained. 'I asked a policeman at the station. PC Roberts, he said his name was. And he said you had a room vacant?' She looked hopefully at the woman whose wary eyes were permanently narrowed by smoke from the cigarette which dangled from the corner of her mouth. She wore a bright red lipstick, applied in an exaggerated Cupid's bow and her frizzy hair was a dubious shade of auburn.

'Well now, I dunno where he got that idea from,' she said guardedly. 'Come from London, eh?' The narrowed eyes took in the short skirt and shapely legs. Could she be on the game? You never could be sure nowadays, and you couldn't be too careful who you let your rooms to.

'Got a job then, have you?' she asked, subjecting Fleur's features and the luxuriant mane of dark hair to embarrassingly close scrutiny.

'Well, no. I'll be looking for one though.'

'So, if you've not come here to work, what brings you to Elvemere?' Ivy asked bluntly.

'I'm here to look up some relatives.' The reply slipped out glibly on impulse. Fleur didn't like the suspicious way the woman was eyeing her and it was the most respectable reason she could think of.

Ivy Franks's face brightened. 'Oh, I see. So it'll only be temp'ry then, will it?'

'I expect so, yes.'

Ivy held the door open. 'In that case, you might as well come in.'

Fleur followed the woman inside with relief. It was past seven o'clock and she hadn't looked forward to searching for digs in a strange town after dark. Inside the basement kitchen of number thirteen it was dim but cheerful. An ancient Aga provided a warm atmosphere. There was a large table in the centre of the room, two comfortable shabby armchairs and a dresser. In one corner there was an archway through which she could see a sink and kitchen cabinet.

'I live down here,' Ivy explained. 'All the rooms upstairs except my bedroom are let to my "perms".'

Fleur frowned. 'Perms?'

'Permanent paying guests,' Ivy supplied. 'There are two flats at the back,' she said proudly. 'Big bedsits with their own facilities. They're more expensive, of course. Young Robbie – PC Roberts – lived in one of them before he got married last year. He said there was no privacy at the Section House.' She removed the cigarette stub for a moment. 'Mind you, I don't encourage my tenants to entertain visitors of the opposite sex,' she warned. 'At the moment I've got a bank clerk in one and the manager of a hardware shop in the other. Most of my perms are business gentlemen, you see. I don't normally take young women.' She sniffed and folded her arms. 'But as you say it's only temp'ry. . . .'

'Oh, yes.'

'I don't do food,' Ivy warned. 'There are gas rings in the rooms and if you've got an electric kettle you can use that. Electric's on a meter.'

'Er – how much?' Fleur asked.

Ivy raised an eyebrow. 'Better have a dekko at the room first, hadn't you?'

The vacant room was at the top of the house and looked out over the central green with its jungle of overgrown shrubs and rusting railings. From up here it looked even more squalid. It was a long, narrow room and held a single bed, a dressing table and chair, a wardrobe and a marble-topped wash stand which doubled as a worktop and table. On the floor was linoleum covered by a narrow strip of threadbare carpet.

'The bathroom's on the floor below,' Ivy told her. 'I've had a shower put in to keep the costs low. It takes less time too,' she added meaningfully. 'There's always a queue for the bathroom of a morning. And in the interests of my gentlemen, I'd be obliged if you wouldn't hang your undies in there. There's a yard at the back with a line.' She named a rent at which Fleur heaved a sigh of relief. It might not be luxurious but at least she could afford it. Until her money ran out.

'I'll take it,' she said.

'Right. Want to go and collect your stuff then?'

'There's only the two cases I brought with me,' Fleur told her. 'I'll come down and get them.'

At the bottom of the stairs Ivy turned to look at her new lodger, her sharp features relaxing into a smile. 'I was just going to make myself a cup of tea,' she said. 'Fancy one, do you?'

Fleur smiled. 'I'd love one. Thanks.'

'Right. You just get them things upstairs and come right down to the kitchen.' There was something intriguing about this girl. She had a foreign look about her that Ivy couldn't place. She could be Spanish or even Cypriot or Maltese. Yet she reckoned she had relatives here in Elvemere. Maybe over tea Ivy could find out who she was and who these relations were she'd spoken of.

'So, you'll be looking for work then?' Ivy poured Fleur a cup of strong tea and passed the biscuit tin across the chenille-covered table.

'Yes.'

'In what line would that be?'

'I'll take anything,' Fleur told her. 'In London I worked in a fish and chip shop, but only because it was all I could get. I'd like to get something better if I could.'

'Waitressing?'

'What I'd really like would be to train for something. I got ten "O" levels before I left school. I would have stayed on for my "A"s but my grandmother was ill so I left school to help her.'

'Granny from foreign parts, was she?' Ivy asked slyly.

'No. A Londoner.'

'I see.' Ivy sipped her tea, peering speculatively at Fleur over the rim of her cup. 'Mum and Dad?'

'My grandmother brought me up,' Fleur said.

'So how's she managing without you?'

'She died a few weeks ago.'

'I see. I'm sorry to hear that.' Ivy lit a fresh cigarette from the stub of the old one and squinted at Fleur through the cloud of exhaled smoke. 'So now you've come to look up the rest of your family?'

'Well, distant relatives really. Yes – probably. But mainly to make a new start.'

'What would their name be then – these relatives? I mean, I might even know them. Same as yours, is it, Sylvester?'

'Er – yes, that's right,' Fleur lied. She realised now that the woman had only offered her tea so that she could quiz her for information.

'But I lost touch with them years ago, so they might not even live here any more.'

Ivy screwed up her face thoughtfully. 'Sylvester. Would that be a foreign name then?'

'Not as far as I know.'

'Well, I can't say I've ever heard of any Sylvesters in these parts. Still I don't know everybody, do I?' She cackled hoarsely. 'They do say the Salvation Army are good at finding lost relatives.'

'Oh – well, I shall have to think about that.'

As soon as she could Fleur made her excuses and left. As she came up the basement stairs into the hallway she met a young man on his way in. He smiled at her. 'Hello there. Have you just taken the top floor front?'

'Thats right, Fleur Sylvester.' She held out her hand and he shook it.

'Tom Markham.' He looked at her appreciatively. 'Well, I must say, it'll be a treat to see a feminine face around here for once.' He lowered his voice. 'It's not too bad here as long as you don't intend to spend the rest of your life in the place. Watch the old girl though. The News Of The World, we call her. She knows everyone's business. Take a tip from me and don't tell her anything unless you want the whole town to know about it.'

Fleur laughed. 'I'd already gathered that.'

He had a nice, unremarkable face with warm brown eyes and floppy brown hair. It was cheering to see a friendly face, but he disappeared into one of the first-floor rooms and when she had climbed the next flight to the top floor and closed the door it hit her quite suddenly how alone she was. Had she done the right thing? Fleur asked herself as she stood at the window looking down into the litter-strewn green. This place looked hardly any more salubrious than Brightman Lane. Would she have done better to have stayed in London where she knew people and everything was familiar? Then she remembered the street fights, the racism and muggings. No. She'd been right to take Grandma's advice and make a fresh start. The future was in her own hands now. And her first priority was to get a job. Things would surely be better once she had settled down.

Fleur spent most of that first week familiarising herself with the layout of the town. On her first morning she discovered to her satisfaction that Victoria Gardens was within easy walking distance of the town centre, which would save on bus fares. At the first newsagent's she came to she invested in a street map and took it into a cafe to study over a cup of coffee and a doughnut. Soon she knew her way around. The Market Square, the Town Hall, the Cathedral and the town's bright new shopping mall soon became familiar territory.

She liked what she saw. For the most part, Elvemere was clean and spacious, a fascinating mixture of the very old and the brand new. It had wide streets with bright, well-stocked shops and plenty of trees and flowers. And everywhere the towering presence of the great Cathedral was like a protective patriarch, enfolding the town in its embrace.

The Cathedral had been a surprise. Somehow she hadn't expected a town as small as Elvemere to have a great medieval cathedral at its heart. She'd always thought that only large cities had cathedrals.

She often reminded herself that this was the place where her mother belonged. She would have known these streets as a child, probably walked these very pavements and looked in these shop windows every day. Sometimes she found herself wondering what Julia was like and what she had made of her life. It struck her once with a small shock that they could pass each other in the street and not realise it.

She invested some of her precious money in an electric kettle, a small saucepan and a toaster. She had to have the means of making herself a cheap meal, eating out was out of the question. Each day she went to the Job Centre and studied the cards displayed there. There were plenty of vacancies for shop assistants and filing clerks, but although Fleur wasn't completely clear exactly what it was she wanted, she knew she wanted something with more of a challenge to it than any of them. She longed for a job that had a future – prospects for improvement; something that would fire her imagination and bring satisfaction. But jobs in this category were clearly going to be hard to find and Fleur's meagre savings were dwindling fast. In the end she was obliged to apply for a job stacking shelves in the town's largest supermarket.

She had been there a little over a month and had almost given up hope of finding anything better when she spotted something that intrigued her in the Situations Vacant column of the local evening paper. The advertiser wanted a general assistant to help in a catering firm. '*The applicant should preferably have some experience in the catering trade, should be willing to work flexible hours and versatile enough to juggle several tasks at once,*' the ad read. '*Initiative and common sense essential.*' Something about the way it was worded stirred Fleur's interest. She had a little experience of the catering trade, helping Dolly with her party buffets. Perhaps that would count in her favour?

Fleur went out to a telephone box to ring the number given in the paper. The pay phone at number thirteen had been installed at the top of the basement stairs and she had already learned that Ivy Franks always left her door open so that she could eavesdrop on all her lodgers' conversations.

A woman with a pleasant voice answered her call and an appointment was arranged for the following evening after work. For the first time since she had arrived in Elvemere, Fleur went to bed that night in a hopeful frame of mind.

Sally Arden was forty-nine and had started her catering business twenty years previously when her husband died suddenly, leaving her a penniless widow with a young son to bring up. Desperate to make some money to keep her home going she had begun in a small way, working from her own kitchen and catering for friends' parties and small functions. But word had soon spread and her business had gone from strength to strength. Now she ran a successful outside catering firm, providing buffets and meals for everything from weddings to boardroom lunches.

She explained all this to Fleur as she interviewed her in the office at her pleasant suburban home. 'I started working from home when my son Peter was little and it's become a habit,' she said. 'It's handy too as I still do all the cooking myself. I can answer the telephone while I'm busy in the kitchen.'

'How many other staff have you got?' Fleur asked.

'None. I still do most of the work myself,' Sally smiled. 'I hire my waitresses on a casual part-time basis and I drive the van myself. But I must admit that I do get tired more easily than I used to and my son has finally convinced me that I really do need a permanent assistant.'

'What would the job involve?' Fleur asked.

Sally laughed. 'A bit of everything, I suppose. I do a lot of preparation in advance, storing food in the freezer, so to begin with you'd probably find yourself spending all day making sandwiches or filling vol-au-vents. On the other hand, I'd need you to answer the telephone when I'm not here – take bookings, that kind of thing.' She smiled. 'When we had a function on I'd need you to come along with me to help set everything up, maybe double as a waitress if we were short-handed, and generally run around for me. That would mean working unsocial hours, I'm afraid. Of course I'd pay you the going rate for overtime, or we could arrange time off in lieu, whatever you preferred.'

Fleur smiled. 'I don't know anyone in Elvemere, so I don't have any social life at the moment. I haven't worked in the catering trade before, but my grandmother used to cater for parties and I usually helped her,' she said frankly. 'I'm quite a good cook too. My grandmother taught me.' She paused, glancing at her prospective employer hopefully. 'My grandfather was from Jamaica and I can make some Caribbean dishes. So maybe when I've got the sandwiches right I could learn to do something more ambitious?'

Sally looked at the girl's eager face and warmed towards her. 'Of course the job can go much further than that if you want it to,' she said. 'If you were interested, I could teach you to cook some of the more adventurous dishes, and eventually how to interview clients and assess their needs – make suggestions, create menus, all that. Then there's the business side of things: the ordering, accounts and book keeping. Can you drive – use a computer?'

Fleur shook her head, her cheeks flushing with excitement. 'No, but I'd love to try all of those things. I'm sure I could learn.'

Sally nodded. 'I'm sure you could too. We can sort out driving lessons and some evening classes for you. And, of course, the more responsibility you can take, the more you'll earn, so it will be worth your while.' She liked the look of the girl. She was intelligent and keen to learn. She was very young, of course, but for all her youth there was an air about her – a presence that Sally found impressive. If she could be trained to work in all branches of the job she could prove an invaluable asset in time. Sally stood up and held out her hand. 'Well, Fleur, you seem prepared to be flexible. If you really think you'd like it we could give it a go. Shall we say a month's trial?'

It was beginning to rain when Fleur got off the bus at the park gates and by the time she reached the Gardens it was coming down fast, large cold drops that quickly penetrated her light summer clothes. Her head down, she ran all the way to number thirteen and had just reached the front door when she bumped into someone coming the other way.

'Oh! I'm sorry. I . . .' Looking up, she saw Tom Markham smiling down at her. 'Oh, it's you.'

He looked at her thin clothes and took her arm. 'Better get in before you get soaked.' Inside she took off her jacket and shook the raindrops from it. Tom looked at her. 'You seem pleased with yourself.'

She smiled at him. 'I've just got a job.'

'I thought you already had one? Whenever I see you you're

rushing off somewhere. We've hardly spoken since the night you arrived.'

She pulled a face. 'I don't call stacking supermarket shelves a job. It's more of a punishment. Anyway, it was only temporary. To keep me going and pay the rent. This is something much better.'

He looked at her glowing cheeks and shining dark eyes. 'Look, do you want to come and tell me about it?' He held out the large newspaper-wrapped parcel he was carrying. 'I've just been out for some fish and chips and I always get too many.'

She hesitated, wondering how Ivy Franks would feel about her going into Tom's room. She had made her disapproval of 'entertaining' only too plain. Besides, since the attack Fleur had fought off she had found herself instinctively avoiding being alone with a man.

'Come on. You'd be doing me a favour by helping me eat them,' Tom urged. 'I'll only put on weight and you wouldn't want that on your conscience, would you?'

She laughed. 'Okay then. You're on.' Tom was nice and she was going to have to overcome her apprehension sometime, and it would be great to be able to tell someone about her good luck instead of shutting herself away alone for the rest of the evening.

Tom's room on the first floor was larger than hers. It had a three-quarter bed and an armchair. Best of all it had its own wash basin. She looked around. 'This is better than my room.'

He filled the kettle and plugged it in, then began to unwrap the fish and chips. 'There are some plates in the bottom of the wardrobe, if you wouldn't mind,' he said. 'There isn't anywhere else to keep them.' He grinned. 'It's hardly The Ritz, is it?'

'It is compared to mine,' Fleur told him. 'You've even got a gas fire. I don't know what I'll do when the weather gets cold.'

Tom struck a match and the fire popped into life. 'Old Poison Ivy will find you an electric fire if you're still here in the winter. But I expect you will have moved on to pastures new with this fabulous new job of yours.' He pointed to the chair. 'Hang your jacket over that to dry,' he invited.

Over supper he told her that he worked as a reporter on the local paper. He'd been born in Elvemere, but spent much of his childhood away at school.

'My dad died when I was ten and my mother went to live with her parents in Yorkshire. My grandfather paid for me to go to boarding school.' He grinned. 'To get me out of the way, I think. They were getting on in years and I was a bit of a tearaway. I did my training on a Yorkshire paper, but I always wanted to come back here so when the vacancy came up on the *Elvemere Clarion*, I applied.'

'It must be interesting, working for a paper?' Fleur remarked.

'Very, even if the hours are terrible. But you were going to tell me about this marvellous job you've landed?'

She shook her head. 'It isn't a marvellous job yet, but it will be. I'll have a chance to build it up, to learn to drive and work with a computer. Best of all it's working with food and people, both of which I like.'

'I think you might have landed on your feet,' Tom told her. 'Everybody in Elvemere knows Arden Catering. Mrs Arden is a very successful lady. She does all the best weddings in the district, engagement parties and so on, plus all the council functions.' He grinned. 'Everything I ever cover for the *Clarion* seems to be catered for by Mrs Arden. There's a lot of one-uppmanship here, you know. I imagine it's become quite trendy to have Arden Catering providing the nosh for your do.'

Fleur's eyes were shining. 'It sounds as if I'm in for a fascinating time.'

'You'll be in for a busy time by the sound of it, what with your driving lessons and your evening classes.'

Tom made coffee after they'd eaten and they sat near the gas fire, their hands round the warm mugs, relaxing and getting to know one another. 'What made you leave London and come here?' he asked.

'My grandmother died and I didn't fancy staying on alone.'

'Why Elvemere though?'

She shrugged. 'Stuck a pin in the map?' she offered.

'Well, your pin struck lucky for me,' he said. 'I've got nothing in common with the two other guys here and working the odd hours that I do, I don't have much social life. It gets lonely sometimes. So if you ever have any time off from all your studying . . .'

'Yes – er . . .' Suddenly Fleur felt a twinge of uncertainty. She glanced at the clock and stood up, handing him her empty mug. 'It's getting late. I'd better go,' she said. 'Thanks for supper and the coffee.'

Tom put both mugs down on the mantelpiece and looked at her anxiously. 'Look, I didn't mean anything, Fleur. I'm not trying to push or anything. It's just that it'd be nice to have someone friendly around.'

Embarrassed, she began to back towards the door. 'Of course. I know. Yes, it would.'

'Look – Fleur.' He reached out to touch her arm. 'If you want company any time, I'm here. Just knock on the door. I won't hassle you. Right?'

She smiled, feeling awkward and foolish. 'Of course, Tom. And – thanks.'

'I've got the car. It's only a clapped-out Metro, but I could take you for a run down to the coast one Sunday, – if you'd like that?'

'Yes. That might be nice. Goodnight, Tom.'

Later, tucked up in bed, Fleur thought about Tom, and their talk over supper, his offer of friendship and tentative invitation. She felt slightly ashamed. She'd always been more than able to stand up for herself, so why had she behaved so stupidly? The man who had attacked her had been a vicious thug. It had been a frightening, humiliating incident, but she had survived and it was unlikely to happen again. Tom was so different; decent and kind. She was going to have to start trusting men again. If she didn't she'd become warped and paranoid. As she closed her eyes she made up her mind to take him up on his offer of a trip to the sea.

Chapter 3

Canvassing was an eye-opener for Julia. She could not believe that she had lived in Elvemere all her life and not known of the conditions under which some people lived. On some of the council estates she was shocked to find that there were homes where there was no floor covering and hardly any furniture. It was the kind of poverty she had previously thought existed only in inner city areas, not prosperous small towns like Elvemere.

It was a far cry from the luxurious home she took so much for granted and she felt slightly ashamed. Yet in spite of her smart outfit and generally affluent appearance, she was greeted for the most part with respect and politeness. There were people who were rude, of course. She had been prepared for that. But she found that most of the rudeness came from the people who had all they needed in life and – if Councillor Eleanor Maitland was correct – never bothered to vote anyway.

Eleanor Maitland was in her mid-sixties. She had been on the council for more than twenty years and was well known for her outspoken views and her toughness. She had taken Julia under her wing from the first and had generously offered to accompany her on the first few forays into the unknown world of political canvassing.

'You'll need a thick skin, my dear,' she said, pulling on her sensible tweed coat and ramming the familiar brown felt hat down over her steel-grey hair. 'A thick skin and a lot of determination. Not only with the voters either,' she added. 'You'll find some of your fellow councillors are hard nuts to crack. It helps to do your homework well – make sure you're damned well right. Don't let the buggers grind you down, in other words.'

Councillor Maitland's gritty obstinacy and doggedness in getting what she wanted for the people she represented had earned her the nickname 'Old Brillo'. It alluded not only to her tightly permed grey hair, but also her abrasive manner. She confided in Julia that not only was she perfectly aware of the nickname, she was actually proud of it.

'I may be a dyed in the wool Tory, my dear, but I stand for the underprivileged. They can't speak up for themselves but I bloody well can. I was one of them myself once and I know what I'm talking about.'

It was no accident that on their first day out together she took Julia to the streets she had never ventured into before, to show her the class from which she herself sprang. In spite of the poverty Julia found there was pride and dignity here too, a resigned acceptance that tugged at her heart-strings and a desire for betterment against all the odds: qualities that unearthed old memories for her.

But, as always, there was another side to the coin. There were those who felt the world owed them a living and would milk the system for all they could get. There were the resentful, suspicious ones; tough unshaven men in string vests who used the kind of language that made Julia's toes curl, and expressed their views of the Tory Party, and Mrs Thatcher in particular, in highly colourful terms. Eleanor was equal to them all.

'All right, lad. Keep your hair on,' she'd bellow good-naturedly. 'Tory we might be but we're on your side, can't you see that? Party politics count for nothing when it comes to local government. We're here to do our best to try and put things right for you, so just watch your language and show a bit of respect.'

Julia admired her enormously. Privately she felt that she could never be as tough or as outspoken as Eleanor if she lived to be a hundred. All the same she was inspired enough to want to try. From Eleanor she learned to handle the insults and swearing with dignity; how to cope with the awkward ones and convince the waverers. There were some it was wisest to walk away from, and those who, with patience and sincerity, could be won over. Eleanor showed her how to spot the difference.

After a particularly gruelling evening of canvassing Eleanor asked Julia in for a much needed cup of tea when she dropped her off outside her house.

'I reckon you can go it alone now, lass,' she said as she filled the kettle. 'You don't need me to hold your hand any more.'

Eleanor still lived in the little house she and her husband had shared since the day they married. It was a tiny terraced cottage in a row originally built for railway workers. It had two rooms upstairs and two down and few modern conveniences, but Eleanor had made it homely and warm. There were hanging baskets and brightly planted tubs in the back yard and her little living-kitchen was bright and welcoming with its yellow curtains and geraniums on the window sill. Looking around her, Julia noticed that the bookcase was full of biographies of eminent statesmen and books written by campaigning politicians.

Eleanor drew the curtains on the gathering darkness outside and turned to look at Julia's doubtful face. 'Don't worry, you're doing fine.'

'I hope you're right.'

'I am!' Eleanor plonked a tray of tea down on the table between them. 'You know, I'm pinning a lot of hope on you, my dear. I can't go on forever. Old Jack Martin's death set me off thinking. I've been on Elvemere Town Council for almost as long as he had and I hope I've done a bit of good in that time. I'd like to think there'd be some like-minded person to carry on the work when the time comes for me to pop my clogs.' She smiled at Julia. 'You've got the background and the education I never had. You've got the *words*. All I ever had was a bloody loud voice and teeth like a bulldog.'

'I don't think anyone will ever replace you,' Julia said with an affectionate smile. 'But I'm deeply flattered that you have so much confidence in me.'

'You'll be all right, lass,' Eleanor said, nodding to herself as she poured tea into willow pattern cups. 'Of course there are those no one will ever help. You'll have to get used to having your teeth kicked in and your heart broken for your trouble. But just keep on believing in the human race, that's the secret. There's an old saying: To be in the weakest camp is to be in the strongest school. Just remember that.'

'I will.' Julia pulled her canvassing schedule out of the bag that contained her leaflets. 'Well, if I'm flying solo I might as well start right away.' She unfolded the paper and spread it on the table between them. 'I think I'll make a start on Victoria Gardens. I can drop the leaflets off on my way home and follow them up tomorrow evening.'

Eleanor smiled. 'That's the spirit, lass.'

As she saw Julia off on the doorstep, she said, 'Oh, by the way. I don't know if you realise it but Victoria Gardens is due for redevelopment.'

'They're surely not thinking of pulling it down?'

'No, they can't. The houses are listed, but the place has been getting steadily more rundown these past years. The plan is to buy up all the occupied houses and renovate the whole place – turn the ground floors into offices and maybe have some luxury flats above. The council's got some vague thoughts about turning a section of it into a health centre – maybe even a new library.'

'I see.'

'But that's all under your hat, understand?' Eleanor tapped the side of her nose. 'I'm only telling you so that you'll be careful what you say when you're round there. Don't make any promises.'

'Right. I won't.'

Julia parked her car near the park gates and set off to drop her leaflets. As she walked round Victoria Gardens she saw what Eleanor had meant about the place being rundown. It was years since she had visited the place. Her school friend, Joanna Bloom, had once lived at number twelve with her family. In those days the houses had been well-kept and the central green neatly maintained with flowers and shrubs.

It was a long time since Julia had thought about Joanna and her Bohemian family. The friendship had been ill-advised, even the teachers at school had tried to warn her against it, but she had been drawn to the other girl like a fly to a spider's web. It had been Joanna who had first persuaded her to rebel against her parents' protectiveness; Joanna who had introduced her to the delights of disco dancing and the heady excitement of pop music. Eventually Joanna had been at the root of her downfall and the secret tragedy that had changed her life and left an indelible blemish on her memory. Julia had never quite forgiven her for that. But it was years since she last saw Joanna. When she had returned to Elvemere the family had packed and gone – no one knew where.

As she pushed a leaflet through the letter box of number twelve she saw that the house was very different from when the Blooms had occupied it. There was a rusty bicycle propped against the wall down in the area; the steps were muddied and the paintwork chipped. When the Blooms had occupied the house the front door had been painted purple, and bright orange curtains had hung at the windows. Inside there had been no carpets, just varnished boards and rush matting, and Julia seemed to remember that all the furniture had been made of bleached pine.

As she went from house to house she found herself remembering so many things about Joanna and her family; things she had almost forgotten. Mrs Bloom with her braided hair and colourful caftans, and Joanna's bearded, sandalled father. She had loved the disorganised chaos in which they had lived, the carefree, casual atmosphere that was so different from what seemed to her the stiflingly ordered life her parents led. The Blooms went to bed, ate and partied just as the mood took them. Joanna and her two older brothers came and went as they pleased, owned their own keys and followed no rules except those they made for themselves. As both boys were musical their home always rang with the strains of the guitar or the latest hits on disc. Joanna's father was an artist so there was always an odour of turpentine and linseed oil in the air. Julia had found it all exotic and exciting.

Joanna was allowed to do all the things Julia was not. She wore mini skirts and daring tops with bare midriffs – later, when the ethnic look came in, she drifted around in Indian cotton skirts that swept the floor and masses of jangling silver bracelets. Her chestnut hair was long and silky straight in the favourite style of the sixties and her green eyes, made up with heavy liner and thick mascara, had the brooding, soot and treacle look that Julia longed to achieve for herself.

May and Harry Philips were so afraid of the modern hippy culture with its shocking sexual permissiveness that they hardly let their daughter out of their sight and monitored her wardrobe carefully. But their claustrophobic watchfulness only served to drive a wedge between them and Julia. The more she saw of the Blooms and their way of life, the more defiant and rebellious she had become. She'd persuaded her parents to let her take a Saturday job in a hairdresser's and with her wages bought some fashionable clothes which she kept at Joanna's and changed into whenever she was allowed out.

It was quite dark by the time Julia had delivered all her leaflets. It had begun to rain too and she was grateful for the warmth of her car. She spent a few minutes arranging her cards in order for the following day's canvassing, then switched on the ignition and headed for home.

As soon as she opened the front door she heard Vernon's voice raised in anger and Charlotte's shrill response.

'You can't tell me what to do. I'm an adult now and it's my decision. If I want to spend my free time working with horses then I *will*, and you can't stop me!'

There was a loud slam as Charlotte banged her bedroom door and Julia gave a sigh of dismay as she began to take off her outdoor things. When she came out of the cloakroom Vernon was coming down the stairs, his face dark with fury.

'That girl! I've always said you're too soft with her. She might have finished at school but she's still got a lot of studying to do, I keep reminding her of it, but will she listen?'

'She does need to have some recreation too,' Julia pointed out. 'I think riding and caring for the horses is good for her. It helps her confidence and develops her sense of responsibility.'

Vernon snorted. 'Huh! As far as I can see she needs no help in the confidence department. And Kath is hardly the best influence on her responsibility-wise. She positively encourages that rebellious attitude of hers.' He looked at her. 'Where have you been, by the way? I have to go out and we should have eaten half an hour ago.'

'Dinner's all ready. I cooked it this morning. It only needs warming in the microwave. I'll see to it now. I did tell you I'd be out canvassing.'

'Did you? Well, I've no time now.' He tapped at his watch. 'I'll have to get a sandwich at the pub after the meeting.'

'In case you want to know, I'm doing rather well with the canvassing,' she told him pointedly as he gathered his briefcase and car keys from the hall table. 'Eleanor says I'm ready to go out on my own from now on.'

'In other words, she's fed up with trailing round with you, eh?' He aimed a kiss in the direction of her cheek. 'Well, if you're really set on putting yourself through this fiasco . . .' He looked at his watch again. 'God! Look at the time. I must go. See you later.'

In the kitchen Julia took the lasagne she'd prepared that afternoon out of the fridge and put it into the microwave. Vernon hadn't said what meeting it was he was going to. She had her suspicions that there was no meeting. He'd been wearing his favourite shirt and had reeked of expensive aftershave. That usually meant only one thing: he was seeing someone again. The signs were all there; the extra meetings, the late nights and unscheduled weekend conferences, the hurried phone calls. Not to mention the tell-tale perfume that lingered about his clothes and in his car. His affairs were usually short-lived and she had become resigned to them, riding out the mingled feelings of anger, humiliation and rejection they gave her. When they had first started, soon after Charlotte had been born, she'd tried confronting him. He had brazened it out, scorning her tears and accusing her of being paranoid. Adamantly denying everything.

She began to make a salad. As Vernon would not be joining them she laid the table in the kitchen, then went into the hall to call Charlotte. When the girl joined her Julia could see traces of angry tears on her cheeks.

'I wish you wouldn't antagonise Daddy,' she said. 'There are better ways of getting round him. You know arguing always makes him lose his temper.'

Charlotte helped herself to lasagne and salad. 'Why should I have to wheedle and coax to get him to let me do something so harmless?' she said rebelliously. 'Anyone'd think I was asking to throw a drugs and sex orgy or something! All I want is to spend my weekends and free time helping Auntie Kath.' She turned large blue eyes on her mother. 'I did as Dad asked and gave up working at the stables till the exams were over. Surely he can't object now I've left school? You will get him to say yes, won't you?'

'I'll try.'

Charlotte stuck out her chin stubbornly. 'Well, you can jolly well tell him that I'm doing it, whether he likes it or not. I've agreed to work at GPC to please him and learn boring computing and book keeping at evening classes. Isn't that enough for him?'

Julia looked up at her daughter. 'I thought you were happy with that?'

Charlotte poked at her food. 'Well, I'm not – not really. You've no idea how stultifying it is. They treat me like the office girl. "*Go and make the tea, Charlotte." "Pop round to the post office, will you?*" They never stop! No one would ever think I was the boss's granddaughter. And I've got to put up with it when all my friends are going off to college or taking their "A"s.'

'But you didn't want to stay on, did you?'

'I'm not academic, Mum. It was a real struggle getting my GCSEs. You know what I really wanted was to go into partnership with Auntie Kath. All I've ever wanted to do was to work with horses, but we both know there's no way Dad would ever agree to that, is there?'

'He just thinks you have a good brain and should put it to better use.'

'Oh, yes? Like running around making tea all day and sitting staring at a flickering computer screen every evening in some stuffy classroom?'

'It won't always be like that. He's actually very proud of you, Charlotte. And he was so pleased when you agreed to join the firm. He's looking to the future,' Julia told her. 'He wants you to begin at the bottom, like he did. One day you could find yourself running the business.'

'Oh, big deal!' she said, unimpressed. 'It's every girl's dream, isn't it – the construction business! What it's really about is that he and Granddad have always been pissed-off that I'm not a boy.'

'Don't talk like that,' Julia said with a sigh.

'Well, it's true,' Charlotte insisted. 'That and the fact that he and

Auntie Kath have never got on. This is a way of getting back at her too.'

'He wouldn't dream of being so petty,' Julia said unconvincingly. 'Look, I'll speak to him later about it. I'm sure he won't mind you going to the stables in your free time if he's approached reasonably.'

'Okay, thanks.' Charlotte helped herself to more salad and ate in silence, obviously appeased. 'How did you get on with your canvassing?' she asked.

Julia smiled. 'I thought you'd never ask! Very well, actually. Tomorrow I'm going solo. Councillor Maitland said she thinks I'm ready to canvass on my own.'

'Really? That's great!' Charlotte swallowed the last mouthful then pushed her chair back. 'Look, I'm sorry, Mum. I'd love to stay and hear all about it but it's the first of these wretched evening classes tonight and I'll be late if I don't go.'

Julia washed up the dinner things by hand. Two place settings hardly justified using the dish-washer. As she worked she heard the sounds of her daughter's hasty preparation for departure and replied to her call as she left, banging the front door behind her. The house settled into silence around her.

It was a solid, well-built house, architect-designed and built by Charlie Grant for them as a wedding present. It had every modern convenience and was equipped with the finest fittings that money could buy. In the hope that his son and daughter-in-law would provide him with several grandchildren Charlie had supplied them with five bedrooms. The house was far too large for the three of them and Julia had never really liked it. The design was unimaginative and even after eighteen years it still looked raw and new with its red brick exterior and large flat windows. But she knew better than to suggest a move to something smaller and more stylishly designed. Charlie and Louise would be scandalised and Vernon would be irritated. It would never happen and it wasn't worth the furore which suggesting it would create.

Julia ran her home and coped with the garden alone, enjoying it as a relaxing hobby. But she could see that if she was elected to the Council she was going to have to think about getting more help, both indoors and out. It was something she hadn't broached with Vernon as yet. He was of much the same view as his father – that a woman's place was, if not permanently in the home, then certainly taking sole responsibility for everything in it.

Her leaflet drop in Victoria Gardens had stirred up old memories and as she washed up Julia let her mind drift back to the late-sixties when she and Joanna had been friends. It had been such an exciting time – 'flower power', 'love and peace', the music of The Beatles and The Rolling Stones, the freedom of the new kind of dancing, so different from the sedate and laboured ballroom dancing they learned at school. And somehow the fact that she was deceiving her parents had made it all the more thrilling.

She and Joanna went to a disco at least once a week and sometimes she would stay at Victoria Gardens for a whole weekend, sharing Joanna's bedroom where the walls were plastered with Andy Warhol posters and pictures of all her pop favourites. On those occasions they would stay out till after midnight. Joanna was boy crazy and used to boast of her sexual exploits, claiming to have had sex with dozens of boys. Julia, with her straight-laced upbringing, had been secretly shocked at the time. Her views were more romantic and idealistic. In spite of the so-called permissive age, she still felt it was wrong to give yourself completely to a person you didn't love, and said so. Joanna laughed.

'It's just a game, you sweet old-fashioned thing,' she laughed. 'A wonderful game. You don't know what you're missing.'

And gradually even Julia had discovered that under the intoxicating influence of a rhythmic beat, strobe lights and the Bacardi and Coke that Joanna had taught her to drink, there was a certain honeyed sweetness to kisses and petting, even with someone she hardly knew. As Joanna had said, it was all a game, and anyway she never let things go too far, even if she did tell the occasional white lie to Joanna.

It had been in the summer of 1970 that Joanna had announced her intention to go to the Isle of Wight for the rock festival. She took it for granted that her friend would go too. When Julia hesitated and shook her head doubtfully, Joanna tossed her long hair petulantly.

'Please yourself, but I shall go of course. It's going to be fabulous. The Stones will be there, Procul Harem, Jimi Hendrix and loads of others. Imagine actually seeing and hearing them in the flesh! If you don't come you'll miss out on something fantastic.'

The more Julia thought about it, the more she longed to go. She racked her brain for a way to get her parents to agree and in the end she came up with an idea. The English mistress at school was getting up a weekend party to go to see an open-air production of A Midsummer Night's Dream in London. It was August and Julia had left school at the end of the summer term but she was still entitled to go. She asked and her parents agreed readily. Their daughter could come to no possible harm under the eagle eye of the elderly Miss Grimshaw. Luckily for Julia it did not occur to them to telephone and check that their daughter had in fact booked.

The two girls hitch-hiked down to Lymington and caught the ferry across to Yarmouth, both of them in a state of high excitement. From Yarmouth it was only a short journey to Afton Down, Freshwater.

To Julia the festival was a revelation. There on the clifftop, in a tiny place renowned for its Victorian values, every pop star she had ever heard of seemed to be assembled. And the mass of young people that grew hour by hour dazed her completely. Joanna took it all in her stride, pointing out the celebrities to her friend as they wandered wide-eyed through the crowds.

'Look, there's Joan Baez – Jim Morrison. I've just seen Tiny Tim and – you'll never guess – *Keith Moon*!'

'Where are we going to sleep?' Julia asked. 'Most people seem to have brought tents and things.'

Joanna looked at her askance. '*Sleep*? How can you even think of sleeping? Oh, I expect we'll find some place to snuggle down when and if the music ever stops,' she said airily. 'Who knows?' She grinned. 'We might get lucky and get to share some gorgeous guy's sleeping bag!'

The weekend became a blur to Julia; an amalgam of pulsating music, good-natured pushing, discomfort, and at times downright squalor. There were times when she was chilled to the bone and others when she was so hungry her stomach hurt. The sanitary facilities were adequate but only just. There was certainly no place to take time over one's appearance, and for the most part people were grubby and dishevelled. But no one seemed to care. The sight and sounds of artists like Miles Davis and Jimi Hendrix, with his exotic personality and colourful clothes, soon made Julia forget her discomfort. She and Joanna spent the first night huddled together under a blanket someone had lent them, hardly able to sleep for the mixture of cold, damp and excitement. But it was on the morning of the second day that Julia met Dean Sylvester. After that the rest of the festival became a mere sideshow for her.

'Need any help?' She'd been looking for some breakfast when the voice behind her spoke.

She turned and recognised the lead guitarist from a minor group called The Sylvas who had impressed both girls the night before when they had heard them play. He was a tall young man with dark skin and a mane of black curls. Julia thought him quite the most attractive she had ever seen. She felt herself blush hotly as he looked down at her appraisingly, his lips curved in amusement.

'We – I was looking for something to eat,' she said.

'The kitchen's over that way.' He pointed. 'Come on, I'll show you.' With an air of complete assurance he took her hand and they began to walk. Julia was astounded. He was so casual and relaxed. It was as though they'd always known each other. And he had a wonderful accent that sent thrilling shivers up and down her spine.

'Enjoying the festival?' he looked down at her with warm melting brown eyes that turned her knees to jelly.

'Oh, yes. We saw your group perform last night. You were fabulous.'

He threw back his handsome dark head and laughed delightedly. 'Great! For that I'll buy you a sausage!'

They ate breakfast together and talked. Julia couldn't get over it. That a man as good-looking as Dean Sylvester should not only notice but want to spend time with her was amazing. His conversation was riveting. He knew so much about pop music, and about all the other artists at the festival. He'd met them all – even performed with some of them – and she listened with rapt attention as he recounted little personal anecdotes about them. The life he led, travelling from place to place and performing with his group, sounded fascinating. And while he spoke he held her hand, or draped an arm around her shoulders. It felt wonderful.

They spent most of that day together. When he was playing he made sure she had a place near the front, flashing her the occasional 'special' smile. When he wasn't he would escort her to where all the most exciting action was. It was almost evening before Joanna caught up with Julia again. She was far from happy.

'Where on earth have you been?' she demanded indignantly. 'You went off to get us some breakfast and that was the last I saw of you!'

'Sorry. I met this marvellous boy.'

'What boy?'

'His name is Dean Sylvester. He's the lead guitarist with that group we saw last night, The Sylvas.'

Joanna's face was a study. 'The tall black guy?'

'He isn't black.'

'Yes, he is – well, partly anyway. Bet you anything. He looks a lot like Jimi Hendrix.' Joanna pouted, clearly resentful. 'What on earth did he want with you?'

Julia blushed. 'Thanks! You'd better ask him. He's coming over.'

But although Joanna tried hard, fluttering her eyelashes and using all her wiles to attract Dean's attention, she did not succeed. To her fury, he had eyes only for Julia.

In the small hours of the following morning, when everything was comparatively quiet, they walked hand in hand round the perimeter of the ground, and in the shade of a group of trees Dean took her in his arms and kissed her. It was the most exciting kiss Julia had ever experienced. She wanted it to go on forever. The previous evening some of the people they'd been with had passed round a joint. Joanna had persuaded her to try a few puffs and she had found the effect surprisingly pleasant. It made her feel relaxed and dreamy. But Dean's kisses were better than any drug – infinitely more exhilarating. Her knees seemed to turn to water as she clung to him.

'You're not going back to find your friend, are you?' he whispered, his warm breath tickling her ear.

She sighed. 'We've only got one blanket between us. It was cold last night.'

'Haven't you got a tent?'

'No.'

He chuckled and pulled her closer. 'I have. I've got a sleeping bag too. Share it with me and I promise I won't let you get cold.'

Julia stood with her hands in the cooling washing up water, her eyes far away as she remembered Dean and that first night together. Never in a thousand years could anyone have prepared her for the ecstatic delight of making love with him. He was gentle, especially when he realised that it was the first time for her. But later, as dawn was breaking and all her shyness and inhibitions had melted, her passion had matched his. By morning she had known that she was hopelessly in love. In spite of Joanna's insistence that sex was just a game, something that you enjoyed and forgot, like a bar of chocolate or a can of Coke, she had known by morning that there could never be any other man for her but Dean.

Even now after all these years she could still conjure up the breathtaking thrill his lips had the power to create; the explosion of sensations she felt at the touch of his hands. Closing her eyes, she allowed herself to visualise his handsome face, the golden skin and beautifully moulded features, the midnight-dark eyes and glorious mass of curling hair. If only he could have turned out to be the man she'd thought he was. If only the tragic disillusionment that had come later had. . . .

The shrill of the telephone startled her out of her dream, jerking her thoughts abruptly back to the present, and she hurriedly dried her hands and went into the hall to answer it.

Charlotte had enrolled at the local further education college for computer studies and book keeping, neither of which aroused her enthusiasm in the slightest. The college, a sprawling red brick complex, was only a ten-minute cycle ride from home and she arrived with time to spare. Parking her bicycle, she went inside to join the other students crowded round the information board in the front hall, all of them checking to see which room their particular course was to be held in. As she scanned the board she became aware of another girl standing beside her.

Charlotte turned with a smile. 'Hi. What have you enrolled for?'

'Computer studies. It's in Room B6.'

'I'm doing that too.' Charlotte looked at her with interest. She guessed that the other girl was a few years older. She looked her over enviously, admiring her figure and striking looks. 'Shall we go up?' she asked companionably.

'If you like.'

As they went up the stairs together, Charlotte said, 'I haven't seen you around.'

'I've only just come here to live,' Fleur told her. 'From London.'

'You've left London to come and live *here?*' Charlotte looked at her in amazement. 'You'll find it a bit tame. I'd give anything to go and work up in London.'

'It isn't all it's cracked up to be,' Fleur said. 'Going up on a day trip or a holiday is one thing. Living there is something else. I lived in the East End.'

Charlotte had already guessed that. She watched the new 'soap' East Enders regularly and had recognised the accent. 'Oh. What's it like – rough?'

'A bit.' Fleur smiled.

Charlotte was fascinated by this attractive older girl with her exotic looks and fascinating way of speaking. She looked so sophisticated and worldly. Why on earth had she wanted to come and bury herself in a dump like Elvemere? Surely she could have had a much more exciting life in London? 'Seriously, though, what made you come here?' she asked.

Fleur shrugged. 'Why anywhere?' She said evasively.

'You must have had a reason though. I shouldn't think many people have actually ever *heard* of this place.'

Fleur resorted to the answer she'd given Tom. 'I stuck a pin in the map.'

'Really? No kidding.' Charlotte was intrigued. It all sounded so wonderfully free and adventurous. 'Have you got a job then?'

'Yes. With a catering firm,' Fleur told her proudly. 'I'm going to learn everything from the cooking to the business side so that I can eventually be my employer's right-hand woman.'

'Wow!' Charlotte was impressed. It sounded a whole lot more interesting than the construction business. 'I have to work in my grandad's office,' she said. 'It's so *boring* you wouldn't believe. I really wanted to work with horses. My aunt has riding stables and I go there and help her whenever I can.' She looked at Fleur. 'You like the catering trade, do you?'

'Yes, I do.'

'Are your parents pleased?'

'Haven't got any. My grandma brought me up. When she died I thought it was time to move out – make a fresh start.' They had reached their room and Fleur turned to the inquisitive younger girl with a smile, relieved that the cross-examination would have to stop. 'Right then. Shall we go in?'

When the class was over and the students began to file out Charlotte pushed her way to the front to catch her new friend before she disappeared. There was no one else in the class she fancied making friends with. All of the boys were spotty and gauche and she didn't know any of the other girls.

'Hi! How did you get on?' she asked breathlessly, catching up with Fleur at the bottom of the stairs.

'Oh, all right, I suppose. I never liked computers much at school but now that I have a reason to be computer literate, as they call it, it makes all the difference.'

'There's a canteen place here,' Charlotte said. 'Fancy a coffee?'

Fleur hesitated, then smiled. 'All right, if you like.'

Over coffee they exchanged names. Charlotte thought the name, Fleur was beautiful. 'I wish I had a pretty name,' she said, stirring her coffee. 'I was christened Charlotte Harriet, would you believe? After both my grandfathers. Isn't it the absolute *pits*?'

Fleur laughed. 'I expect people call you Charlie.'

'Good heavens, no!' Charlotte looked shocked. 'That's what my granddad is called, so at least I've been spared that.' She took a sip of her coffee, studying Fleur over the rim of her cup. 'So – tell me about yourself. I don't get to meet many Londoners.' She licked her lips and asked the question she'd been wanting to ask all evening. 'You're not actually English, are you? I mean – not, well, *completely*.'

'My grandfather was West Indian,' Fleur told her. 'Apart from that I'm English. I was born here and so was my father. In fact until I came here I'd never been out of London, apart from a day trip to Southend.'

'West Indian, eh?' Charlotte rested her chin on her cupped hands and looked at Fleur. 'How fascinating. You're very beautiful,' she said candidly. 'I'd give anything for hair like that. And those eyes. I've always wanted brown eyes. They're more – I don't know – mysterious, I suppose.'

Embarrassed by the girl's scrutiny, Fleur looked up at the clock on the wall opposite. 'I'll have to go,' she said. 'There's a bus at half-past and if I miss it, I'll have to wait half an hour.'

'Of course.' Charlotte sprang to her feet, gathering her books together. 'I'm starting driving lessons the moment I'm seventeen. When I've passed my test I expect Mum will let me borrow her car. I'll be able to give you a lift home then.' She fell into step with Fleur's long-legged strides. 'Where do you live by the way?'

'Victoria Gardens.'

'In a flat?'

'A room.'

Charlotte sighed with envy. The girl had it made. A room of her own, a job and the independence and freedom to organise her own life. It sounded marvellous. 'I wish I were in your shoes,' she said wistfully. 'I bet you have no one telling you what time to be in and what you can and can't do.' They had reached the main entrance and she paused to pull on her jacket. 'My bike's over there in the bike sheds. See you next week then?'

'I expect so.' Fleur watched the other girl hurry off with a wry little smile then turned towards the bus stop thinking wistfully of the obvious contrast between the two of them. She wouldn't mind going home to a mother who was waiting eagerly to hear how the class had gone; who had a tasty supper ready and a hot water bottle warming her bed. Briefly she wondered how a cosseted girl like Charlotte would cope with living alone in a cramped single room, making her own scratch meals and sleeping in a narrow, lumpy bed. The girl had no idea. She didn't know she was born!

But as Fleur began to walk towards the bus stop she reflected that there was a certain engaging charm about pretty little Charlotte Grant. She was like a friendly puppy; bouncy and uninhibited – taking it for granted that her company would be welcome. That kind of confident personality only came from a stable home background, she told herself sadly.

Fleur's first week at her new job was mainly routine. She buttered bread till her arms ached, learned how to mix the various fillings, wrap, pack and label for the freezer. She also became acquainted with the appointments book in the office so she could deal with bookings if Sally was out. But on Saturday evening the monotony of the week's routine was relieved when she attended her first function, a twenty-first birthday party in one of the town's smartest suburbs.

At the client's home Sally quickly showed her how to assemble the long trestle tables, to spread the snowy cloths so that they fell exactly to the ground and arrange the coloured swags. Sally always took along her own silver candelabra and flower arrangements as well as cutlery and napkins, and she showed Fleur how to fold them deftly into pretty shapes. She learned how to arrange the food attractively on dishes and lay it all out on the tables. Later, wearing the smart black skirt and white blouse that Sally had provided for her, and with her hair carefully plaited and tamed, she circulated along with the hired waitresses among the guests with trays of wine,

At the end of the evening Sally complimented her. 'You're picking it all up very well, Fleur,' she said. 'Several people have asked me who my attractive new assistant is. You have a very pleasant way with people.'

Fleur found herself unable to stop smiling. She had enjoyed the evening very much. Getting the job with Sally was a real piece of luck. For the first time she felt she had made the right move in coming to Elvemere. Even the chore of packing everything up afterwards seemed pleasurable. She was looking forward to tomorrow with anticipation. This was the Sunday that Tom was taking her down to the sea for the day.

'Oh, I *love* the country,' Fleur said, looking out of the car window as they drove, admiring the gently undulating Norfolk landscape. They had left the busy dual carriageway now and were on the quieter country roads. The trees were beginning to turn from green to gold and the fields were already brown with newly turned furrows.

'I hardly ever saw trees and fields in London,' she told Tom. 'Oh, it's so fresh! You can really breathe out here.' She rolled down the window and took a deep draught of the air. 'Mmm – I believe I can smell the sea already!'

Tom laughed. 'That'll be the muck spreading,' he joked. 'They do a lot of it at this time of year.' He glanced at the girl sitting beside him. She really was quite beautiful with her warm olive skin and flashing dark eyes, alive with excitement. Ivy had hinted at some kind of mystery attached to her new lodger. She had told him with an air of gloomy foreboding that in her opinion Fleur had *foreign blood*. Her inquisitive remarks had led him to believe that she suspected him of knowing more about Fleur than she did. Obviously the old girl had observed their growing friendship with a more than casual interest and was hoping he would be able to satisfy her curiosity. She had certainly looked disappointed when he told her he knew no more than she did. Nevertheless, his natural journalist's interest made him wonder about Fleur, her background and sudden unheralded arrival in Elvemere.

'So – you're glad you chose this neck of the woods now, are you?'

She turned to him with a smile. 'Yes. I like my new job and the town.' She paused. 'I'd like somewhere better to live though. I'm not looking forward to spending the winter in that poky little room.' She looked at him. 'I've been meaning to ask, who lives in the room on the first floor at the back – the one with the little balcony?'

On her trips into the back yard to peg out her washing she had been intrigued by the little white-painted wrought-iron balcony. She indulged herself with dreams of what it would be like to occupy the room behind it. There were two half-glazed doors opening out on to the balcony and she imagined herself sitting out there on warm summer evenings or Sunday mornings with her coffee. If it were hers she would put out hanging baskets and trailing ivy – perhaps even buy herself a sun lounger and use it for sunbathing. She had never known the pleasure of a garden, but that balcony would be the next best thing. There must be a nice view over the park from up there too.

'It's one of the flats. Derek Jones lives in it,' Tom told her. 'He's the tall thin guy with the moustache. He manages the hardware shop in the High Street. Ivy tells me he's divorced. But he's moving out shortly – to share a house along with a friend apparently.'

'Really?' Fleur bit her lip with excitement. 'Would she let it to me, do you think?'

'If you want it, you'd better ask quickly.' Tom looked doubtful. 'And I warn you, she doesn't usually keep female tenants permanently.'

'I know. The rent might be more than I can afford too,' Fleur said.

'I've no idea what she charges for the flats. You'd have to ask.' Tom pointed as they rounded a bend in the road. 'Hey, look, there you are – the sea.'

Fleur sat up straight, peering intently through the windscreen. There it was, a shining silver ribbon etched against the blue of the sky in the distance. She drew in her breath sharply. 'Oh! Isn't it lovely? I can't wait to get there.'

Tom laughed and pressed his foot firmly on the accelerator. 'Right. Have you there in five minutes flat!'

Fleur hadn't know quite what to expect of the Norfolk coastline.

She had known it would not be like Southend but she had not been prepared for its wild beauty. She was enchanted by the many different kinds of seabirds, crowded together to feed on the saltmarsh as they drove along the coast road. And, as they entered the little fishing village of Ormsburgh, the delightful brick and flint cottages, built around the tiny harbour.

For what was left of the morning they explored the streets which converged on the harbour, and Fleur marvelled at the colourful cottage gardens, overblown now, but still bright with dahlias, asters and chrysanthemums. In the tiny natural harbour, boats were moored, tossing gently on the incoming tide, their sails furled, whilst out to sea the waves rolled in, capped with white foam. Fleur was enchanted by it all.

'Can we walk along there?' She pointed to the dunes. 'Is it safe?'

'Course it is.' Tom took her hand. 'I know this bit of the coast like the back of my hand. We used to come here for holidays when I was a kid.' It was impossible not to catch some of her enthusiasm. Even though the place was a familiar childhood haunt to him he found that he was seeing it afresh, through her eyes. 'We can walk as far as you like. Don't you want to eat first though?' he asked. 'I know I do.'

It was only with reluctance that she allowed herself to be drawn inside a harbourside pub for lunch. But even there she was intrigued by her surroundings. The centuries-old walls were whitewashed and the heavy oak beams black with the smoke of the years. Small round tables with wheel-back chairs were clustered around a huge open fireplace in which burned a fragrant log fire. Behind the bar stood a smiling landlord and his wife, waiting to serve them.

Tom ordered ploughman's lunches for both of them and it was only then that Fleur realised how hungry she was. She applied herself with zest to the ripe Stilton cheese, salad and home-made crusty bread.

'So you want to go for a walk after lunch?' Tom asked.

Fleur nodded. 'Yes, please. I want to see it all.'

'I warn you, walking on soft sand can be tiring.'

'I don't care.'

An hour later, replete with lunch and the local real ale, they began their walk. Tom admired Fleur's stamina as she strode along beside him. As she walked her cheeks were whipped to a glow by the wind and her eyes shone.

'You never told me your real reason for choosing Elvemere,' he said.

'I told you – I stuck a pin in the map.'

'Ivy mentioned that you had relatives here.'

She turned to look at him, her eyes clouding. 'What else has she been saying about me?'

'Nothing. Just that. It's not true then?'

Fleur paused. 'It might be.'

'That's rather an oblique remark.'

She stopped and sank down on a hummock of wiry grass. 'Let's have a breather, shall we?'

'Suits me.' He sank down beside her and pulled himself a long blade of grass, looking at her thoughtfully as he wound the wiry length around his finger. 'Was it just something you told her to keep her quiet then?'

'About having relatives here? No, not exactly.' She paused, following his example and pulling herself a piece of grass. 'As a matter of fact, my mother came from here.'

He stared at her. 'Your mother?'

'Yes. I don't remember her. She left me with my grandparents when I was a baby. They brought me up. Before my grandmother died she made me promise to try and find her. But that's only partly why I chose Elvemere. If I ever do look for her it'll only be because of my promise. There's absolutely no reason why I should want to find a mother who couldn't care less about me. Anyway, for all I know she probably left here years ago.'

'I see. What about your father?' Tom asked casually. He was trying hard to hide his rising curiosity. Whether Fleur knew it or not she *had* come here because of her mother, and one day she would have to face the fact. But he sensed that she might be put off if he showed too much curiosity.

'My dad?' She shrugged. 'Haven't a clue. He abandoned my mother before I was born, and he died soon after.'

For a long moment they were both silent. Fleur looked at the sea and wondered at its vastness. This morning in the distance it had looked so dreamy and idyllic. Later with its little white waves it seemed almost playful. Now it looked hostile and threatening. It made her shudder a little.

But Tom's curiosity would not let him alone. It rubbed insistently like a stone in his shoe. 'Your father – was he . . .?'

'Half-West Indian.' She turned to look straight into his eyes. 'My grandfather was black. That's what you and Ivy have been dying to know, isn't it? Well, you can tell her now. And I daresay that when she knows that she'll be sure to turn down my request for the flat.' She got up and brushed down her jeans. 'But I'll tell you this – my granddad was the finest man I've ever known. He was kind and

68

honest and good and I loved him very much.' She began to walk back towards the village. 'You were right, Tom,' she said over her shoulder. 'Walking on these dunes is harder than I thought.'

He had to run to catch up with her. 'Fleur – wait. I didn't mean to pry. And I wasn't trying to find out about your private affairs. If I was clumsy and I upset you, I'm sorry. Really sorry.'

She walked on for a moment without speaking, then turned and he saw the brightness in her eyes. 'It's okay, Tom,' she said softly. 'It doesn't matter.'

He caught her by the shoulders and pulled her round to face him. 'Yes, it does matter! I wasn't trying to find out so that I could tell Ivy. Surely you didn't think that?'

'I don't know what I thought.' She shook her head. 'No, of course I didn't.'

'You don't have to be so defensive. I'm sure you've every reason to be proud of your grandfather. Look, Fleur, you do trust me, don't you? I wouldn't do or say anything that would hurt you.' He brushed a strand of windblown hair away from her face and cupped her face between his hands, looking deep into her eyes. 'You do believe that, don't you?'

Eventually she nodded. 'Yes. I trust you, Tom.'

'I'm glad.' He took her hand. 'Hey, they do fantastic cream teas at the Lifeboat Cafe. I could murder one, couldn't you?'

She laughed. 'You bet!'

By the time they got back to Victoria Gardens it was dusk and a chill wind had replaced the balmy breeze. Fleur shivered a little as she got out of the car. 'Thanks for a lovely day, Tom.'

He bent his head to look up at her. 'Don't run off like that. I thought we'd have a coffee or a nightcap when I've put the car away.'

'Oh, all right then.'

Tom rented a lock-up garage a couple of streets away and as he drove off Fleur let herself into the house. She'd only just closed the front door when Ivy poked her head round the corner of the basement stairs.

'Have a nice day at Ormsburgh, did you, Miss Sylvester?'

'Lovely, thanks. And please call me Fleur.'

Ever since she had first arrived, Ivy had steadfastly refused to call Fleur by her christian name.

She emerged into the hall and Fleur saw that she was wearing her fur fabric jacket and pearl stud earrings. 'I've just come in myself – been out to tea with my friend, Mrs Jennings,' she volunteered. 'A real lady, Mary is – fallen on hard times since her husband died. He was a gambler, you know.' She shook her head and drew in her breath with a hissing sound. '*Terrible*. Poor Mary never knew what she was going to have to manage on at the end of each week when he was alive, then when he passed on she was left without a penny. She has to go out cleaning now to eke out her pension. Shocking, isn't it? Especially at her age.'

'Yes, that's very sad.'

Ivy folded her arms and leaned against the side of the stairs, clearly preparing herself for a long gossip. 'She only cleans for the best people, of course. Three days a week she goes to Mrs Charlie Grant. That's Grant Philips the builders, you know. Lovely place they've got. Every modern convenience – carpets up your ankles! Mary says it's a pleasure to work there, and Mrs Grant is ever so generous with her.'

'That's nice.' Fleur put one foot on the stairs. 'Well – better go, I suppose.'

Ivy peered at her. 'Early night then, is it? Tired after all that fresh air?'

'No. It's just . . .'

The front door opened and Tom came in, rubbing his hands together briskly. 'Brrr, the evenings are getting really chilly now. Never mind, that coffee will soon . . .' As his eyes adjusted to the dim light in the hallway he noticed his landlady standing in the dark recess near the basement stairs. 'Oh, hello, Ivy. Didn't see you there.'

'Evening, Tom. *Well*—' she smirked ' – sorry if I've kept you, Miss Sylvester. I expect you'll be wanting to go up and – er – take your things off.'

'What was all that about?' Tom asked with a grin as they reached the top of the stairs.

'Oh, nothing much,' Fleur stopped outside his door, her face still burning at Ivy's suggestive remark. 'Look, Tom, I'm a bit tired. It must have been all that fresh air. I think I'll leave the coffee for tonight, if you don't mind.'

'Hey, come on.' He reached out to touch her shoulder. 'It's not what Ivy said, is it? You know what she's like – always making pointed remarks. Take no notice. She doesn't mean anything.'

'I know. It's not that . . .'

'Well, if you're sure?'

'I am – really. Another time, eh?'

He paused, then stepped closer. 'I've been meaning to ask you,

Fleur, did you leave anyone special back in London? Is there a boyfriend? If there is . . .'

'No!' His face was very close to hers and she turned her head away, her heart pounding uneasily. To her annoyance the memory of the attack she had suffered still affected her. She forced herself to swallow the panic that rose in her chest, reminding herself firmly that Tom was nice. He was decent. Not like that animal. 'No, there's no one,' she said.

'Any special reason?'

What did he mean by that? 'No. I just never seemed to have time for socialising.'

'Well, I won't pretend I'm not pleased about that.' He bent his head to rub his cheek against hers. 'Goodnight then, Fleur. And thanks for coming out with me today. I enjoyed it very much. More than you know.' He looked into her eyes. 'Can we do it again some time?'

'Yes. Yes, I'd like that.'

'And maybe next time we can have that nightcap?'

'Yes mayb—' The word was stifled as his lips covered hers. It was a chaste kiss, soft and undemanding. She should have enjoyed it, but she couldn't submerge the spectre that had haunted her for weeks. The violent image of her sadistic attacker, bent on inflicting pain and humiliation, rose again behind her closed eyelids. Once again she could feel his rough hands on her flesh and the evil smell of him filled her nostrils. She bore it as long as she could, then, with a strangled gasp she pushed Tom away, holding her hands protectively in front of her.

'I – I'm sorry. I have to go. I'm sorry, Tom – *sorry*.' She backed away and ran up the stairs to her own room, shutting her eyes to the dismayed look on his face. Closing the door of her room, she leaned against it as she waited for her heartbeat to slow and the tumult of nauseated panic to cease. What she'd done was unforgivable. She'd hurt him without meaning to. And after he'd treated her so well. What she'd just done had ruined the delightful day they'd just spent together. But the feeling of revulsion had been so strong, so inescapable. It seemed to swallow her up, squeezing the breath from her body until she thought she would suffocate. It was triggered by Ivy's knowing smirk and suggestive remark, then Tom's unwitting entrapment of her as she stood with her back to the wall, her escape blocked by his body.

When would the memory ever go away? she asked herself despairingly. When would she feel free to form a normal relationship again?

71

She lay awake for a long time, thinking regretfully of Tom and wondering how she could explain her strange behaviour, make it up to him. But it was only as she was drifting into sleep that something quite unrelated that Ivy had said suddenly rang a bell in the back of her mind. She had mentioned that her friend Mrs Jennings worked for a family named Grant. She had heard that name somewhere recently – but where? Then she remembered – the young girl in the computer class. Her name was Grant. On the brink of sleep Fleur wondered drowsily whether she was from the same family.

Chapter 4

Julia parked the car under a street lamp and stepped out into the rain. This was the last evening. Just one more street to canvass and then it would be in the laps of the gods, or rather the voters. One more night of uncertainty before tomorrow.

Polling day! The very thought of it made her stomach churn with apprehension. Although Eleanor had urged her to be positive, she kept guarding against disappointment by telling herself that she wouldn't really mind if she didn't get in.

Putting up for the council had been much harder than she'd envisaged. She'd certainly worked hard, but over the weeks of canvassing she had learned that wasn't enough. She had at least to appear strong – to convince people, make them believe she was sincere. And she was. She genuinely wanted to represent them as best she could, to serve her community, although for now she wasn't committed to any particular cause. The trouble was that everyone seemed to want something different. How did you convince them all that you had their best interests at heart when a lot of the time you didn't agree with their views? When it came to the crunch you could only really be yourself and if that wasn't enough, then so be it. Twenty-four hours from now she would know just how convincing she'd been.

She had left the Mapleton Estate till last and the notorious Scrimshaw Street was the very last on the list. She locked the car carefully, put up her umbrella and lowered her head against the lashing rain as she stepped out along the puddled pavement.

Scrimshaw Street was unfamiliar territory, as so many of the other streets had been. She was beginning to realise how little she knew about the town she had grown up in, or the people who lived in it. This street was lined on either side with mean little red brick council houses, built between the wars. Many of the council estates she had

73

canvassed were well kept, with neat gardens and fresh curtains at the windows. Some of the tenants had bought their houses and took a pride in them, paid their rent and council tax regularly and kept control over their pets and children. Not so here in Scrimshaw Street. Eleanor had warned her what to expect here and now Julia saw that she hadn't exaggerated. Most of the front gardens were overgrown and strewn with rubbush, broken and discarded toys and rusting bicycles. Derelict-looking cars were parked on the pavements and the atmosphere of despair and apathy was almost tangible. The only advantage was that being a wet evening the street was free from marauding children.

Julia stood with her hand on the gate of number one, hesitating. From the cards attached to her clipboard she saw that the tenant here was a Miss Brownlow. Glancing up, she saw that there were no lights on. Maybe she was out. She was tired and it was getting late. Was it really worth canvassing a street like this? she wondered. Would these people actually bother to turn out to the polling station tomorrow? From the look of things they had little to lose or gain from exercising their right to vote, especially for a mere by-election. But this was the last street so she might as well go ahead now that she was here. She pushed open the rickety gate, walked up the path and knocked.

Somewhere inside she could hear a baby crying. She was struggling to hold on to her clipboard whilst folding her umbrella when the door opened an inch or two. She looked up to see a young girl looking at her inquiringly through the gap.

'Yes?'

'Good evening. Miss Brownlow?'

'That's right.'

Julia went into the routine that felt almost parrot-like by now. 'Hello, I'm Julia Grant, your Conservative candidate at the by-election tomorrow,' she said. Holding her umbrella and clipboard in one hand, she extended her fingers through the four-inch opening. The girl ignored them but Julia smiled and managed to hold her eyes. 'I'm sorry to call so late and I don't want to take up your time, but I wonder – can I count on your vote?'

The door closed abruptly and for a moment she thought she was being summarily snubbed, but the next moment she heard the chain being released and to her surprise the girl opened the door and held it wide. 'You'd better come in,' she said. 'You look as if you're getting wet out there.'

A little taken aback, Julia shook the raindrops from her umbrella and stepped inside. The poverty of the little house shocked her.

There was no floor covering, even on the stairs, and the dark brown paintwork was chipped and peeling. The only light came from candles stuck into bottles, and shadows danced and leaped as the draught from the door stirred the flames. Julia saw now that the girl was no more than eighteen. She was very thin and her long fair hair was tied back with a piece of tape. Her skirt and cardigan, although clean and tidy, were clearly far from new. In the hall stood a pram in which a baby stirred restlessly.

'Go through,' the girl invited. 'Sorry about the mess but I couldn't get the washing dry today.'

There was a small fire burning in the living-room grate. Around it was a clothes horse hung with gently steaming nappies and baby clothes. Although spotless, the room was furnished very basically with a table, two chairs and one armchair covered in faded tapestry which the girl now indicated to Julia.

'Take the weight off your feet for a minute.' She looked towards the door. 'I put the baby out in the hall. The steam from the washing makes him chesty,' she said.

'Yes. Yes, I see.' Embarrassed, Julia sat down and looked again at her clipboard.

'Do you live here alone, Miss Brownlow?'

'That's right. Just me and baby. It's Tracey, by the way. Can I get you a coffee? I was just going to have one.'

'I don't want to put you to any trouble. I only came because . . .'

'It isn't any trouble,' the girl interrupted. 'It's nice to have a bit of company to tell you the truth.' Without waiting for Julia's reply she went into the kitchen and came back with two mugs on a tin tray. 'I've got a little spirit stove,' she explained. 'So that when they cut off the electric I can still manage.'

Julia took the mug from her, suddenly understanding the candle-light. 'They've cut off your electricity supply? But that's terrible! Do they know you have a tiny baby?'

'Oh, yes.' Tracey sounded resigned. 'But you can't have what you can't pay for and that's all about it. I just can't seem to manage on the benefit money and if I got a job I'd have to pay someone to look after baby.'

'How old is he?'

'Three months.' The girl sat on one of the chairs and pushed a stray strand of hair behind her ears. 'To tell you the truth, I wouldn't trust any of them round here with him anyway,' she said. 'Only interested in the money, they are. Know how to charge too! And God knows what they'd do with him once my back was turned.'

Julia took a sip of her coffee and tried to hide her horror and

75

distress at the girl's plight. 'What about the baby's father?' she ventured. 'Wouldn't he pay something towards his child's keep? Couldn't the Child Support Agency make him?'

Tracey lifted her shoulders in a small helpless gesture. 'They'd have to find him first,' she said. 'Soon as he knew I was pregnant, he took off. I haven't seen him since, and if his mates know where he is they're not saying.'

'Your parents then?'

Tracey gave a wry little grin. 'There's only Mum and she don't want to know. She don't want her new boyfriend to know she's got a daughter my age. He's younger than her, see? She's frightened of losing him. She says I'll just have to manage the same as what she did.' Tracey looked around her with a resigned sigh. 'I know I was dead lucky to get this place, and once I get myself sorted I'll make it nice. I just need to be able to find a job where I can take Damian.'

'Damian?'

'My baby.' As though on cue he began to cry again and Tracey got up and went into the hall, returning with the child in her arms. 'He's hungry. Do you mind?'

'Not at all. Please go ahead.' Julia watched as the girl unbuttoned her blouse and gave one breast to the hungry baby who sucked greedily, his big blue eyes fixed on his mother's face and his fuzz of fair hair transformed by the flickering candlelight into a shining halo. As he fed he made satisfied little grunting noises and suddenly a memory that Julia thought she had buried forever flooded back with sharp and painful clarity.

She hadn't breast fed Charlotte, but she'd fed Dean's child, Fleur, for the first few weeks of her life. Now, watching the young mother and child wrapped in the sharing of this intimate and tender moment, she felt a lump tighten her throat and quick tears stung her eyes.

Tracey looked up at her. 'They wanted me to have him adopted when he was born,' she said. 'But how could I? Look at him. It's not his fault he's here, is it? I'd *never* part with him, whatever they did to me. He's all I've got.' She wrapped her cardigan round the baby's head and hugged him closer. 'I'm not a tart you know. I trusted his dad. I really loved him.'

As she transferred the child to her other breast her eyes were dreamy. 'We spent hours planning the way it'd all be when Rick found a job. We were going to get married with me in a lovely white dress – in a church and everything. I'd was training to be a hairdresser. I was good at it too. I had a job and I used to go to college one day every week. I had to give all that up to have

76

Damian.' Her eyes hardened. 'Still, better off without a guy who lets you down like that, eh? We'll get through somehow, Damie and me.' She looked at Julia hopefully. 'I hadn't even thought about voting tomorrow, but if you could do something about getting some of the factories round here to have creches so's single mums like me could go back to work and take the kids with us, I'd vote for you then all right, no sweat. I can think of a good many others round here who would too.'

Julia felt ashamed not to be able to promise. 'If I'm elected I'll certainly do all I can,' she said. 'It's a shame, being forced to live like this when you're willing to work.' She opened her handbag, fumbling for her cheque book. 'Look, how much is your electricity bill?'

Tracey flushed and waved her hand. 'No! Please, I wasn't looking for no handouts. I don't want you to think I was whingeing. My Giro comes any day now and then I'll pay it. We'll be all right, really.'

'Have you had anything to eat today?'

Tracey nodded. 'I'm okay – honest. Soon as the Giro comes I'll go round the supermarket, do a big shop.'

They went into the hall together and suddenly Tracey put the baby into her arms.

'Here, just hold him a minute while I straighten the pram, will you?'

Julia held the sleepy baby while Tracey rearranged the blankets. The warm feel of his fragile little body through the shawl and the sweet milky scent of him tugged at her heart.

'Thanks.' Tracey took him back, tucking him up warmly in his pram. 'Goodnight, Mrs Grant.' She opened the front door for Julia. 'It was really nice meeting you. Good luck for tomorrow. Us single mums want more like you sticking up for us.'

Julia sat in the car and watched the curtain of rain that streamed down the windscreen. What would that young woman say if she knew just how much they had in common? The difference was that Tracey had the guts to stand by her child, to struggle to keep him, whilst Julia had abandoned her baby in favour of an easy, soft life. If that girl knew what she was really like she wouldn't vote for her in a thousand years!

Holding the tiny baby in her arms had been so evocative, reminding her of things she hadn't even thought of for years. Suddenly she was back in Brightman Lane, Hackney, with Dolly and Maurice Sylvester, in the cramped little flat over the shop where

Dean had taken her after those three terrible months of touring with the group.

When Dean had impulsively asked her to stay with him after the Isle of Wight pop festival she had been delirious with happiness. Swearing Joanna to secrecy, she had telephoned her parents with a story about the old schoolfriend she had met during the weekend school trip to London, the job she had been offered and the flat she would share with two other girls who were now university students. They'd been a little apprehensive at first about the suddenness of her leaving home, but she'd talked them round. She'd felt a little ashamed at the readiness with which they had believed her lies, but the heady prospect of being with Dean, of being part of his career and helping him climb the spangled ladder to stardom, had eclipsed any guilt she might have felt.

She could not have foreseen the squalor and disquiet of the weeks that followed. The snatched meals and boredom of waiting around for endless hours while Dean was at concerts, rehearsals or just out searching for an agent or anyone who would give the group a recording contract. Worst of all, sharing accommodation with a series of fellow artists in flats that seemed to grow progressively more squalid. Sometimes, when a gig went on till the small hours, they even used the van as sleeping quarters, all of them sharing the confined space. At times like this it was only Julia who suffered from the extreme discomfort. The other members of the group, including Dean, were usually too stoned, either on drink or dope, to notice.

After the first few weeks of ecstatic lovemaking it was only too clear from Dean's attitude that for him the novelty had worn off. He'd even begun to hint that maybe she'd be better off at home. Julia was devastated. She was disillusioned with the kind of life they were living. It was not what she had been led to expect; a fact of which she constantly reminded him. She repeatedly pointed out that it could all be remedied if they just got a little place of their own. Why didn't he want to please her when he had said he loved her so much? she demanded.

Dean grew impatient with her, tired of her constant complaints. He was bored with her and did nothing to conceal the fact. She whined and nagged day and night, her nerves torn to shreds by his indifference. And the more she nagged, the more he ignored her. Only the other members of the group seemed affected by her truculence and soon they began to complain about it to Dean.

When she first discovered she was pregnant she thought that surely Dean would now be shaken into making a commitment? The

78

realisation that he had no intention of doing any such thing brought her to the brink of panic. How could she have a baby when they had no proper home? When she asked him this, and he casually suggested that she should have an abortion, she became almost hysterical.

Finally the other members of the group gave Dean an ultimatum: either she went or they did. That was when, in sheer desperation, he took her to Hackney, to his parents, Dolly and Maurice.

Julia sat in her car outside the little house in Scrimshaw Street, the rest of her canvassing forgotten. Oblivious to the damp and cold, she made herself relive that May evening at the hospital when Dolly had sat with her all night, sharing the pain while holding her hand and telling her how proud she was of her, and how much she and Maurice looked forward to the grandchild they would hold in their arms tomorrow. Kind-hearted Dolly, and Maurice with his gentle face and soft brown eyes, were good people, the best. But even Dolly couldn't help her bear that other pain – far worse than the pangs of childbirth. The excruciating, heartbreaking pain of knowing that Dean didn't want her; had never really loved her – couldn't care less whether she lived or died. And, in spite of Dolly's reassurance, Julia sensed that he wasn't coming back for her.

She remembered the weary weeks that followed, the sleepless nights, the endless routine of feeds, bathing and washing clothes for a child for whom she could feel nothing. The little girl with black curly hair, dark eyes and olive skin who was so like Dean and whose grandparents doted on her, was merely the symbol of her own folly and wasted life.

Week followed week and her belief that Dean must know the baby was born and come for them became an obsession. Then at last he came, unheralded one weekend, only to tell her that this would be the last time. He should never have taken her away from her own environment, he told her. Their relationship had been doomed from the start. His career was what he wanted to concentrate on – the only important thing in his life. He had been offered the chance to go to America and wanted to take it.

'Go home, Julia,' he had urged her. 'Go home where you belong and take the baby with you. I'm not cut out to be a husband and father. I don't think I ever will be.'

The cruel words rang in her head long after Dean had left. Every time she looked at the child she felt mocked and cheated – trapped into an endless round of poverty and helplessness. Homesickness for her parents and the comfortable life she had given up ate into her soul like acid until she was reduced to a mental and physical wreck, Unable to eat, sleep or even think logically.

The decision to leave the child with Dolly and Maurice, to go home and make a fresh start hadn't seemed momentous at the time. It had come to her in the early hours of one morning as she lay awake after a another sleepless night. The thought had hit her with a blinding clarity. Suddenly it all seemed ridiculously simple – like a revelation. It was the answer to all her problems and she couldn't imagine why she hadn't thought of it before. She had always known that taking Fleur home with her was out of the question. Her parents were still happily under the impression that she had a job in London and was sharing a flat with friends. She had written regularly, her letters filled with fabrications about the good job she had, the happy and fulfilled life she was enjoying. Arriving home with a baby of mixed blood would shock them more than words could tell. None of them would ever survive the stares and the gossip of all their acquaintances in Elvemere. It would ruin everything: her father's business, her mother's social standing in the town. Julia could not subject them to it.

She had done it without giving herself time to think, rising early and writing the note, packing her few clothes. As she stood looking down at the sleeping dark-haired baby, she had felt a slight pang, no more. She knew that Fleur would be cared for and loved here with her grandparents. She had no fears about that. No one could love her more than they did. This was where she belonged, with her own people. Julia, her mother, belonged elsewhere.

She had been home for almost a week before it hit her. She missed her baby with a crippling guilt and an ache in her heart that was almost unendurable. The tight bud of mother-love, that had never fully opened, suddenly flowered with as much pain as birth and death combined. It was almost as though she had left a part of herself behind. The anguish was made worse by the fact that there was no one she could tell, no one to confide in. Every time she saw a pram she had to force herself to resist looking into it. Children at play brought a lump to her throat, as did the sight of a pregnant woman or a young couple absorbed in their new baby. And all the time she had to hide these feelings, suppress her agony and force herself to smile.

Meeting Vernon had helped a little. Handsome and personable, newly home from university and fired with ideas for the family business, he had lifted her spirits and restored her confidence. Her parents were pleased at their friendship and so were Vernon's. The two of them were almost precipitated into marriage, urged on by the prospective merging of the two firms. Julia had allowed herself to be carried along on the tide of approval. Life with Vernon would be safe and comfortable. She did not feel the headlong excitement she had experienced with Dean, but it didn't matter. Marriage to Vernon would be safe. Never again need she know heartbreak or loss. Little did she know!

Their engagement was a foregone conclusion and within a year they were married. It had taken years and another baby girl in her arms finally to obliterate the pain of losing Dean and baby Fleur. But tonight she had remembered the way she had felt as though it were yesterday. Tracey Brownlow had made her realise anew how despicable, how cowardly, her action had been. Tracey would never abandon her child. She would stand by him whatever happened. And when he grew up he would be proud of his mother and all that she had sacrificed to keep him. If only Julia could have had an ounce of Tracey's courage all those years ago, how different life might have been. But perhaps it was not too late? If she were to be elected tomorrow, maybe she could try to pay back the debt she owed.

Starting the car, she began to head for home. On the corner of the next road a fish and chip shop was doing good business. The bright lights from its windows shone out through the driving rain, making the pavements glisten. On impulse Julia stopped the car and got out to join the queue.

Ten minutes later she was knocking on the door of number one Scrimshaw Street again. Tracey opened the door a crack and peered out into the gloom.

'Who is it? Oh, Mrs Grant!'

Julia thrust the newspaper-wrapped parcel into her arms. 'Here, have supper on me,' she said. 'You have to keep your strength up for Damian's sake.' And before Tracey could argue she had fled to the shelter of the car, started the engine and headed once more for home.

It was almost midnight the following night before the count was completed. Julia had been up since seven, dividing her day between the polling station and party committee rooms. She had been here in the school hall since nine o'clock when the polling stations closed. She had watched the sealed black ballot boxes arrive and seen their contents tipped on to the waiting tables. Sitting mesmerised, she had watched as the tellers sorted the papers and bundled them, later meticulously recording the votes on the forms provided. She had watched as the column with her own name at the top lengthened. Success became at first hopeful, then likely. Finally the knot in her stomach tightened as that likelihood became a definite possibility.

She had applied for two tickets to attend the count, hoping that Vernon and Charlotte would accompany and support her, but both had announced that they were too busy so in the end her parents had come. Harry and May sat on their hard chairs at the back of the hall, looking weary as the waiting hours ticked by. But now the final lull had arrived and the tellers sat back, rubbing their stiff necks and heaving sighs of relief as they waited for the Recording Officer to make his final calculations.

Harry and May roused themselves at the prospect that the result was at last imminent, welcoming Julia who joined them looking pale and tense. May reached into the bag she had brought and produced a flask of hot coffee. She poured it into three mugs, handing her daughter and husband one each.

'Here, I'm sure we can all do with this.'

But before Julia could raise the mug to her lips, the Recording Officer rose from his seat in the centre of the hall and nodded to the four candidates to join him. On trembling legs, Julia crossed the hall to where the small hopeful huddle had gathered. It was through a daze that she heard him tell her she had received the greatest number of votes and was therefore the elected candidate.

The other three melted away and, in a kind of dream, she was mounting the steps of the platform for the announcement. A storm of applause greeted it and the first person to congratulate her was Eleanor Maitland.

Flinging her arms around her she said, 'Well done, girl. You're going to be the best councillor Elvemere has ever seen. Sock it to them, lass! Drag them into the twenty-first century. *I know you can do it!*'

Julia knew then that she had been handed the biggest challenge of her life. Briefly she heard an echo of Tracey Brownlow's words. *Us single mums want more like you sticking up for us.* Till last night she'd had no special cause to fight for. Now she had. People were counting on her. She wouldn't – couldn't – let them down.

At the back of the hall May Philips looked at her husband with a smile. 'Well, Harry, she's done it. Aren't you proud?'

He sighed and pushed at the bridge of his glasses. 'Of course I'm proud, dear,' he said. 'She's done well – very well.' But privately he was remembering Charlie Grant's words and wondering just what his daughter had let herself in for.

Chapter 5

'Well, I think that about wraps it up for tonight, unless there's any other business?'

Vernon, who was chairing Grant Philips Construction's monthly board meeting, looked up at his father and father-in-law, hoping that neither of them would bring anything further up. He had an urgent appointment at eight and it was already twenty to.

Charlie Grant cleared his throat and nodded to the secretary taking the minutes. 'Right, that's it, Jennifer, lass. You can go now.'

'Thank you, Mr Grant.' The girl closed her notebook and left. When the door had closed behind her and his father remained seated, taking out his pipe and tobacco pouch, Vernon's heart sank.

'Now then – there's this business about Victoria Gardens,' the older man began, packing tobacco carefully into his pipe.

Vernon groaned inwardly as he glanced at his watch. He'd certainly be late if they got on to that. 'Nothing's been settled about that, Dad,' he said. 'It's only a wild rumour as yet.'

'Don't you believe it.' Charlie waved him to silence. 'It'll go ahead all right. I had it on good authority – from Jack Martin, not long before his last heart attack, that the Gardens were definitely scheduled for redevelopment.' He frowned impatiently at the two doubtful faces opposite him. 'You have to get in on these things before they become public knowledge,' he said, accentuating his remark with a thump on the table. 'How do you think we've been successful in all our other council ventures? By getting inside information and then getting off our arses before anyone else. That's how!'

Harry Philips frowned. 'Do you think perhaps it was just a bit of guessing on Jack's part, Charlie? After all, he hadn't been attending council meetings regularly for some time and might have been out of touch or got the wrong end of the stick – anything.'

'Not Jack,' Charlie said vehemently. 'In all the years I knew him he was never out of touch. He was very seldom wrong about anything either. Had a nose for these things did Jack. He may have been badly over the last couple of years but he was far from senile. Now . . .' He leaned his arms on the table. 'His information was that there's to be a new library built on the town side of the gardens and a health centre on the side nearest the park. In between, there'll be offices at ground level – solicitors, accountants, that kind of thing. All top-class professional people, 'cause from what I can make out the rents'll be upper limit. Then, this health centre – it's to be the kind of place where they have everything under one roof. You know, dentists, doctors, physio-what-you-m'call-'ems. You know, like a kind of health *supermarket*.' Pleased with his own joke he leaned back, waving his pipe at them expansively. 'That whole area will be completely refurbished. The job'll be worth a packet. If we get in sharp like we could get that contract, and the money we make out of it will help finance the new executive estate at Meadowlands. Plans for that should be passed at the next meeting.'

'But we haven't done that kind of thing before, Dad,' Vernon pointed out. 'It'd take ages and we want to get on with the Meadowlands project.'

'So – we take on more men,' his father said.

Vernon frowned. 'Yes, but so far we've always built from scratch. Those buildings are listed so we wouldn't have a free hand. We'd have to abide by strict specifications. And another thing: once you start pulling old buildings like that about, you never know what you're letting yourself in for. We could end up out of pocket.'

'Never!' Charlie leaned back and lit his pipe. 'Trouble with you, Vernon, is you've got no vision. You might be good at the business side of things, but it's *vision* you want! The ability to see ahead like I've always had. Make no mistake, we wouldn't be sitting round this table now if it hadn't been for my business instincts. Just you get that architect feller we used for Meadowlands to do some preliminary plans, lad. He'll know all about listed buildings – what you can pull down and what you can't. He should do, he bloody charges enough! You get on and cost the job out and I'll drop hints in all the right places. Then we'll sit back and wait till the time's right.'

'When it's announced officially, you mean?'

'Oh, before that, lad. *Long* before. You can leave that part to me.' Charlie tapped the side of his nose. 'I'll get wind of it on the grapevine.'

'At a Lodge meeting, you mean?' Vernon said with a wry smile.

'All right, but don't knock it! I mean GPC to be first in with a chance. If our ideas are original and the estimate pleases them we'll get the job. We can juggle with the figures when we've got them good and interested.' He puffed hard on his pipe, then blew out a cloud of smoke and looked at the other two. 'I mean it. I've set my heart on this one. Handle it right and we'll get Meadowlands off the ground without having to go cap in hand to the bank, so think on.'

Vernon nodded. He had to admit that getting the contract for Victoria Gardens would certainly be a coup. And if his father's business methods were less than ethical, they certainly weren't new. 'Right, I'll get on to it.' He looked from one to the other of the older men. 'Well, if that's all . . .'

'What about the new secretary?' Harry asked. 'We haven't talked about that at all yet. I seem to remember at the last meeting there were about a dozen applications. Don't we need to make a shortlist – arrange a date for interviewing? After all, Jennifer's notice will be up the week after next.'

'I've already chosen a secretary,' Vernon said, shuffling his papers. 'Someone I know was among the applicants. She's very competent and experienced – up with all the latest computer skills. In fact, I think she'll make a very good PA once she's settled in.'

Harry frowned. 'You mean, you've already engaged her?'

'Subject to a few loose ends, yes.'

'Isn't that rather irregular, Vernon?' He looked across the table at his partner. 'Did you know about it, Charlie?'

He shrugged. 'Not till now, but it's Vernon who'll have to work with the woman most of the time and if he's happy with her, I'm content to trust his judgement.' He glanced at his son. 'Who is it anyway? Anyone I know?'

'I don't think so. Her name is Mrs Hanson. She lived in Elvemere as a young girl, until she married and went to live in America. Recently she was divorced and now she's come back to settle here.'

'An older woman then?'

Vernon lifted his shoulders. 'Well – older than Jennifer. Who can tell nowadays? At least she won't be running off to start a family.'

'That's a point.' Charlie sucked on his pipe and regarded his son speculatively. One of Vernie's old flames? Ah, well, it was nothing to do with him, or with Harry Philips either if it came to that. Just so long as you kept your private life and business in separate watertight compartments and didn't mess around with other men's wives, nothing could go too badly wrong. At least, that had always been his maxim. Aloud he said, 'Right then. If there's nothing more

I suggest we all retire to The Hat and Feathers for a little libation, as they say.'

'Not for me tonight, Dad,' Vernon said, gathering up his papers and pushing them into his briefcase. 'I've got to be somewhere else and I'm already late. See you at the office tomorrow. Goodnight.'

In the car park of the GPC building the two older men got into Charlie's Mercedes and headed towards the town and their favourite hostelry.

'A great pity we've lost old Jack, you know,' Charlie said thoughtfully as he negotiated the traffic in the town centre. 'A good friend and ally, he was. We'll miss him.' He glanced at his partner. 'Julia's done well to get in. Pleased, was she?'

Harry nodded. 'According to her mother she's working very hard at it already. Out all hours apparently. Seems she's taking her duties very seriously.'

'Mmm. Let's hope she remembers which side her bread is buttered, 'specially as she's on the planning committee,' Charlie said dryly. 'She could be a big help to us if she plays her cards right.'

Harry bit his lip. He'd been secretly dismayed when he heard that his daughter was to be involved with planning. Privately he considered it bad enough her being elected to the Town Council, but being on the planning committee would put her in an impossible situation. Charlie had absolutely no scruples when it came to business. When he decided to put the pressure on he could be quite ruthless. In his book anything was fair and the word 'corruption' simply wasn't in his vocabulary. Although to his shame Harry had benefited amply from his partner's devious methods in the past, he had no wish to see his daughter mixed up in them.

'I hear that Councillor Mrs Maitland has been a great help to her,' he said into the silence.

'Lena Maitland, eh?' Charlie gave a snorting chuckle. 'There was a lass for you, if ever there was one. I could tell you a tale or two about her! She and I almost got engaged once, you know. Oh, years ago when we were both n'more than kids. Chucked me for that Jim Maitland. A plate-layer on the railway! I ask you! Real choked I was at the time. Still, reckon I had a lucky escape, eh? She's turned into a right old battle-axe since. Left-wing as they come, even if she does pretend to be Tory.'

Charlie turned into the car park of The Hat and Feathers and neatly parked the Merc in his favourite space. 'You want to have a word with your Julia, Harry lad,' he said, unfastening his seat belt.

'You know, father to daughter, like. I've warned our Vernon – wives want keeping under your thumb. Give these modern lasses an inch and before you know it they've taken the whole of the bloody M1! Maybe you could tip her the wink about this council thing; point her in the right direction.' He punched Harry's shoulder playfully. 'Young chaps nowadays can't hold a candle to us old 'uns when it comes to knowing how to handle a woman, eh, Harry lad?'

'No, well . . .' Harry Philips coughed nervously. 'I daresay you're right.' He turned to look at his partner. 'About this new secretary . . . Don't you think we should make a proper shortlist and interview everyone? It doesn't seem very fair the way Vernon's handling it.'

Charlie turned to look at him. 'Like I said, he will be working with her most of the time so let him have the choice. You see, Harry, the trouble with Vernon is that he's got no imagination. He can't see any further than a balance sheet. Sometimes he complains we don't give him enough say in things, so I reckon this is a good way to let him think he's making a decision.' He nudged Harry in the ribs and winked broadly. 'Take my tip and let him have his head on this one, Harry. It'll keep him quiet – for the time being at least.'

After Vernon had watched the two older men drive away he got into his own car and drove off in the opposite direction. His destination was the Fairwoods Country Club and Motel halfway between Elvemere and Merifield, the nearest village.

When he drew on to the forecourt he felt a little frisson of excitement at the thought of the coming meeting with Jo Hanson. So far they'd only spoken on the telephone and that was when he'd suggested meeting away from the office instead of for the usual formal interview. The Fairwoods Country Club had been her idea. It was where she'd been staying since her recent return to England.

When he'd received her application and read the little note she'd enclosed in a separate sealed envelope he'd been surprised. He hadn't seen her for something like twenty years, just before she'd run off with an American airman and got married.

They'd had a brief, torrid affair the year before he had married Julia – when he was twenty-three and just beginning to work for his father. Jo had been seventeen at the time, but more exciting and passionate than any other girl he'd known. Certainly more experienced. Their affair had been too frenetic and fiery to last and had burned itself out after a couple of months, after which the American serviceman had loomed on to the horizon, presumably sweeping her off her feet. But Vernon had never forgotten Jo. She wasn't the kind of girl a man easily forgets.

Switching off the engine, he adjusted the rearview mirror to examine his reflection, wondering if she would think he had changed. Taking out his comb, he flicked it through his hair, grateful it was still thick and wavy. The streaks of silver over his ears were attractive and sophisticated, he had been told. Sexy even. Anyway forty-three wasn't exactly over the hill, was it? He was in his prime.

Would she have changed? he wondered. He pictured the long thick hair, a rich dark red like old mahogany, and the sultry green eyes that could burn with passion or flash with temper. Oh, yes, Jo had been a powerfully attractive woman, even at seventeen. Had, marriage and divorce dimmed and disillusioned her, or would her experience of life have brought a fascinating new depth to her character? There was only one way to find out, he told himself.

He saw her at once, sitting alone at a table in the corner of the garden bar were they had arranged to meet. She didn't see him at first and he had time to observe her from the doorway. She looked a little older, more mature, but it suited her. The lines of her jaw and cheekbones, softly blurred in her teens, were now sharper and more defined, deepening the shadows under cheekbones and eyes. And the hair . . . He was pleased to see that its colour was as rich as before. The style was different, of course. He missed the luxuriant waist-length sweep he remembered, but the short sophisticated feathery style she wore now accentuated the new sensual contours of her face.

She turned towards the door, saw him and lifted her hand. As he returned her wave and crossed the room towards her he saw that her eyes were the same. Large and lustrous, a deep, deep green, the heavy lids giving them that mysterious brooding look he remembered so well. He felt his stomach lurch.

She stood up and held out her hand. 'Vernon. How lovely to see you again after all these years.'

He shook her hand. 'Jo. How are you?' He took in the charcoal grey suit and silky cream shirt, the understated gold jewellery. Her taste in clothes had matured too, along with her figure; a little more rounded, perhaps, but still as stunning and alluring as ever.

'I'm fine. It was very good of you to agree to meet me here. So much nicer than a formal interview.' She sat down again and indicated the chair next to her. 'I took the liberty of getting you a whisky and dry ginger. That used to be your favourite, didn't it?'

'Still is. Fancy you remembering.' He sat down and lifted the glass, intrigued by the slight trans-Atlantic accent she had acquired. He remembered the way those husky tones had once had the power to make his heart race.

'Here's to the future. I hope you're going to like working at GPC.'

'I'm sure I shall. I must say it was marvellous of you to offer me the job so promptly. Are you sure it's all right with your father?'

Vernon felt his colour heighten. Did she imagine he was still running around like an office boy as he had been before she left? 'I don't need his permission,' he said stiffly. 'I'm the firm's general manager now.'

'Of course. I'm sorry.' He was aware of her, watching him from under lowered lids as she took a sip of her own drink. 'I've brought you my references,' she said, opening her handbag. 'They're all from my previous employers in the States, of course, but you could always ring them for quick confirmation.'

'I wouldn't dream of it.' He waved away the handful of letters she passed him. 'Put them away. If I can't take the word of an old friend . . .'

'So – when would you like me to start?'

'In two weeks' time, if that's all right? Meantime you must come into the office one day soon and look round – let Jennifer acquaint you with the routine.'

'Jennifer?'

'My present secretary. The girl who's leaving. She's getting married and going to live down south. She's been with me since leaving school and she's very good, but now that I'm replacing her I'm looking for someone who can eventually take more responsibility – work on her own initiative, more of a PA in other words. We're taking on more and more work all the time, you see. There are plans for going much further out of town. I have to be away from the office more and I need someone capable to leave in charge.'

She smiled. 'Sounds fascinating.'

'Your salary will be adjusted once that happens, of course.'

'Of course.'

'I'm sure you'll make a very capable PA.'

'It's in line with the work I've been doing over in the States. I was with a real-estate company in Denver for the past two years, so I hope I shall live up to your expectations.'

'I'm sure you will.'

She regarded him in that direct way of hers that made his spine tingle. 'What have you been doing all these years, Vernon?' she asked. 'It's so long since I left Elvemere, I've got an awful lot of catching up to do.'

'Well, as you must have realised, the family firm has expanded. I'll have to take you on a guided tour of all our sites.'

'I've certainly noticed a lot of changes. I'd hardly have recognised the place, the town has grown so.'

'We've been responsible for a large part of that. I daresay you've seen the new industrial estate? We were heavily involved in that. We've been very successful since we merged with Philips Electricals.'

'Yes, I wondered about the Philips part. That wouldn't be the Harry Philips who used to have the little electrical shop in the High Street, would it?'

'That's right. He branched out into plumbing and heating later. When Dad heard he was planning to expand, he offered him a partnership.'

'Well, well! His daughter Julia and I were friends at school. I wonder what became of her?'

Vernon cleared his throat. 'As a matter of fact, I – er – married her.'

She threw back her head and laughed. 'I *see!* A family merger in more ways than one. How is she?'

'As a matter of fact she's just been elected to the Town Council,' Vernon told her. 'She's so busy I hardly ever see her these days.'

She looked at him speculatively. 'Do I detect a slight note of resentment?'

He laughed. 'Good heavens, no,' he lied. 'Julia and I have always done our own thing. I've always believed that women should use their skills and talents in whatever way they can.'

'I see. Any little Grants?'

'One. A daughter, Charlotte.'

'Congratulations!'

'Oh, she's hardly little any more – sixteen – just passed her GCSEs.'

'And going into the family business?'

'Yes, but I'm insisting she does it from the bottom up, just like I had to.'

'In this day and age?' She looked at him, one eyebrow raised. 'Are educated young people still willing to join their family businesses on those terms?'

'Oh, yes! She's quite happy about it. She's a bright girl. She knows she can only benefit in the long run.' Vernon wasn't too keen on the way the conversation was going. It made him feel very attached and very old. 'But that's enough about me,' he said with a light laugh. He leaned forward and treated her to his special intimate smile. 'What about you, Jo? What brought you back to Elvemere?'

'I'd had enough of America, especially after my second divorce.' She glanced up at him. 'Oh, yes, I'm afraid marriage has been a bit of a non-starter as far as I'm concerned. I've decided to concentrate on my career from now on.'

'So you decided to come home.'

'Yes. I was never all that keen on life in the States anyway. Somehow I never really seemed to fit in. I think I've always been essentially British.'

He tossed back the last of his drink. 'Well, their loss is our gain. Another drink?'

She looked at her watch. 'No time, I'm afraid. I'll have to be going.'

'Oh. You're not still living here then?'

'No.'

To his considerable disappointment she began to gather up her bag and gloves. 'I'll walk you to your car,' he said quickly.

As they crossed the forecourt he wondered where she was going. Did she have a date – was there already a new man? 'You've found somewhere permanent to live then?' he asked. 'If you'd told me you were looking I could have helped you.'

'I've bought a house in Hazel Grove just off the Merifield Road. Do you know it?'

Vernon grinned. 'I should do. It's one of ours. We built that estate soon after we merged. They're nice houses. Small but well-planned.'

'Yes, compact and warm. That's one thing one gets used to in the States. Central heating and air conditioning are counted as necessities over there. I moved in last week.' She turned to smile at him as she unlocked the door of a little scarlet Mazda. 'I'll have to give a house warming party. You must bring your family round. It'd be fun to see Julia again.'

Vernon watched as she settled herself into the driving seat and fastened her seat belt. 'Give me a ring and say when you'd like to come into the office and look round,' he shouted, stepping back as she started to move the car forward.

She smiled up at him through the window. 'I will – soon.' Bye, Vernon. And thanks again.'

Walking to his own car he felt flat. The meeting had disappointed him. She'd given not the slightest indication that she remembered the passionate affair they'd enjoyed. He sighed. He'd been fooling himself. What had he expected? He reflected that he had probably been one of many such lovers in those far off days. Why should she have remembered him? Since then she had been halfway round the world and had two husbands, whilst he had scarcely stirred from Elvemere, Grant Philips Construction and Julia. As he headed back to Elvemere he wondered whether to tell his wife that her schoolfriend, the former Joanna Bloom, was back in town? Then, for reasons he was reluctant to acknowledge, he decided against it.

'I'd like to stay on permanently, if that's all right with you, Mrs Franks?'

Fleur had come down to the basement flat to pay her rent and felt that the time was right to broach the subject of the flat. Her little room under the eaves was bitterly cold now that the winter was close on the heels of autumn. Derek Jones had already moved out and she knew the flat hadn't been advertised yet.

Ivy looked up from counting the notes in her hand and took the half-smoked cigarette from her mouth. 'Oh, you would, would you?'

'But not in the room I'm in now.' Fleur took a deep breath. 'I hear you haven't advertised Mr Jones's flat.'

'Oh?' Ivy's eyes narrowed. 'And where did you hear that?'

'You mean, you have?'

'I might and I might not have. But what would you want with a flat anyway?'

'I could make more of a home of it,' Fleur said. 'And I like the little balcony. I've seen it from the garden.'

'Mmm, I daresay you would like it – along with a good many others.' Ivy stuffed the notes into her capacious handbag, put the smouldering cigarette back between her lips and folded her arms. 'I could let that flat ten times over if I'd a mind to. And I seem to remember telling you I was only letting you have that room on a tem'pry basis.'

'That's right. Which is why I'd like to rent the flat,' Fleur said firmly. 'I've got a steady job and I'm willing to pay the same rent as Mr Jones.'

'Oh! I expect you know what that is too, do you?'

'Not exactly, but obviously I'd expect it to be more than I pay now.'

'Too right it is! In fact I was thinking of putting it up,' Ivy said. 'I could double what I ask for that flat if I'd a mind to. My trouble is, I'm my own worst enemy. Too soft by half, I am.'

Fleur turned away, trying to hide the irritation she felt. Ivy was playing her like a fish on a line and she wasn't having it. 'I see,' she said. 'In that case, I'd better give you my notice. I don't want any favours, Mrs Franks, but now that the winter is almost here I'll have to find something more comfortable.' At the door she turned. 'Shall we say a fortnight's notice as from today?' She was almost through the door when Ivy said, 'Hang on – wait a minute! You're a bit sharp off the mark, aren't you? You might give a body a chance to think, springing things on me like that.' She regarded Fleur speculatively. 'I expect you want to stay here to be near your feller. That it?'

Fleur frowned. 'Feller?'

Ivy winked. 'Come off it. You know who I mean. Young Tom.' She smirked. 'Planning some romantic little candle-lit suppers for two, are you?'

'I just want somewhere to live, Mrs Franks – somewhere a bit better than where I am now. It has nothing to do with Tom.'

'Why has he been dropping hints about you then?'

Fleur felt her colour rise. 'What kind of hints?'

'About how he hoped you'd be staying on permanent like.' Ivy nodded and grinned knowingly. 'Reminding me what a nice girl you are and what a good tenant; hinting that he'd like me to let you stay here.'

Fleur felt resentment pricking at her. What made Tom think he had the right to speak on her behalf? She could fight her own corner. 'I did mention it to him, but you're quite wrong, Mrs Franks. Tom and I are friends – nothing more,' she said. 'I'd no idea he'd said anything to you, and if you're putting the rent up it'll probably be out of my reach anyway so maybe I should forget it.'

'Now then, no need to get uppity,' Ivy chided. She looked at Fleur's indignant expression for a moment, then said, 'Okay. I've got used to you now and you've been a good tenant so far. Better the devil you know, I suppose. You can have it for what Derek paid. That suit you?'

Fleur's heart gave an excited leap, but she kept her voice level. 'Thank you, Mrs Franks, that'll be fine.'

'You can move your stuff in any time you like seein' it's empty and you're all paid up.' She treated Fleur to one of her rare smiles. 'You're right to keep that young Tom in his place,' she said. 'Too much casual sex these days, if you ask me. Only starts 'em thinking they own you. Oh, and by the way, I think it's time you started calling me Ivy like the others.'

'Of course. There's just one thing . . .'

Ivy lit a new cigarette from the disintegrating stub of the old one, squinting up sideways at Fleur as she did so. 'Go on then. I can always say no.'

'Would you mind if I decorated it? The flat, I mean.'

Ivy gave a cackle of laughter. 'Why should I mind that? S'long as you don't want to paint it black with sky blue pink spots, you can do as you like.'

Fleur was settling down well to her job with Arden Catering. As well as the evening classes in computer studies, she had begun a course of driving lessons. She had very little free time but that was the way she liked it.

Sally Arden had discovered that Fleur had a light hand with pastry and had taught her to make the quiches that she was famous for as well as some of her other celebrated recipes. In return Fleur had given Sally some of the Caribbean recipes she had learned from her grandfather which Dolly had cooked regularly when they were together as a family in Hackney.

As they worked together in the gleaming kitchen that Sally had had built on to her home, Fleur learned more about her new employer; about the brief marriage that had ended so tragically and her dedication to her only son, Peter, whom she had worked so hard to send to his father's old school just as they'd always planned. Peter Arden was now an under manager in a large London hotel.

'He could have done anything,' Sally told her. 'Medicine, law, journalism. But that was what he'd always wanted. Of course I insisted that he must do it the right way,' she added. 'He took a course in business and hotel management at college after leaving school, then he went to work in a large hotel in Switzerland for a year. He's had experience in every department from the kitchens up. He could turn his hand to the job of anyone in the hotel from the maître d' and chef to the manager's secretary or receptionist.'

'He sounds very efficient,' Fleur said.

'Oh, he is. He has the charm and diplomacy to go with it too. And the good looks,' Sally added. 'I'll show you his photograph some time.'

But Fleur had already seen Peter Arden's photograph. It was once when Sally had forgotten her reading glasses and sent Fleur up to her bedroom for them. Out of a silver frame on the little table beside her bed a handsome dark-haired young man smiled. His hair was thick and well-groomed and his eyes a soft, twinkling hazel like his mother's. Fleur had guessed at the time that he must be Peter.

As Christmas approached Arden Catering grew very busy indeed. As well as the usual parties there were the more formal buffet dances and executive Christmas lunches, given by various local

94

firms. One of these was a boardroom lunch at the premises of Grant Philips Construction on the industrial estate.

They arrived early with their assortment of boxes and equipment, and were shown up to the boardroom by an exquisitely groomed woman with red hair. Fleur set to work, laying the long table with Sally's snowy damask cloth and elegant cutlery and glasses. Working quickly and deftly as she'd learned, she folded the napkins into water lily shapes and set the pretty flower arrangement of bronze and yellow chrysanthemums in the centre of the table.

When it was done she joined Sally in the small adjoining kitchen where she was carving the pre-cooked turkey and unpacking the vegetables from their insulated boxes. In places like this where there were no cooking facilities, a hot lunch was more of a challenge, but Sally had the task worked out to a fine art.

'You can change now, if you like,' she told Fleur over her shoulder as she put plates to warm in the microwave they took everywhere with them. 'Then take the wine out of the cool box and uncork it. By the time I've dished up they'll be ready for their pre-lunch drinks.'

At exactly twelve-forty-five the door opened and the party came in. They seemed to be in a jovial mood and Fleur was waiting with her tray of drinks: sherry, dry and medium, orange juice or mineral water. There were two older men, whom she took to be Mr Grant and Mr Philips; a younger, rather suave-looking man in what looked like an Armani suit; the elegant woman who had shown them to the boardroom; and two other men whom she gathered were a senior sales executive and a transport manager. They took drinks from her tray and chatted in a relaxed way. Fleur was just about to go back into the kitchen when the man in the designer suit stepped in front of her.

'*Hello* there! I don't think I've seen you before.'

She smiled. 'No, I've only worked with Mrs Arden since October.'

He gave her an appraising look. 'And unless I'm mistaken you don't come from around here.'

'No. From London.'

He nodded wisely. 'I knew it. The young women in this part of the world just haven't the style. I could see at once . . .'

'I'm sorry but I'll have to go,' Fleur said, edging away. 'There's only Mrs Arden and me and I think your meal is ready to serve.'

'My dear, of course. Thoughtless of me. What's your name?'

'Fleur.'

He smiled. 'Charming. Well, Fleur, we don't stand on ceremony here so there's no need to be afraid.'

'I'm not!'

He laid a warm hand on her arm. 'My wife and I were thinking of having a party at our home for New Year. If we engage Mrs Arden to do the catering, I shall insist on making it a condition that you'll be coming along too.'

'I see – er – thank you, but I would anyway.'

'Well, isn't that stroke of luck? I shall speak to her about it this evening.'

Fleur went quickly into the kitchen with her empty tray and closed the door. Sally looked at her flushed face.

'Did you have a job to get away?'

'You saw then? Who was that man who was talking to me?'

'That's Vernon Grant. He's the boss's son and general manager of GPC. He's got a bit of an eye for a pretty girl, so I hear.' She laughed. 'But you've just discovered that! I'm sure you can cope.'

Fleur said nothing, deciding that the man's behaviour must be an occupational hazard. She served the starter, a delicious concoction of prawns and grapefruit. Vernon Grant kept giving her encouraging smiles as she worked her way round the table. To her embarrassment he even attempted once to draw her into the conversation. She suspected that he'd already taken more than a glass or two of something alcoholic before the party began. Beside him sat his private secretary, the sophisticated red-head with the slight American accent whose name she now knew was Mrs Hanson. She looked increasingly annoyed each time her boss addressed Fleur with such familiarity, and twice she saw her lay a discreetly restraining hand on his wrist and give him a reproachful look.

In the kitchen she told Sally of the embarrassing situation. 'I wish he'd stop,' she said. 'Can't he see that I'm just trying to do my job? I'm being discreet and unobtrusive just like you've taught me, but he isn't making it very easy.'

Sally smiled. 'Don't worry. This is the first time you've encountered a man like that but I'm afraid it won't be the last. Try to ignore it.'

'I think he's had a bit too much to drink.'

'I'm sure he has,' Sally said wryly. 'Just keep reminding yourself of how awful he's going to feel when he's sober.'

'And his secretary looks so annoyed,' Fleur said, watching as Sally sliced the delicious home-made chocolate gâteau.

The older woman paused in her work and frowned thoughtfully. 'You know, I have the oddest feeling I've seen that woman somewhere before. It's been bothering me ever since we arrived.

96

Apparently she's fairly new here – been living in America. But I could have sworn . . .'

'I wouldn't have thought there were many like her around,' Fleur remarked as she loaded her tray with plates. 'If you'd met her before, you'd remember.'

'Yes, and if you ask me she's got trouble written all over her,' Sally said quietly.

Joanna Hanson drove her car into the garage and unclasped her seat belt. Vernon turned to her.

'It's very good of you to do this for me, Jo, but I would have been perfectly all right.'

'All right my foot,' she said bluntly. 'The police are especially vigilant at this time of year and you must be way over the limit. I'll make you a pot of strong black coffee and then later, when you've sobered up enough, I'll drive you back to the yard to get your own car.'

Vernon got out of the car and followed her into the house. As she unlocked the front door and they stepped into the hall, he looked around with admiration. She had made good use of mirrors to enhance the space in the small square hall. Twin gilt-framed ones were placed on either side, facing each other and reflecting light from the window, and the rose pink carpet and white walls helped provide a warm welcoming feel to the house. 'Well, I must say, this is very nice,' he said, nodding his approval.

'I'm glad you like it.' She took off her coat and held out her hand for his. 'I like nice things. My parents favoured a rather spartan way of living. My tastes are a little more affluent. My last divorce settlement was generous, so why not?'

'Why not indeeed!' Vernon walked through into the living room where glass doors gave on to a circular conservatory filled with green plants and cane furniture. The living-room chairs and carpets were of soft cream leather, strewn with pastel-coloured cushions, and the walls and lampshades were a delicate shade of peach. He noticed that there were two original paintings by lesser French Impressionists on the walls. As he sank into one of the cream leather chairs Joanna slid a CD of Vivaldi's Four Seasons into a music centre discreetly concealed on a book shelf and a moment later the lush string music billowed into the room.

He leaned back to close his eyes. 'Mmm, very restful.'

'I'll make you that coffee,' she said.

After a few minutes he got up and followed her through to the kitchen. The decor here was in pale shades too, ivory cupboards and worktops, beige and white ceramic tiles on the floor. Only the curtains added a splash of colour with their design of sunflowers.

The coffee machine was already bubbling and Joanna had laid a tray with cups and put a jug of milk into the microwave to heat. Vernon looked around him with interest.

'Funny, although we built these houses, I've never been into one of them after it was occupied,' he remarked. 'Except for the show house, this is the first one I've ever seen furnished.'

She glanced at him. 'I don't suppose there's any reason why you should.' She turned to look at him. 'Vernon, don't you think you should ring your wife? She'll be wondering where you are.'

He leaned against the worktop and folded his arms. 'She's sure to be out,' he said gloomily. 'Since she got elected to the council she's hardly ever in.'

The microwave pinged and Joanna took out the jug of milk and set it on the tray. 'Poor Vernon. Are you feeling terribly deprived?'

He shrugged. 'Not particularly. I must admit I don't enjoy eating alone, though.'

'What about little Charlotte?'

'She's hardly ever there either.' He looked at her. 'It isn't easy, you know, living in a house of women. They gang up on you.'

She picked up the tray and headed for the living room again. 'I'm sure that can't be true.'

When they were seated on the settee with the coffee table drawn up before them, Joanna looked at him. 'If you don't mind me saying so, Vernon, I really don't think you should drink so much.'

He looked at her. 'Give me one good reason . . .'

'Because you can't handle it,' she told him bluntly. 'Well, you did ask. Take this lunchtime, for instance.'

'What about this lunchtime?'

'Chatting up the waitress. Couldn't you see you were only embarrassing the poor girl?'

'Was I?'

'Of course you were. Then saying you were going to engage that catering firm for a New Year party at home.'

'What's wrong with that? Julia will be far too busy to bother with catering for her own parties now she's on the council.'

'Oh, she *asked* you to book them, did she?'

'No – but she'd want me to. It'll be a surprise.'

'And if she's already booked another firm?' He stared at her. 'There, see what I mean?' she added. 'You're so used to making decisions in the office, Vernon. You're overworked – showing all

98

the signs of executive stress. It's a good job you've got me to help you now.'

'Believe me, I know that. I'm already wondering how I managed before you came,' he said. 'I can't tell you how wonderful it is to have someone sympathetic to talk things over with.'

'Don't you ever talk to Julia about business, Vernon?'

He shrugged his shoulders. 'Julia and I stopped talking – about business or anything else – years ago.'

She poured the coffee, put milk into her own and gave him his black. 'There, drink that. It'll clear your head.'

He sipped the strong brew, looking at her thoughtfully as he did so. 'Now if I was married to someone like you, Jo . . .' She laid a hand on his arm.

'Vernon, tell me something. I noticed that none of the wives are on the board of directors. Is there any reason?'

He shook his head. 'Only that Dad is old-fashioned about things like that,' he told her. 'Doesn't believe that women have heads for business. Ma has some shares in the firm – well, she put up so much of the money in the beginning. But she's never taken up her position as a shareholder. It's largely on paper, for tax purposes, I suppose.'

'You mean, she doesn't demand to have her say – doesn't use her vote on any proposals?'

'Well, no.'

'And what about Julia?'

'She's never asked. But even if she had, I could hardly demand she had a seat when Ma hasn't.'

'Are there any shares for sale, Vernon?' She looked at him closely.

'We're not a public company, you know.'

'I know, but that doesn't stop people from investing in GPC, does it?'

'I suppose not. I've never thought about it. No one outside the family has ever offered.'

'Well, I'm offering now.'

He stared at her. 'Are you serious?'

'Never more so. I told you my divorce settlement was generous. What better firm to invest in than the one I'm working for?'

'I'd have to put it to the next meeting. And I'm not sure that it would be acceptable to have an employee holding shares.'

'Some firms actually *offer* their employees shares. It makes them feel they have a stake in their company's future.'

'Well, just leave it with me. It won't be till after Christmas now.'

She leaned across and covered his hand with hers. 'Are you feeling more relaxed?'

He smiled. 'A little. This is a very relaxing room.'

She stood and picked up the tray. 'Tell you what, why don't you go upstairs and have a lie down for an hour? I'll wash these cups and tidy up a bit. I'll call you at six o'clock.' At the foot of the stairs she directed him. 'It's the door facing you at the top of the stairs. Help yourself.'

When Vernon opened the door at the top of the stairs he found himself in what was obviously Joanna's bedroom. It was decorated in dove grey and pink, with fitted cupboards and dressing table in ivory and silver. He took off his jacket and trousers and slid under the frilled coverlet. Minutes later he was fast asleep.

When he awoke it was dark. He was about to reach out to switch on the bedside lamp when the door opened and Joanna came in. He saw that she wore a dressing gown, or rather a négligée. It floated around her as she came into the room, the light from the landing silhouetting the outline of her body through the filmy material.

'Don't switch on the light,' she said. 'I'll draw the curtains first.' She pulled the cord and the velvet drapes swung across, enveloping the room in a cosy intimacy. She turned to him. 'That's better. You can switch on the light now, if you like. I've just had a bath. Would you like one before you go home?' She sat down on the bed and looked at him and as she did so the years rolled away. She was even more beautiful now than she had been at seventeen. He sat up in the bed and raked a hand through his hair, acutely conscious of his dishevelled appearance.

'Sounds like a good idea,' he said.

'It seems odd, seeing you in my bed.' She reached out to touch his cheek. 'It's all so long ago, isn't it, Vernon?'

He swallowed hard. 'I – thought you'd forgotten all that.'

She smiled. 'Oh, no. I could never forget, could you?'

'No. It was too special.'

'Was it really? Was I someone special to you, Vernon – or just another little bimbo?'

'You were never that.'

'No?' She leaned towards him and the soft lace and chiffon of her négligée fell away. Her breasts were clearly visible and he caught his breath. Her lips brushed his. 'You're still a very attractive man,' she breathed against the corner of his mouth. 'Even more attractive than you were all those years ago. But I expect you know that. I expect there have been dozens more since me – since Julia even.'

It was a question rather than a statement and he looked into the direct green eyes that were so close to his. 'There have been a few. I might as well be honest.'

'For me too,' she said. 'But at our age experience is everything, don't you agree? We have no illusions, no expectations. Just desires and needs.' She slipped her arms around his neck and kissed him. 'I suppose you'd better get up now,' she said as their lips parted. 'Julia will be worrying about you.'

'To hell with Julia,' he said raggedly as he pulled her roughly to him again.

The flat on the first floor of thirteen Victoria Gardens was really no more than a glorified bed-sit. It had been converted from what had once been an elegant first-floor drawing room. The deep fireplace alcove had been made into a bedroom area, the fireplace itself being boarded up and disguised as a dressing table. There was a built-in wardrobe cupboard and just enough room for a single bed and bedside table. The whole area was closed off from the rest of the room by heavy curtains. Another corner was partitioned and equipped as a tiny kitchenette, with a sink, cooker and cupboard.

What was left of the room was spacious and airy, the best part in Fleur's eyes being the French windows that gave on to the little balcony overlooking the garden.

After she moved in Fleur spent every spare moment decorating. Tom helped, but by now he knew her well enough to respect her independence and only gave his assistance when invited to. She painted the walls of the living room white and bought a brightly coloured floral border which she applied at waist level. 'To help lower the ceiling,' as she explained to Tom on the Sunday afternoon before Christmas when she invited him in to see her finished work.

He laughed. 'How can you *lower the ceiling* and why would you want to?'

'Because this room was once much larger,' she told him patiently. 'So now that it's been chopped up, it looks out of proportion. The border helps rebalance it.'

He saw that she was right and was impressed. He had to admit that she seemed to have an instinct for interior decoration. The whole place had been completely transformed since Derek Jones had lived in it.

She had papered the bedroom area with a pretty sprigged paper and bought herself a duvet cover and pillow cases to match. She'd also found a pretty table lamp with a soft pink shade that gave the room a soft warm light. The whole effect was completed by the two coats of brilliant white paint with which she had covered the dingy beige woodwork.

'When I can afford it, I'd like to get a new carpet and some covers for the armchairs,' she told Tom as she looked around the room with satisfaction. 'There's one of those discount warehouses out at Merifield. I'd like to have a look sometime.'

'Well, if you're serious, I'll take you,' he said. 'But surely you don't want to waste your money on a rented flat? You never know, you might want to move to something better in a year or two – even buy a place of your own.'

'I shan't,' she said firmly. 'I like it here. It's just the right size for me and I'd never get anywhere as cheap. Just as soon as the spring comes I'm going to transform the balcony. Just you wait and see.' She hugged her arms around herself gleefully. 'I'm *really* looking forward to that. I'm going to paint the wrought ironwork white and I'll have hanging baskets and tubs. A whole riot of colour. My own little corner. Maybe I'll get some of those wind-chimes to hang up, to play me to sleep on warm summer nights.'

He grinned. Her enthusiasm was so infectious that it was impossible not to be affected by it. 'You and your old balcony,' he teased. 'Well, when you're lugging bags of compost up the stairs and hanging from the railings by your eyelashes with a paintbrush in your teeth, maybe you'll let me help?'

'I'll manage, thanks.'

He regarded the stubborn set of her mouth, a little wounded by her rejection. It was impossible not to admire the stoic, independent way in which she struggled to manage alone. He just wished she'd unbend a little towards him. They'd known one another almost three months now and yet, to his disappointment, their relationship was no closer than when they'd first met.

'Miss Emancipation, aren't you?' He reached out to brush her cheek with his knuckles, his eyes wistful. 'I wish you'd let me inside that reinforced steel barrier sometimes, Fleur. I mean it when I say I want to help, you know. There are no conditions – no strings. I just want to do things for you because I like you very much.'

'I know, Tom. And it isn't that I don't appreciate it. I like you too, really.'

'Then why?' He took a step towards her and put his hands on her shoulders. Immediately he felt her stiffen just as she always did at his touch and for a second anger warmed his blood and sharpened his voice.

'You see? There you go again! Am I really so repulsive to you, Fleur? If I am you only have to say so and I'll . . .'

102

'Oh, please don't be angry, Tom. It isn't that.' His sudden abruptness disturbed her and she drew away, turning towards the window. 'It's not what you think, but I can't explain. Don't ask me. Maybe – maybe it would be better if you left now.'

For a moment he stood looking at her straight, unyielding back, wondering whether to do as she asked and leave. But if he left now it would be for the last time, and somehow, in spite of her apparent coolness, he knew that neither of them wanted that. He had to make her trust him if they were ever going to get anywhere and he sensed that they had arrived at a watershed.

He moved to stand behind her as she looked down into the rambling garden below. Her arms were wrapped protectively around herself and he looked at the tense fingers that clutched each upper arm.

'Did something happen to you, Fleur?' he asked softly. 'Is it something to do with your childhood – the time before you came here?'

'I had a *wonderful* childhood!' She spun round to face him, her eyes bright and defensive. 'No one could have had a better family. I miss them very much and . . .'

'And *what*?' He put his hands on her shoulders, firmly this time, drawing her towards him. 'Tell me, Fleur. Did you love someone? Did he hurt you? Is that why you ran away?'

'*I didn't run away!*' She tried to push him away, but he held her fast. She lowered her eyes, refusing to meet his insistent gaze. 'Let me go, Tom. You've got no right to question me like this.'

'Maybe not but I still think we should talk,' he insisted. 'Come and sit down, Fleur. I'm your friend. You can trust me, I promise you that. There's something bothering you. It's eating at you and it's time you got it off your chest – for your own sake.'

The feel of his hands on her shoulders was sending spirals of panic through her chest, making her want to scream. She could feel her breathing become so shallow it was making her hot and dizzy. As the room began to spin she opened her mouth to shout at him to leave her alone – to go away and mind her own business. But as she looked into his eyes and saw the respect and genuine concern in them the words died in her throat. Suddenly she realised how long it was since she'd shared her anxieties with another human being; how long since she had confided in anyone or poured out her innermost fears. She felt the panic and tension slowly seep out of her like air from a burst balloon and suddenly, without warning, tears welled up in her eyes and began to trickle down her cheeks.

She laid her head against his chest. 'Oh, Tom, I'm sorry. I never meant to hurt you. You don't deserve this.'

'You haven't hurt me.' His arms closed gently around her. 'I just wish *you* weren't hurting so much. Darling, can't you tell me why you're so reluctant to trust me? You must know how much I care about you by now.' He led her to one of the armchairs and knelt beside her, holding both her hands.

'You're right,' she said slowly, her mouth dry. 'It was something that happened – just before I left Hackney. And I suppose I did run away.' Her hands gripped his tightly. 'I never ran away from anything in my whole life till then, Tom, and I despise myself for it.'

'Maybe if you tell me about it you can stop running,' he said gently. 'At least in your mind.'

'I told you that I promised my grandmother to come and look for my mother,' she began. 'But I don't think I ever would have come to Elvemere if it hadn't been for . . .' She paused, biting her lips.

'Yes. Go on.'

'I stopped a gang of skinheads from beating up an Asian boy one night. It was outside the fish and chip shop where I worked.'

He smiled. 'That sounds like you.'

'A policeman happened to come along and I made the leader of the gang look silly in front of him.' She shuddered. 'They don't let you get away with a thing like that. Not where I come from. I suppose I should have known they'd try to get even.'

He held her hands tightly. 'What happened?'

'Nothing for a while. Except that I suspected that someone had been following me home for some time. I guessed it was them – or rather him. I thought he was just trying to intimidate me, scare me to get his own back. Then, one night, a few weeks after Grandma died, he was waiting for me. He cornered me in the alley next to the flat where we lived.' She raised huge haunted eyes to his and he felt his blood turn to ice. 'He attacked me. He tried – tried to . . .' She broke off as her mouth dried again.

'Say it, Fleur,' he urged. 'Get it out in the open once and for all, that's the only way you'll ever be free of it.'

She swallowed hard and took a deep breath. 'He tried to rape me. He didn't, though. I fought him off. I had a heavy torch with me and I managed to hit him with it, then I kicked him – where it hurt most. Somehow – I'll never know how – I managed to get indoors before he recovered.'

The expression on her face told him she was reliving the terror of that night and he drew her into his arms and held her close. 'My poor Fleur,' he whispered, stroking the thick soft curls. 'But he didn't succeed. That's the important thing. You won. Just hang on to that.'

'But he *did* win,' she insisted. 'He drove me out of my own home. I was afraid to stay there alone after that. Don't you understand, Tom? Afraid is something I've never been, and I can't forgive myself for it!'

'You didn't report it to the police?'

She shook her head. 'It would have been his word against mine. I've heard of girls who report attacks like that. Everyone blames them – says they asked for it. And I felt bad enough as it was. Dirty and disgraced. I didn't *want* anyone to know. You're the first person I've ever told. All I wanted at the time was to get as far away as possible.'

'So you came to find your mother?'

'*No.*' She shook her head adamantly. 'I came to Elvemere because it was the only place I could think of.'

'Fleur.' He took her face between his hands and looked into her eyes. 'Listen, if you want to find her, I can help. It wouldn't be difficult. I have access to the archives at the paper. There'd be a report of her marriage or clues of some sort – bound to be in a town this size. If you could just give me as many details as you can have . . .'

'*No!*' Fleur shook her head. 'There isn't any point, Tom. The time when I needed a mother is long past. I've got a job I love and my own home. I'm my own person and I'm happy. I don't need *anyone* now.'

He shook his head slowly. 'We all need someone, Fleur. You're no exception.'

For a long moment she looked at him, then she let out a long shuddering breath as the last of the tension left her. 'Thanks, Tom.'

'Don't thank me. The offer is there. All you have to do is ask. As for the rest, I'm proud to be the only person you've told,' he said. 'And you can rest assured that nothing you've said will go further than this room. All I want now is to make it up to you – if you'll let me? In whatever way I can.' Very slowly and tenderly he drew her towards him and kissed her. This time her lips were soft and responsive, melting into his. He pulled her to her feet and for the first time her arms went round him and he felt her body relax in his arms. For a long time she stood in the circle of his arms, just holding and being held.

'Only a few days till Christmas,' he said looking at her. 'What are you going to do about it?'

'I haven't given it a thought,' she confessed. 'I suppose I've deliberately pushed it to the back of my mind. It hasn't been hard, Sally and I have been so busy. Last year I still had Grandma.' She smiled reminiscently. 'She loved Christmas. Even though I wasn't a kid any more she still hid my present and made me hang up a stocking. We still had a tree and decorated the flat. She belonged to a Christmas Club – saved up for it for months so we could have all the things she loved.'

'You must miss her.'

'I do.' She looked at him. 'You must be planning to go and spend it with your mother.'

'No. Mum's met someone and wrote to say he's taking her away for Christmas.' He smiled. 'I'm glad for her. She spent years nursing my grandparents and it's time she had a life of her own again.'

'Do you like him, this man?'

He shrugged. 'Haven't met him yet, but if he makes her happy, who am I to say whether I like him or not? The fact is, Fleur, it looks as if you and I are both at a loose end for Christmas, so how about sharing it?'

She smiled, feeling suddenly light as a bubble. 'Oh, Tom, that would be lovely! Spending Christmas here will make the flat feel like a real home!'

Chapter 6

The New Year began for Arden Catering on the afternoon of December 31st with preparations for the party at the home of Mr and Mrs Vernon Grant. Sally had taken the booking when Fleur was out and she had only noticed it in the book the day before they closed for the Christmas holiday. She'd been surprised to see that in spite of his obviously tipsy mood Vernon Grant had obviously meant it when he said he would be booking Arden Catering for a party at his home. Sally was surprised too.

'Mrs Grant junior has always done the catering for her own parties,' she remarked as they packed the van. 'But I suppose her time must be fully taken up now she's been elected to the Town Council.'

Fleur rarely had time to read the local paper and, as she had not been in Elvemere long enough to qualify for a vote, the local by-election had not particularly interested her. She looked up as she carefully stowed the microwave in its padded box into the van. 'The Town Council? That sounds important.'

Sally gave a rueful grin. 'That's what a lot of them like to think,' she said. 'If you ask me these local councils have had their day. If things were run at County level there wouldn't be so much wheeling and dealing going on.'

'Wheeling and dealing?' Fleur shook her head. The complexity of small-town politics was unfamiliar territory to her and at that particular moment she was more concerned with making sure her change of clothes and the little vanity case she always used was in the van before she climbed into the passenger seat. But instead of getting into the driving seat beside her, Sally stood at the window and said, 'Not there, Fleur. I'd like you to drive this evening.'

She felt her cheeks burning and her heart quickened with a

mixture of excitement and apprehension. 'Oh! Do you really think I should?'

'I don't see why not. You've been having lessons for several weeks now and I seem to remember you telling me you'd applied for your test.'

'That's right,' Fleur told her. 'I'm taking it next month.'

'Then what are you waiting for? The sooner you get behind the wheel and get as much practice as you can, the better. From now on you can consider yourself Arden Catering's official driver.'

'What about the L plates though?'

Sally laughed. 'No problem. I found a pair at the back of a shelf in the garage the other day. They're the ones Peter used when he was learning. I always knew they'd come in useful. Just wait a second while I attach them.'

Fleur enjoyed the drive across town to the suburb where the Grants lived. It was a pleasant district, and although it was winter and the trees were bare she could well imagine how leafy and delightful it would be in summer. As she drove into the drive of the large square house and parked carefully and unobtrusively close to the side entrance, Sally turned to her with a smile.

'Well done! You should pass the test first time if that's a sample. And while we're on the subject of tests, unless you particularly want to continue, I don't think you need any more computer classes. You're managing very nicely on what you've already learned. I was very impressed the other day when I went to check and saw that you'd updated all our customer files.'

For the past few weeks, while she wasn't working in the kitchen, Sally had encouraged Fleur to use the computer in the office and she had devised a new method of keeping track of their stocks, making it easier to see at a glance what provisions they needed to reorder. She'd also invented a system for circularising clients in order to up-date them on their services. She'd viewed it as more of an experiment than anything else and now blushed with pleasure at Sally's appreciation.

'Thanks. They were just some ideas I had.'

'No, thank *you*. They work extremely well. You've worked very hard since you've been with me, Fleur, and come up with some very sound ideas. I sometimes wonder how I ever managed without you.'

They began to unload the van and carry the equipment inside. Fleur looked round the Grants' kitchen admiringly. It was large and spacious, fitted with light oak cupboards and smooth green-tiled worktops with concealed lighting. It was equipped with every kind of gadget and modern convenience imaginable. 'I wish all the kitchens we had to work in were like this,' she remarked.

'No shortage of money here,' Sally told her. 'Grant Philips made their pile out of the building boom, though apparently Charlie Grant was a poor boy who made good. There are those who say he did it on his wife's money, but he must have had the know-how and the business acumen to make it work.'

As they made the final preparations Sally asked what kind of Christmas Fleur had had.

'Fairly quiet. It was nice spending some time in my new flat,' she said. 'Tom shared Christmas Day with me as he wasn't going home. We had turkey and a tree – all the usual things. He brought his portable telly with him and we watched some of the shows, and in the afternoon we went for a walk down by the river.'

'Tom – that's the boyfriend, is it?'

'He's a neighbour. He has a room in the same house and he's a journalist on the local paper. He's just a friend.'

As they worked on in silence Fleur wondered why she had been so quick to deny any kind of affection between herself and Tom. Christmas Day had been a delight. They had bought each other small presents and spent the day together, quietly enjoying each other's company. He'd been sensitive and considerate, careful not to push their new understanding too far. There had been kisses, and they'd held hands, but he had made no attempt to take their relationship further. As Tom was on duty for the paper on Boxing Day, covering various sporting events, he'd had only one day off and now he had gone up to Yorkshire at his mother's invitation, to spend the New Year with her and no doubt to be introduced to the new man in her life. Somewhat to her dismay Fleur was finding that she missed him a lot more than she had expected to.

'He has no family then?'

'Who?' Fleur realised that Sally was still talking about Tom. 'Oh, Tom. There's just his mother, she lives up North.'

'But he spent Christmas with you?'

'Only because he had to work on Boxing Day and his mother was going away. He's taking some holiday and spending a couple of weeks with her now.'

Sally smiled a little at Fleur's defensiveness. 'You do like him though?'

'Yes, of course I like him.'

'I'm glad.' Sally smiled. 'You should have more social life, Fleur. I worry about that sometimes. With us working the hours we do.'

'Tom works strange hours too. Did Peter come home to spend the holiday with you?' She asked, anxious to change the subject.

Sally shook her head. 'Working in the hotel business, it was his busiest time. He's coming home for a few days at the end of January when the seasonal rush is over. It's a dead time for catering too and so far there are no functions booked, but there'll be plenty for you to do in the office and the kitchen.' She laughed. 'You needn't worry, I shan't be laying you off.'

The buffet table was to be laid out in the dining room which was decorated with evergreens and a large Christmas tree decked out in red and gold. Sally put the finishing touches to her flower arrangement while Fleur changed out of her jeans into her dress and did her hair. She had just joined Sally in the dining room when the door opened and a woman came in. She wore a plain but exquisitely cut black evening dress and her delicate bone structure was enhanced by the expert cut of her blonde hair. Her only jewellery was a single diamond on a fine gold chain and earrings to match. Sally looked up with a smile.

'Good evening, Mrs Grant. I hope everything is to your satisfaction?'

Julia looked around the room briefly and nodded. 'It all looks very nice indeed.' She looked at her watch. 'The guests will be arriving soon. You will be ready to serve them drinks?'

'Of course. Hot punch as you requested as well as the usual choice of sherry and fruit juice.'

'That's fine. I thought we'd eat at about half-past ten. We'll open the connecting doors between here and the drawing room just before.' Julia cast an eye over the table then turned away as the door bell was heard. 'It all looks delicious. I'm sure it's all going to be a great success. Thank you.'

Fleur looked at Sally. 'So that's Mrs Grant.'

'*Councillor* Mrs Grant now,' Sally reminded her.

The large drawing room was beginning to fill and Fleur was circulating with her tray of drinks when Charlotte suddenly appeared. She wore more make-up than usual and her hair was a glorious explosion of tiny spirals. Over her glittery party dress with its minuscule puffball skirt she carried a coat. 'Anyone seen Mum?' she asked no one in particular. 'Oh, *Fleur*. What are you doing here?'

'I work for Mrs Arden, remember?'

'Yes, of course you do. I suppose I might have known.' She pulled a face. 'Doesn't she give you New Year's Eve off?'

Fleur smiled. 'I'd rather be working.'

'You've got to be kidding! I'd rather be anywhere than here,' Charlotte said, lowering her voice. 'Did you ever see such a collection of wrinklies? I'm off to the Dramatic Society bash. A lot of my friends are members and they always put on a good party for New Year.'

'Well, I hope you have a good time.'

Charlotte laughed. 'I intend to! Gotta go. See you at college next term.'

'Well, no. I won't be coming back.'

'Oh – you're kidding?' Charlotte frowned. 'Lucky you! Still, I'm not surprised. I wish I'd picked up computing as quickly as you. I was always a complete prat at it at school and I'm not much better now. I reckon I'll still be there when I'm as old as this lot! Oh well, see you around, I expect. Happy New Year, Fleur!' She waved a carefree hand and disappeared into the throng of party guests.

Charlie and Louise Grant were the first guests to arrive and as soon as Charlie had made sure his wife was busy talking to Vernon, he buttonholed his daughter-in-law.

'So – I hear you've wangled yourself on to the planning committee then?'

'There was no wangle about it. I was asked to be on it.'

'Never mind. Just as long as you use the opportunity to help your family, eh?' Charlie took a sip of his drink and eyed her thoughtfully. 'No doubt you'll have heard about this redevelopment planned for Victoria Gardens. So what's to do about it then? When are things likely to start moving?'

Julia sighed. 'Father, you know I can't discuss things like that with members of the public.'

'*Members of the public*!' His florid complexion deepened to purple. 'I'm your bloody father-in-law, for Christ's sake, girl! Not some faceless punter.'

'I know that, but you're still a member of the public as far as the council is concerned.' As more guests began to arrive she seized the excuse to escape with some relief. 'If you don't mind, I'll have to leave you for a moment. Perhaps there'll be a chance to talk later?'

He watched her go resentfully. He'd never really liked his daughter-in-law. Stuck up little bitch! If it hadn't been for the chance of that merger he might have tried to warn Vernon off. Who did she think she was? Just because her grandfather was a doctor and she'd been to some snotty private school. He had a pretty good idea the marriage wasn't a roaring success either, especially now

111

that she'd got herself elected to the council. And the way Vernon looked at that new secretary or Personal Assistant or whatever he called her proved his point. What did she *personally assist* him with? wondered Charlie. If he wasn't getting his leg over there Charlie was a Dutchman! He'd be a damned fool not to after all! Charlie looked around the room. The fact that the lovely Jo Hanson was noticeably absent from this little soiree went some way to proving his point.

His eyes lighted on his wife on the other side of the room. Louise was talking to May Philips. He always enjoyed pulling old May's leg – taking her down a peg. Almost as stuck up as her daughter. It was a damned good thing old Harry was down to earth. He was ridiculously easy-going too. Never put up much of a fight about anything, silly old sod.

'Now then, May,' said Charlie, swaggering over to join the two women. He was rewarded with a warm blush from his partner's wife who could read all the signs that Charlie was out to embarrass her.

'Good evening, Charles.'

May's insistence on calling him that never failed to set his teeth on edge. Who did she think he was – the heir to the throne? He noticed that she was wearing a dress of coffee-coloured lace. It had a flesh-coloured underslip which intrigued him. He stared pointedly at her bust. 'You're looking 'specially sexy tonight, m'dear,' he said, watching with satisfaction as the colour spread to the roots of her hair. He took a step closer and lowered his voice to an undertone. 'Between friends, is that your skin I can see through all those holes?'

May's face turned crimson. 'Indeed it is *not!*'

He chuckled. 'Pity. Thought for a minute you'd come out without your bust bodice. I like to see a woman with a good bosom on her. Lou will bear me out in that, won't you, Lou?'

His wife gave him a push. 'Behave yourself, Charlie.' She nodded towards his glass. 'How many of those have you had?'

'Not enough yet, lass. When I've had enough I start chasing women and saying outrageous things!' He chuckled, holding up his glass to May. 'Here's to ladies with lovely curves. Long may they quiver.'

Kathleen Grant had arrived at the party when it seemed to be in full swing, and now wished she hadn't come at all. Family parties were one thing, this was something else. There was hardly anyone she knew here. It seemed that even Charlotte had escaped.

She stood on the fringe of the group looking acutely uncomfortable. The chignon she had forced her long hair into was coming

112

down and the long black velvet dress that did little to enhance her tall thin figure had seen better days. If only she had worn something less formal. The other women were wearing more festive dresses in pretty colours. She felt positively funereal. The fact was that she never really felt at ease in anything other than jodhpurs and sweaters. Looking round at the assembled guests, all chattering and clearly enjoying themselves, she wished again that she'd stayed at home. This really wasn't her scene at all.

'Can I offer you a drink?'

Kath looked up to see a young woman standing before her. She was striking-looking with a beautiful golden complexion, dark eyes and curling black hair. Her short black dress revealed long shapely legs in sheer black stockings which reminded Kath painfully of the reason she preferred jodhpurs and had worn a long dress this evening. Years of riding and the outdoor life had given her the muscular legs of a carthorse. Suddenly she became aware that the girl was still holding out her tray and smiling.

'Drink?'

'Oh! Yes – thank you.'

'There's hot punch,' Fleur said, indicating the sugar-frosted glasses. 'Or there's sherry – medium and dry, or orange juice.'

'The punch looks nice.' Kath took a glass and sipped at it. 'You're new, aren't you?' she said, wanting to hang on to the girl for as long as she could. 'I mean – I haven't seen you around before.'

'I've been here a few months,' Fleur said. 'I moved here from London last autumn.'

'I see. Like this job?'

'Very much, thank you.'

'I'm Kathleen Grant, by the way. Vernon is my brother.'

'Oh, you must be the lady who owns the stables. Charlotte has told me a lot about you.'

Kath smiled and began to relax. 'You know Charlotte?'

'Yes. We met at evening classes. We've both been doing computer studies.'

'I'm very fond of Charlotte,' Kath said. 'I once cherished fond hopes that she might come and work for me when she left school, but her father had other ideas.'

'Yes. She told me that.' Fleur looked around uneasily. She had no wish to be overheard discussing the party's host and could see several people whose glasses were empty. 'I'm sorry but I'll have to go now,' she said with an apologetic smile. 'It was nice meeting you.'

'Yes. Maybe we'll . . .' Kath trailed off, seeing Vernon frowning at her reproachfully. He came across the room towards her.

'Hello, Kath. Can't you find anyone to talk to?'

'I don't know anyone here.'

'You know Julia, me – Ma and Father and the Philipses. You don't have to hob-nob with the hired help.'

'She's a very nice girl.'

'That's hardly the point. I daresay she'd like to get on with what she's being paid to do. Come and talk to Ma. She says you haven't been round to see her for weeks.'

'I wouldn't have thought you'd be too worried about that!'

'No? Well, since you've brought up the subject of family problems, I'd be grateful if you'd discourage Charlotte from spending all her spare time round at the stables. She has a lot to learn and I want her to get on with it.'

'I don't ask her to come, Vernon. I can't help it if she loves working with horses.'

'It wouldn't have anything to do with the fact that she's cheap labour, would it? Oh, don't think you can pull the wool over my eyes, Kath. I know how devious you can be and I won't have my daughter exploited.'

She flushed angrily. 'And just what is it *you're* doing? She seems to be nothing more than an errand girl at your office.'

Vernon's nostrils flared and the colour left his face. 'Mind your own bloody business and leave my daughter alone,' he hissed at her between clenched teeth. 'You just can't stop meddling in other people's lives, can you? First it was Julia and her crazy local government fad. Now it's Charlotte. Just because you couldn't hang on to that husband of yours for long enough to persuade him to get you pregnant!'

As he turned on his heel and walked away Kath felt herself shaking with fury and frustration. It was so like Vernon to make a vile remark like that in a situation when she couldn't retaliate without making a scene. She took a long drink of her punch and tried to swallow her fury with it. *Damn Vernon to hell!* He'd always been a perfect little shit, ever since he was a small child. The moment her parents had produced a son they'd had little time for her, a fact which he quickly latched on to. As a boy he'd lied about her, told tales and got her into trouble at every possible opportunity. She could see his angelic little face now, smirking with satisfaction as he watched her being smacked and sent to bed without supper for something *he'd* done. And as they'd grown older the situation had worsened. Vernon had seemed to have all the

114

advantages. Whilst she'd grown into a gangling, ungainly teenager, he had developed into a debonair and outwardly charming young man. His success with the opposite sex had been phenomenal. He had delighted their parents by marrying the right girl and opening up the opportunity for a family merger for the business, whereas all Kath had achieved was a childless failed marriage and a riding school that barely paid its way.

She decided she must leave. No one would notice her absence anyway. She put down her glass and began to move towards the door, but Julia caught her in the hall as she was putting on her coat.

'*Kath*! I'm sorry I haven't had time to have a word with you before. It's lovely to see you. It's been ages.'

'Don't worry, Vernon has already had a *word* with me, as you put it,' Kath said, her lips still quivering. 'It was nice of you to invite me, Julia and I know *you* mean it when you say you're pleased to see me. I wanted to come if only to congratulate you on getting elected. But I think it would be better if I left now – before there's an atmosphere.'

Julia's heart sank. Vernon and his sister had never hit it off and of course Kath was right when she said that their animosity would create an atmosphere. It seemed impossible for them to be in the same room without sparks flying. But she liked her sister-in-law and hated the thought of her going home alone and upset on New Year's Eve.

'Take no notice of him,' she said hopefully. 'Do stay. I'm sure your mother wouldn't want you to leave. Come and say hello to her and your father at least.'

Kathleen shook her head. 'I'd rather just slip away quietly, if you don't mind.' She bent to kiss Julia's cheek. 'Thank you for inviting me. Goodnight.'

'Well – if you really must. I'll ring you. We'll have coffee or lunch some time soon.' Julia watched her sister-in-law go with genuine regret. Kath had had a difficult, disappointing life. It wasn't her fault that she was sometimes touchy. Surely Vernon could have made an effort for once?

On the far side of the room Charlie nudged his wife. 'Bloody hell, I've just seen our Kathleen. What the flippin' heck has she got on? She looks like a flaming stick of liquorice!'

Louise shook her head. 'Don't be so cruel, Charlie. It's not her fault she's no fashion sense. Where is she? I must go and have a word with her.' But Charlie grabbed her arm.

'I think she's leaving. Let her go. If she stays and knocks back a few she'll start airing those barmy left-wing ideas of hers. Better let well alone. We don't want her embarrassing us, do we? She's better off stopping at home with those damned nags of hers. Come to think of it, she gets more like them every time I see her!'

As he spoke his eye was drawn to a middle-aged woman who had just arrived. He detached himself from his wife and made his way across the room towards her.

'Well! As I live and breathe. If it isn't little Lena Maitland!'

Eleanor turned to look at him. 'Hello, Charlie. Not so little nowadays! And no one has called me Lena for years.'

'I daresay.' He put his empty glass on the tray of a passing waitress and took a full one. 'A lot of water has gone down the plughole since you and I were snogging behind the bike sheds, Lena. How have you been then, eh, lass?'

'I've been fine. Busy of course. No need to ask how you've been.'

'Not so bad – not so bad at all, thanks. I hear you've been giving our Julia a bit of a bunk up. Good of you, that.'

'I set her off in the right direction, that was all. She's a very bright and capable woman. She doesn't need any help from me.'

'Oh, I'm sure she'll make a damned fine councillor given time. I daresay they're lucky to get her.'

'Too true.' Eleanor smiled ruefully. She'd heard a little about Charlie's resistance to his daughter-in-law's ambitions in local politics from Julia herself. What was the old hypocrite up to?

Charlie took a swig of his drink and shuddered slightly. *Ugh! Sherry!* A woman's tipple if ever there was one. Tasted like bloody cough syrup. Where did they keep the hard stuff? he wondered. He regarded Eleanor speculatively over the rim of his glass. She would be about two years younger than him, but she'd worn well. She was still a handsome woman. He could still fancy a bit of slap and tickle with her, especially if it proved worthwhile. It didn't look as if he was going to get much inside information out of Julia. Have to box clever though. Lena was nobody's fool.

'Tell you what, Lena,' He lowered his voice conspiratorially. 'You and I will have to have a bite of supper one of these evenings, just the two of us. Catch up on all the old gossip.'

'My door is always open. I'm your councillor, in case you've forgotten,' she reminded him. 'I represent your ward.'

'Yes, yes, I know all that. I was thinking more on friendly lines,' Charlie said with a sly wink. 'I'll give you a ring in a day or two, eh? I'm sure you can – what's the expression these days? – find a window in your busy schedule for a friend as old as me.' He chuckled to himself as he tossed back the last of the despised sherry. That

was the tactic. Don't *ask* them, tell them what you're going to do –
and then do it.

Fleur was on her way through the hall to the kitchen to refill her
tray when Vernon caught her.

'Well, *hello* there – Fleur, isn't it?'

'Good evening, sir.'

'Oh, surely there's no need to be so formal? We're almost old
friends, aren't we?' She made herself smile. 'That's better!' He took
a step towards her. 'Anyone ever tell you you've got a lovely smile,
Fleur?'

She edged towards the kitchen door. 'I'd better go and . . .'

'Don't run away. Look, I just wanted to apologise for my sister.
She was the tall woman in black velvet who was monopolising you.
She's a bit of an odd-ball. All she cares about is horses. People
don't really rate for much with her. I hope she didn't keep you
from your work?'

'Not at all.' His nerve almost took her breath away. After the
remorseless way he had chatted her up at the boardroom lunch! 'I
didn't realise she took me for a horse.'

'*What?*' He stared at her, then saw the joke. 'Oh – I see what
you mean!'

'And I thought she was very nice actually.'

'Really? Oh, well, that's all right then.'

'Vernon! There you are.' Julia stood in the doorway. 'I've been
looking for you. I want to announce that we're about to eat. Are
you coming?'

He moved away looking sheepish. 'Right. Just coming. I was just
– just . . .' He looked at Fleur. 'So if you could make sure the wine
is really well chilled?' he said with a change of tone.

'Of course, sir.'

He walked past Julia into the dining room. She looked at Fleur.
'Is everything all right?'

'Yes, thank you. I'll tell Mrs Arden you're ready for us to serve
the buffet now, shall I?'

'I'd be glad if you would. And as my husband says, the wine
should be well chilled, especially the champagne.'

'It's been on ice ever since we arrived.'

'I thought it would be, knowing how efficient Mrs Arden is.' Julia
took a step towards her, her eyes puzzled. 'Excuse me, but haven't
I seen you somewhere before?'

'Not that I remember.'

'You haven't been with Mrs Arden for long then?'

'Just since September.'

'Oh, I must be mistaken then. I could have sworn... Wait a minute, you didn't come to my daughter's last birthday party, did you?'

'No. I'm new to Elvemere.'

Julia looked puzzled. 'Odd. I'm sure we've met somewhere. Never mind.' She shook her head. 'We'll open the double doors between the two rooms now and then you can serve.'

'Certainly.'

'You really mustn't mind Charlie's teasing.' Louise was looking at May Philips with some concern. Charlie had really gone over the top tonight. He'd made a target of poor May ever since she'd arrived, and he'd flirted with that Councillor Maitland woman and generally made a nuisance of himself with his outspoken remarks. She intended to give him a piece of her mind when they got home.

May sniffed. 'A joke is a joke, Louise,' she said in wounded tones. 'But the remark he made about my dress was really quite offensive.'

'I know it might've seemed that way, love, but he doesn't mean anything, you know. It's just his idea of fun.' Louise laid a placatory hand on the other woman's arm. 'He was brought up in a very outspoken home. I was too if it comes to that. Us Northerners don't mince words, you know.'

'But you do know where to draw the line, Louise. Charles doesn't seem to give a fig for people's feelings.'

'Ah – now that's something I've been meaning to mention to you,' she said.

'Feelings?' May looked nonplussed.

'No. The way you always call him *Charles*. I think I ought to tell you that he hates it. It might be the reason why he goads you like he does.'

'I was brought up to call people by their proper names,' May said stiffly. 'It's only polite and courteous.'

'Mebbe so, but it isn't very *friendly*, is it? See, Charlie thinks you're being – well, stuffy, and it gets up his nose.'

'I can't help the way I was brought up any more than he can,' May said pointedly.

'But everyone calls him Charlie. They always have. Even his mum called him that.'

'Yes. Well, I'll try to remember,' May said. 'Now I think I'd better go and find Harry. I can see Julia is about to tell us that supper is being served.'

Louise watched her go with a sigh. May had been like this for as long as she had known her and that was a good few years. She'd never be any different now. Her old dad would have described her as toffee-nosed. She could hear him now explaining to her the difference between gentry and snobs. *'There are them as was born wi' a silver spoon in their gobs and them as looks as if they was born wi' a stink under their nebs. It pays to know t'difference.'* She smiled to herself as she moved with the rest of the guests towards the dining room. May was definitely one of them wi' a stink under her neb!

At midnight everyone gathered for the chimes of Big Ben, toasted each other and sang 'Auld Lang Syne'. As soon as everyone had begun to drink again Vernon sneaked away upstairs to the bedroom he shared with Julia. Closing the door carefully, he lifted the telephone and dialled. After a moment or two he was rewarded with the sound of Jo's sleepy voice.

'Hello – who is it?'

'It's me darling, just calling to wish you Happy New Year.'

'I was asleep,' she told him petulantly. 'Did you have to?'

'Don't be cross. I miss you,' he whispered.

'I bet you do. You sound drunk. I expect you've been having a whale of a time – never given me a thought.'

'That's not true. Would I be ringing you now if it were?' He cradled the receiver close to his ear. 'I wish I was there with you now.'

'Then what are you waiting for?'

'Be reasonable, darling. You know I can't come now. I really wish I could, though. When we're apart, just thinking of what you do to me nearly drives me mad. It's sheer torture.'

'I'll let you demonstrate that next time you're here,' she said with a husky laugh.

'Tomorrow?' he asked, encouraged. 'Can I see you tomorrow?'

'I suppose you can try.'

'I can't promise a time or anything, but I'll come round when I can.'

'In that case, darling, you'll have to take the risk that I might well be out, won't you?'

'Yes, but I . . .' Vernon found himself holding a dead line. Joanna had hung up.

It was one-thirty when the last of the party guests departed. Sally and Fleur had already cleared away the leftovers, washed up and packed most of their equipment. There was just the table to dis-

119

mantle and pack away. As they stood in the kitchen waiting Sally explained to Fleur who the guests were.

'The big man with the white hair was Mr Grant Senior and the lady in the pink dress with the sequin embroidery and all the jewellery was his wife.'

Fleur smiled. She'd already gathered that. Mr Charlie Grant was as bad as his son, though less subtle. Twice he had pinched her bottom as she circulated with her drinks tray, but she had decided to say nothing about that, assessing for herself that he'd obviously had more than enough to drink.

'Then the dignified little woman in the coffee lace is Mrs Philips. Her husband is the nice dapper little man with the thinning grey hair and gold-rimmed glasses. They are Mrs Grant Junior's parents.'

Fleur looked up with interest. 'Oh, her name was Philips before she was married then?'

'That's right. May Philips was Doctor Geoffrey Bishop's only daughter. He was Elvemere's best loved GP some years ago. She was his receptionist and they were very close. It caused a bit of a sensation when she married Harry Philips.'

'Why was that?'

'He was just a poor electrician in those days,' Sally explained. 'I was still at school at the time but I still remember the talk. But Harry turned out to be a local lad who made good and Doctor Bishop came round to it in the end. The Philipses still live in the family home, Gresham House, a big Victorian place on St Paul's Green. It always used to be known as Doctor's House when I was a child.'

For the past hour Fleur had been stifling yawns and longing for her bed, but now she was suddenly wide awake. *Gresham House.* Surely that was the name of the house on the scrap of paper with her mother's address scribbled on it? *Philips – Julia Philips!* Was it possible that the woman she had spoken to earlier this evening was the same one who had abandoned her illegitimate baby daughter in the East End of London twenty years ago?

Fleur pictured the cool attractive woman in her elegant home, surrounded by family and guests. The very thought seemed ludicrous. Yet the more she thought about it, the more she realised that too many details fitted for it to be a mistake. It was more than likely that she had actually seen and spoken to her mother this very evening and been unaware of it. She had never meant to seek her mother out when she came to Elvemere, yet it seemed that fate had somehow stepped in and found her anyway. The question was – now that she knew, what did she do about it?

Chapter 7

It began to snow again as Julia turned into Scrimshaw Street. The covering of white that gave most things a sparkling, pure look merely made the mean little pebble-dashed houses appear grimmer and even more uninviting than before. As Julia stood shivering on the doorstep she fervently hoped that Tracey had found the money to pay her electricity bill. It must be freezing inside. She turned up the collar of her sheepskin coat against the falling flakes and put the suitcase she was carrying down on the step.

The curtain twitched and Tracey's face appeared momentarily at the front room window before she opened the door. She looked pale and hollow-eyed as she greeted Julia. 'Come in out of the cold, Mrs Grant. Sorry to keep you waiting, only Damie isn't very well.'

Julia could hear the baby's fretful wailing as she stepped into the hall. 'Poor little boy. Has he got a cold?' she asked. 'I've brought a few things for you,' she said. 'I don't want you to think I'm unloading all my unwanted rubbish on to you, but Charlotte, my daughter, is about your size and she's so wasteful with her clothes. Most of these are almost new.'

Tracey smiled and some of the colour seemed to come back to her cheeks. 'It's very good of you, Mrs Grant. I'm ever so grateful. Come through.'

In the living room Julia was glad to see that a bright fire was burning. 'You applied for the extra benefit I told you about then?' she said. Tracey nodded.

'They never let on about these things till you ask, do they? It isn't much but it does help.' She watched with eager eyes as Julia opened the suitcase, exclaiming with delight at the soft woollens and other barely worn garments cast off by Charlotte. Picking up a red cashmere sweater, she held it to her cheek.

'Oh, Mrs Grant, this is lovely! Are you sure your daughter doesn't want it?'

Julia smiled. 'That colour is just right for you, and yes, I'm quite sure. Charlotte asked me to drop them off at the Oxfam shop this morning but I thought you might like to have first pick. Whatever you don't fancy can still go there.'

'Will you stay and have a coffee?'

Julia shook her head. 'I'm meeting a friend in town in ten minutes. I just thought I'd pop in on you first.' She looked at the girl's pale face. 'You're looking very tired, Tracey.'

'I know. I've had some sleepless nights with Damian. It started as a bit of a sniffle but now it's gone on his chest.'

Julia looked into the pram at the baby who had settled into a restless sleep. He looked flushed and she could hear him wheezing softly as he breathed. 'Have you taken him to the doctor?'

'No. I know I should but I haven't liked to take him out in this weather. It's about a mile to walk and the air's been so cold and frosty. I just kept hoping he'd pick up.'

'When I've seen my friend, I'll come back and take you,' Julia said.

Tracey shook her head. 'Oh, no, I couldn't . . .'

'Yes, you could. No arguing. It's for Damian and it won't take long. The doctor will probably put him on some antibiotics – have him well again in no time.' She looked at the girl with concern. 'Maybe we should ask him to check you over too? You look as though you could do with a tonic. Are you sure you're all right?'

'Yeah – yeah, I'm fine.'

'Getting enough to eat? Warm enough?'

Tears welled up in Tracey's eyes and she sat down suddenly on the only armchair. 'Oh, Mrs Grant – I wasn't going to say anything but it's Rick.'

Julia frowned. 'Rick?'

'Damie's dad.'

'He's back? You've seen him again?'

'Oh, yes, I've seen him.' Tracey said bitterly. 'Turns out he's been inside all this time. Breaking and entering – says it weren't his fault. He got mixed up with the wrong people, apparently. Anyway, he's out now and he's got no job and nowhere to go.'

Julia began to see. 'So he thought he could move in with you?'

'That's it. He says it ain't fair that I've got a house and money to live on when he's got nothing. He says I owe him.'

'That's ridiculous. You owe him nothing.'

'There's no way I want him back, Mrs Grant, but he keeps on

and on coming round. He makes sure the neighbours hear too – banging on the door, shouting and going on till I let him in. I'm so ashamed.'

'You must tell the police,' Julia said.

'He says if I do, he'll tell them I'm on the game – that I ill treat Damie – and then they'll take him away from me.' Tracey began to cry, her thin shoulders slumped and her hands over her face.

Julia watched her helplessly. Patting her shoulder in an attempt to reassure her, she said, 'Anyone can see that you don't ill treat your baby, Tracey. And you know that I'd vouch for your character any time.' Opening her bag, she pressed a clean handkerchief into Tracey's hand. 'Here, dry your tears.'

'Thanks.' She blew her nose. 'You've been so kind, Mrs Grant, but you don't know what Rick's like.'

'I can't see that there's any way he can do what he threatens. It's all bluff.'

Tracey turned haunted eyes to hers. 'I haven't told you the worst. He said that if I make it tough for him he'll make sure Damie's got the bruises to prove what he says is true.'

'He said *what*!' Julia was shocked.

'He says he's desperate enough to do that, and that if I force him to it it'll be my fault! He really scares me, Mrs Grant. He's not the same person he used to be. His eyes look wild and strange and he shouts and acts really violent. I reckon he must be on something.'

'Drugs, you mean?' Julia was seriously concerned now. 'Look, Tracey, I've got to go now but I'll be back later. I'll take you and Damian to the doctor's and then I think we should go and see Social Services and ask what they can advise.'

'*No!*' Tracey was twisting the handkerchief between her fingers. 'Look, I don't want to get him into trouble. That'll only make things worse. Maybe if I tell him about you – warn him off, – he'll keep away.'

'I think we both know that he won't, don't we, Tracey?'

They looked at each other for a long moment, then Tracey took a deep breath and made herself smile. 'Look, Mrs Grant, I feel a lot better now I've told you, but there's no need to go making a big thing of it. Rick never used to be bad. I daresay he never meant what he said. He'll probably calm down when he's had time to think. He might never come back again. Maybe he'll get a job – go away, anything. I shouldn't have said anything to you. Let's just forget it, shall we?'

Outside as she got into the car Julia's heart ached for the girl and her child. They had looked so vulnerable in the cold, bare little house. She couldn't stop herself thinking that but for the grace of God and a good family home she might easily have been in the same position.

Sitting at the wheel, her eyes staring unseeingly through the windscreen at the soft flakes of snow, she remembered the child she had left. She had been a strong healthy little baby. But suppose she had become ill like Damian? In her mind she heard a baby's pitiful crying and saw the little tearstained face and arms held out to her. Suppose her baby had died? She would never have known. There was no way she could ever find out. Taking a deep breath, she shook off the tortured thoughts and turned the ignition key. She would help Tracey all she could. It was almost as though she were being given a second chance. At least she could see that this girl was not driven to take the drastic action she had.

Julia found Eleanor waiting for her at a corner table in The Apple Tree, the small restaurant near the Cathedral where they often met. She hurried across to her.

'Sorry I'm a bit late, Eleanor. I went to visit Tracey Brownlow and found her in a bit of a state.'

Eleanor smiled. 'It's all right. You're a councillor now. Your time isn't completely your own any more.' She poured Julia a strong cup of coffee from the pot she'd already ordered.

'Her baby is poorly and I promised to go back later and take her to the doctor's.'

'Can't she take him herself?'

'She would have done but it's a long walk and he has what sounds very much like bronchitis to me, poor little scrap. She quite rightly didn't want to take him out in the cold air.'

'I know you feel she's a deserving case, Julia, but you mustn't let yourself get too involved, you know,' Eleanor warned. 'People will put on you if they think you're a soft touch.'

'Not Tracey. She's a very independent young woman.' Julia dropped sugar into her cup and stirred thoughtfully, wondering whether to ask for the older woman's advice. Seeing her worried expression, Eleanor said, 'What is it? Some kind of problem?'

'Yes, I'm rather concerned for her. It's the ex-boyfriend, the child's father. It appears he's been in prison and now he's out and pestering Tracey to take him in.'

Eleanor shook her head. 'If you take my advice you'll keep out of it, Julia. Next thing you know he'll be living with her and you'll be labelled an interfering busybody.'

'It's not quite that simple. It sounds as though he's on drugs,'

Julia said. 'He's threatening the baby; using him to get at her. And if she gives in and lets him move in, I think she and the baby will be seriously at risk.'

'Oh, dear, poor child.' Eleanor sighed and sipped her coffee thoughtfully. 'Of course what we badly need here in Elevmere is a women's refuge.'

'You mean, there isn't one?'

Eleanor shook her head. 'I've been trying to get one for a couple of years, but it's hopeless. Everyone just seems to want to shut their eyes to the fact that there are battered wives and kids in Elvemere. It doesn't go with their image of the tranquil life of a cathedral town.'

'Maybe it's time the issue was raised again. We could try, couldn't we?'

'Maybe. With your help they might start taking notice. But I wouldn't hold my breath if I were you!'

'We could lobby some of the other women councillors,' Julia suggested. 'You said Victoria Gardens was going to be redeveloped. Couldn't the council rent us one of those houses as a temporary measure? I noticed there were two or three empty when I was canvassing.'

'That's a good idea, but I doubt if you'll persuade the council to spend any money on it. It would need furnishing and decorating for a start, then there'd be heating and lighting. It costs more than you think – a lot more.'

'Surely Social Services and local charities would help, and I'm certain we could get volunteers to help – even some of the women themselves. There's something else I'd like to raise too: the problem of young mothers who can't go to work because the factories don't have creche facilities,' Julia said. 'It would save so much in State benefits if only employers would provide this simple service. If people were made aware of the problem . . .' She broke off as she saw Eleanor's rueful smile.

'I'm afraid you've got an awful lot to learn about people, Julia, lass,' she said. 'Specially those with money and power. It's one thing getting them to recognise a problem – quite another getting them to put their money, or their application, where their mouth is.'

'Yes, but surely . . .' Julia broke off as a woman who had just come into the restaurant attracted her attention. Something about the way she held her head and the chestnut hair triggered recollections. Then suddenly the memory clicked into place and she realised she was looking at someone she hadn't seen for more than twenty years. 'My God!' she exclaimed.

Eleanor looked up and followed her gaze. 'What? Who is it?'

'Joanna Bloom! I'm almost sure that the woman who just came in – the one who's just sat down at the corner table – is an old schoolfriend of mine.'

'Really?' Eleanor smiled. 'Well, what are you waiting for? Go over and say hello. I've got to go now anyway.' She gathered up her gloves and various bags of shopping. 'See you at the meeting on Wednesday.' She reached across the table to pat Julia's hand. 'Good luck with the Brownlow girl, and remember what I said – keep your distance.'

Julia watched Eleanor leave and poured herself another coffee, her eyes still on the woman in the far corner. What if she went over and it wasn't Joanna after all? But if it wasn't then this woman bore her an uncanny resemblance. She was older, of course, more mature, but then she would be. Her hair was different and her style of dress much more conservative, but still . . .

Sensing someone's scrutiny, the woman turned and looked directly into Julia's eyes. Their gaze held for a moment, then Julia smiled and the woman rose and came across.

Standing by the table she said, 'It *is*, isn't it? You're Julia Philips.'

'Hello, Joanna. I recognised you the moment you came in. You haven't really changed at all.'

'Nor you!' Joanna laughed. 'What a fantastic piece of luck, meeting you like this. I've been meaning to look you up ever since I got back to Elvemere, although I didn't really expect you to be here still.'

'How long have you been back?'

'Not long.'

'Please, sit down and join me.' Julia looked at her watch, remembering Tracey. 'I don't have long but I'm dying to know what you've been doing all these years.'

They ordered another pot of coffee and Joanna lit a cigarette. 'I've been in America for the past eighteen years,' she volunteered when the waitress had withdrawn. 'I'm afraid I've two failed marriages behind me, both to Americans. After my last divorce I suddenly got this yen to come home, so here I am.' She shrugged. 'That's all. Nothing exciting really. I see you're married,' she observed, looking at Julia's left hand.

'Yes, I married Vernon Grant, remember him? We have a sixteen-year-old daughter, Charlotte, so I've been busy looking after her since she was born, but I've just been elected to the Town Council.'

'Of course! I didn't connect the new Councillor Mrs Grant with the little Julia Philips I went to school with.' Joanna leaned across the table. 'I take it your mad passionate affair with the pop guitarist fizzled out?'

'Yes.' Julia coloured. 'No one knows about that so I'd be glad if . . .'

'I'd keep it under my hat?' Joanna laughed. 'My dear, what do you take me for? Heaven knows there are plenty of skeletons in my closet.' She chuckled huskily as she stubbed out her cigarette. 'God! We were a pair of wild little devils in those days, weren't we?'

Julia nodded half-heartedly and looked away. 'I suppose we were. It was the age we grew up in, I daresay.'

'The crazy permissive sixties.' Joanna sighed. 'What fun it all was. I'd do it all again, given the chance, wouldn't you?'

'Not really.' Julia picked up the bill and began to gather her things together. 'It's been lovely seeing you again, Joanna, but I have to go now. Council business.'

'Of course. Mustn't keep you from your good works, must I? We'll have to get together and have a girls' night out some time, eh? I'm sure there's a good club around someplace where we could have some laughs and relive some of the old days. I'll give you a buzz, shall I?'

'Yes – fine. Bye then, Joanna.'

'Bye.'

Joanna smiled as she watched Julia go. Now that she had met the competition she felt more confident than ever. Poor hidebound, suburban-minded little Julia. She'd always been so scared to try her wings – until that weekend at the Isle of Wight Festival when she'd fallen like a ton of bricks for that dishy exotic-looking guitarist. What was his name? Shane, Wayne? No Dean – that was it! Dean Sylvester. What had *really* happened after she ran off with him? Joanna wondered. Had she discovered the heady delights of flying – or flown too close to the sun and singed her feathers badly? One thing was as sure as hell: she didn't want to talk about it. Did Vernon know about her escapade? Obviously not. She poured herself another coffee and mulled over the interesting possibilities of his accidentally finding out. Then she decided that for the moment that was one trick she'd keep up her sleeve.

Tracey emerged from the doctor's sugery looking relieved.

'Its' only a slight chest infection,' she told Julia. 'I've got a pre-scription for some penicillin and Doctor Moss thinks he'll be as right as rain in a couple of days' time.'

In the car Julia glanced at the girl sitting beside her. 'Did you ask him to take a look at you?'

'No.' Tracey shook her head. 'I'll be fine now I know that Damie's okay.'

'I've been thinking, Tracey, you need a job and I need someone to help me out now that I'm out so much on Council business. How would you feel about doing some cleaning for me? You could bring Damian with you of course.'

Tracey looked at her. 'It's ever so good of you, Mrs Grant, but it's this benefit problem. I'd lose my Family Credit.'

'I'll pay you below the ceiling,' Julia said. 'It won't affect that. And if I want to give you something extra occasionally, to get things for the baby, then that's between you and me.'

Tracey's cheeks turned pink with pleasure. 'Well, I'd love that, if you're sure?'

Julia smiled. 'I am. So that's settled then. You can start as soon as Damian's better and fit to go out again.'

'Apart from anything else, it'd be great to get out of the house for a few hours each day.'

Julia glanced at her. She looked so young and so vulnerable sitting there clutching the baby. By 'getting out of the house' Julia took her to mean out of the way of Rick and his demands. This way she would be able to keep an eye on them both. She smiled as she drew up outside the house in Scrimshaw Street, convinced she'd done the right thing. 'Just give me a ring when you're ready to start, Tracey,' she said. 'And feel free to ring me if there's any kind of problem too, won't you?'

Fleur took her driving test on the last Wednesday in January. Luckily the worst of the snow had thawed and the day dawned crisp, dry and sunny. After an early breakfast her driving instructor took her out for a warm-up drive before dropping her off at the test centre.

'Don't look so worried!' he urged her 'You're going to pass with flying colours. Next time I see you, you'll be smiling all over your face.'

She swallowed hard. 'I hope you're right.'

'I *am* right.' He looked at his watch. 'Well, this is it. Good luck!'

Fleur got out of the car and walked up the steps, wishing that Tom could have been here. She had purposely kept the date of her test from him, afraid that he might postpone his holiday. If she passed she would be able to surprise him when he came home.

As she gave her name at the desk and felt her heartbeat quicken she took a firm hold on herself. *You're not on trial for your life*, she admonished herself. *It's only a driving test. Pull yourself together!*

'Miss Sylvester?'

A portly, stern looking man in a tweed cap and trench coat was peering enquiringly at her.

'That's right.'

'Will you come with me, please?'

Forty minutes later Fleur emerged from the driving school car feeling dazed and disbelieving. She'd convinced herself that she'd got all the Highway Code answers wrong and still couldn't quite believe she had actually passed. She tried to recall the formal and impersonal phrase the examiner had used, intoning the words as a matter of habit. '*I am pleased to tell you that you have achieved the standard necessary and passed your Ministry of Transport driving test.*' As though it was a mere matter of routine!

She was still standing on the pavement looking dazed when a voice behind her said, 'Hi! You must be Fleur.'

Turning, she saw a tall young man smiling at her and recognised him at once from his photograph. She'd known Sally was expecting her son home today but hadn't expected to meet him like this. 'Y-yes,' she said shakily.

He held out his hand. 'I'm Peter Arden.'

'I know. I – I mean – hello.'

He laughed at her bewildered expression and pointed to the slip of paper in her hand. 'I take it you've passed?'

'Yes.' She shook her head. 'I'm still trying to take it in. It's amazing.'

'Not from what I've heard.' He nodded towards a smart little sports car standing at the kerb. 'I've come to take you home.' He raised an eyebrow at her. 'Want to drive?'

She looked at the pristine little car and shook her head vigorously. 'No! I'd probably crash the way I feel at the moment. That would ruin everything, wouldn't it?'

He smiled. 'Okay, I'll let you off.'

As she fastened her seat belt, she said, 'I live in Victoria Gardens, do you know it?'

'Yes, but I'm not taking you there,' he told her. 'Mum has prepared a special celebration lunch for you.'

'But she didn't know I'd pass.'

'She was pretty confident you would. But she reckoned that if by some unlucky chance you didn't, you'd need consoling anyway.'

'Your mother is a wonderful woman,' Fleur told him. 'She's been so kind to me.'

He grinned. 'She is a pretty remarkable woman, but from what I hear she's found her ideal assistant.'

'I love the job. That makes it easy.'

'I've been taking a look at the work you've done on the computer,' he said. 'Mum never really got the hang of it, you know, but now that she's got you she's beginning to reap the benefit.'

Fleur blushed with pleasure at the compliments. This was turning out to be her day!

Sally was waiting for them. The table in her dining room was spread with her best cloth and laid with her finest crystal, silver and china, and the delicious aromas drifting through from the kitchen made Fleur's mouth water. Sally hugged her warmly when Peter announced that she'd passed her test.

'Congratulations! You've done so well. Barely five months since you joined me and look what you've achieved already.'

'With your help,' Fleur reminded her.

'Nonsense. I'm lucky to have you.' Sally poured three glasses of wine and raised hers. 'Here's to our future success! And I can tell you now that from this week on you'll be getting an extra little something in your pay packet.'

The lunch was delicious with all three of them in a celebratory mood. Afterwards Sally insisted that Fleur must take the rest of the day off, instructing Peter to drive her home. In the car he glanced at her.

'Well, I have to say that you look a lot more cheerful than when I picked you up this morning,' he remarked. 'You looked lost then. Now you're positively glowing.'

She smiled happily. 'It's been a day I shan't forget in a hurry. When I think of the way things were for me just six months ago, I can hardly believe my luck.'

When Peter stopped the car outside number thirteen Victoria Gardens she turned to him. 'Thanks for bringing me home.' When he hesitated she said, 'I suppose – I mean – would you like to come up for a cup of tea?'

He laughed. 'Why not? I'd love to.'

He seemed impressed by the flat and her plans for it.

'I can't wait for the spring,' she told him as they stood at the window. 'I'm going to make a feature of the balcony. Paint the wrought ironwork white and have hanging baskets and things. I can just see myself having breakfast out here on warm summer mornings.'

'Yes, I can see that it could be very pleasant.' He looked at her. 'Fleur – Mum's appointment book doesn't seem too full for the next few days so I know you're not busy. Will you have dinner with me one evening before I go back to London?'

Her eyes widened with surprise. '*Me*? Well, yes. Yes, I'd like that.'

'So would I.' He stood looking at her with open admiration till she felt her cheeks flush.

'I – I'll put the kettle on,' she said, turning away. 'We'll have that tea.'

Over the teacups he told her a little about his job as under manager at the large London hotel where he worked, and his ambition to take over as manager one day. His enthusiasm for his work matched her own. She found her mind wandering as he spoke. He was so good-looking. She wondered what kind of social life he had in London and how many smart, attractive girls he knew – and why he clearly thought she had no social life of her own beyond work. It also occurred to her to wonder what Sally's reaction would be to their going out to dinner.

Ever since the New Year party at the Grants' house she'd had mixed feelings about her own background. Discovering who her mother was, suddenly and by accident like that, had plunged her even deeper into the identity crisis she'd struggled with for most of her life. It was just as Dolly had said; Julia Grant née Philips had clearly been born into an upper-middle-class family. She was used to an easy, comfortable way of life, had never had to worry about trivialities like paying bills or where the next meal was coming from. So being thrust headlong into the Sylvesters' lifestyle must have been traumatic to say the least. Life in the meagre little flat in Hackney was so far removed from her own comfortable life that she had been prepared to abandon her child in order to get away from it. Surely a person as shallow as that could have little character? Why should anyone want to waste sentiments like love or respect on a woman so weak and ineffectual that she had set more store on physical comforts than the welfare of her own child? Julia Grant did not deserve to be her mother, Fleur told herself stoutly. She was *lucky* to have been brought up by Dolly and Maurice Sylvester. They were each of them worth a dozen Julia Grants! She would make something of herself; she would succeed without any help from her.

Yet in spite of what the positive side of her mind told her she found herself unable to shake thoughts of Julia out of her head. When she closed her eyes at night the cool, assured voice rang again in her ears and she saw the slim, graceful figure, the delicately

131

boned face and blonde hair, so very different from her own. It seemed so strange to think she had stood in the same room as her natural mother, near enough to smell her expensive perfume, close enough to have been able to reach out and touch her, whilst at the time neither of them had been aware of it.

The disturbing feelings and emotions she went through were a total enigma to Fleur; a bewildering tangle she found impossible to unravel. She longed to talk to someone about them, yet she could not bring herself to tell anyone about her discovery, not even Tom. It was all too close – too intensely personal. Was it hatred that was preventing her from forgetting Julia Grant? Did something deep inside her crave for revenge? Or was there some other, inexplicable reason why thoughts of Julia refused to leave her dreams and waking hours?

'A penny for them?' Peter was looking at her closely.

She shook her head, focusing her eyes on him. 'What?'

'You were miles away.'

'Oh, sorry. It's been quite a day.'

'You're tired. Time I was going anyway.' He stood up. 'I'll see you tomorrow, I expect?'

'Yes. I'll be at work as usual.'

'I'll look forward to seeing you.' He took her hand and held it for a moment. 'Goodbye, Fleur.'

The following morning Peter told her that he had booked a table for that evening at the Fairwoods Country Club in Merifield. It all sounded very grand and she began to have doubts. He had booked it without asking her if she was free and she wasn't at all sure that she wanted to be taken for granted. Besides, she didn't have a thing suitable to wear to a place like that. But in the end Peter's charm won.

'I know it's short notice,' he said with his special smile. 'I should really have asked you first. But I'll be gone the day after tomorrow and I'd really like us to spend an evening together.'

'That's all right. As it happens I've nothing else planned,' she heard herself saying.

In her lunch hour she took the bus into town and looked around the boutiques. Luckily she'd just received her pay cheque and she decided that if she went easy on food this week she could afford a new dress as well as the rent. The choice wasn't easy, but she finally chose a soft wool dress in glowing garnet red. By a stroke of luck it was left over from the winter sale which was just ending and she was thrilled to find that she could afford a pair of shoes to match.

Peter picked her up at eight o'clock that evening and they drove out to Merifield. He admired the new dress, telling her how well the colour suited her. Privately she thought he looked very handsome in his dark grey suit and impeccable shirt and tie but she was too diffident to tell him so.

The restaurant was plushy, with soft lighting and discreet music playing in the background, and there was a small dance floor in the centre of the room. The waiter showed them to their table and gave them each a menu. Fleur glanced at the prices and almost gasped with shock, but a glance at Peter's cool assurance told her that he was obviously quite used to eating in expensive restaurants.

She concentrated on the various dishes on the menu, mentally translating the names of the dishes from what she could remember from her schoolgirl French. She eventually decided on a seafood cocktail to start, with *Coq au vin* to follow. Peter ordered the same.

By the time they reached dessert several couples had got up to dance and the tiny dance floor was filling up. Peter looked at her inquiringly. 'Would you like to dance while we wait for our dessert?'

Fleur stood up and took his hand. She thought this kind of dancing only happened in old films. It seemed unreal and almost laughable, but when Peter's arm encircled her and they began to move in time to the music on the crowded little floor she soon forgot her misgivings and began to enjoy herself.

'I'm afraid it's too crowded for proper dancing,' he said. 'At least, the kind you get at a disco.'

She smiled at him. 'It doesn't matter. I don't like discos much anyway. All that noise. You can't hear yourself think!'

He laughed and rubbed his cheek against hers. 'Thank you for coming out with me this evening, Fleur,' he said softly. 'I'm really enjoying myself. I hope you are too?'

'I am. Thank you for asking me.'

'I think my mother was very lucky to find you.'

'I'm the lucky one,' Fleur told him. 'She offered me a job just when I needed one badly. I love working for her.'

'She's very fond of you, you know,' he said softly. 'Concerned because she's afraid you don't have enough fun.' His arm tightened around her waist.

Fleur made no reply. Was this evening just a thank you for being a good employee? she wondered. Had Sally persuaded her son to give her poor hard-worked assistant an evening out? As he smiled down at her she, quickly admonished herself for the ungrateful thought.

It was as they were sitting down again that she noticed a couple who had just come in. A waiter was showing them to a table tucked discreetly away in a quiet corner on the far side of the room. Although the lighting was dim she recognised the man as Vernon Grant. The woman, on the other hand, certainly wasn't Julia. She had short red hair and wore a beautifully cut dress in a stunning shade of green. Fleur racked her brain to remember where she had seen her before. Then it came to her. Of course! She was Vernon Grant's personal assistant. She had been at the Grant Philips Construction company's Christmas boardroom lunch.

Peter ordered liqueurs with their coffee and Fleur felt relaxed as she sipped the thick, sweet liquid. She wondered now why she had felt so apprehensive about coming here this evening and why she had been so suspicious of Peter's motives in asking her out. As they circled the small floor once again she couldn't remember enjoying herself so much. Then suddenly she was shocked to see it was after midnight.

'I hadn't realised it was so late. The evening has gone so quickly! I really should go,' she said apologetically.

He looked amused. 'All right, Cinderella. I'll settle the bill while you get your coat.'

Outside the air was frosty and sharp. Stars twinkled in the sky and the moon was almost full. Her spirits buoyed by the good food, the wine and Peter's company, Fleur looked up and took a deep breath of the fresh, frosty air. 'Oh! What a beautiful night!'

'Isn't it?' He slipped an arm around her waist and drew her close as they walked. When they reached the car he turned her towards him. 'I've enjoyed your company very much, Fleur. I'll be visiting again soon and I'd like us to see more of each other.'

She smiled. 'I'd like that too.'

When he drew her gently towards him she did not resist. His arms were firm, holding her close, and his mouth on hers was warm and sensual. 'You're lovely, Fleur,' he whispered. He kissed her again and when their lips parted, he whispered, 'You know what's happened, don't you?'

'Happened?'

'It began yesterday, didn't it? One of those special, rare once-in-a-lifetime things – the minute we met. Don't say you weren't aware of it too?'

'I – don't . . .' She was unable to finish the sentence. She'd certainly felt attracted to him, but if she'd allowed herself to think of it at all she would have assumed that it was wishful thinking – imagination. What he was implying had a slightly unreal, dreamlike feel to it. He gave her no time to think about it. His lips were on hers again and she allowed her lips to part eagerly for his kiss as he unbuttoned her coat and pulled her closer.

'Oh, Fleur, I wonder if you want me as much as I want you?' The hard warmth of his body pressed close to hers was intoxicating and she let her head fall back as his lips moved from her mouth to her neck, pausing sensuously at the little pulse that throbbed at the base of her throat.

He took her face between his hands, looking into her eyes. 'I can't take you home,' he said breathlessly, 'and perhaps your place isn't such a good idea either. Will you wait in the car while I see if they've got a room here?'

Suddenly she came down to earth. The euphoria of the past moments evaporated abruptly as she realised what he had in mind. She stared at him. '*No!*'

He looked surprised. 'But why?'

She pulled away from him, shaking her head. 'I don't know. It just – doesn't feel right. It makes me feel like a . . . I think I'd like to go home now, if you don't mind.'

His face fell. 'Of course. Just as you wish. I'm sorry.' He let her go abruptly and unlocked the car door. They got in and for a moment or two sat silently side by side. Then he turned to her.

'I'm an insensitive idiot, rushing you like that. It must have sounded almost insulting to you, Fleur. I'm sorry. Can you forgive me?'

'Yes. Yes, it's all right.' She was stiff with misery. He thought she was easy. A mixed-race cockney girl might be a new experience for him. What was it his type called it? *A bit of rough*? She cringed with humiliation at the thought. She had thought him so attractive – been so flattered when he had asked her out for dinner. She had let him kiss her – almost believed . . . She shuddered.

He was looking at her. 'Fleur?'

She shook her head. 'Look, I know people – some girls – do this kind of thing, but I'm not one of them.' She broke off. She sounded so stuffy and prudish. There was no way she could begin to explain how she felt so she might as well give up trying. He probably wouldn't be interested anyway. 'Please, could you just drive me home?'

'Of course. Anything you say.' He started the car and backed it out of the parking space. As they turned and headed for the entrance gates the car's headlights raked the forecourt. In the brief flash from the lights Fleur saw a couple walking hand in hand towards the country club chalets. She had only a momentary glimpse, but it was enough to recognise them. It was Vernon Grant and his PA, Jo Hanson.

Councillor Harold Jeffries, Mayor and chairman of Elvemere Town Council, looked at his watch and cleared his throat. 'I think that concludes our meeting for tonight, ladies and gentlemen.' He glanced at the Town Clerk who was taking the minutes. 'So unless there is any other business . . .'

'There is something I'd like to bring up.' Julia's voice shook slightly as she rose to her feet and all eyes turned on her. This was the first time she had actually spoken since being elected. She had told Eleanor she would keep quiet until she had something of importance to say. Now she definitely felt she had.

'Yes, Councillor Grant?' Councillor Jeffries glared at her over the tops of his spectacles in the manner he reserved for new councillors who threatened to get too big for their boots. He hoped she wasn't planning anything lengthy. Sports Night was on TV and he'd just catch it if he started out now.

Julia took a deep breath. 'It has only just come to my attention that there is no women's refuge in Elvemere.'

A general rumble went round the council chamber and someone said, 'There's one in Merifield.'

'Merifield is ten miles away,' Julia remarked. 'A woman with small children and no transport can't go that far.'

'Why not? What's wrong with public transport?'

'In the middle of the night? When she's traumatised by a violent husband or partner?'

A buzz of disapproval went round and the chairman tapped his gavel. 'This is an issue which has been brought up before, Councillor. It was intensively discussed and at the time we all agreed that it was out of the question. It would be exceptionally expensive and I personally do not feel that the cost would be justified.'

'I think it would,' Julia said boldly. 'How many of the councillors here have actually looked into this need? Battered wives and violent men are not confined to large inner city areas,' she said. 'Neither are single mothers.'

'They're a drain on our resources already!' shouted a voice at the back.

Julia's colour rose. 'Mainly because of the men who have deserted them and reneged on their responsibilities!' she said. 'And in many cases these young women have no wish to be a drain on anyone. They would like to work and be independent. In some cases they have been trained in skills, – often paid for out of our taxes, which

136

are being wasted. If employers would only provide creche facilities . . .'

Her words were lost in the ensuing uproar and Eleanor who sat beside her whispered, 'Now you've done it! At least seventy percent of the council is made up of employers of one sort or another.'

'Then I hope they're listening,' said Julia unrepentantly.

Once again the chairman banged his gavel. 'These are issues that need careful analysis and debate,' he said.

'If I might make a suggestion?' Julia was on her feet again. Her blood was up now, her eyes shining and her cheeks pink. Without waiting for permission she went on, 'There are two empty properties in Victoria Gardens. One of them might be rented by the council and used as a women's refuge. I'm sure that I could get voluntary help and the various local charities would . . .'

'The area known as Victoria Gardens is already under discussion for redevelopment, as I believe you are aware, Councillor?'

'I know, but as a temporary measure – surely . . .'

'I'm sure that everyone will agree that this is not a matter that can be discussed at such short notice and with so little information available.'

There were calls of, 'Hear, hear!'

'Then can it be put on the agenda for a future meeting?'

Councillor Jeffries spluttered into his handkerchief, blew his nose loudly and glared furiously at Julia. 'Your remarks have been minuted, Councillor Grant. There are a great many other issues associated with your proposal which need to be considered.' Before Julia could speak again his gavel came down for the last time. 'I now bring this meeting to a close.' He glanced up at the ancient council chamber clock. 'At nine-thirty-five precisely.' Damn and blast the woman! By the time he got home now Sports Night would be all but over.

As they filed out of the large semi-circular council chamber Eleanor gave Julia a pat on the back. 'Well done!'

She pulled a face. 'I didn't get very far with it, did I?'

'You raised the matter. That's the important part,' Eleanor said. 'I purposely kept quiet and let you get on with it, but when it's formally brought up you can count of my support. And, as you say, we'll lobby some of the other women councillors in the meantime. Coffee?' she looked at Julia inquiringly. 'My place if you like. Or we could go to The Feathers for a drink.'

'I'd love to but I feel I should get home,' Julia said. 'I don't get to see as much of Charlotte as I'd like. Vernon's sister Kath sees more of her than I do. Charlotte spends every spare minute round at the stables and I daresay she'll be there even more when the lighter nights arrive.'

How is the Brownlow girl?' Eleanor asked.

'The baby is better,' Julia told her. 'Unfortunately the child's father is still causing problems, demanding money she can't afford to give him. I just hope he doesn't do something violent. We really do need that refuge, you know, Eleanor.'

'I know, my dear. And we'll get it, you just see. If we stick together we'll win through in the end.'

Charlotte was already in when Julia got home. She was in her room, watching television. Julia asked her if she wanted a hot drink but she said no. She seemed disinclined to talk either, much to Julia's disappointment. As her daughter grew older the gulf between them seemed to be widening. She watched a little TV herself downstairs in the living room, trying to unwind after the meeting, but her mind was so full of her plans that she found it impossible to concentrate and switched it off. She looked at her watch. Half-past eleven. Vernon was very late. She decided to go up.

She didn't know how long she had been asleep when he came in. She woke to hear him stealthily creeping around, undressing in the dark, and reached out to switch on the bedside lamp. Half in, half out of his underpants, he looked up, startled.

'Oh! I thought you were asleep – didn't want to wake you.'

'What time is it?' She peered sleepily at the face of the alarm clock by the bed. 'Two-thirty! Where have you been till now?'

'Round at Dad's. Where did you think I'd been?' He pulled on his pyjamas and went into the bathroom. 'We had a lot to discuss.'

'You must have done. Was Daddy there?'

'No.' The tap running and tooth-cleaning sounds drowned his next remark. He turned off the bathroom light and came back, climbing into bed beside her.

'What were you discussing?' she asked.

He punched his pillow and lay down with his back to her. 'For heaven's sake, Ju, it's late. I'm sure you wouldn't be interested but if you really need a blow by blow account, could we have it in the morning?'

'If you like.' Julia was vaguely aware of a scent that certainly wasn't his usual aftershave. It was a feminine perfume, though not one she had ever used herself. She sniffed. It was familiar yet elusive. Who was it this time? she wondered resignedly. Switching off the bedside lamp she lay on her back, staring up into the darkness. Although he had the duvet over his head she could tell that Vernon was awake too.

138

'Do you know who I saw a few weeks ago?' she asked.

'No idea,' he grunted.

'Joanna Bloom. Remember her? Only her name is something else now. Hinton . . . Hampson or something. She's been divorced twice – been living in America.'

He paused then said, 'Really?' After another pause he turned over and she felt his breath on her cheek. 'It's funny your mentioning her. I meant to tell you. She applied for a job at GPC and got it. She's working as – working in the office. But then, I suppose she told you that?'

'No, she didn't.' Julia frowned into the darkness. 'How odd. I wonder why?'

'God knows.' Vernon punched his pillow again. 'She's only just started. Maybe she didn't even know she'd got the job at the time.'

'Maybe not.'

'Better get some sleep then.' He pecked her cheek and turned over again. ''Night.'

'Goodnight.' She remembered now where she'd smelt that perfume before.

Fleur was busy cleaning the flat on Sunday morning when there was a knock on her door. She opened it to find Peter Arden standing outside on the landing. Her heart quickened with surprise.

'*Oh*, hello.'

'Your landlady said it was all right to come up. I hope you don't mind?'

'No.' She was slightly at a loss to know what to do next when he suddenly produced a bouquet of flowers from behind his back.

'I brought you these.' He grinned disarmingly at her nonplussed expression. 'Well, I suggest that you either put them in water or hit me over the head with them.'

She laughed, taking the bronze and yellow chrysanthemums from him. 'They're lovely. Thank you. Would you like some coffee? I was just going to make some.'

'I thought you'd never ask. That would be very nice. Thanks.'

As she put the flowers into her one and only vase she said, 'I thought you were going back to London today?'

'I am, but I wanted to come and see you first.'

'There was no need.'

'I think there was. I wanted to say how sorry I am for the mess I made of things on Friday evening, Fleur.'

'That's all right. I'd already forgotten it,' she lied.

'Then will you come out to lunch with me before I leave? Give me the chance to make a new start?'

She hesitated. She'd been going to wash her hair and catch up on some jobs. Besides, she wasn't exactly sure just how she felt about him yet, or whether a new start was what she wanted.

'Please come,' he said.

She looked at his contrite face and appealing brown eyes and capitulated. The least she could do was to give him a chance to make amends. 'Okay,' she said. 'Can you give me about ten minutes to change?'

They drove out to a small country pub that Peter said had a reputation for good food, and ate roast beef and Yorkshire pudding. As she attacked the meal with relish Fleur couldn't help thinking of the frozen meat pie she had planned to defrost for lunch.

'When I first came to Elvemere I had this freezing cold little room at the top of the house,' she told him. 'All I had was a kettle and a toaster so you can imagine what kind of meals I had.'

He regarded her across the table. His first impression of her, with her fiery gypsy eyes and endless legs, could not have been more wrong. He saw now that the light in her eyes and the firm set of those luscious lips belonged to a girl determined to get the best she could from life. He admired that, and at the same time found her air of assurance challenging. There was also an intriguing air of mystery about her.

'Tell me, why did you come to Elvemere?' he asked.

'Mainly to get away from London after my grandmother died.'

'But why here?'

'I'd heard the name.' She shrugged. 'It seemed as good a place as any other.'

'And you have no family at all now?'

'Who needs family?' The moment the words had left her lips and she saw the spark of curiosity brighten his eyes she regretted them.

'That sounds intriguing,' he said. 'Are there some some skeletons rattling around in your family cupboard then?'

'Not at all, as far as I know. I only meant that I intend to stand on my own feet.'

'I see.' He looked at his watch apologetically. 'I'm sorry, Fleur but I'll have to take you home now. I'm on duty this evening so I'll have to be on my way.'

As they drew up outside thirteen Victoria Gardens he turned to her. 'I won't get a chance to visit again for some time unfortunately.'

She nodded. 'I understand.' Was this the polite brush-off,

140

intended so as not to leave her working relationship with his mother strained?

He leaned towards her and kissed her softly. 'What I said on Friday – about something special happening between us – it wasn't just a line, you know. I meant it.' He reached out to draw her closer. 'I really do want to see you again, Fleur. I'm going to have a problem waiting till my next visit. Can I ring you?'

'You could, but there's only the communal phone in the hall. It isn't very private.'

He looked into her eyes. 'Is there any chance you might come up to London – stay for a weekend? We could have a good time. I could book you a room at the hotel – get tickets for a show. Please say you'll come.'

'Well – I don't know.'

'Will you at least think about it?'

'Yes. All right. I'll think about it.'

'I'll ring you in a few days to see if you've made up your mind.' He kissed her again.

She stood waving on the pavement as he drove away. On Friday evening she'd been so disappointed in him, but today everything had been different. Now she believed he was sincere. She drew in a deep breath of the cold winter air and found that it tasted like champagne. It made her feel as light as air. Victoria Gardens with its rusty iron railings and ragged frost-bleached grass was suddenly transformed and the raw damp wind felt as warm as a spring breeze. She climbed the narrow stairs on dancing feet, happier than she ever remembered feeling. As she took out her key to unlock the flat a voice from behind her spoke.

'Hi there dreamy! I'm home.'

Turning, she came face to face with Tom. 'It's great to see you. I've missed you so much.' He was looking at her expectantly. 'That's your cue to say you've missed me too,' he prompted. 'Well – do I get a kiss?'

She smiled. 'Of course I missed you. Did you have a good time?' She put her hands on his shoulders and gave him a peck on the cheek.

He drew back his head and looked at her ruefully. 'Is that all the welcome I get? Here I am, back after spending two weeks in the frozen North, missing my girlfriend like crazy, and all I get from her is a chilly little peck on the cheek?'

It took an effort to stop herself from retorting that she wasn't his girlfriend. Instead she said, 'Sorry, Tom. You took me by surprise. Look, come in and have some tea – tell me all about your holiday.'

He followed her into the flat, only slightly mollified. He felt puzzled and uneasy. There was something about Fleur, something he couldn't quite pin down. Then his eyes fell on the vase of flowers by the window; expensive flowers, their rich glowing colours brightening the cold winter light. Something had happened in his absence, and he had the distinct feeling that it wasn't to his advantage.

Chapter 8

'So – did you ask them?'

They were driving towards Merifield and Vernon glanced apprehensively at Joanna. It was the question he'd been dreading. 'I mentioned that you had some money to invest and that you'd like to give GPC the benefit.'

'Yes, and . . .'

'You have to take these things a step at a time, you know.'

'Yes?' When he didn't reply she gave an impatient little snort. 'So are you going to tell me what they said?'

'Dad says he doesn't believe in employees having a financial interest in the firm.'

'What do you mean, *Dad says*? Don't the rest of you get any say?'

'Of course we do.'

'All right then, what did *you* say?'

Vernon drew the car on to the forecourt of the Fairwoods Country Club and switched off the engine. He'd been nursing the vain hope that they could put off this discussion until the end of their weekly rendezvous. 'I pointed out that we could always do with extra resources, of course, and Harry agreed with me. But it wasn't any use. When Dad has made up his mind about something, there's no moving him.'

'But he's in a minority of one! Don't you have the chance to vote on proposals?'

'Look, Jo, even if he agreed to accept your investment, he'd never agree to you taking a seat on the board. He's old-fashioned about that kind of thing. Julia's mother put some money into the firm when they merged but she doesn't have a directorship either.'

'*What?*' Joanna stared at him. 'Why do these women put up with it? Your father is more than old-fashioned, he's a bloody dinosaur!

143

I blame the rest of you for standing for it. As for you and Harry Philips, you're just a pair of yes men. I can't believe you just sit there like a couple of nodding dogs and let him have things all his own way?'

'We don't – not all the time. Dad did build the firm, remember, Jo. He has the largest financial share in the business and he does know what he's talking about.'

'And you have the necessary negotiating skills to get his projects off the ground. Wake up, Vernon! Where would the firm be today if you hadn't pulled off all the land deals? It's time you made him sit up and take notice for a change instead of sitting there and agreeing with everything he says.'

'Maybe so,' he mumbled non-commitally, and looked at her inquiringly. 'Let's not spoil our time together talking business, Jo. Now – do you want to eat first or . . .'

'I'm not at all sure that I want any *or* tonight,' she said petulantly.

He ran a hand through his hair. 'Oh, for God's sake, don't tell me you're going to sulk about it? This business has nothing to do with our relationship. We agreed on that.' He reached out for her but she pushed his hand away. She could hardly say so, but as far as she was concerned it had *everything* to do with their relationship. 'I'm sorry, Vern, but I don't feel like it tonight. I've had a splitting headache all day.'

'I see. You might have said so before we drove all the way out here. Do you want me to drive you home then?'

'Yes. I think that would be best.'

As he turned the car he said, 'By the way, I've been meaning to ask you, why didn't you tell me you'd seen Julia?'

'I didn't think it was important.' She turned on him irritably. 'Do I have to report back to you on who I've seen every time I go into town?'

'When it's my wife I would have thought you might mention it, yes. And why didn't you tell her you were working for GPC?'

'Because it was obvious she didn't know, that's why. She didn't even know I was back in England!' She turned to look him squarely in the eyes. 'If it comes to that, why didn't *you* tell her?'

'We don't discuss the firm much, I told you that. I didn't think she'd be interested.'

'Well then, there's your answer – neither did I.'

'Didn't it occur to you that once she did know she might think it odd you hadn't mentioned it?'

She turned to him. 'Vernon, Julia is your problem. What she

144

thinks *odd* is a matter of supreme indifference to me! Now, are you going to drive me home or do I have to call a cab?'

The drive back to Joanna's house was silent and strained. When Vernon stopped the car outside her house, he turned to her. 'Do I get a nightcap?'

'If you want to make it yourself.' She got out of the car and strode up the front path. Vernon locked the car and followed. They normally spent their evenings together at the Fairwoods to avoid the attention of Joanna's neighbours and he was acutely conscious of the BMW's conspicuous gleaming silver bulk standing outside the house. 'Would you like me to put the car in the garage?' he asked as she unlocked the front door.

'*My* car is in the garage,' she told him brusquely. 'Besides you won't be staying long enough to cause any gossip, will you?'

Once inside the house she took off her coat and headed for the stairs. 'You know where the kitchen is,' she said over her shoulder. 'I don't know what you're having but I'll have a coffee.'

He'd made it by the time she reappeared. She had changed out of the suit she wore for the office into jeans and a sweater and had removed all her make-up. Vernon poured the coffee and handed her a cup. 'Don't be like this, Jo,' he said. 'If you make an atmosphere in the office tomorrow everyone will notice. They'll start to think there's something going on.'

She laughed dryly. 'Then they'd be wrong, wouldn't they?'

'Look, it's only that I'm treading carefully over your investment,' he said. 'Using a little diplomacy. I'm sure I'll get Dad to accept it eventually.'

'*Really*? How kind of him,' she said caustically. 'That's not what you said earlier. You said that once he'd made his mind up there was no moving him.'

He winced. How could he have said that? He ran a hand through his hair. 'What I meant was that you can't bulldoze him into things. You have to be tactful with Dad. Once he's agreed to accept your investment we'll let him think it's his idea to invite you on to the board.'

'Maybe you'd rather I tried a bit of feminine guile,' she said with a brittle little smile. 'He obviously thinks that women were only put on earth for one purpose. What do you think, Vernon? Is it worth a try?'

'Don't be flippant!' He moved across to sit beside her on the settee. 'Just give it a bit more time, Jo. I promise you I'll get you in eventually.' He slid an arm around her. 'Come on, don't let's waste the time we have to spend together. You're surely not going to let this one little setback spoil what we've got, are you?'

She remained stiff and unyielding in his arms as he kissed her, offering no response to the hand that pushed up her sweater and fumbled with the fastening of her bra.

'Oh, Jo, let's go upstairs,' he murmured, his breath warm and moist against her neck. 'It seems ages since last week. I can't wait to . . .'

'Well, I'm sorry, but you're going to have to, Vern.' She pushed him away and stood up, straightening her sweater and smoothing her hair. 'I'm tired and I think you should go now. You know I don't like people seeing your car standing outside. And neither should you. It's careless and indiscreet.'

'Let's go back to the Fairwoods then. It's not too late.'

'No!' She was suddenly irritated by the sight of him sitting there on the settee with his crestfallen expression and untidy hair. She went into the hall and returned a moment later with his coat. 'Goodnight, Vernon.' She held it out to him. 'And for goodness' sake, do something about your hair before you get home. It's standing on end.'

Getting up, he snatched the coat from her hands, his face dark with anger as he self-consciously smoothed his ruffled hair. 'If you want that seat on the board you're going the wrong way about it, Jo,' he warned.

'Really? If that's a threat it's a pretty empty one. You don't seem to have much clout with the firm from what I can see.' Her eyes narrowed. 'And while we're on the subject, Vernon, if you want the luxury of a discreet mistress, I'd say that *you* were going the wrong way about it!' She strode to the door and flung it open. 'Drive carefully,' she called after him. 'But then you always do, don't you?'

The house was in darkness when he let himself in. His heart sank. It was like this most nights now. No wonder he looked elsewhere for amusement, he told himself self-pityingly. There was a light showing under Charlotte's door, but he didn't go in. His daughter and he were barely speaking these days. She persisted in defying him, going off to his sister's stables at every possible opportunity. He was convinced that she did it to spite him, and Kath encouraged her, revelling in the girl's defiance. At the office Charlotte was sullen and moody, doing the minimum of work with the maximum of resentment. If only she could have been a boy, life would have been so much easier.

As for Julia, she was always busy with her council business. If she wasn't out at some meeting or other she was working on something at home. There was no family life in the house any more. And now Jo had started to be difficult. It was the last straw. Until tonight he had at least had these Thursday evenings to look forward to. There had to be some way he could persuade his father to accept her on to the board of directors. He locked up and began to ascend the stairs. It had been a bloody awful day. Might as well have an early night and write it off.

To his surprise Julia was awake. She was sitting up in bed and had obviously been working on some papers. A council agenda and her reading glasses lay on the duvet. Now she was watching a documentary on the portable TV. She looked up, surprised when he came in.

'Hello. You're early.' She snapped off the TV with the remote control.

'I know. Chap I was meeting couldn't make it. Something about his car breaking down.'

'I see. Well, an early night will do you good.'

He looked at her. She wore a filmy nightgown in a flattering shade of pink trimmed with black lace and she'd done something different with her hair. Had it cut, restyled or whatever they called it. 'Everything all right?' he asked her.

'Fine thanks.'

'Charlotte okay?'

'Seems to be.'

'Right.'

In the bathroom he hurriedly undressed, showered and brushed his teeth. When he emerged she'd already put out the light on her side of the bed and was lying down. He climbed in beside her and switched off his own light.

'You're looking very lovely tonight, Ju,' he said quietly into the darkness. Reaching out he put a hand on her thigh and rolled her towards him. 'It's ages since we made love. There never seems to be time or an opportunity these days.'

'You're so often late.' She paused. 'I thought you'd lost interest.'

'Ju! How could you think that?' His hand travelled upwards to cup her breast and he raised himself to lean over her. 'We really should make more time for each other, shouldn't we?'

'I suppose we should.'

'I do still find you attractive, you know – very much so. You've kept your figure and you always look nice.' He kissed her and pulled up the silky material of her nightdress to stroke her hip and slide his hand over the smooth curve of her stomach. Pushing the gown above her breasts he nibbled at the soft nipples and felt them

147

harden at the touch of his tongue. 'You're a very desirable woman, Ju. You still excite me,' he whispered huskily. Unable to contain his arousal any longer, he moved urgently over her acquiescent body and entered her in one strong thrust.

Perversely, Joanna's angry, vindictive rejection had excited him more than her normal eager response, creating an urge to vent his anger on her in a sexual way. He had left her house in a highly aroused and frustrated state. Had that parting shot of hers about driving carefully held a snide criticism? he wondered. He recalled the comment about him and Harry being nodding dogs and smarted. How he wished now that he'd insisted on staying and proving to her that he was no pushover to be manipulated and threatened. He would have shown her who was boss. Nodding dog indeed!

Now, as Julia lay submissively beneath him, he envisaged over-powering Joanna, imagined her cries – first of alarm at his anger and the power of his masculine dominance, then of ecstatic response as she happily surrendered to his passion. Julia's surprised compliance was a poor substitute for the splendidly explosive climax he and Jo would have achieved, but it was better than nothing.

He came quickly and rolled away. 'Sorry about that,' he gasped. 'It's been so long, hasn't it? We could try again if you like, but I'm not sure if I . . .'

'It's all right,' she said quickly. 'I'm fine, honestly.'

Julia lay on her back staring up at the ceiling. What had happened she wondered, to make Vernon feel amorous towards her tonight? Was she standing in for someone? Was that someone Joanna? And if so – why?

She lay quite still, listening tensely as his laboured breathing slowed and then deepened. Released from his pent-up frustration, he was already asleep whilst she felt only revulsion mingled with a sense of treachery. Getting up quietly she went into the bathroom and pulled off her crumpled nightdress, dropping it into the soiled linen basket. Then she showered away all traces of Vernon's duplicity.

As she lay on the brink of sleep, memories of Dean returned unbidden to haunt her last waking thoughts. Those first blissful weeks they had shared seemed so long ago. Like all half-buried memories the barbs and the sharp edges of the ill-fated affair had become blurred and softened by time. She forgot the squalor, the discomfort and neglect, remembering only the blissful nights when there was nothing but love.

Dean may have proved false in the end but at least for a little while he had made her feel vibrant and alive – a passionate flesh

148

and blood woman. Vernon only ever made her feel used and exploited. He had always been a selfish, uncaring lover, concerned only with his own gratification. She was so used to his ways now that it was hard to believe she had once known an intense, all-consuming love. Far easier to believe was the bitter pain of the final betrayal that had ended it all. She thought guiltily of the baby girl she had abandoned, Dean's child; then briefly of pathetic little Tracey Brownlow, struggling with the potentially dangerous results of her own folly, bravely making the kind of sacrifices that she herself had shirked.

Perhaps she deserved the reward she had reaped. Her marriage had been dead for years, but there was no way she would ever be able to end it whilst the two families were so closely intertwined in the business. Happy or unhappy, she was trapped.

Fleur was alone in the office when the telephone rang.

'Good morning, Arden Catering. Can I help you?'

'Fleur! It's me, Peter.'

'Peter!' Her heart quickened at the sound of his voice. 'If you want your mother, I'm afraid she isn't in. She's snatched a free hour to go to the hairdresser's.'

'No, it's you I want. I'm glad I've caught you alone. Any chance of coming up to London next weekend?'

She caught her breath. So soon! She had half thought his invitation was a spur-of-the-moment idea he'd forget once he was back in his own environment. 'Well, I don't know,' she hedged. 'I don't *think* we've got any functions booked but I'll have to have a look in the book.'

'Come off it, Fleur. You know there are no bookings. Mum has arranged to go away next weekend and she kept it clear. I checked when I was home.'

Fleur frowned, a hint of resentment prickling. If he'd known there were no bookings, why hadn't he asked her before he left? He was taking her for granted again. 'Then can you wait till I see if *I* have anything booked?' she said. 'I do have a life of my own too, you know.'

'Of course. I'm sorry, Fleur. I would have mentioned it before but I had to check my work rota. I couldn't do that till I got back.'

'No. I see.' She held the phone away from her, one hand over the mouthpiece. What should she do? He sounded sincere. She wanted to go and yet . . . She counted to fifty, then she took her hand from the receiver.

'Peter? Ah, you're still there. Sorry to keep you. As it happens I do seem to be free next weekend.'

'That's great!' He sounded genuinely delighted.

'So – what did you have in mind?'

'I thought you could come up on Friday evening and stay until Sunday evening,' he said. 'I'll book you in here at The Ascot. It's my weekend off. I'll get tickets for a show for Saturday evening. Is there anything you particularly fancy seeing?'

Fleur's heart stirred with excitement. 'Oh, well, as a matter of fact I'd love to see *Phantom of the Opera*,' she said.

'Right. *Phantom* it is.'

'Unless you've already seen it?' she said quickly.

'No need to worry about that. I've already looked up the trains and there's one that gets in to Liverpool Street at seven-twenty. I'll meet you, all right?'

'Yes, fine.'

'I'm looking forward very much to seeing you again, Fleur,' he said softly.

'Are you? That's nice,' she said.

'Look, just one thing, Fleur. No need to mention the weekend to Mum, okay?'

She frowned. 'If you say so. But why?'

'It's just that I've always liked to keep my private life separate and you know what mothers are like.'

'I don't actually, but of course I won't say anything if you don't want me to.'

'Thanks. See you on Friday evening then. Can't wait.' Bye, darling.'

'Goodbye, Peter.'

Fleur sat looking at the telephone for several minutes after she'd hung up, that 'Bye, darling' still echoing in her ears. Was she right to go up to London and spend a weekend with Peter? She wanted to very much. Ever since he'd gone back she thought about him constantly. But why not tell Sally? It felt wrong. What was the real reason he didn't want her to know? It wasn't as though there was anything to hide. Did he feel that she might disapprove? She quickly dismissed her concern, telling herself that Peter must have his own reasons. She put the thought out of her head and began looking forward to the weekend.

She saw him as soon as she got off the train, standing head and shoulders above everyone as he stood at the barrier. He didn't see her right away and for a moment she watched him raking the faces of all the passengers as they passed him. Then he spotted her and his face lit up.

'Fleur!' He held out his arms and she went into them. Passers by smiled at the sight of the handsome young couple embracing. 'It seems ages since I saw you,' he said, looking down into her face. 'Let me take your case. I've got the car. Or are you hungry? We can have something to eat now if you want?'

'No.' She laughed. 'I can wait till later, thanks. It is good to see you, Peter. I've looked forward to it all week.'

'Me too.' He put her case down again and drew her into his arms, kissing her. She struggled free, laughing and embarrassed. 'People are looking.'

'Let them.' He put an arm around her, pulling her close to his side as they walked. 'They're only jealous, especially the men.'

The Ascot was a small but elegant hotel overlooking Green Park. As they went in through the revolving door Fleur was impressed by its slightly old-fashioned air of affluent gentility. The decor was stylish yet discreet; the carpets deep and the lighting soft. At the reception desk she signed in and then they went up in the silent lift to the third floor. Peter opened the door for her with a flourish.

'Welcome to The Ascot, madam.'

Fleur looked around the comfortable room with delight. There was a large bed with a draped satin cover and quilted headboard. The built-in furniture was white and gilt and there was a lovely view of the park through the two long windows. Through the open bathroom door she glimpsed gleaming tiles, a pink suite and soft cream carpet. She turned to look at him.

'Oh, Peter, it's lovely!'

'There's TV and radio. A hair dryer if you need it, and tea and coffee-making facilities.' He smiled at her. 'Not that you'll be spending much time in here. I've got all sorts of things planned for us.'

She threw her arms around his neck. 'Oh, Peter, I never expected anything this grand. Do you know, I've never actually been in a hotel before, let alone one like this.' She peered at him doubtfully. 'It isn't costing you a fortune, I hope?'

He laughed. 'That's something you needn't bother your head about. I'm under manager, remember? I do have certain perks. Now, I'll leave you to unpack. Pick you up in an hour and we'll have dinner here. All right?'

She made the most of the hour, taking a luxurious bath in the elegant bathroom and changing into the dark red dress she had bought for their dinner date at New Year. When he knocked on the door she ran to open it, her cheeks flushed with anticipation. His admiring expression told her all that she wanted to know.

They dined downstairs in the hotel dining room where the food was even more delicious than that at the Fairwoods Country Club. Fleur enjoyed every mouthful. Peter had ordered wine, choosing carefully from the wine list. She found it sweet and refreshing and she lost count of how many times he refilled her glass. By the time they had finished Fleur felt pleasantly relaxed. When Peter asked her if she would like to go on to a club and dance she was surprised.

'It's eleven o'clock,' she said.

He laughed. 'You're in danger of sounding like a country cousin, my sweet,' he said. 'The night is still young.'

He took her to an intimate little club well known for its jazz and they danced in the dim, smoky atmosphere, pressed close together and barely moving on the tiny crowded floor. Fleur had more to drink. She hardly knew what was in her glass except that it never seemed to be empty but it didn't seem to matter very much. Peter was reassuring, insisting that most of it was tonic water.

They finally arrived back at The Ascot at two a.m. Fleur felt as though her feet hardly touched the ground and Peter collected her key from the night porter and escorted her up to her floor.

Turning the key in the lock he pushed open the door for her. She smiled at him. 'Aren't you coming in? I can make you a cup of coffee.'

Inside the room she groped around for the light switch and suddenly the situation seemed overwhelmingly funny. She began to giggle. 'Peter – where are you? I can't find you. It's dark and . . .' In the darkness she stumbled against him. His arms closed around her and he held her close.

'I believe you're ever so slightly drunk, my darling,' he whispered in her ear.

'No, I'm not,' she said indignantly. 'How can I be?' She wound her arms around his neck. 'It's just that I need to hold onto you because – because I can't seem to stand up very well.'

He put his arm behind her knees and scooped her up. The room seemed to spin around her dizzily until she felt herself deposited on the softness of the bed. Peter switched on the bedside lamp and smiled down at her in the soft diffused light.

'There, that's better. Now I can see you.' He kicked off his shoes and lay down beside her, pulling her into his arms again.

She smiled hazily, snuggling against him. 'Mmm. That's comfy. I like it here – being with you – like this.' The room was still spinning as her lips parted eagerly for his kiss and when he began to undress her she felt her heartbeat quicken. The sensation of his hands exploring her body was heady and sensuous. It made her ache for more, and when he left her for a few moments to undress she received him back with open arms, thrilling to the touch of his naked flesh against hers – offering herself with avid abandonment.

Looking down at her Peter held both her hands in his. 'Better get something sorted out first sweetheart,' he said. 'You're on the Pill I take it?'

She stared up at him. 'No.'

He smiled reassuringly. 'Okay, just as long as I know. Wouldn't do to take any risks, would it?'

It didn't occur to Fleur to be surprised that he had come prepared with condoms. And if he was surprised to find her a virgin he didn't say so. To begin with he was as gentle as his arousal allowed, but when they made love for the second time he found her less submissive, assuming a more assertive role and delighting him with her uninhibited passion. Dawn was breaking before they finally slept, their exhausted limbs entwined amidst a tangle of crumpled sheets.

Fleur was first to waken. For a few moments she could not make out where she was, then she turned and saw Peter's head on the pillow beside her and slowly the events of the previous night came back to her. She blushed as she remembered the abandoned sensuality of the night before and decided to get up before Peter wakened. But as she was starting to get out of bed he stirred and opened his eyes.

'Hello, beautiful,' he said sleepily, throwing a restricting arm across her. 'Where do you think you're going?'

'I was going to get dressed,' she said.

'I prefer you as you are.' He raised himself on one elbow to look down at her. 'You know, you could be a model, Fleur. You have the most beautiful body. Those page three girls have absolutely nothing on you.'

She shook her head and tried to sit up. 'Peter – don't. You're embarrassing me. I want to get up.'

He laughed softly. 'You weren't embarrassed last night. And there's no hurry to get up. We have all day.' He pressed her back against the pillows and began to kiss her breasts, circling each nipple with his tongue until he drew little moans of pleasure from her. 'All day to make love, my darling,' he whispered seductively into the hollow of her throat as his hands caressed her. 'Isn't that a delicious prospect?'

Although the affects of the vodka had long since faded her head was beginning to spin again. Peter's lovemaking was far more intoxicating than any alcohol and under the irresistible persuasion of his teasing, questing lips and fingers she abandoned her inhibitions once again, giving herself up to her own clamouring urges.

At the theatre that evening they sat hand in hand. Fleur was enraptured by the ambience, the music and romance of the story, the sheer spectacle of it all. But as much as she enjoyed the show she was impatient to be alone with Peter again. Afterwards they went back to the hotel to eat a late dinner, then up to Fleur's room where they fell eagerly into each other's arms again.

Long after Peter had fallen asleep Fleur lay awake, her body still tingling, every nerve singing, vitally alive and glowing from their love making. These two days had been a revelation. She would not have believed it was possible to feel like this. Till now love and desire was something she had only read about. If she'd given them any thought at all it was to doubt their existence – to believe they were nothing but fantasy. Something dreamed up by authors in order to sell books. Now she knew better. Everything the books said was right. She was in love with Peter, in love for the first and last time. So much in love with him that she would have done anything he asked.

She thought of Sally and wondered what she would think when she knew they had spent this weekend together. Surely she would not be angry at the small deception, especially when she realised how much in love they were? She raised herself on one elbow to look down at Peter's sleeping face. He was so handsome. She loved him so much that just looking at him like this brought a lump to her throat. It was hard to believe that so much happiness was possible.

At the station the following afternoon he saw her on to the train and kissed her goodbye.

'When shall I see you again?' she asked, holding on to his hand till the very last minute.

'I'll ring you,' he said. 'I don't know when I'll be free again, but I'll ring.'

As the train began to move she asked, 'Peter – will you write to me?' She visualised the pleasure of getting a letter from him – reading the special intimate things he might write – writing back.

He laughed and shrugged his shoulders. 'I might. I'll see. I'm not very good at putting my thoughts on paper.'

'Just a few lines, please.'

He was walking with the moving train, but the distance between them was lengthening and she was forced at last to let go of the hand she held. There was something odd about him this afternoon.

This morning when they first wakened he had been as warm and passionate as before, making love to her even more urgently because it would be the last opportunity for a while. But ever since lunch he had seemed restrained, almost distant, as though he was locked up inside himself, afraid to display his feelings. Perhaps he felt as sad as she did at saying goodbye. As the train reached the end of the platform she leaned out of the window to wave, but to her dismay he had already turned and started to walk away.

She sat down in her corner seat, puzzled and slightly troubled. Why couldn't he have stayed until the train had gone? But he was a man, wasn't he? Men were sometimes reluctant to reveal the depth of their feelings. Maybe he wanted to be by himself. Tomorrow, or maybe the next day, he would telephone and everything would be all right. And they would write to each other – wonderful poetic letters that would almost make up for the distance between them.

She closed her eyes, beginning already to compose her first letter to him – shutting out the other occupants of the carriage along with the rest of the world. Enclosed in her own private world she indulged herself with thoughts of Peter, reliving the blissful two days and nights they had shared.

Eleanor Maitland was making her bedtime drink that Sunday night when a knock on her front door made her look up in surprise. She slipped the chain on and opened it a crack to peer out cautiously into the darkness.

'Who is it?'

'It all right, Lena, it's me, Charlie Grant.'

'Charlie?' Eleanor closed the door and slipped off the chain, opening it again to reveal her childhood friend standing on the doorstep. 'I hope there's nothing wrong?'

'No, no. Nothing to worry about. I was passing and I thought you might like to see this.' He tapped a flat brown paper parcel under his arm. 'Well, are you going to ask me in, lass, or do I have to stand here and freeze?'

'Sorry, Charlie.' She opened the door. 'Come in, of course. I was just making myself some cocoa, would you like some?'

He pulled a face. 'Cocoa? I'll pass on that, if you don't mind. I always say it's only for old maids and invalids.'

'I might still have a drop of whisky in the cupboard, left over from Christmas.'

He grinned. 'Now you're talking!'

In the living room she took the whisky bottle from the sideboard cupboard and poured him a glass. 'Well – are you going to show me what's in the parcel then?'

'Oh, yes. I almost forgot.' He removed the paper and held up his offering. 'I found this the other day when I was having a bit of a clear out. An old school photograph, look. You and I are both on it. Your Jim an' all. I thought you might like to have it so I've had it framed for you.'

'Oh, Charlie!' Eleanor took the photograph and studied it carefully, her eyes misty. 'How thoughtful of you.' She sighed as she looked at the rows of childish faces ranged in tiers against the background of the Victorian school building. 'It all seems so long ago, doesn't it?'

'It does that.' He stood looking around him. 'Fancy you still living here, Lena,' he said. 'How many years is it?'

'Forty-two,' she told him. 'The last fifteen alone. It suits me, this little place. All my memories are here. Moving to some big posh house is all very well, but we're not all rolling in money like some I might mention, Charlie Grant.'

He sipped his whisky and smacked his lips appreciatively. 'Mmm – don't know about rolling in it. Not as well off as some folk think,' he said, making himself comfortable in the armchair by the fire. 'Thing is, Lena, strictly between ourselves, I'm hoping to get the contract for the redevelopment of Victoria Gardens. Our plans for Meadowlands Park have been passed okay. It's going to be the most upmarket project we've ever tackled, is that, but it's going to stretch our resources to the limit and the bank could prove to be tricky over the loan we need to get things up and running.'

'Oh? Why's that?'

'Oh, don't get me wrong, they haven't turned us down,' he went on. 'Our credit's good, but we still have a substantial loan outstanding and it'd be a lot more comfortable not to have to ask. The Victoria Gardens contract would just about save our bacon if you know what I mean.'

She nodded. 'I do. But I don't quite see how I can help, Charlie.'

He cleared his throat. 'Well, all I really need to know is, when are they likely to offer the job for tender and what kind of sum are they prepared to spend on it? Julia's on the planning committee, of course, but you know what new brooms are like. She's as tight as a tick. Can't get a dicky bird out of her.' He leaned forward towards her. 'You're on the finance and general purposes committee aren't you? You must have some idea. Now, Lena, I'm sure you know that anything that passes from you to me will be strictly between ourselves. Goes without saying, eh?' He winked.

'Yes, it does, Charlie, but I'm afraid there's nothing I can tell you.'

His jaw dropped. 'Oh, come on, lass. We go back a long way. Surely you can do me a small favour like this? I wouldn't ask if it wasn't vital.'

'I know you wouldn't, but I really can't help, Charlie.' She paused, biting her lip. 'But as you say, we do go back a long way and there is one piece of advice I can give you, off the record.'

'Yes?'

'Give the whole idea up.'

'Give it up! Why?'

She sighed. 'I shouldn't be telling you this but it'll be public knowledge very soon anyway. The plans for redeveloping Victoria Gardens have been abandoned, or at least shelved for the foreseeable future. Since the community charge came in the budgets have gone haywire. The council won't be making any major changes until they've have had time to sort out a new financial programme.'

Charlie stood up and put his glass down on the mantelpiece with the thump of finality. For a moment he stood staring pensively into the fire, then he looked up at her. 'I appreciate your telling me this, Lena,' he said. 'You're a pal.'

'I'm just sorry it had to be bad news, Charlie.'

He nodded thoughtfully. 'Don't know about that. Forewarned is forearmed, as they say. You might have done me more of a favour than you realise.' He stepped up to her and put his arms round her waist, then he kissed her full on the mouth. 'You always were a grand lass, Lena. Thanks. And thanks for the whisky too.'

Fleur was letting herself into the flat when a step on the stairs made her turn. As his head came level with the landing Tom's face lit up with pleasure at seeing her.

'Hi! You're back then.'

'Yes, I'm back.' She was irritated. She'd hoped to get in without being seen. All she wanted was to be by herself. Now Tom would expect to be invited in to hear all about the weekend she was supposed to have spent in Hackney with her grandmother's friend.

'How was it then?'

'Fine, thanks.'

'I'll make you a coffee, if you like?'

'It's all right. I can make one for myself.' His hurt expression immediately made her regret her terse reply.

'I just thought you might not have any milk,' he said apologetically.

'I like it black anyway.'

'Right then.' He backed away. 'I'll leave you to unpack in peace.'

She relented. 'No. Look, sorry if I was sharp, don't go.' She took her key out of the lock and pushed the door open. 'Come in. Tell me all the latest gossip.'

As she took off her coat, he busied himself filling the kettle and plugging it in. 'You had a good time then? You look positively blooming.'

'Thanks.' She came and stood with her back to the worktop in the tiny kitchen. 'Look, Tom, there's something I think I should tell you.'

He turned to look inquiringly at her in the act of pouring hot water into the mugs. 'Yes?'

'I didn't quite tell you the truth – about this weekend, I mean.'

'No?' He handed her a mug of black coffee.

'I didn't go to Hackney. I stayed at The Ascot Hotel in Park Lane.'

'Wow! very posh. Don't tell me you've won a . . .'

'With Peter Arden. Sally's son.'

'Oh!'

'Yes. We – I'm in love with him, Tom.'

He stood looking at her. 'What you're saying is that you slept with him.'

'Please, don't make it sound sleazy. It isn't. I'm really happy. Happier than I ever thought possible.'

'Really? I'm glad for you.' He put his untouched coffee down on the worktop. 'Right then. If there's nothing else you want to tell me, I'll go.'

'Please, Tom, don't be difficult about it. Don't spoil it for me.'

'*Difficult*? What the hell do you expect?' He rounded on her. 'Do you want me to stay so that you can tell me all the intimate details and gloat? So that you can enjoy watching me curl up with misery. Is that it?'

'Misery?' She stared at him, shocked and dismayed by his reaction. '*No!* Tom, how can you say that?'

'Oh, come *on*! You must have known how I felt about you,' he said, his voice thick with emotion. 'Ever since you first came here I've hoped that we might get closer. I've waited, thinking you were still traumatised over your bad experience. I've been patient, waiting for you to come to me when you were ready, in your own time. What a prize bloody *idiot* I was! This Arden guy crooks his little finger and you go haring off to London. He wines and dines you

158

and before you know it – bingo! He's got you into bed! Simple as that!'

'It wasn't like that, Tom. You're making it all sound cheap and sordid.'

'Then how was it? You haven't known him five minutes. How can you be in love with someone you hardly know?'

'I don't know. I just *am!*'

'I see. There's nothing more to be said then, is there?' He walked to the door. 'Goodnight, Fleur.'

'Tom – wait. Don't go like that. I still want us to be . . .'

He spun round to look at her, stopping her words with his wounded expression. '*Friends*? Is that what you were going to say.' His eyes were bright with anguish. 'For Christ's sake, spare me that old chestnut, Fleur. At least have the decency to spare me that!'

Vernon's weekend had been hellish. He hadn't seen Joanna since their quarrel and he could only guess at what was going through her mind. He'd spent Saturday on the golf course and Julia had invited both sets of parents round for the day on Sunday so there was no escape. After they had eaten a late lunch his father took him to one side.

'Can we have a word, Vern?' He glanced around him and lowered his voice. 'In private, I mean. Perhaps we could go to your study?'

'Of course.' Inside the study Charlie took the high-backed leather swivel chair behind Vernon's desk, leaving him to draw up a hard chair for himself opposite. It was typical and Vernon tried unsuccessfully to rise above the resentment that rankled. He looked inquiringly at his father.

'What is it, Dad? Problems?'

Charlie lit his pipe and regarded his son through a cloud of blue smoke. 'How much cash was Mrs Hanson thinking of investing with GPC?'

Vernon's eyebrows rose in surprise. 'I don't know.'

'You don't *know?*' Charlie glared at him. 'You come to a board meeting with an investment proposal without knowing how much the punter's got to invest? Well, I think you'd better find out then, don't you?'

'But you turned the offer down,' Vernon protested.

'Yes – well, something's come to my attention since that meeting.' Charlie regarded the glowing bowl of his pipe. 'We won't be getting the contract for the Victoria Gardens redevelopment so if there's any extra cash going, I think maybe we should look into it.'

'Why won't we be getting the contract?'

'They're shelving the project. Seems the community charge has thrown the council's budget out of kilter. Oh, they might do it at some later stage but that'll be too late for us. I want to get Meadowlands under way before the bubble bursts. I want it doing *now*!' He thumped the desk to reinforce his statement.

'I think I should warn you, if she invests money she's going to want a directorship,' Vernon pointed out.

'Is she now? Doesn't want much, does she? Damned cheeky bitch. Well, we'll meet that one when we come to it.'

Vernon shifted uneasily on his hard chair. 'Look, shouldn't Harry be in on all this?'

Charlie waved his pipe, scattering hot ash across the pristine desk top. 'We'll let him in on it when I've tested the ground. You know what an old woman he is, forever putting obstacles in the way. Now . . .' He leaned forward. 'When can you find out what she's thinking of investing with us?'

'Why don't you ask her yourself?'

Charlie grinned knowingly. 'She's your personal assistant. You're the one with the – what shall we call it? – *intimate inside knowledge.*' He leaned back, enjoying his son's obvious discomfort. 'No, what I mean is, ask casually. I don't want her getting her hopes up. If she's got nowt but a few piddlin' hundred to put in it won't be worth bothering with, and certainly not worth a directorship. I can't help thinking that if she was that well off she wouldn't be living in Hazel Grove and working for us.' He gave Vernon a meaningful look. 'Not even as your PA. But you did mention a substantial divorce settlement so maybe it's worth asking.'

'I'll sound her out in the morning.'

Charlie stood up. 'Right. Do that. And let me know as soon as you can.' He walked to the door. 'Better get back now before the womenfolk send out a search party!'

As Vernon parked the BMW in his parking space, Joanna's little red Mazda pulled up beside him. Opening the window he gestured to her to do the same. She frowned at him as she wound the window down and he noticed that she still looked far from happy.

'What is it, Vernon?'

'I want to talk to you.'

She got out of the car and locked the door. 'There's nothing to talk about.'

'Yes, there is. Get in here with me for a minute. I don't want to talk in the office with all the staff flapping their ears.'

Something about the urgency of his tone made her hesitate.

Slipping her keys into her handbag, she walked round the car and got into the passenger seat. 'Well?' She raised her eyebrows at him challengingly.

'I have to ask you something?'

'Go on then – ask.'

'How much were you thinking of investing with GPC?'

Her eyes flickered and he knew he'd got her full attention. 'Why do you want to know?'

'Isn't that obvious?'

'Your father has agreed?'

'He might. I've been working on him all weekend. He just might agree when he's satisfied himself as to just how . . .' He cleared his throat. ' . . . how serious you are.'

'*Seriously* serious.' Joanna leaned back against the seat. 'I know that the company is trying to launch into up-market residential properties starting with Meadowlands Park,' she said slowly. 'I know how much initial investment these ventures require from my own experience in real estate, and I also know that GPC has a lot of cash tied up in land, materials, not to mention payments still outstanding on an existing bank loan.'

He nodded. 'You've done your homework, obviously.'

'Well, it is part of my job after all. The fact remains, GPC's cash flow is strictly limited.'

'True. So?'

'So I thought perhaps five hundred K might help for starters.'

He stared at her, his eyes popping, momentarily stunned into silence. 'Five hundred thou'? Half a *million*? You're joking!'

'I'm not in the habit of joking about large sums of money. And there's more where that came from.' She smiled. 'I don't want to appear vulgar, do I?'

'But – so *much*? I mean how – where . . .?'

'Where did I get it? I told you I had a good settlement from my ex. He happened to own the real-estate business I worked for and he made quite a lot of money out of it. I made good and sure that I had my own share of the business, so I had that as well as my settlement. I sold it before I left the States – at a very good profit, I might add.' She laughed. 'Don't worry, Vernon. The money is there all right. It's all kosher, legal and above board.'

He closed his gaping mouth and took a deep breath. 'But the house you bought. And the car, your job here, your lifestyle . . .'

'Isn't that of a wealthy woman? You're right, Vernon. But living a life of pampered luxury isn't what I want. I consider myself far too young to spend my time and money on luxury cruises and face

161

lifts,' she told him. 'I like money for what it can do. I want to make it work for me. I love a challenge. It's what life is all about as far as I'm concerned right now. Pampered luxury can come later.'

He nodded. 'I think you should see Dad as soon as possible.'

'What about my seat on the board?'

He smiled wryly. 'I think you hold the trump card as far as that's concerned,' he said. As she made to get out of the car he laid a hand on her arm. 'And what about us, Jo? Are we still on? Am I forgiven?'

Glancing round the car park to make sure they were not observed, she leaned across and kissed him, her mouth moist and seductive and the pressure of her hand warm on his thigh. He reached out to pull her closer.

'Oh, Jo, I've had a hell of a weekend. I was so worried you might not want . . .'

'Shhh.' Very gently she extricated herself from his arms. 'Later darling. Business first, pleasure later. Maybe we could meet at the Fairwoods this evening?'

'Yes. I'll ring and make a booking.'

She smiled her sultry smile at him, running the tip of her tongue along her upper lip. 'Then I can show you just how grateful I really am.'

Fleur watched for the postman every morning, running downstairs as soon as she heard the rattle of the letterbox, but to her disappointment there was no letter from Peter. She decided to write to him anyway, but it wasn't as easy as she'd thought. Putting down in words what she felt was so difficult. When she read it through afterwards it all sounded so schoolgirlish and inadequate. She kept the letter that finally satisfied her, slipping it into a drawer and promising herself that she'd post it if she didn't hear from him by next weekend.

Arden Catering had gone through the usual post-Christmas lull and now the bookings were beginning to come in again. Through the lull Sally and she had been working hard, stocking up the freezers so that when the functions began again they would have plenty of ready-prepared foods to draw on. Each afternoon Fleur worked in the office, making sure the paperwork, orders and accounts were up to date. But being restricted to the kitchen and the office had become tedious and by the time they set out for their first party, a twenty-first birthday celebration, both were glad to be back in harness.

As they loaded the van Fleur wondered whether Sally had heard from Peter. His lack of communication had made her uneasy. She wondered whether he was all right. She had telephoned The Ascot twice to find out why she hadn't heard from him, to be told on the first occasion that he was out; on the second that he was too busy to come to the telephone. Finally she decided to come right out and ask Sally.

'Have you heard from Peter lately?' She tried to sound as casual as she could as she climbed into the van's driving seat.

'Yes, I had a long letter from him just this morning,' she said as she fastened her seat belt. 'As a matter of fact he sprung some rather surprising news on me.' She turned to look at Fleur. 'How would you feel about managing on your own for a few days?'

'You're planning to go away? When?'

'In April. Peter has announced that he's getting married and he wants me to go over to Switzerland for the big day.' She turned to smile at Fleur. 'Thanks to your efficiency I shall be quite confident to leave you in sole charge, as long as you're happy about it.'

'Yes . . .' Fleur's mouth had dried so that speaking was difficult. 'Yes, of course,' she said. She ran her tongue over her dry lips and took a deep breath. 'I'd no idea that Peter was engaged.'

'Neither did I. Not officially anyway. Lorraine is Swiss. They met when he was working in Switzerland and she was working in London until recently.' She smiled. 'She's a really lovely girl. I've met her several times. Her father has a lovely hotel on the outskirts of Geneva. She and Peter have been seeing each other for about two years, but I didn't know it was this serious until now.'

'I see.' Fleur had to grip the steering wheel tightly to stop her hands from shaking.

'It seems that the wedding is to be in a little church by the lake,' Sally went on. 'It will be so beautiful there in the spring. So romantic.'

Numb with shock, Fleur scarcely heard as Sally chattered on excitedly about her future daughter-in-law. It was like a slap in the face, hearing so suddenly that Peter was to be married. He had never even mentioned a girlfriend. But then he hadn't given much away at all, especially about himself. How could she have been so easily taken in? Surely there had to be some mistake, she told herself disbelievingly – a misunderstanding?

'She's going to make the perfect daughter-in-law,' Sally was saying. 'I've always wanted a daughter so naturally I can hardly wait. When they're married they're hoping to run a hotel of their own in Switzerland. Lorraine's father has already started looking out for one for them. She turned and noticed Fleur's shocked expression for the first time. 'Fleur! Are you all right, dear?'

She shook her head and forced a smile. 'I'm fine. It's just – just a surprise, that's all'

'You're not worried about managing on your own? It will only be for a few days. And it won't be for a while yet.'

'No. I'm not worried at all.' Fleur swallowed hard at the lump in her throat that threatened to choke her.

'I could always get someone in to help you if you're at all doubtful.'

'No, really, I'll look forward to it. Fleur swallowed hard and turned to smile at her employer. 'Congratulations, Sally,' she said. 'I'm very happy for you.'

Chapter 9

Charlie Grant leaned back in his chair. The pad before him on the desk was covered with calculations and his heart was pounding with excitement. When Vernon had named the sum the Hanson woman was thinking of sinking into the business, he'd been floored. *Gobsmacked*! His mind had been on overdrive ever since. What couldn't GPC do with that kind of input? Especially just now! It meant that the idea that had been in his mind ever since his visit to Lena was an actual possibility. This could turn out to be the biggest opportunity he'd ever been offered.

It would need to be handled carefully, of course, he told himself, drumming his fingers on the desk, especially in view of who the investor was, but the breathtaking idea that filled his mind eclipsed all his reservations. The thing was to get on with it. Strike while the iron was hot. No good dithering about till things went off the boil. If he waited for Harry and Vernon to ruminate over his idea and come up with all the inevitable objections it would be too late. Vernon he could easily sway. It was Harry who was the fly in the ointment. He was always so afraid to try anything new and daring. No, best to have all the loose ends tied up and put it to them both as a package – *a fait accompli*. After all, he was really only obliged to consult them over incurring debts, not investments.

A couple of confidential phone calls to his solicitor had reassured him on the few possible stumbling blocks and cleared up some vital queries. Now everything looked set fair. He rubbed his hands together gleefully. It couldn't be better. He buzzed his secretary.

'Ask Mrs Hanson to come in here, will you, Phyllis? And then see that I'm not disturbed for half an hour.'

He looked up when Joanna walked into the office. She was a damned good-looking woman right enough. No wonder Vernon was taken with her. But her money was far more attractive than her face and figure – to him at any rate. Better not let her think he was snatching her hand off though. The impression he would convey was that they were doing *her* a favour by letting her into the firm. He gave her his most affable smile.

'Have a seat, Mrs Hanson. Or may I call you Joanna?'

'Please do.' She sat in the chair opposite, crossing her shapely legs. She looked as cool as a cucumber. But then she had every right to.

Charlie leaned back. 'Vernon tells me you have some spare cash you'd like to invest with us. We feel very flattered that you have so much faith in the firm.'

'Does that mean you're accepting my offer?'

She didn't beat about the bush! But that was all to the good. 'In principal, yes,' he said cagily. 'Though there will be a few technicalities to iron out, of course. As a matter of fact I have a new project in mind and the input of fresh money could be a help.'

'The Meadowlands Park Estate, you mean?'

'Ah, no.' Charlie smiled and tapped the side of his nose. 'Better than that. Something even more ambitious. What I have in mind will finance Meadowlands and bring all of us a substantial income for many years to come,' he said. 'But I don't want to say anything further on the subject till my partners and I have had a meeting to discuss the possibility.'

'I take it that I will be invited to this meeting, Mr Grant?'

He glanced at her. One look into those calculating green eyes told him that she was not a woman to be trifled with. There was no pulling the wool over her eyes either. She already worked for Vernon and had access to the firm's books, so she was well aware of their delicately balanced financial situation. She knew exactly what she was doing right down to the last detail. He reminded himself to have a private word of warning in Vernon's ear about her. A woman like this could eat him for breakfast and be looking around for afters before he knew what had hit him. He cleared his throat. 'Is that what you'd like?'

'I'd go further than that, Mr Grant. In fact I'd like it to be perfectly clear from the start that unless I have an active partnership, the deal is off.'

Charlie gritted his teeth and kept the benign smile resolutely glued in place. 'I had thought a directorship . . .'

'I hardly think so, Mr Grant. Theoretically, any employee can be a director. With the kind of investment I'm prepared to offer . . .'

Charlie held up his hand. 'All right, lass. Fair enough. A partnership it shall be.'

'With the accompanying bonuses, reimbursements and expenses, of course. I would also like to be appointed Company Secretary,' she said coolly.'

Charlie's eyes bulged with astonishment. '*Oh*! I thought you'd want to give up your status as an employee?'

'Oh, no, Mr Grant. I have no intention of becoming some kind of sleeping partner. I would hope to play a much more useful part in the firm's running.'

Charlie was completely thrown. 'Well, I don't know . . .'

'You need have no worries. I can assure you that I am up to the job. You are aware of my experience in real-estate management.'

'I am. Yes.'

'And I have to say that I feel a partnership is a small return in view of the risk I'm taking.'

'You drive a hard bargain, lass.'

'Not at all.' Joanna smiled icily. 'I think it's best to put our cards on the table so that we know exactly where we each stand right from the outset, don't you?'

'Oh, by all means.' Charlie fiddled with the pencils in the pen tray on his desk. 'Er – in view of the terms you're asking for I shall have to speak to my son and my partner before I accept your offer, of course.'

'Really?' She looked surprised. 'Surely you're not obliged to do that, Mr Grant. As chairman of the company you are surely authorised to accept investements at your own discretion?'

'Ah . . .' Charlie coughed. 'Well, yes, of course you're right. I see we'll have a lot to discuss, Miss – er – Joanna. I'll call a board meeeting for tomorrow and introduce you then.'

'I shall need to be reassured on the terms before I attend any meeting, Mr Grant,' she told him. 'And I would also like to have prior knowledge of this new project you're planning before I make my final decision to invest. After all, it is a lot of money.'

He stared at her, momentarily rendered speechless. *Bloody cheek*! This woman was going to need very careful handling. He was half tempted to tell her what she could do with her money and chuck her out here and now. Then he remembered how much she was offering and the exciting plan already more than half worked out in his mind.

'As a matter of fact, you're the first person I've even mentioned it to,' he told her. 'Even Vernon doesn't know about it yet, and you want me to confide in you?'

She smiled. 'I'm afraid so, yes. You can be sure that it will be strictly between ourselves, especially if it's to be my money financing it.'

'Company money,' he corrected her. Nevertheless, he saw her point. 'All right then,' he said at last. 'Stay behind after work this evening and I'll tell you a bit about it. I'll agree to the terms you've mentioned, provisionally of course, and we'll work out the details of your partnership. But you must understand that your acceptance into the company must be above board. The whole thing must at least *appear* to be finalised at the meeting. Then, all things being equal, we'll get you registered and have my solicitor draw up an agreement.'

She smiled triumphantly. 'I knew you'd see it in a positive way, Mr Grant.'

'I'll see you here in my office after work then.' Charlie made a note on his pad and buzzed the intercom to let her know that the interview was at an end. No harm in reminding her that he was still the one in charge.

She stood up and came round the desk, offering her hand. 'Thank you, Mr Grant. I'm sure neither of us is going to regret the decision.'

He stood up, taking her hand briefly. 'I trust not, my dear. I trust not.'

He watched her walk from the room with resentment fermenting inside him like rising yeast. She'd got a bloody nerve, screwing him to the floor like that. But she'd got what he wanted so he was going to have to bite his tongue and make her look tempting to the others. It was going to take all the bravado he could muster.

Fleur stood in the draughty hallway at thirteen Victoria Gardens, the receiver of the payphone in her hand as she waited patiently. It was several minutes since the receptionist at The Ascot had gone to find Peter. It was a good job she had brought plenty of change with her. Any moment now her time would run out.

This was the third time she'd tried to ring him since Sally had mentioned his engagement. She kept telling herself that there had to be some simple explanation. Perhaps he hadn't told his mother that he had broken off the engagement. He seemed to keep his private life very much to himself. Maybe he had been putting it off, afraid that she would be disappointed – upset. There was a click at the other end and the receptionist's voice spoke.

'Miss Sylvester?'

'Yes, I'm still here.'

'I'm sorry but Mr Arden isn't answering his office phone or the one in his flat.'

168

'Oh, could you please try and find him for me?' Fleur begged. 'I've been trying to get him all week and it's very important.'

'Well, I'll try and find out whether he's in the hotel.'

She had only just gone when Fleur saw the digital readout flashing. Her time was up. She hastily put more money in before she was cut off. These pay phones seemed to eat the money.

'Having trouble, are you, dear?'

She turned and saw to her dismay that Ivy was standing at the top of the basement stairs, half hidden in the shadows, her eyes glinting with curiosity. 'No – just waiting,' she said. 'It's a long distance call. A private one.'

Impervious to subtleties, Ivy ignored the hint. In fact the news that the call was private only increased her curiosity. 'Oh, dear,' she said. 'You haven't had bad news, I hope?'

'No, nothing like that.'

The front door opened and Tom came in, bringing with him a gust of raw February air. His leather jacket was spattered with rain. He glanced at her and then at Ivy. 'Everything all right?'

'It's just Fleur,' Ivy said. 'She's making an important long distance call. Seems to be having a bit of trouble getting through.'

'I *am* through,' Fleur said through clenched teeth, her nerves shredded. 'I'm just waiting for – for the person I'm ringing to come to the phone.'

Summing up the situation, Tom walked to the top of the basement stairs and took Ivy's arm firmly. 'You were asking me to have a look at your television the other day,' he said. 'Why don't I come down with you now, before I take my coat off?'

They had just disappeared down the basement stairs when she heard the telephone click and Peter's voice at the other end made her heart leap with relief.

'Fleur? What's wrong? I was in a meeting.' He sounded irritable. 'Is there something wrong with Mother?'

'No, nothing like that. Sally's fine. I'm sorry, Peter, but I had to speak to you,' she said breathlessly. 'I've been trying to get you all week.'

'Yes?'

His abruptness made her feel tongue-tied. 'I – you didn't write,' she said lamely.

'I told you, I'm no good at putting thoughts down on paper. You haven't dragged me out of a meeting just to say that, surely?'

'No.' She took a deep breath. 'Peter, I think there's some kind of misunderstanding here. Your mother seems to think that you're engaged – getting married in April. To a Swiss girl called Lorraine.'

169

'Oh.' There was a small silence, then he said. 'So – what of it?'

Her heart turned to ice as she clutched the receiver. 'You mean – it's true?'

'Yes, it's true.' He sounded irritated. 'My mother would hardly have made it up, would she?'

'But I thought – I thought maybe there was some mistake – that she'd got hold of the wrong idea.'

'Look, I'm sorry if you think I should have told you, Fleur, but we had a great time together, didn't we?' he said. 'You surely didn't think there was any more to it than that?'

She swallowed. It was like a horrible dream. Soon she'd wake up and find it was all nonsense. 'But I *did*, Peter!' She felt her cheeks growing hot as the full implication of the situation hit her. 'Did you imagine I was the kind of girl who'd spend a weekend with just *anyone*?' Her mind was whirling with images of the two of them in that hotel room, naked in each other's arms – making frenzied, abandoned love, totally immersed in one another. And all the time it had meant nothing – less than nothing to him. He had simply been using her, amusing himself while his fiancée was absent.

'Fleur, look, let's be realistic about this. It was no big deal,' he was saying unbelievably in her ear. 'We both enjoyed ourselves, didn't we? You had a luxury weekend, good food and wine, a show. I thought you understood from the start that it was just fun – time out for us both.'

She could hardly believe what she was hearing. He made it sound as though it had been some kind of deal – sex in return for a good time. She opened her mouth to speak, but no sound would come from her constricted throat.

'For heaven's sake, Fleur,' he went on. 'Get real for God's sake! You got as much out of it as I did, so what are you complaining about? There's no harm done. We haven't hurt anyone.'

A dozen angry retorts sprang to her mind, but they all died before she could voice them. Clearly there was nothing she could say that would make any impression on him. He would not be interested in her hurt feelings and she was already too ashamed to risk more humiliation.

She took a deep breath to steady her voice. 'I'm sorry, Peter. We seem to have got our wires crossed. I don't want to be in your debt. I'll send you the money for my room and for the theatre ticket.'

'Oh, my God!' She heard him groan impatiently. 'Don't be so bourgeois. I don't want your money. It was fun – a laugh, that's all. Look, I think you're a great girl. You don't owe me anything.'

Her hand tightened round the receiver. The word 'bourgeois' had

170

stung her acutely. He probably thought she was too ignorant to know what it meant.

'A laugh. That's how you see it?'

'Yes, of course. Let's just remember it like that. I thought you were a modern, liberal-minded girl.'

'Let's face it, Peter, we both know what you thought I was.'

'You're over reacting,' he said coldly. 'But if you feel that way, it's your problem, not mine. And if I were you I wouldn't get any ideas about running to my mother and playing the wronged little innocent.'

'Don't worry. I think far too much of Sally to let her know what kind of man her son is!' Still shaking with anger she hung up and rested her burning forehead against the cold wall, feeling as though the pain inside her chest would suffocate her. She'd been a challenge to him, nothing more. She wouldn't sleep with him on their first date and he couldn't resist trying again to prove to himself how irresistible he was. And she had fallen for it, taken the bait like a fool. She could still scarcely believe she could have been so naive.

Another of Ivy's tenants came in, nodded 'good evening' to her and went on his way up the stairs. As soon as it was quiet again Fleur lifted the receiver and dialled the hotel's number again. When the receptionist answered she inquired what the cost of a weekend stay at The Ascot plus the cost of a theatre ticket. When the girl told her she caught her breath. It was more – much more than she had thought.

Upstairs in the flat she took out the tin in which she had been saving money for the balcony. Ever since she moved in she had been putting her spare change in the tin ready for the day when she would buy the paint, the hanging baskets and plants for what she thought of as her little corner of heaven. She sat on the bed and counted the money. It was about half what she needed. She would have to live cheaply all next month, but she was determined not to be in Peter Arden's debt. Hot tears stung her eyes and thickened her throat. She swallowed hard and dashed away the wetness with the back of her hand. She hadn't cried since Grandma died and she *wouldn't* cry for him. He wasn't worth it. But the hurt and humiliation wouldn't go away. It was worse than the shame and outrage of what had happened in the alley all those months ago in Hackney. At least her attacker had made his intentions to hurt and humiliate perfectly clear. That skinhead had had more integrity than Peter Arden, the first man she had trustingly given her love to. She had always thought herself streetwise, a good judge of character, yet it seemed she was more naive than a babe in arms.

171

At last she gave in and let the tears trickle unchecked down her cheeks. Keeling over sideways on the bed, she drew up her knees and wrapped her arms around herself until she was curled into a tight ball. What was it about her that made people see her as some kind of expendable commodity, to be used and tossed aside? Why did she appear so insignificant and worthless?

A sudden soft tapping on the door startled her. She sat up and brushed the tears from her face with her fingers. It would probably be Ivy, come to probe, having scented a juicy piece of gossip. She sat quite still. If she ignored her she might go away.

But a moment later the knock was repeated and Tom's voice said softly, 'Fleur, are you in there? Are you all right?'

She stood up and went across to the door, smoothing her hair as she went. 'Yes – yes, I'm fine.' Standing close to the door she sensed that he was still on the other side and after a moment's hesitation she unlocked it. Ivy had ears like a bat. If she heard them she'd be up in a minute herself. Opening the door a couple of inches she looked out at him. 'It's all right. I'm fine, really.'

He peered at her. 'You don't look it. What's wrong, Fleur? Can I do anything?'

She opened the door and let him in. 'I'm all right. But thanks for asking.' She made herself smile at him. 'Would you like a coffee?'

He stood looking at her, unconvinced, his eyes searching hers. 'Do you want to talk about it?'

She turned away to fill the kettle, busying herself with mugs and the milk bottle. 'It's just – oh, nothing really. A little disappointment, you could say. I'll get over it.'

'It's him, isn't it? Arden. He's let you down.'

She turned to look at him, her chin held high and her eyes dry. 'Not really. I read him wrong, that's all. I thought our relationship meant something – was worth more.'

'What's he done?'

She shrugged. 'He hasn't actually done anything. I found out that he's engaged – getting married in April.' She waved a hand at him as though to erase the angry expression from his face. 'No, Tom, it's *me*. People are more open-minded nowadays. I was brought up by my grandmother. She always believed that love was a precious gift that you only gave to someone special. I suppose that's just stuffy and old-fashioned nowadays.'

'I don't happen to think so.'

'I didn't understand that the time Peter and I spent together – what happened between us – was just meant to be for amusement.

172

I should have seen it for what it was and taken it lightly. It's my fault. I've been naive and stupid.'

'No, you haven't! Don't say that.' Longing to comfort her, he took a step towards her then stopped, his hands clenched at his sides. 'Look, I've always respected your privacy, Fleur, so I'm not going to force my company on you. I won't invade your space, but you know where I am if you need me. Right?'

She nodded. 'Thanks, Tom.' The kettle boiled and she made the coffee, handing him a mug, glad of something to keep him a few minutes longer.

As he sipped the hot brew he looked at her. 'Why don't you try to trace your real mother?' he said. 'I think you need to, Fleur. I think it's what you came here for, whether you realise it or not. And I don't think you're ever going to be really happy till you do it. You see, even if you don't actually contact her you'd . . .'

'I know who she is,' she interrupted.

He stared at her. 'You *do*? But how . . .?'

'By accident as it happens. I knew her maiden name, you see. We came face to face at a party we catered for just after Christmas. Sally was giving me the background of the guests there and Ju— her name came up.'

'And you're leaving it at that? You don't intend to take it further?'

She shook her head. 'She wouldn't want that, Tom.'

'There's no way you can know that for sure?'

She shook her head. 'It's obvious. She has a happy marriage, another daughter, a comfortable lifestyle. People look up to her.' She smiled wryly. 'If she was ashamed to own me all those years ago, just think how devastated she'd be if I suddenly turned up now!'

'Are you going to tell me her name?'

She shook her head. 'No, Tom.'

'You can't trust me – because I'm a newspaper man?'

'No. I'm not going to tell you because I'm determined to forget it. I need to build a life of my own. I want to be my own person. I can't do that if I have a shadow hanging over me.'

Tom drank the last of his coffee and put his mug down. 'I understand. At least, I *don't* but I do respect your decision.' He stood up. 'I meant what I said, Fleur. If you need me, just call. Goodnight.'

'Goodnight, Tom. And thanks.'

She sat for a long time just staring at the door. At that moment its closing seemed a kind of symbolic gesture. She had thrown away something valuable. Tom still cared about her as a friend, but she felt that the closeness, the tenderness that had started to blossom between them at Christmas, was dead. She herself had killed it, tossed it aside for something false and worthless just as her mother had tossed her aside all those years ago. The feeling of sadness and regret almost overwhelmed her. She had just said that she was determined to build an independent life – to be her own person. Well, she'd made a fine mess of things so far. Everything, all of it, was her own stupid fault. She'd got no more than she deserved. But at least she could try to learn from her mistakes.

The council meeting had gone well. The last item on the agenda had been Julia's proposal for the opening of a women's refuge in Victoria Gardens.

She had not been idle since the last meeting, spending the intervening time as usefully and productively as she could. On Eleanor's advice she had been careful to obtain all the information she could about opening a women's refuge. She had been to see Social Services and inquired into all the peripheral requirements: insurance, fire regulations and local by-laws. She had even been in touch with the owner of the empty property in Victoria Gardens. Communicating through the agent who was handling the house she had ascertained what the rent was likely to be. Now that the council had shelved their plan for redevelopment it could be a long-term proposition which would obviously make it more attractive to the owner.

The planning committee's site inspection team were unable to find any fault with the location and there had been no objections raised. Julia had even spoken to some of the local women's groups and persuaded them to donate furniture and help with the redecoration.

There were those on the council who were against the idea, some of them women, but when it came to a vote at the meeting she won with an easy majority, a vote that clearly had the approval of the spectators in the public gallery.

As usual the press was represented at the meeting and after the proceedings had been declared closed and the councillors had begun to leave the council chamber, a young man approached her.

'Mrs Grant, I'm Tom Markham of the *Elvemere Clarion*. I was very impressed with the way you put your case this evening. Will you give me a few words for my paper?'

Julia smiled. 'There isn't much I can tell you,' she said.

'I realise that. What I'm more interested in is the personal angle. This is obviously something close to your heart. Is there perhaps some special reason?'

174

Julia flushed. 'I represent the people who voted for me, Mr Markham. Some of those are women who have special needs that have not been provided for in our town. I believe it is time they were.'

'Do you expect to get overall support on this one, Mrs Grant?'

'I believe it's something close to the hearts of most women.'

'And yet there were women councillors who voted against it this evening.'

'Perhaps their comfortable lifestyles mean that they are not fully aware of the problem.'

'And you obviously are, in spite of your own lifestyle. Would you say that your own experience is what makes you a champion of these women?'

Julia looked into the clear eyes of this young man and suddenly saw herself reflected. What was it that made a comfortably off middle-class housewife feel so deeply committed to abandoned and badly used women and their children? The answer to that was firmly locked up in her own past and not to be dragged out for public scrutiny.

'It's a fact that in spite of all the principles upheld by the feminist movement, women will always continue to be very vulnerable in certain circumstances,' she said carefully.

He nodded, the eyes still on her, his pencil poised. 'Would you like to elaborate on that for me?'

Eleanor had warned her about charming young journalists who smiled and noted your remarks, only to distort and quote them grotesquely and damagingly out of context in their papers next day.

'Only to say that although women have won a lot of battles on the equality front, human nature hasn't changed much since time began,' she said. 'As long as woman is the sex that gives birth she will always have a weak spot in her armour. And as long as there are unscrupulous men to exploit that vulnerability, they will continue to take advantage of the fact.'

He raised an eyebrow at her. 'That sounds rather cynical, Mrs Grant. Would you describe yourself as a feminist?'

'Good heavens, no!'

'A man hater then?'

She laughed. 'Heavens above! Is that how I sound to you? I'd like to go on record as saying that I couldn't be more happily married. I have a wonderful husband and daughter and an ideal family life. It's that very thing that makes me appreciate that not all women are as lucky as me.'

'You have first-hand knowledge of the other side of the coin, obviously.'

She met his eyes without flinching. 'Yes.'

'So you'd say that it's a case of "there but for the grace of Go..."?'

'Of course I'd say that. Any compassionate woman could.'

Tom's pencil scribbled half a page of illegible hieroglyphics, then he looked up at her. 'Is there anything else you'd like to tell me about yourself, Mrs Grant?'

His engaging grin amused her. She found it impossible not to smile at his audacity. 'No, Mr Markham, I'm afraid there is not. I think that will have to be all for now.'

'Just one more thing. At the last council meeting you mentioned the lack of creche facilities that would enable local young mothers, single and married, to get back to work.'

'That's right, I did.'

'I was wondering, as a member of one of Elvemere's leading business families, are you hoping that Grant Philips Construction will back you up and lead the field locally in this?'

Julia flushed. 'That is something that I haven't discussed with my family yet. But I'd very much like to think that I could persuade the board of directors to think seriously about it.'

'Good.' Tom looked up with a persuasive smile. 'I have a photographer waiting outside. Could we have one shot for the *Clarion* – please, Mrs Grant?'

She shook her head. 'Oh, I don't think so. Not now.'

'I'm sure it would go a long way to help your cause,' he said persuasively. 'The people you are trying to help – and those who voted for you – would be reassured to see how hard you are fighting on their behalf. A picture would remind them of who they're reading about.'

'Well...' Julia hesitated. 'All right then. Just the one.'

The photographer was a young woman. Her dark hair was cropped close to her head and she wore motorcycle leathers and a gold nose stud. She was totally professional, brisk and efficient, knowing exactly what she wanted. She took several shots of Julia alone in the council chamber, sitting in her place, pen in hand, her papers spread out before her, then, with a word of thanks and a nod to Tom she was gone. A moment later Julia heard the roar of a motor cycle from the car park outside as she sped off to her next assignment.

She had begun to pack her papers back into her briefcase when

Tom asked her quietly. 'Obviously you have the vision to put yourself in the position of one of these vulnerable women, Mrs Grant.'

She stopped short and gave him a startled look, her heart suddenly quickening. 'What do you mean?'

'Exactly what I say. You are clearly an intensely sympathetic person, a woman with deep emotions and a strong social conscience. And you say that you have a daughter of your own. You must have felt for these women – imagined for yourself what it must feel like to be abandoned with a small child; left to bring up a baby alone?'

'Yes. Yes, of course I have.'

'Then perhaps you could describe for our readers the way it is.'

Julia took a deep breath. The room felt suddenly much too warm. She had brought this interview to an end once so just what was this persistent young reporter trying to get her to say?

'It isn't possible for anyone truly to know what that is like without having experienced it,' she said slowly. 'But I have met a young woman who is in the unfortunate position of being a single mother, abandoned by the father of her child who has since subjected her to threats and violence. So I do have some first hand knowledge through her.'

'Really? You wouldn't like to give me her name? Would she be willing to give me an interview?'

'No, Mr Markham, I certainly will not give you her name. And if you don't mind, I really would like to go home now.'

'Of course.' Tom flipped his notebook shut and slipped it into his pocket. 'Forgive me. I shouldn't have asked, though I would have made sure that she remained completely anonymous. Thank you for your cooperation, Mrs Grant, and good luck with your project.' He smiled disarmingly and held out his hand. 'Goodnight.'

After he had gone she went to the ladies' cloakroom for her coat. As she took out her comb and ran it through her hair she was shocked to realise that she was trembling. She stood for several minutes gazing at her reflection in the mirror. Of course she knew how it felt to be abandoned with a small baby. Who better? She was sincere in her desire to do her best for these women, but she had to admit to herself that her motives were not entirely selfless. In some obscure way she hoped to make good her past shortcomings – salve her conscience. But was it all going to get out of hand? Had she the courage to follow it through? Had she bitten off more than she could chew? The young reporter's direct questions had unnerved her and for the first time the icy finger of doubt sent a shiver down her spine.

177

'*Buy* Victoria Gardens ourselves! Instead of the council – all thirteen houses?'

'That's what I said. Yes.'

Harry Philips stared disbelievingly at Charlie Grant across the boardroom table. This was the first he'd heard of his partner's latest scheme. He cleared his throat and surreptitiously fingered his collar. For some time now he had had his doubts about Charlie's state of mind. There were times when his high-flown plans bordered on megalomania. He'd thought Meadowlands Park a touch too ambitious with its top-of-the-range executive homes complete with saunas and swimming pools, but this one went further than any of his past excesses. To take on the rebuilding of Victoria Gardens as well as Meadowlands looked dangerously like over-reaching.

'I really don't think that even with an injection of new money from this mystery investor . . .' he began. But Charlie waved both hands at him, his face almost obscured by the cloud of smoke emanating from his pipe.

'I've already looked into all that. The investor I mentioned is waiting outside at this moment and I'd like to invite her to join us at this point.' He rose from his chair and went to the door.

Harry turned an expression of outrage mingled with bafflement on Vernon and mouthed, 'What's all this about?'

He tried to look non-commital and reassuring at the same time, thankful that there was no opportunity for him to explain. His father returned with Joanna following in his wake. She wore a bottle green velvet suit and her auburn hair gleamed like a polished chestnut. She carried the gloss of confidence like an aura. Charlie indicated a chair for her and resumed his own seat.

'Mrs Hanson is here tonight for a special purpose,' he said. 'She is the person who has expressed a wish to invest some money in GPC. A very substantial sum of money. I outlined for her earlier what I have put to you at tonight's meeting and now the proposal is open for discussion.'

'Surely this is all most irregular?' Harry said boldly. 'Discussing an item on the agenda prior to the meeting with a person not even on the board? It's unheard of!'

'Mrs Hanson will automatically become a director of GPC as from today,' Charlie told him with a reproving glare. 'She will also be a full partner,' he added quickly. 'I think, Harry, that even you can hardly grudge her that when she is investing the sum of half a million pounds with us.'

'*Half a million* . . .' The rest of the sentence was smothered by

178

Harry's handkerchief as a coughing fit convulsed him. He looked at his son-in-law with watering eyes. 'Were you aware of this, Vernon?'

He fidgeted nervously. 'Well, I . . .'

'What does it matter? We all know now,' Charlie boomed. 'The important thing is how to use the cash most effectively. That is why I propose we put in an offer at once for Victoria Gardens while the opportunity is there, and put into operation ourselves what the council had in mind. That way all the profits will be ours.'

'It's a very risky project,' Harry said, shaking his head. 'Restructuring property as old as that. All kinds of problems could arise. Those houses are early-Victorian which means they'll be listed too. We wouldn't have a free hand in altering them.'

Charlie sighed. The objections were exactly what he had anticipated from Harry and they had all been brought up before. 'Nothing we can't cope with,' he said with a dismissive wave of his hand. 'I'm an experienced builder, remember, Harry. I'm prepared for things like that. As long as we leave the period façades unaltered, we can do what we want to the interiors.'

'I see. You've looked into all that too?'

'Yes. Don't worry. We'll take it all in our stride.'

'And in the meantime what about Meadowlands Park?' Harry asked. 'Do I take it that is to be shelved?'

'No. Meadowlands can go ahead using Mrs Hanson's investment,' Charlie said. 'The bank will give us a loan for the Victoria Gardens job. It's more gilt-edged than a housing estate – less of a gamble.'

'You seem to have researched all this very thoroughly,' Harry said. 'Haven't you taken a lot for granted? There's an awful lot for us to agree on and I'm not at all sure . . .'

Charlie waved an impatient arm. 'No good coming to a meeting with some half-cocked pie-in-the-sky idea, was it? I had to make sure it was workable first.'

'What about the bank loan?' Vernon asked. He'd been watching Joanna out of the corner of his eye. He was acutely aware that she was waiting for him to make a contribution. She'd already described him as a nodding dog. His father glared at him.

'What *about* the bank loan?'

'I take it you'd like me to get on to it at once?' He already knew that Bill Watts, the manager of Ffloyd's Bank, was in his father's lodge. He assumed that Charlie had already made sure no problems were anticipated. 'Do you want me to handle it?'

'I have made some tentative inquiries,' Charlie said guardedly. 'I think I can confidently say that the loan will be forthcoming. I'll let you know when I want you to set up a meeting with them to negotiate the terms. This scheme will be of enormous benefit to the town, especially now that the council has abandoned the scheme. Victoria Gardens has been rundown for years, getting more and more of an eyesore. This way it'll be a smart, functional area instead of a near slum. We shall provide upmarket dwellings and professional premises too. We'll be doing the town a service.'

'And you feel confident that the bank will lend the money even though we still have part of a previous loan outstanding?' Harry inquired.

'Yes, it will all be taken care of in due course,' Charlie said.

'It seems to me that an awful lot has already been taken care of behind everyone's back,' Harry said, his colour rising. 'And may I ask what kind of partnership arrangement is to be made with Mrs Hanson?'

'I was coming to that. Mrs Hanson is to become a full partner,' Charlie told him. 'With the usual entitlements. She will hold the same number of shares as the rest of us and the remainder of her investment will go as uncalled capital.' He cleared his throat. 'She will also become our Company Secretary as well as acting as Vernon's personal assistant.'

Harry looked at him askance. 'Company Secretary! May I be so bold as to ask at what salary?'

'Double what she is receiving now, plus a percentage of GPC's profits.'

All the colour drained from Harry's face. He'd picked up the atmosphere and heard the gossip around the office about Vernon and this Hanson woman. He hadn't believed any of it – till now. He took a deep breath and tried in vain to keep his voice steady. 'I see. So it's all cut and dried, is it? I'm sorry but I can't seem to remember a vote being taken on this. Can you, Vernon?' He coloured and looked away. Harry nodded. 'Ah! I see that you were in on all this too. It seems that I am the only one not to have been consulted.'

You're being consulted now, old lad,' Charlie blustered.

'Being *told*, you mean! It all smells very strongly of conspiracy to me. Well, I'm sorry but I'm not prepared to stand by and have you all ride roughshod over me. I must make a stand. I'm afraid I can't agree with any of it.'

'I don't have to ask the board when it comes to accepting an investment. I'm sure I don't need to remind you, Harry, that a limited company is structured for expansion. Anyway, you're out voted. Three to one.'

'Of course. You've already made sure of that.' Harry rose

unsteadily to his feet, the colour rushing back into his pale cheeks. 'In that case I have no alternative.' He gripped the edge of the table. 'For some time past I have had my doubts about the way this firm was being run. I respect your position as chairman, Charlie, but not when you persist in making decisions without putting them before the board in the proper way. You may be able to manipulate your son, but not me. Oh, no, not me. Not this time.' He walked stiffly to the door. 'You will receive my formal resignation first thing in the morning. Goodnight.'

As the door closed behind him Vernon turned an appalled face towards his father. 'Shall I go after him?'

But Charlie's face was unconcerned as he waved his pipe dismissively. 'Let him go,' he said scathingly. 'He's been a dead weight for years now. Time the silly old sod retired anyway.'

'Do you want me to go round to the house and talk to him?'

'No, leave it. If he crawls back tomorrow, all well and good. If not, well, so be it.'

'But what about his share of the business?' Vernon asked.

Charlie shrugged. 'We'll buy him out if that's what he wants,' he said. 'It's a damned nuisance but it can't be helped. We're better off without him, lad. Just forget it and let's get on with more important things.' He leaned forward. 'Victoria Gardens now. What I thought was that we could convert those top floors into luxury flats. They must have a glorious view over the park and the river. We'll install lifts of course. The two lower floors will be state of the art offices – maybe a couple of houses knocked into one will make a top-class health centre . . .'

'In other words, all the things the council had in mind,' Vernon put in.

Charlie grinned. 'And more, lad. Much more. For instance, I thought we could make a feature of that rubbish dump in the middle. A garden where folks could sit and enjoy the sunshine – with seats and flower beds, a fountain and maybe a statue or something tasteful in the centre.'

Vernon had a wild vision of a rotund facsimile of his father smiling benignly down on his *pièce de résistance*. He'd be after an OBE or a bloody knighthood next! For the first time he began to doubt the wisdom of the scheme.

'Yes, everything the council would've done.' Charlie went on with a satisfied smirk. 'Except that with Grant Philips Construction doing it, it'll be a hundred percent better! *And* the proceeds will be all ours.'

181

'Won't we be plain Grant Construction with Harry gone?' Vernon asked.

Joanna laid a hand on Charlie's arm and leaned forward to flash her most dazzling smile at him. 'Might I suggest Grant *Hanson* Construction?' she said innocently.

Julia had just taken off her coat in the hall when the telephone rang. She lifted the receiver.

'Hello, Julia Grant speaking.'

'Julia, it's Mum. Thank goodness you're in.' May sounded upset. 'Your father has just come home. He's in a terrible state. He's walked out – resigned.'

'*Resigned*? From GPC? You're joking!'

'Believe me, joking's the last thing on my mind. He walked out of the board meeting. Came home pale and trembling, looking like death. He frightened the life out of me. It's a wonder he didn't have an accident, driving home in that condition. I've just packed him off to bed. He won't tell me the full story, but it seems that Charlie and Vernon have taken on a new partner behind his back. He says they did it on purpose to force his resignation. He's absolutely devastated. Can you find out what's going on and let me know, Julia?'

'Vernon isn't home yet, but as soon as he comes in I'll ask him about it. Tell Daddy to try not to worry. I daresay it's all a storm in a teacup.'

'I'm afraid it's more than that. He keeps muttering something about Mrs Hanson. It seems she's putting some money into the firm. He says she's taking his place on the board, but that can't be right, can it? I thought she was Vernon's secretary.'

'Yes, she is.' Julia frowned. *Joanna*? 'Look, Mum, I haven't an idea what it's all about, and this is certainly the first I've heard about a new partner. Let me talk to Vernon and get back to you.'

'All right, dear. I'm sorry to worry you with it at this time of night, only your father is so upset. I'm just going to take him some brandy.'

'Tell Daddy to try not to worry. I'll be in touch first thing tomorrow. Try and get a good night's sleep. Things always look better in the morning. Goodnight.' Julia rang off. What on earth was going on? She knew Vernon wasn't home. His car hadn't been in the garage when she put hers away. She ran upstairs and tapped on Charlotte's door, but she wasn't home either. She sat down on the bed, suddenly aware that she had no idea where her husband or her daughter were. She remembered her words to the young reporter: *I couldn't be more happily married. I have a wonderful husband and daughter and an ideal family life.* God! It couldn't be further from the truth! Vernon and she lived virtually separate lives and as for her relationship with Charlotte, since the girl had left school it was like living with a stranger. Should she have allowed Vernon to push her into the firm when she clearly wanted a career with animals? Had she allowed him drive a wedge between her only daughter and her? The truth was, she'd been so busy trying to get her seat on the council at the time that she hadn't given it a thought one way or the other. No one had. They hadn't asked Charlotte what she wanted – hadn't really cared whether she was happy or not. And now they were reaping the result.

Walking slowly back downstairs she lifted the telephone and dialled Kath's number. When her sister-in-law's clipped tones replied she gave a sigh of relief.

'Kath, it's me, Julia. Is Charlotte there?'

'Yes, she came over straight from work to help me bed down the horses. She stayed on for supper and to watch the show jumping on TV. Is anything wrong?'

'No. It's just that I don't like her cycling all that way home in the dark.'

'That's all right, I'll bring her home in the Land Rover,' Kath said. 'I usually do anyway.'

Julia bit her lip. She hadn't even known that!

'I can put her bike in the back.' Kath was saying. 'Are you all right, Julia? You sound a bit upset.'

'No. It's just that I've had rather a day of it. And to top everything, Mum has just rung to say that Daddy isn't well. Some trouble at a board meeting upset him.'

'I'm sorry to hear that, love. Maybe he's sickening for something. There's an awful lot of 'flu about. People are at a low ebb at the end of winter, aren't they? I hope he'll soon be better. I'll bring Charlotte home as soon as the programme is over. I'm sorry you were worried. She really should have left you a note or something.'

'Thanks, Kath. Goodnight.' Julia put the telephone down with a sigh. None of them ever left notes for each other. Probably because none of them cared enough. With a pang of envy she pictured her sister-in-law and daughter relaxing together companionably over supper trays in front of the TV. Maybe she had never been cut out to be a mother.

Joanna lay with her head on Vernon's chest under the duvet.

'It was wonderful, wasn't it?' she sighed.

He knew she wasn't alluding to their recent lovemaking, but the meeting which had ended an hour ago. Her mind had been focussed on it ever since. 'You're pleased then?' he asked superfluously.

'Delighted.' She stretched her arms luxuriously. 'In fact I'm going to give a party to show just how delighted I am.'

'Party? Isn't that a bit over the top?'

'It'll just be for all you Grants and some of the senior staff,' she said. 'I'll have it here at home. You can bring Julia.'

He stared at her. 'You can't be serious?'

'It would look a little strange if I didn't invite her, wouldn't it, darling? Anyway, she's going to have to get used to sharing her husband with me now that I'm one of his business partners.'

Vernon shifted uncomfortably. 'I'd rather keep our relationship separate.'

'I really don't see how that's going to be possible.'

'Julia is going to be pretty upset about what happened to her father tonight.'

She raised herself on one elbow to look at him. 'He was getting on anyway, wasn't he? Coming up for retirement age?'

'Yes, but all the same, to go like this . . .'

Her eyes clouded. 'Well, of course if you feel you should be at home soothing her troubled brow, you'd better go.'

'It isn't that.'

'Then what is it?'

'You don't understand, Jo. Harry Philips has been Dad's partner ever since the firm expanded, ever since . . .'

'Ever since you and Julia got married and made it all possible?' Joanna supplied. 'What are you afraid of, Vernon? I expect Harry will still want to be a sleeping partner, but if he wants his share of the business he can have it. I can even lend the firm the money to pay him off if need be. When this Victoria Gardens development gets off the ground the firm will be in clover. We're right in the middle of a property boom, in case you hadn't noticed.' She looked at him. 'My God, I do believe you're afraid of Julia.'

'Of course I'm not!'

'Right then. If she doesn't like it, hard luck. What can she do about it?'

'Nothing, I suppose.'

'Then how about giving me all your attention for a change?' She cupped his face in both hands and kissed him, pushing him back against the pillows. 'I read somewhere that power was an aphrodisiac,' she murmured in his ear. 'And I'm just beginning to think there might be something in it!'

'You really should have let your mother know where you were,' Kath said as the Land Rover trundled along the bumpy drive from the stables.

'What does she care where I am?' Charlotte said truculently. 'Half the time she never even looks into my room anyway. Now that she's *Councillor* Mrs Grant she's got no time for me.'

'You don't really believe that, Charlotte,' Kath said, turning the vehicle on to the road. 'All mothers care about their daughters. You wouldn't like it if she was constantly poking her nose into what you were doing, would you?'

'I suppose not.'

'Of course you wouldn't. But you shouldn't cut yourself off from her all the same.'

'She's not interested.'

'Has it ever occurred to you that she might like it if you showed a little interest in *her* from time to time? When was the last time you asked her how her life was going?'

The girl beside her sighed. 'Okay, but it isn't as simple as you think. You should have been my mother, Aunt Kath. You and I have far more in common than Mum and me. And as for Dad . . .'

'Your dad wants the best for you.'

'He wants the best *out* of me, you mean,' Charlotte said bitterly. 'He's never forgiven me for not being a boy. And Granddad has never forgiven him and Mum for not producing one. Sometimes I wish there was no family firm. I wish I had sisters and brothers and that Mum stayed at home all day cooking lovely meals instead of rushing out to Marks and Spencer's at the last minute for something quick for tea. I wish that Dad went to work in a factory, a shop, a *coalmine* – anything so that we could live a normal family life like other people.'

Kath laughed. 'Other people's lives always look better than your own. I often wonder if there's any such thing as a normal family? Let me ask you something. When you're married, will you want to spend your entire life in the kitchen? Especially when your family hardly notice your existence.' She looked at the girl. 'Try and talk to your mother, Charlotte.'

'I would if she was ever there.'

'There must be plenty of times when you're both there. You're important to her, believe me. She's lucky to have you. You're lucky to have each other.' Kath glanced at her niece's wistful face. 'Promise me something – promise you won't ever use me to get at her?'

Charlotte looked shocked. 'I wouldn't do that!'

185

'Oh yes you might – without realising. You're always welcome at the stables, you know that. But come because you want to, not as some kind of rebellion.'

Charlotte grinned. Sometimes Aunt Kath could almost read her mind. 'I love working with you at the stables. I'll always want to come, you know that. But okay, I promise.'

They were driving along the Merifield Road and suddenly Kath turned left into a road of smart modern houses. 'We'll nip through here,' she said. 'It cuts off the traffic lights and the town centre. I've found you can save about ten minutes by taking this shortcut.'

The houses were neat and the road well-lit. Charlotte looked out with interest. 'This is Hazel Grove. Joanna Hanson lives down here somewhere,' she said. 'She's Dad's PA. The girls in the office call her Joanna the Hun. She's always trying to get round me, telling me how she and Mum were at school together and what fun they had. But since I've made sure she knew that I wasn't going to suck up to her, she's treated me like the other girls in the office. They all think she's an absolute *cow* with that awful put-on American accent of hers. She's unbearably bossy and she has a vile temper. Do you know, she hasn't been working for the firm for five minutes and already she's had the cheek to . . .' She broke off as she saw a familiar silver BMW parked in the drive of one of the houses. 'Hey, that looks like Dad's car.'

'Surely not? Where?' Kath slowed down and as she did so the front door of the house opened and two people came out. In the shaft of light spilling out through the open door Kath could clearly see that the woman wore a dressing gown. As they drove past she reached up to wind her arms around the man's neck, standing on tiptoe to kiss him. Kath caught her breath and pressed her foot down hard on the accelerator, hoping to speed past before Charlotte recognised Vernon.

They drove on in silence for a few minutes, then Kath stole a glance at her niece. The girl's face was white with shock.

'Did you see?' she whispered.

'There's probably a very innocent explanation,' Kath began unconvincingly.

'There's an explanation all right,' Charlotte said bitterly. 'My father is a cheat. I've suspected it for a long time and now I've seen the proof.'

186

Chapter 10

It was just after midnight when Vernon arrived home. Julia was waiting in the sitting room. When she heard him stealthily crossing the hall she got up and opened the door. 'Vernon.'

He stopped halfway up the stairs to look down at her. 'Julia! You startled me. You shouldn't have waited up.'

'What happened at the meeting, Vernon?'

'Happened?'

'Don't look so surprised. You must have realised that Mum would ring me. Daddy is in a terrible state. She was dreadfully worried about him. She said something about his resigning.'

He shrugged. 'Oh, it was a storm in a teacup. You know board meetings. There was a bit of a disagreement. It'll blow over.'

'I don't think so. By the sound of things it was a lot more serious than that. He's extremely upset, Vernon. Is it true that you've taken Joanna Hanson into partnership?'

'She's investing quite a lot of money with the firm. Dad's repaying her with a partnership. Nothing wrong with that, is there?'

'It must be a substantial sum.'

'It is.'

'So if she's got that kind of money to invest, why GPC?'

'Why not? She said she'd like to invest in the firm she works for. She has faith in us.'

'Evidently! So – if it's as straightforward as that, why is Daddy so upset?'

Vernon sighed. 'Look, Ju, it's late. And let's face it, company business is not exactly your strong suit, is it? Let's get some rest now and I'll try and explain it to you over breakfast.'

'No, now, Vernon.' She held the door of the sitting room open and stood back. 'I want you to explain it to me now. I need to understand what's going on. It's my father who is involved, don't forget.'

With a resigned sigh he followed her into the room and sat down. 'Your father is annoyed because he wasn't consulted at an earlier stage,' he said. 'That's all there is to it. Jo sounded me out first because she works for me. That was only natural. I spoke to Dad and he worked the whole thing out with Jo before he put it to a meeting. But only because he wanted to be sure it was workable so as not to waste everyone's time. Unfortunately Harry saw it as some kind of conspiracy. He wouldn't wait to hear an explanation.'

'And that's all it was?'

'Absolutely.' He shook his head. 'Your father has been looking very tired these last few months, Ju. Maybe you should persuade him that it's time he put everything on hold and took an extended holiday. When he's feeling more himself he'll probably see things more rationally.'

Julia paused. She had to agree that her father had been looking strained lately. Maybe there was something in what Vernon said. She decided to go round and see her parents in the morning and try to smooth things over – persuade them to take a holiday somewhere warm and sunny. She looked at Vernon. 'Right. So Joanna is to become a partner. Obviously she won't want to remain as your secretary?'

'Personal assistant,' he corrected. 'Yes, she does want to carry on, as a matter of fact. She'll be holding the position of Company Secretary as well from now on. She has a real interest in the firm and a flair for the business too. She's a definite asset.'

'I see. I'm glad,' she said dryly. She gave him a hard look. 'I take it you and she have been celebrating?'

He coloured slightly. 'No. What makes you say that?'

She glanced at her watch. 'The time for one thing. The lipstick on your collar for another.'

His hand went guiltily to his collar. 'Oh, that. I daresay there's some on Dad's collar too. She was excited – you know, elated. It's been quite a night for her.'

'I can imagine.' Julia got up and walked into the hall, starting to go upstairs without another word. Board meetings never lasted this long, even given that this one had been out of the ordinary. It was clear from Vernon's demeanour that he had been with Joanna. He reeked of guilt – and of her perfume again. It seemed that little by little she was gradually insinuating herself into their lives and it looked as though there was little Julia could do about it.

'Charlotte in?' Vernon asked as they reached the landing.

'Yes, she's in bed. Asleep too by this time, I should hope.'

Charlotte had arrived home looking pale and preoccupied. Kath hadn't stopped for coffee or a chat, but had driven straight off after taking Charlotte's bicycle out of the back of the Land Rover. In the hall the girl had looked at her mother, then suddenly thrown her arms around her neck and hugged her.

'Darling! Are you all right?' Julia had asked, holding her at arms' length and searching her face. Charlotte was not normally given to displays of emotion, but she just shook her head, saying that she was tired, and went straight upstairs to bed. It had been a night of unusual and inexplicable happenings, Julia told herself as she undressed. Bewildering and exhausting. Her euphoria over winning the battle for the women's refuge was almost forgotten. So far none of her family even knew – or seemingly cared – about her victory.

But their ignorance was not to last for long.

The first reaction came with a telephone call from Charlie at eight o'clock the following morning. Julia had just come down when the telephone in the hall began to ring. She picked it up immediately.

'Elvemere 58498.'

'Julia?'

Recognising her father-in-law's voice she said, 'Oh, good morning, Charlie. I'll get Vernon.'

'No! It's *you* I want!' Charlie bellowed down the telephone. 'What the *hell* do you mean by it, eh?'

'I'm sorry. Mean by what?'

'Don't come the innocent with me, girl! All this crap in the *Clarion* this morning, that's what! All this twaddle about a women's refuge in Victoria Gardens. What the hell do you think you're playing at?'

'A refuge is badly needed, Charlie. I don't see why it need affect you.'

'Well, you bloody soon will! And what about this hare-brained notion about a creche at GPC? First I've heard of it, but then I'm only the managing director!'

'I was speaking off the cuff. But you must admit that it is a good idea?'

'Oh, *is* it? Well, thanks for telling me. I'm supposed to start providing for unmarried mothers and their brats now, am I? You'll have me changing nappies next! If you ask me, I think you're getting too big for your britches, madam!'

Julia winced and held the receiver away from her ear. 'I'm not deaf. There's no need to shout. There's no need to be coarse either,

Charlie. I think that as one of the largest business concerns in the town, we should set an example.'

'*We*? Who's this *we* when it's at home?' Let me tell you something, girl. You didn't get the lifestyle you enjoy today by my behaving like some kind of charity! And the running of GPC is nowt to do with you anyway, so just keep your opinions to yourself!'

'Really? I was under the impression that this was a family firm . . .'

'Not *your* family. Not any more,' he interrupted. 'Your father – the Philips half – opted out as from last night. Anyway, never mind bloody creches. It's Victoria Gardens that bothers me. How far has this refuge garbage gone? Tell me that.'

'It's under negotiation at the moment, but as the council have agreed I can't see why it shouldn't go ahead as soon as we can get up and running. And I honestly don't see why you're so upset.'

'You don't, eh? Well, perhaps you'd better ask Vernon just how it will affect me – and you too in the end! Go ahead with this and you'll be taking the bread and butter out of your own mouth, woman. Maybe even jeopardising your daughter's future too! So *think on*!'

There was a loud clatter as Charlie banged down the receiver and Julia was left staring into the receiver, her ear still singing from his vociferous assault.

In the morning room the table was laid for breakfast, but neither Charlotte nor Vernon was down yet. Tracey had already arrived and had picked up the morning papers from the front doormat and put them on the table. Julia saw that the *Clarion* was open at page two and there, staring up at her, was her own picture. The headline read,

NEW COUNCILLOR CHAMPIONS BATTERED WOMEN.

Below was an account of the council meeting and Julia's successful result. The article went on to say that plans had been passed for number six Victoria Gardens to be refurbished as a women's refuge. There then followed some of her comments as made to the young reporter. '*Although happily married with a young daughter, Councillor Mrs Grant is obviously a champion of single mothers,*' it read. '*A sympathetic and compassionate woman, she identifies strongly with their plight and in spite of some local opposition has vowed to see that Elvemere leads the field in seeing that they receive a fair deal. As the daughter-in-law of Mr Charles Grant of Grant Philips Construction she says that she intends to arrange for her family firm to set an example by opening Elevmere's first free industrial creche*

190

so that the young single mother can get back to work without her income being eroded by the necessity of paying for child-minders.'

'You've seen it then? Good for you. It's a really good photo, isn't it, Mrs Grant?' Tracey stood in the doorway, the vacuum cleaner in her hand. 'I hope you didn't mind me reading it.'

Julia looked up. 'No, not at all, Tracey. I told you I'd do my best and I will, but I'm afraid that even now we're going to encounter some opposition.' She smiled. 'Never mind. We expected that, didn't we? Where is Damian?'

'Asleep outside in his pram. It's quite warm this morning,' Tracey said. 'Feels like spring's on the way at last. All right if I get on with the sitting room, is it?'

'Yes, of course.' Julia sat down and poured herself a cup of coffee, reading the article through again. Would Charlie really do anything to stop her? Why was he so angry? Would he refuse to open a creche for mothers with small children who wanted to get back to work? It was true that his workforce was predominantly male, but there were women working in the office and in the canteen too. She knew for a fact that several of them left their children with minders. It need only be a small creche, easily staffed. She would organise it herself if only Charlie would agree.

Charlotte appeared. She still looked pale. She took a slice of toast and buttered it, still standing.

'Are you all right darling?'

'I'm fine.' Charlotte avoided her mother's eye as she took a bite of the toast.

'Why don't you take a day off? You're looking a bit peaky.'

'No, I can't.' Tracey switched off the Hoover and Vernon could be heard coming downstairs. Charlotte stopped eating. 'Look, Mum, I've got to go. I'll take this with me.' She pushed the rest of the toast into her mouth and made for the back door.

Julia called after her, 'Charlotte! Don't run off like that. You haven't even had a drink of . . .' But she was too late. Even as she spoke she heard the door slam.

'Was that Charlotte?' Vernon asked as he came into the room.

'Yes. She said she was in a hurry.'

'Who was on the phone?'

'Your father. He was annoyed – well, no furious is more like it.' She pushed the paper across the table towards him. 'Apparently because of this.'

Vernon scanned the article briefly, then, his mouth sagging with disbelief, he read it through again more slowly. When he had finished he looked up at her, his eyebrows almost meeting in a

191

frown of horror. 'Are you completely *mad*? My God! No wonder Dad was annoyed. You realise what you've done, don't you?'

'Only that I'm hoping to provide a much-needed service,' Julia said calmly. 'I can't see what all the angst is about. I grant you that I should probably have mentioned the creche before, but it only occurred to me when I was talking to the reporter. I . . .'

'Sod the *creche*! You've only thrown a spanner into the works of Dad's latest pet scheme.'

'What scheme?'

'Now that we have Joanna's investment, he's planning to buy Victoria Gardens and refurbish it in much the same way as the council intended.'

She stared at him. 'As a speculation, you mean? But isn't that a bit of a risk? Not to mention a costly project.'

'You're right on both counts. But Dad is confident that it's just what GPC needs to put us among the most highly acclaimed in the construction business. There could even be an award for the project. Conservation and design, that kind of thing. Plus the fact that it'll send his stock soaring locally. But if you go and tie up one building out of the thirteen . . .' He peered at the article again. 'Number *six*, it says here. Christ! That's slap bang in the middle of the terrace. It would render the whole scheme a total impossibility! What respected firm of accountants or solicitors would rent an office next door to one of these women's refuge dumps? Squalling kids and shouting matches going on all day.'

Julia shook her head impatiently. 'It won't be like that. And it won't be a dump. If you ever discussed the firm's business with me I'd have known about all this before I started. As it stands now, I was in first so why should I stand down?'

Vernon buttered a piece of toast, momentarily silenced. He could hardly tell her that he had only heard of the plan himself at last night's meeting. It would make him look as weak as Harry where his father was concerned. 'You've never been interested in the firm before,' he said morosely.

'How would you know that? As it happens I would have enjoyed working with you once Charlotte started school – as your secretary, personal assistant, anything. I was never offered the opportunity.'

'Julia! Let's face it. You've neither the qualifications or the aptitude for that kind of job,' he said scathingly. 'You married me virtually straight out of school.'

'That's not to say I couldn't have learned. I didn't leave my brain at the altar steps along with my name, you know.'

He shook his head. 'We've had all this out before. Dad doesn't believe in wives getting involved. You're just annoyed because Joanna has the job and now a stake in the firm too. She's got a fabulous head for business.' He looked at her. 'From what I can make out, you and she were always rivals as young girls.'

'Oh, she told you that, did she? You've discussed me?'

'No, of course not. It was just in passing.'

Julia got up and began to clear the table. 'Isn't it time you went to the office?' she asked dismissively.

Vernon looked at his watch and sighed. He wasn't looking forward to the coming interview with his father, knowing that he would be in the line of fire for Julia's actions. 'Look, Ju, there must be plenty of other empty houses in the town. Couldn't you find somewhere else for this refuge place?'

'No!' She looked at him, her face alight with determination and her mouth set in a firm line. 'The plans have been passed for this one. Charlie might be able to make you dance to his tune, Vernon. But after the way my father has been treated – and the way Charlie spoke to me this morning on the phone – I intend to have my way over this.'

Her election win and her council work had proved to her that she didn't always have to stand down and give way to others as she had in the past. She had already seen that people had begun to respect her for standing firm. And she was damned if she was going to give in over this, her first real victory. She wasn't prepared to take any more brow beating from Charlie either. This time he'd gone one step too far.

Speechless with surprise, Vernon stared at her back as she walked out of the room. Julia had always been so compliant. He'd never seen her in this mood. But he had to find some way to make her change her mind. If he didn't, his life at work wouldn't be worth living.

He stood up, wiping his mouth with his napkin. 'You're right. I'd better go. Maybe we can talk about this later.'

'Maybe,' she said over her shoulder. 'Not that talking will do any good.'

When Vernon arrived at Joanna's house he saw from his watch that it was already after nine. As he rang the bell and waited on the porch he wondered if she had already left for the office. But when she answered the door to him it was clear that she wasn't going in. She still wore her dressing gown and her head was swathed in a towel.

'Vernon!' She looked slightly put out. 'I can't stop now, I'm afraid.

I'm in a hurry. Charlie and I are seeing the firm's solicitor this morning, then I've got an appointment with my bank manager. Later on I've got that Arden Catering woman coming to talk about the arrangements for the party.'

'This won't take long,' he said tetchily, pushing past her into the hall. 'It's a bit more important than parties. Something's come up that I think I should warn you about.'

With ill-concealed irritation she closed the front door. 'What can possibly have come up overnight that's so important?'

'This for a start.' Vernon picked up the *Clarion* from the hall table. It was still folded and Joanna obviously hadn't looked at it. He shook it open and held it under her nose. 'Julia is planning to open a women's refuge, right in the middle of Victoria Gardens. The plans were passed at a council meeting last night. When Dad read about it this morning the proverbial hit the fan in a big way, as you can imagine.'

Joanna was staring at the headline and photograph of Julia on the front page. 'Christ! I can imagine.' She looked at him. 'But surely if you just explain she'll back down and find somewhere else?'

'I wish you were right!' He sighed. 'Unfortunately Dad got in first while his temper was still at boiling point. Tact is hardly his strong suit at the best of times. He really blew his top at her and now she's digging her heels in and refusing to back down.'

'She'll give in in the end. Shall I have a word with her?'

Vernon gave her a wry smile. 'I hardly think that would help, do you? She's pretty sore about her father's resignation and your part in it.'

'My part? I had nothing to do with his resignation.'

'You were the cause of it – indirectly.'

'Oh?' Her eyebrows rose indignantly. 'Well, in that case, maybe I should withdraw my offer!'

He sighed. 'Don't be silly. You know I didn't mean that. I'm just trying to make you see it from her point of view.'

Joanna looked at the hall clock. 'Look, Vernon, I really can't spare the time to talk about it now. I'm going to have to hurry. All this is trivial – a storm in a teacup. We'll think of something to make Julia change her mind. It shouldn't be that difficult. I'll talk to Charlie about it when I meet him.' She pecked his cheek briefly, took him by the shoulders and gave him a push towards the door. 'Off you go now, and try not to worry. Everything is going to be just fine.'

194

When Charlotte spotted Fleur standing at the bus stop her heart leaped with hope. Seeing her unexpectedly like this was like the answer to her prayers. She waved frantically and shouted.

'Hi, Fleur! Haven't seen you for ages. Not since that party at New Year. How are you?'

Fleur smiled. 'I'm fine. How's college?'

The other girl jumped off her bicycle and pulled the machine off the road on to the pavement. 'Crummy as ever,' she said disconsolately. 'Like work.'

'Go on, I bet you're getting the hang of it all nicely by now.'

The smile left Charlotte's face. 'As a matter of fact, life's just one big pain in the bum right now.' She paused. 'Fleur – look, I'm glad I've seen you. I was going to come round to your place later for a chat.'

'Were you?' Fleur was taken aback. 'Well, that would be nice. I've got a flat now, with my own kitchen and everything. I've decorated it since I moved in. I'd love you to come and see it.'

'A flat – where?'

'It's the same address.' Fleur looked at the girl's troubled expression. 'Was there some special reason you wanted to see me? There's nothing wrong, is there?'

'Yes, there is as a matter of fact.' Charlotte sighed. 'I haven't really got any friends, you see. Not real friends. At least none that I could talk to. Not about this. You don't belong here in Elvemere and you're not connected with my family or anything so I feel I can confide in you.' She smiled, a wry, apologetic little smile. 'I hope you don't mind? It sounds an awful cheek put like that, sort of like making a convenience of you. If you think it is, just say.'

'I don't think it's a cheek, and I'd love you to come round.' Fleur looked up as the bus arrived and pulled into the layby. 'Look, come this evening if you like – around seven. It's thirteen Victoria Gardens – flat two.' She jumped on to the bus platform and turned to wave. Charlotte waved back as she remounted her bicycle.

'Thanks, Fleur. See you.'

She found a seat, paid her fare and settled down to think about the brief conversation she had just had with Charlotte Grant. The girl had looked so worried. What on earth was it she wanted to talk to her about? The irony of her remark suddenly struck Flew. *You don't belong here in Elvemere, and you're not connected with my family.*

Maybe she should not have encouraged the girl to visit her. Perhaps it was a mistake to get involved. What would she say if she knew that there was indeed a very strong connection between them

– that Fleur was in fact her half-sister? Strangely enough the irony of their relationship had not struck Fleur until this moment. It was odd; they were related and yet they were not. A sister was someone you'd known all your life – someone who shared the same parents. In all probability Charlotte had never even heard of Dean Sylvester and certainly knew nothing of the segment of her mother's life which included him. All the same the relationship, tenuous as it was, could not be denied and it gave her a totally new view of the younger girl.

They were not at all alike. Charlotte was small and fair, the very opposite to her. Julia's second daughter took after her. No one would ever connect Fleur Sylvester with Julia Grant – which was just as well, she told herself, because there was no way she would ever want them to. And yet, she felt a sudden protective affinity with the young girl who was her half-sister, wondering why she was so unhappy. She made a silent vow to help in whatever way she could.

Standing in the hall of Sally's house, taking off her coat, she heard her employer on the telephone. As she walked into the office Sally was just putting the receiver down.

'That was Mrs Hanson,' she said, looking up. 'You remember, the PA lady from Grant Philips? She wants to arrange a party for next week. I said you'd go along and discuss menus with her.' She scribbled the address on the pad and tore off the top sheet, handing it to Fleur with a smile. 'You can handle this one on your own. See how you get on.'

Fleur looked at the address. 'Hazel Grove. Those are the nice houses off the Merifield Road, aren't they? Is she having the party at home?'

'Yes. It's to be a fairly small affair, colleagues from work and a few friends. She hasn't decided yet whether to make it a dinner party or a buffet. You can talk to her about that. I've made an appointment for twelve-thirty. She'd like you to be on time as she has to be at the office for two.'

Fleur arrived at the house in Hazel Grove with five minutes to spare. She parked the van in the driveway and walked up to the glazed porch. As she waited for Joanna to answer her ring at the bell she looked down at herself regretfully. If she'd known that Sally was going to send her out on a preliminary visit she would have worn make-up and put on something more business like; as it was she was wearing jeans and a heavy sweater, her hair tied back in a loose knot. Sally had assured her that she looked fine, but remembering Mrs Hanson's consistently well-groomed appearance, Fleur doubted whether she would agree.

Her doubt was confirmed when Joanna opened the door and stared at her coldly. 'Yes? What is it?'

'I'm from Arden Catering,' Fleur nodded towards the van which had the name painted on the side in large letters.

'Oh?' Joanna looked her up and down. 'I was expecting Mrs Arden herself.'

Fleur felt resentment at the woman's arrogant manner, but she forced a smile. 'I'm Fleur Sylvester, her assistant. I think you'll find me efficient,' she said briskly. 'Mrs Arden and I work very closely together.' She held up the briefcase in which she carried the file of menus, the order book and diary. 'I think you said you had a limited time to spend, Mrs Hanson. Shall we get started?'

Clearly taken aback by Fleur's businesslike manner, Joanna held the door open. 'Yes – yes, of course. Come in.'

In the living room she offered Fleur a comfortable chair and seated herself opposite. 'I'll show you the other rooms in a moment,' she said. 'I'm undecided whether to have a dinner party or a buffet with cocktails.'

Fleur took out her notepad. 'What kind of party is it to be?' she asked. 'Some kind of celebration – birthday, anniversary? Or is it a business affair?'

'Both, really.' Joanna smiled and seemed to relax a little. 'Though quite informal. As a matter of fact, it's to celebrate my promotion with my firm.'

'I see. That would be Grant Philips Construction?'

Joanna's eyebrows rose. 'You know?'

'We did the catering for your Christmas lunch.'

'Ah, of course.' Light dawned on Joanna's face. 'I remember you now. I didn't recognise you in those – er – clothes.'

'So you'll be inviting your colleagues from work?'

'Fellow management,' Joanna corrected with a little smile of triumph. 'I've just been made a director.'

'I see. Congratulations. Your fellow directors then. How many would that be? And are there to be any other guests?' She reflected that if Joanna was going to need drawing out like this, she was likely to be here all afternoon.

Joanna crossed her perfect legs and smiled smugly. 'I'd like to make a magnanimous gesture and invite all the senior members of the workforce,' She said. 'Foremen, salesmen, negotiators and so on. I've been counting them up and it comes to about twenty altogether.'

197

'In that case I would recommend a buffet with drinks,' Fleur suggested. 'Twenty would be rather a lot round a dinner table at one time. Besides, if you're going to invite people from different levels of the firm, it might be better if you were free to circulate among them. That way no one will feel awkward and out of their depth.'

Joanna looked impressed. 'Of course. How clever. Why didn't I think of that?' She got up. 'Let me show you the conservatory. I think that might be the perfect place to lay out a buffet.'

After Fleur had approved the conservatory they sat down again and she opened her briefcase. 'I can show you the selection of menus we have for buffets,' she said. 'They are all worked out at so much per head, including wines. Spirits and other drinks are extra, the amount being up to you. Unless you want to provide your own, of course. We also hire out glasses and cutlery at a small extra charge, and extra stacking chairs. But we bring trestle tables, tablecloths, candles and table flowers as standard.'

'I see. It all sounds very suitable indeed.' Joanna looked at the selection book Fleur passed her, which was illustrated with coloured photographs. She studied them all carefully and then turned back to the most expensive.

'I'll have this one,' she said. 'I want to launch my new status with the firm in the most appropriate way.'

Fleur interpreted this as making an ostentatious impression. In other words, showing off. But it was none of her business. She was just delighted that she was getting a good order. She added up the cost of Joanna's total requirements on her calculator and passed her the estimate. Joanna glanced at it briefly and nodded.

'Thank you. That will be absolutely fine.'

Fleur smiled and made a note of her client's choice on her pad.

They settled the date – a Saturday evening two weeks ahead and Fleur closed her pad and slipped everything back into her briefcase. 'I think that's all for the moment then, Mrs Hanson.' She stood up. 'We'll send you a detailed invoice through the post in the normal way and if you'd just confirm it in writing, giving us a close estimate of the number of guests?'

'Of course, naturally. And thank you very much for your advice.' Joanna looked at her watch. 'It's taken less time than I expected. Please, won't you join me for a drink before you go?'

Fleur shook her head. 'I'm driving, thank you.'

'A coffee then. I'm going to have one before I go to the office. The kettle has boiled. Please join me, Miss – er – I'm sorry but I've forgotten your name?'

'Sylvester. Fleur Sylvester.'

'Of course.' Joanna had not forgotten the name at all, she just wanted it confirming. The moment the girl had given it, it had rung a distant bell at the back of her mind. It wasn't a name one heard every day and it brought back memories. 'Of course, *Fleur*.' She smiled. 'May I?'

'Yes – please do.'

'And you will have a quick coffee, won't you? It's chilly outside and you must have fitted me in in your lunch hour.'

'Well all right then. Thank you.'

During her brief absence Fleur pondered over the woman's change of mood. She was certainly a lot less frosty than when she'd opened the door.

When Joanna returned and put the tray down between them on the coffee table Fleur caught her looking curiously at her. 'You're not local, are you, Fleur?'

'No. From London. I've been here since last autumn.'

Joanna handed her a cup of coffee and sat down opposite again. 'Your name – it's quite unusual. I once knew someone of that name. He played the guitar with a pop group called The Sylvas.' She smiled. 'Oh, long before your time of course. Dean Sylvester was his name.'

Fleur's eyes widened in surprise. 'You knew him? He was my father.' The words were out before she had time to think.

'*Really*?' Joanna was smiling. 'How extraordinary. How is he? What is he doing these days?'

Fleur hid her face in her cup. 'When I say that he's my father it's true, but I never actually knew him. He and my mother parted before I was born. He died in America; some years ago.'

'Oh, how sad! So – your mother brought you up alone?' Joanna's eyes glittered in an almost predatory way and Fleur suddenly sensed that she was on thin ice. She looked at her watch and put her cup down on the coffee table.

'I'm afraid I'll have to go now, Mrs Hanson,' she said, gathering up her things. 'I have another appointment in ten minutes and it's on the other side of town. Thank you for the coffee. As I said, we'll be in touch.'

'Of course. I mustn't keep you.' Joanna went to the door with Fleur and saw her out. As the van backed out of the drive and drove away she stood watching thoughtfully. There was more to that girl than met the eye. There was no doubt that she was telling the truth when she said that she was Dean Sylvester's daughter. She was the absolute image of him; the same flashing dark eyes,

199

tumbling black hair and honey-coloured skin. But who was her mother? Why had the girl clammed up at the mention of her, and, what was much more to the point, why had she left London to come here to a backwoods town like Elvemere?

She closed the door and went upstairs to collect her coat. Standing on the landing she allowed her mind to drift back to that pop festival on the Isle of Wight. She recalled the year 1970 – remembered so clearly Julia's passionate crush on the handsome young guitarist and her uncharacteristically wild and defiant behaviour in running off with him. Fleur looked about the right age. It all fitted. Although Joanna had been jealous at the time, she'd kept her mouth shut when she came home about where Julia really was. In truth she'd rather lost interest once she began her fiery and exciting affair with Vernon. But, thinking about it, maybe it was providential that she'd remained silent at the time. A pound to a penny Vernon hadn't a clue about Julia's little escapade. She'd practically said as much on the one occasion they'd met, in the coffee house just after Christmas. If what Joanna suspected were true she might well have a powerful trump card up her sleeve. But first she must be absolutely sure of her facts.

On the way home from work that afternoon Fleur stopped off at the DIY centre on the outskirts of town and bought a tin of white paint for the balcony. She intended to make a start the coming weekend so that it would be dry long before she wanted to use it. Already she had planted pots of daffodils and tulips and was eagerly waiting for them to come into bloom. After paying for her weekend in London she had had to abandon the luxury sun lounger she had set her heart on, but she had found two little wrought iron chairs and a tiny table in a junk shop and bought them very cheaply. The man in the shop told her they had come out of an old pub that had been demolished. They were black at the moment but she intended to paint those white to match the balcony railings.

As she carried the can of paint up the steps of number thirteen Tom passed her on his way out.

'Hi! You've decided to make a start then?'

She smiled. 'Hoping to, this weekend. If it rains I shall do my table and chairs inside.'

'Well, remember to keep the windows open for ventilation,' he warned. 'I take it you've got the correct sized brushes?'

Her face fell. 'Oh, no! What an idiot I am. I forgot all about brushes. I could have got them at the same time.'

'I'll get them for you, if you like? I'll be passing the DIY centre in the morning.' He paused. 'If you don't mind my saying so, Fleur, I think you're going to need more paint than you've got there.'

'Am I?'

'Yes. You'll need some undercoat too. It's a good while since that balcony has been painted.' He hesitated. 'Strictly speaking you should rub the railings down thoroughly and paint them with some rust inhibitor first.'

Fleur's heart sank. It was going to cost more than she had thought by the sound of it. 'Oh, should I? It's all going to take more time than I thought.'

'Worth it, though, if you want it to last.' He paused, looking at her thoughtfully. 'I could get the other stuff for you when I get the brushes, if you like?'

'No, it's all right. I'll get it all.' She could hardly explain to him why she couldn't afford the extra materials at the moment, but she saw from the look on his face that he took her refusal of help for a rebuff. 'Thanks for the advice though,' she said, too late.

'That's okay. Just as you like.' They looked at each other awkwardly for a moment, then he said, 'I'm just off to interview a local author.'

'Are you?'

'Yes. I was going to get a takeaway on my way back. Share my supper with me?'

'Oh.' She bit her lip. 'I'm sorry, Tom. I have a friend coming round.'

'I see.' His smile faded and he backed away. 'It's okay. Just a thought. Well – see you around then.'

'Yes. 'Bye, Tom.' She watched with a heavy heart as he walked up the street. They had been awkward with each other since her affair with Peter. He had kept his distance as he had promised, careful, as he put it, not to invade her space. She would have loved to have supper with him like they used to do. She longed to have back the comfortable relationship they had enjoyed before. She missed him and had often thought she should make the first move. But she worried that if she tried to re-establish their friendship he would think she was merely using him. Tonight was the first time he had offered anything more than courtesy and she had been obliged to turn him down, giving him the impression that she was still keeping him at a distance.

Charlotte arrived on time and Fleur answered the door to find the girl standing outside holding a bowl of blue and pink hyacinths.

'A house-warming pressie,' she said, holding them out. 'Or I suppose I should say flat-warming.'

201

'Thank you. They're lovely!' Fleur unwrapped the bowl and put it on the table, bending down to inhale their fragrance. 'Oh, they smell gorgeous, don't they? Shall I take your coat?'

Charlotte took off her coat, looking around at the room. 'This is lovely, Fleur. So cosy. Did you really do all this decorating yourself? You are clever. I wouldn't know where to start.'

'It was a question of needs must,' She laughed. 'It was so dreary when I moved in. Something had to be done. I've got it almost as I want it now, though I'd like to buy some new furniture when I've saved up enough. Come and look at my balcony.' She opened one of the French windows to show the other girl. 'I got the table and chairs from a junk shop. I'm going to paint everything white and then I'll have hanging baskets and pots full of flowers. I can't wait for the summer when I can sit out here and have my meals in the sunshine.'

Charlotte looked at it all with a wistful expression. 'You are lucky, Fleur. I wish I had somewhere like this.'

'But you live in a beautiful house with a big garden,' she said. 'I bet you have a lovely bedroom with your own television and everything. You have a family, Charlotte. Nothing can make up for that.'

'Don't you believe it! Anyway it isn't a real family. I've always wished I had brothers and sisters. A house full of fun and laughter. Sharing things together, that's a real family.'

Fleur went into the tiny kitchenette to make coffee She glanced at Charlotte as she carried the tray through and put it down on the table. 'Is that what you wanted to talk about?' she asked. 'Trouble at home?'

'In a way.' Charlotte sighed. 'Having plenty of money isn't everything, you know.'

Fleur handed her a cup of coffee and sat down opposite. 'What's wrong, Charlotte? You can talk to me if you want to. As you said, we don't know any of the same people so it won't matter to me. And I promise not to gossip. It wouldn't be wise to have a loose tongue in the job I do.'

'I know.' Charlotte sipped her coffee and smiled at Fleur over the cup's rim. 'It's not just that, though. It's funny, isn't it? I hardly know you really and yet I know deep inside that I can trust you.'

Pleasantly flattered, Fleur nodded. 'It's like that with some people.'

Charlotte frowned, searching her mind for the way to begin. 'Yours was a happy home, wasn't it?' she said. 'Before your grandmother died, I mean.'

'Yes, very happy. We didn't have any of the things you have –

202

money and luxury. Where we lived was cramped, noisy and dirty. But we did have lots of love and when Grandpa was alive there was always music and laughter.'

'Our family isn't like that,' Charlotte told her. 'Sometimes days go by and we hardly see each other, let alone sit down to eat together. I don't think my mum and dad have ever got on. I wonder sometimes if they ever really loved each other.'

'What makes you say that?'

'They're always quarrelling. Dad's always been really patronising towards Mum, as though he wanted to make her think she was really thick. I think she's been trying to prove something to him with all this council work and stuff. He has affairs though, so I don't suppose he's even noticed how hard she's trying.'

'Affairs? Other women, you mean?' Fleur remembered the two occasions on which Vernon Grant had tried to chat her up and reflected that Charlotte was probably not exaggerating.

'Yes. He always has. Funny how parents think that kids don't notice things. I was beginning to think he'd stopped but last night I found out that he's at it again – this time with the most awful woman imaginable: his personal assistant, Mrs Hanson.'

Fleur swallowed her involuntary gasp of surprise. 'You say you found out? Are you sure? I mean, you're not just jumping to conclusions?'

'No, I'm positive. I saw them coming out of her house. She was wearing a dressing gown and they were actually *kissing*,' Charlotte said, wrinkling her nose with disgust. 'Not just a casual peck either, a real state of the art *snog*. Doesn't take much imagination to work out what had been going on. Imagine, at *their* age! The worst part is that I have to work in the same office, running errands for her – being bossed around, just as if she owned the place! I hate her *guts*, Fleur.'

Fleur said nothing. Clearly Charlotte wasn't yet aware that the woman she hated so much was now a partner in the firm.

'Poor Mum,' the girl went on. 'I'm beginning to see what it must have been like for her all these years.' She paused, her lip trembling, and Fleur could see that the girl was fighting back tears. 'The thing is . . .' She swallowed hard. 'What should I do about it?'

'What *can* you do?' Fleur asked, wondering if Joanna's affair with Vernon Grant was the reason she had been given a partnership in his firm? 'Does anyone else know about it?'

'My Aunt Kath was with me when we saw them,' Charlotte said. 'She was driving me home from the stables and she took a short cut down Hazel Grove. Aunt Kath is Dad's sister. They've never got on either. She saw them too, but I can't talk to her about it. At least not till I've got my head round it all. There was ever such a funny atmosphere at the office today too. Apparently Mrs Hanson has been given some kind of promotion. She was out with Granddad all morning and she's talking about throwing a party to celebrate. It all looks jolly fishy, doesn't it? And what's worse is there's a rumour flying round that Grandpa Philips has resigned because of it!' She looked appealingly at Fleur. 'I don't know what's going on, Fleur. All I do know is that I hate it. Because of that woman, everything's being torn apart! What would you do if you were in my place? Would you tell Mum or keep it to yourself?'

Fleur found her own emotions stirred by Charlotte's revelation. *What would you do if you were in my place?* Part of her insisted that if Julia was being betrayed it was no more than she deserved. It was a case of 'what goes around, comes around'. But another part of her hated seeing what it was obviously doing to Charlotte.

'You say your dad has had affairs before,' she said carefully. 'This one will probably fizzle out like the others did so surely it would be wisest to keep what you saw to yourself?'

'Fizzle out? When she's working so closely with him? Not very likely, is it?' The other girl shook her head. 'The awful part is seeing them getting away with it – cheating Mum behind her back.' Charlotte chewed her thumb nail. 'Mum knew Mrs Hanson years ago when they were both young,' she said. 'She married an American and went to live over there. I wish she'd stayed! As far as I know Mum isn't friendly with her now. I don't think they've even met since Mrs Hanson joined the firm. Do you think they could have fallen out all those years ago and now Joanna is getting even?'

'Surely not.' Fleur was silently piecing it all together. She remembered seeing Joanna Hanson and Vernon Grant together at the country club on the night she had dined there with Peter Arden. It looked as though their affair had been going on for some time, so Charlotte was right about that. And if Joanna had been Julia's girlhood friend it was quite possible that she knew about her teenage affair with Dean Sylvester. Alarm bells began to ring inside Fleur's head and she wished fervently that she hadn't blurted out the fact that Dean had been her father.

Charlotte was still talking. 'Well, why else would the wretched woman come all the way back here from America and get a job at GPC?' she said plaintively. 'Her being so high-powered, you'd have thought she'd head straight for London.'

'Without knowing all the details, I couldn't even guess, Charlotte.'

204

Fleur refilled both coffee cups, her mind spinning. 'My advice is to leave it for a while,' she said. 'Feel free to come round and see me whenever you want to talk. That might help.'

Julia was busy in the kitchen. She was taking extra trouble preparing the evening meal in the hope that perhaps this evening they would all get to sit down together for once. First she wanted to find out what Charlotte had been so upset about last night. Then there was a lot she wanted to talk to Vernon about, but that would have to wait until Charlotte had gone to bed.

She had had a shock when she went round to her parents' house that morning and saw her father, still in bed where May had insisted he remain. His face looked an unearthly grey against the whiteness of the pillows. She had tried to reassure him that all would be well; to convince him that no one really wanted him to resign.

'You are still the same valued member of the firm you always have been, Dad,' she told him, squeezing his hand. 'I'm sure Charlie will realise that once he's had time to pause and think things through.'

But Harry had seemed too tired and dispirited even to care. All the fight seemed to have drained out of him, a fact which alarmed her even more than his appearance.

Downstairs she urged her mother to telephone the doctor. 'Better to be on the safe side,' Julia said, anxious not to worry May. 'I'm sure he's just physically and emotionally exhausted, but I think it would be wise to have him checked. Besides, he might feel better just talking things through with another man. You know how well he gets on with Doctor Frazer.'

May nodded. 'I think you're right. I'll give him a ring.' She shook her head angrily. 'That Hanson woman has a lot to answer for.'

'To be fair, I think it was more Charlie,' Julia said. 'You know how carried away he gets when he has a new idea. He was extremely rude to me on the telephone this morning when he read the report in the *Clarion* about my women's refuge. He'll probably be round later to see Daddy with an apology and some kind of peace offering.'

'Between ourselves, I hope he isn't,' May confided. 'I really don't feel I could be civil to the odious little man if he showed his face here today. The years I've put up with his appalling manners and vulgarity because he was your father's business partner! Daddy is coming up to retiring age anyway. He's been looking tired for months now. We could be having such a pleasant time together if only he'd just let go.'

Julia gave her mother a hug. 'Sometimes things work out for the best, Mum. Don't put any more pressure on him. We'll just play it all by ear, eh?'

May kissed her daughter's cheek. 'Yes. As you say, we'll wait and see what happens.'

She'd rung half an hour ago to tell Julia that Doctor Frazer had called and advised Harry to take it easy for a few days and then book the two of them on a long holiday somewhere warm and sunny. Afterwards he'd told May confidentially that Harry was suffering from severe stress and that retirement seemed a good idea.

'If only retiring had been *his* idea though,' she said with a sigh. 'It's this business of being edged out that has upset him so.'

'Tell him it isn't worth making himself ill for,' Julia told her.

'By the way, dear, Charlotte has just arrived,' May said. 'She heard about her grandpa's resignation at the office today. I've asked her to stay and have dinner with us. She's upstairs with her grandpa now. She'll cheer him up so much, bless her.'

'Oh, that's nice. I'm glad she's come to see you. Look, Mum, if you get the chance, will you try and find out if there's anything worrying her? She came home looking like death last night and she was out of the house like a whirlwind this morning. I didn't get the chance to talk to her.'

'Leave it to me,' May said. 'Charlotte and I have always been good friends. I'm sure she'll tell me if there anything wrong.'

Julia sighed as she turned back to the kitchen. It would be just the two of them then. Well, at least it would be a chance for her to talk to Vernon.

Charlotte sat beside her grandfather's bed and looked with some dismay at his ashen face.

'It's not true, is it, Grandpa? You haven't really resigned?'

He turned his head and smiled at his only grandchild. 'It's good of you to come and see me, Charlotte, love, but you mustn't worry your head with my problems. Your grandma thinks it's high time I retired anyway. Maybe I'll do best to take notice of her.'

'Yes, but only if it's what *you* want,' she said. 'I don't see why you should go just because Mrs Hanson wants your place.'

'Is that what they're saying?'

Charlotte reddened. 'You know what offices are like. What they don't know they guess at. That's why I'm here – partly. I wanted to see you, of course, but I want to hear from you what really happened?'

He reached out and took her hand, squeezing it warmly. 'It's all very simple, my love. Mrs Hanson has been made a partner and there are some new ideas planned that I can't go along with. I was angry when I walked out of the meeting and said I was going to resign. But I haven't done so formally. Not yet.'

'Well I think you should stay on and fight them if you don't agree,' she told him. 'After all, you're a partner too, aren't you?'

'I'm afraid I'd only be out-voted,' Harry said wearily. 'It's not worth the bother.'

Charlotte edged her chair closer to the bed. 'Grandpa – I've found something out. It's been worrying me and I don't know what to do. I think I should tell you.'

Harry lay back against the pillows and closed his eyes with a sigh. 'What is it, sweetheart? You know I'll help if I can.'

'It's Dad – and Mrs Hanson. They're – you know – having an affair. And it's not just talk. I know it's true because I've seen them.'

Harry's eyes were open in an instant. He pulled himself up in bed and stared at his granddaughter. '*Seen* them. My God, child, what do you mean?'

'Last night, when Aunt Kath was driving me home. We passed her house – Mrs Hanson's, I mean. Dad's car was outside and they were kissing each other. *Really* kissing, I mean, not just a friendly peck.' She paused to bite her lip nervously. It was the first time she had ever spoken to her grandfather about such intimate matters. 'And that's not all. She – she was wearing her dressing gown.'

For a moment Harry was lost for words. Fury filled his breast. He'd always known that Vernon was a philanderer. For years he'd despised him for the dance he'd led Julia. In a way he blamed himself for turning a blind eye to it because of the business, and for encouraging the marriage in the first place. But for Vernon to be so careless as to let his own child witness his depravity . . . His fingers tightened round Charlotte's as he fought for control. 'I daresay there was some simple explanation for what you saw, love. Go along now and don't worry about it any more.'

'But what about Mum? You don't think I should tell her?'

'No! Don't tell anyone. Let your old granddad do the worrying for you, there's a good girl. I'll get to the bottom of it. I'm sure it wasn't what you thought.' He bent forward to kiss her forehead. 'Off you go downstairs now. It'll be nice for your grandma to have someone to eat with. I'm having mine up here tonight.'

She looked anxious. 'You're not ill, are you, Granddad? I haven't upset you and made you worse?'

'Bless you, no, my love.' He smiled at her indulgently. 'You could never make me feel anything but better.'

At the door she paused. 'Will you tell Grandma – about Dad and – and *her*?'

He smiled and shook his head at her. 'I told you not to think about it any more. Off you go now and put the whole thing out of your head. Grandma has made one of her famous chicken pies. You can tell her I've been lying here sniffing the lovely smell of it cooking and I'm feeling quite peckish after all.'

When the door closed behind her he lay back against the pillows, feeling a sudden surge of adrenaline revitalise him. Charlotte's discovery about Vernon and Joanna Hanson had only confirmed what he'd suspected himself for some weeks. Damn that bloody little creep and his sordid affairs! Damn Charlie Grant too! The last thing he'd do was to resign now. If he did, he'd be playing right into their greedy hands. Why should he stand down and let the three of them have it all their own way? Oh, no!

A flash of inspiration brought the colour flooding back into his cheeks as an idea began to take shape in his head. There was a way that he could put a stop to all their little games and do as Angus Frazer had advised too. The plan ballooned inside his head, exploding as gloriously as a firework. He lay back with a smile of satisfaction curving his lips. He'd make Charlie Grant eat humble pie yet. For all his bombastic ways, he'd find out he wasn't as clever as he thought.

Chapter 11

When Charlotte had left, Fleur washed the coffee cups and tidied the flat. It was still only seven o'clock. She'd heard Tom come in about ten minutes ago and as she worked kept picturing him in his room upstairs, eating his solitary Chinese takeaway. Was she being stubborn, refusing to make the first move? He had left it up to her after all, knowing that she hated to be pressured. Finally she made up her mind. Tidying her hair before the mirror and applying a dash of lipstick to give her confidence, she opened the door and walked determinedly up the stairs to knock on Tom's door.

When he opened it he looked surprised. 'Fleur! Is something wrong?'

She smiled wryly. 'No. I just wanted to see you, that's all. If you remember, you invited me to share your supper earlier.'

'You said you were entertaining a friend.'

'Not entertaining exactly. It was only Charlotte, a girl I met at the computer course I was on. I saw her this morning and she asked if she could drop in for a chat.'

His face cleared. 'Oh, I thought – oh, well, never mind that.' He held the door open. 'Come in.'

She grinned at him mischievously. 'I thought you'd never ask.'

Inside the room she saw that he had already eaten. A plate with crumbs showed that he had made do with a sandwich. 'I haven't interrupted you supper, have I?' she asked.

'No.' He whisked the plate out of sight. 'I've already eaten. I didn't bother bringing anything in. I wasn't very hungry actually.' He looked at her. 'Have you had yours? I mean, you hadn't changed your mind about the takeaway, had you?'

'I just wanted to see you, Tom. I think it's time we had a talk.'

'Oh? Yes, of course, if that's what you want.'

She came straight to the point. 'I've missed you, Tom.' She held up her hand. 'Okay – maybe I've got a nerve, saying that after – well, what I did.'

'No.' He shook his head. 'It wasn't your fault. You fell in love. That can happen to anyone. I'm just sorry it didn't work out.'

'Yes, well, it's over now.' She paused, searching for words. It was harder than she'd hoped. He was doing his best to make it easier but she still didn't know what he really felt about her. She cleared her throat. 'Look, Tom, I'd really like it to be as it was before.'

'I don't think that's possible, Fleur.' He paused, his face serious. 'I wonder if you can possibly know how it makes a guy who cares for you feel, telling him you're in love with someone else?'

She saw the hurt in his eyes and realised how much it cost him to say that. 'I'm sorry, Tom. I was such a fool. If it makes you feel any better I have paid for the mistake I made.' She turned towards the door. 'Well, if you feel that it can never be the same between us, I can't say I blame you.'

As she reached the door he moved to stand in front of her. 'Maybe it can't be the same,' he said. 'But we could try to start again. If you're really sure that's what you want?'

'Oh, Tom.' She looked at him, her eyes bright. 'I do. I really do.'

'On your terms. No strings. No obligations.'

'Right.'

For a moment they stood looking at each other, then Tom's face relaxed and they both laughed, releasing the tension between them.

'Shall I go and get that takeaway?' he asked.

'No. I'll make us an omelette. What would you like, mushroom or Spanish?'

Downstairs in Fleur's flat she made the omelettes while Tom assembled a salad and buttered bread. They chatted over the meal, sharing companionable anecdotes about their respective jobs, filling in the weeks between when they'd seen little of each other. It was after they'd washed up and were sitting with their coffee that Tom suddenly said, 'There's something I should tell you, Fleur.'

'Yes?'

'I'm moving from here shortly.'

Her heart sank. 'From Elvemere? You've got another job?'

'Oh, no. Just from this house.'

'I see.' She glanced at him uncertainly. 'Was it – because of me?'

'Partly – and partly because I had an offer I couldn't refuse. I'm going to share a house – with a colleague, someone from the paper.'

She smiled. 'Oh, that's nice. Wow! A whole house! It'll be a great improvement on this.'

210

'Well, not the whole house; two rooms and the use of the rest of it. Yes, it will be an improvement.'

She frowned, waiting for more. If he was happy with the arrangement why was he so hesitant? 'So what's the problem? Is there something you haven't told me?' she prompted.

'I'm just coming to it.' He cleared his throat and looked at her. 'It's just that the colleague – the person I'll be sharing with is – well, a girl.'

'Oh, I see.' Fleur put her cup down.

'No, you don't! Her name is Sadie Freeman and she's a photographer on the *Clarion*. She only started a couple of months ago. She's very good. In fact, I happen to think she's pretty special.'

'*Special?* Well, yes, you must think so if you're going to move in with her.'

'I'm *not* moving in with her. Not in the way you mean, anyway. And when I say she's special, I mean talented – at her work. She really wants the chance to go for photo-journalism and I'm sure it won't be long before she lands a good job with one of the national dailies. A relative died recently and left her a bit of money, that's how she's managed to put down the deposit on the house. It's only a little terraced place in Park Row. She needs someone to share to help with the mortgage. She put a notice on the board at work and I applied. That's all there is to it, Fleur.'

Only slightly reassured she asked, 'When are you planning to move in?'

'At the end of the month. My rent here is paid up till then.'

She looked at him mournfully. 'It won't be the same here without you.'

He smiled wistfully. 'I wish you really meant that.'

'But I do.'

'Well, it's only on the other side of the park. I'll be able to invite you over and make you a proper meal. Sadie got a bargain in that house. It's been nicely modernised, central heating and everything. You'll love the kitchen. Pine cupboards and blue and white tiles. I'm having the ground-floor rooms all to myself and the use of the kitchen and bathroom.'

'What's she like – this Sadie Freeman?'

'Not at all like you.' He laughed. 'I suppose she's what you'd call a feminist. Very tough and competitive. She has her hair cut in one of those spiky styles, rides a motorbike and wears leather trousers. You could describe her as formidable.'

'You make her sound like a monster!'

He laughed. 'No, she's not really, just what you'd call assertive. I

211

guess she's had to be to get where she is. She's fantastic at her job and a good sort when you get to know her. You must meet her sometime. I'm sure you'd get along.'

'Mmm. Well, we'll have to see, won't we?' Fleur picked up her cup and drank the last of her coffee. 'Tom, can I ask you a favour?'

'Fire away.'

'Will you help me paint the balcony? After what you said I don't think I really know enough about the job.' She grinned wryly. 'How's that for assertive?'

'Don't be daft. Of course I'll help.' His face broke into a broad grin. 'This weekend?'

'Ah – no, not this. I can't afford the extra stuff you said I'd need yet.'

'It won't cost that much. I thought you were saving up.'

'I was, but I spent the money.' She looked at him from under lowered lashes. 'I sent it to Peter Arden to pay for everything he spent on me that weekend in London.'

For a moment he stared at her, then he reached out and pulled her into his arms. 'Oh, Fleur.'

She buried her face against his shoulder, grateful that she didn't have to meet his eyes. 'I wanted to be independent of him, Tom, done with him for good. But all that is over now. I don't want to talk about it any more. All right?'

He held her away from him so as to look into her eyes. 'More than all right. It's wonderful. I was afraid you might still be carrying a torch.' He kissed her softly. 'You know how I feel about you, Fleur. Nothing you could ever do would change that.'

He'd half expected her to stiffen and begin to push away, but to his surprise she stayed where she was, her body relaxed and her head against his neck, her soft black curls tickling his nose. After a moment, much to his delight, he felt her arms slide around his waist as she sighed and nestled closer. Raising her face to his, she said, 'Let's not talk about feelings, Tom. Not for a while. Just let's enjoy starting again and being together – like this.'

He looked into her eyes and gently kissed the mouth she offered, deeply grateful for the warm vitality of her body in his arms and the responsive mouth under his. He resolved that he would tread carefully this time, feel his way tentatively back into their relationship. He wanted to tell her how much he loved her; how desperately he had missed her; of the sleepless nights he had spent, wondering if he would ever stand a chance of getting her back again. But he knew that to pour out his heart to her now would be a mistake. Fleur was a girl who must feel sure enough, *free* enough, to share

212

her emotions without obligation. Hers was an independent spirit that would only be captured when she was truly ready. The facet of her character that had once filled him with resentment now made him love her all the more.

For a while they sat silently, warm and content, hands clasped, fingers laced, cheek against cheek. For the moment words were unnecessary.

'Tell me what you've been doing?' Fleur said at last.

'I've started reporting on council meetings. It can be fascinating. Funny too, sometimes.' He reached inside his jacket and pulled the front page of the *Clarion* out of an inner pocket. 'Did you see my piece in the paper this morning?' The paper was folded into a small square but as he smoothed it out for her she found herself staring down at a photograph of Julia Grant.

'Sadie took that,' he told her. 'It's good, isn't it?'

But Fleur only nodded abstractedly. She was reading the article and marvelling at the sheer hypocrisy of the woman.

'What do you think?' Tom said. 'She's doing a good job, I reckon. A lot of councillors just sit there and never open their mouths, let alone try to actually *do* something for the community.'

'Maybe she just wants to get noticed,' Fleur said scathingly.

'Well, if she does at least she'll be doing these poor women a good turn.'

'If it comes off,' Fleur said. 'Probably only a lot of hot air.'

'No, I think she's sincere. The plans have been passed and she's done quite a bit to get the thing off to a good start. I talked to her for a long time after the council meeting and I get the impression that she's a deeply sincere woman. She certainly seems to have a strong affinity with single mothers.'

'*So she should!*' Fleur was suddenly aware that she'd spoken the heartfelt thought aloud. Tom was looking at her, his eyebrows raised in question.

'What do you mean?'

She bit her lip. 'Nothing. Just that any worthwhile councillor should be able to put themselves in the shoes of less fortunate folks.'

'True.' Tom laughed and folded the paper up again, stuffing it back into his pocket. 'Hey, know what? I could murder another coffee, couldn't you?'

'Yes, okay.'

'I'll make it. You sit tight.'

As he began to get up, she reached out and took his hand, drawing him down beside her again. 'Tom . . .'

'Yes?'

'Stay here with me tonight.'

Sorely tempted, he looked into her eyes for a long breathless moment, trying to interpret what he saw there. There was so much. She was tense, maybe even a little nervous but certainly very vulnerable. Leaning forward, he kissed her gently.

'No, love. Not this time. Not yet.'

She held on to his arms, refusing to let him go. 'Why not?'

Now he saw something else in the velvet brown eyes. There was still that deep insecurity she had always tried so hard to hide. Laid bare like that for him to see, it made him slightly ashamed, though he could not have said why. And it made him even more determined to love and protect her.

'We're starting again, remember?' he told her gently. 'From day one. No strings, No obligations. That applies on both sides. Better not to rush things. I want you to be good and sure first, Fleur. When and *if* we decide to take things a step further, I don't want it to be casual. I'd like it to be a real commitment. That's important to me.' He bent to cup her face with his hands, kissing her. 'Now I'll make that coffee.'

It was some time before Fleur slept that night. Lying in bed she went over what she and Tom had said to each other. Had he thought she was throwing herself at him? Maybe she had been in a way. She was so anxious to prove something, both to herself and him. Peter had made her so insecure. Secretly she was afraid of losing Tom again, especially now that he was going to live in the same house as the girl she thought of as her rival. Tom obviously admired and respected this Sadie he talked of so glowingly. Could those feelings develop into something deeper once they were living under the same roof?

She turned over and rearranged her pillow, trying hard to think of something else. The article Tom had written about Julia Grant's plans for a refuge for battered wives was interesting. What would Julia's fellow councillors think, she wondered sleepily, if they knew that their altruistic colleague had herself once been a single mother? What a flurry that would cause!

Suddenly she remembered Joanna Hanson's probing questions this morning and was wide awake in an instant. Already she was trying to steal Julia's husband. If she found out that Julia had had a daughter prior to her marriage to Vernon Grant, she could cause havoc. Joanna was a woman who would have no qualms about breaking up a family or setting people against one another. She

214

would ride roughshod over anyone who got in her way in order to get what she wanted. It was all there in those hard green eyes.

Fleur stared into the darkness, imagining the chaos a disclosure like that could create. *But she would have to prove it before she dragged me into her tacky little plans*, she told herself. And for that she would need Fleur's cooperation. She sighed and closed her eyes again. If Mrs Hanson was hoping for that she was about to be sadly disappointed.

Fleur and Sally arrived in good time to set up the buffet in Joanna's conservatory. On occasions like this where there weren't too many guests Sally preferred to keep a low profile. She herself would remain behind the scenes to replenish plates and uncork fresh bottles of wine. Only Fleur would circulate with trays before and after the guests had helped themselves to the buffet table.

The table looked attractive with an arrangement of spring flowers and yellow candles. Joanna had chosen the deluxe menu, which included smoked salmon, caviare and oysters. Privately Fleur considered it one of the less tempting menus with its array of rich and indigestible luxuries and she wondered what the guests from the lower echelons of GPC would make of it. She guessed – rightly, as it happened – that most of them would much rather have had a selection of cold meats, ham and chicken, with perhaps a whole salmon, and simple salad accompaniments, but as she and Sally worked together in Joanna's exquisitely appointed kitchen she kept her opinion to herself. After all Joanna was paying well so who was she to argue?

Joanna was edgy. This evening was important to her. Since Harry Philips had walked out of the meeting at which she had been appointed a partner no one had seen or heard anything from him. It was the one cloud on her horizon. She would have preferred all the partners to approve of her elevation. The resignation he had threatened had not been delivered – or at least not as far as she knew. Vernon refused to talk about him and Charlie too was keeping his mouth tightly closed on the subject. Working on her own initiative, she had sent him and his wife May an invitation to the party. Now she wondered if she had done the right thing. To exclude him would have looked bad, seeing that he was still to all intents and purposes a partner in the firm, and anyway she doubted whether they would come. But if the Philipses did turn up their presence could make the most awful atmosphere and cast a shadow over the whole evening. It was something she was going to have to deal with if and when.

Looking into the kitchen she was reassured by the sight of Sally Arden, looking brisk and businesslike in her black and white striped apron as she went about the preparations. She was also glad to see Fleur, though for different reasons. The girl was to be her trump card. She could make the difference between the success of Charlie's plan and its failure. For the past few nights Joanna had lain awake, wondering what she would do if the girl went down with 'flu or had some kind of accident at the last minute.

Joanna could hardly wait to see Julia's face when she subtly presented her with the little surprise she had up her sleeve. The coincidence of the girl's name and those distinctive looks was too much to swallow. Fleur Sylvester was Dean's daughter and her sudden appearance in Elvemere seemed to point to the fact that she was here to contact her mother – Julia. Clearly the whole thing was being kept secret. The fascinating question was, *why*?

Joanna had rehearsed what she would say over and again, getting the innuendos just right and watching for the tell-tale signs. She had worked out that she couldn't lose. The more she thought about it, the more sure she was that Fleur was Julia's daughter, but even if her hunch was wildly off the mark Julia would hardly want to go out of her way to prove her wrong, especially when not even her closest relatives knew of her clandestine run-away affair with Dean Sylvester.

Charlie and Louise were the first to arrive and Joanna greeted them effusively, ushering them into the living room and making sure that they had a drink. It was the first time she had met Louise since she had been back in England. There had been no love lost between them all those years ago at the height of Joanna's red hot relationship with Vernon that had been the talk of Elvemere. Louise had had ambitions for her beloved only son, and they did not include his being ensnared by the girl she looked upon as the town tart. Harsh words had passed between them; words which Joanna looked forward to seeing her swallow this evening. She hoped they would choke her.

As she took Louise's fur coat she could hardly conceal a smile at what it revealed. The turquoise blue evening dress Louise wore was as tight as a second skin. Joanna resisted the temptation to shield her eyes from the dazzling glitter of beads and sequins that encrusted it, struggling against the competition of dangling diamante earrings and matching necklace. She reflected wryly that the woman looked as though she had fallen off a Christmas tree.

216

'I'm so glad you could come, Mrs Grant,' said Joanna, smiling sweetly. 'It's so long since we last met. We must have a lovely cosy chat about old times someday.'

When she'd gone Louise jabbed Charlie in the ribs. 'She may have had two rich husbands and a haircut, but she's the same devious bitch she always was, if you ask me,' she remarked. 'Wouldn't trust her as far as I could spit!'

Charlie glowered at her. 'No one *is* asking you, so just keep your opinions to yourself, Lou. She's an important member of the firm now, remember? And not afraid to put her money where her mouth is. She's a talented businesswoman, not a spotty teenager any more.'

Louise took a glass of wine from Fleur's tray and turned her back on her husband, her face crimson with annoyance. 'They'll find out,' she muttered under her breath. 'Once a bitch, always a bitch.' All the same, she already knew that Joanna wasn't to be seen off with bribes and threats this time. She had power now; the power that comes with money. The kind no one, especially Charlie, could resist.

Vernon and Julia put in an appearance soon after. By contrast to her mother-in-law, Julia wore a plain black cocktail dress which Joanna instantly recognised as a Jean Muir.

The first arrivals stood on opposite sides of the room, sipping their cocktails uneasily. There was obvious tension between Charlie and his wife and Julia seemed ill at ease with her in-laws. Joanna tried hard to draw all four into conversation but she was grateful when more guests began to arrive, easing the tension. Soon she was circulating among them, making sure that glasses were full, people were mingling and conversation flowed without constraint.

'I'm sorry Charlotte couldn't come,' Julia said when Joanna appeared at her side. 'She'd promised to go to her aunt's this evening and she'll be staying over.'

'I understand. Don't worry about it,' Joanna said generously. 'This kind of affair can't seem very exciting to a sixteen year old.'

'She asked me to thank you for the invitation though,' Julia lied. What Charlotte had actually said was that she wouldn't go to Joanna's party if she were hung, drawn and quartered and served up as kebabs! 'It's bad enough having to see Joanna the Hun at the office all week,' she said vehemently. 'Without actually spending my precious free time in her company!'

'I haven't congratulated you yet on your – promotion in the firm,' Julia said.

Joanna smiled. 'Thank you. You and I haven't had that little get together we promised ourselves yet either, have we? I've been hoping that we might meet and work something out regarding your

217

women's refuge project,' she said. 'It's unfortunate, I know, but it's so silly to be at loggerheads when it's all in the family, isn't it?' She lowered her voice. 'I know Charlie can let that straight-from-the-shoulder attitude of his get out of hand at times, but I'm sure his heart is in the right place.'

'Are you?' Julia said coolly. 'As far as I'm concerned it's a question of first come, first served. And it happens that I was there first.'

'Well, I'm sure we can work something out between us,' Joanna said placatingly. Out of the corner of her eye she'd just seen Fleur come into the back the room with a fresh tray of drinks. She edged herself strategically into Julia's line of vision. 'Never mind business now. You're here to enjoy yourself tonight,' she said with a smile. 'I want to hear *all* about what you did after I left Elvemere. We really do have an awful lot of catching up to do.'

'There's nothing much to tell,' Julia said. 'Compared to you I've had a very uneventful life – till now.'

'Ah, that's what you say.' Joanna gave her a knowing little smile. 'But maybe it wasn't quite as uneventful as you'd have us believe.' Her timing perfect, she shifted slightly to reveal Fleur who was now moving among the other guests just a few feet away. Joanna pretended to notice her for the first time. 'Oh, by the way, have you met that girl who works for Sally Arden? Strikingly attractive, isn't she? Quite exotic. You know, looking at her reminds me of someone. Can you guess who?'

Julia glanced in Fleur's direction. 'I have met her before. As for reminding me – I don't know. She's certainly attractive but . . .'

'You don't happen to know what her name is?' Joanna asked. Julia shook her head, looking puzzled.

'Fleur. Pretty, isn't it? Though not entirely suitable for someone so tall and dark. I always think of girls named Fleur as blonde and petite. She's not local, of course. Tells me she's from London, but you can hear that from the accent.' She took a sip of her Martini, watching with narrowed eyes, noting with satisfaction the heightened colour as Julia's gaze followed the girl.

'Yes,' she went on, 'Fleur *Sylvester*, she tells me her name is. That's a clue. Now who does she remind you of, darling?'

Julia's heart seemed to freeze. She shook her head. 'I'm sorry, I can't see any likeness. I've no idea who you mean.'

'Really? You do surprise me. Sylvester? It doesn't ring any bells?' Joanna shrugged. 'Oh, well, never mind. It was just an idea. Oh!' She waved to someone on the other side of the room. 'There's Bob Jefford and his wife. Forgive me if I have a word with them. See you later . . .'

218

Julia watched her weave her way through the guests. She felt strange and unreal. It wasn't possible. There was no way that Joanna could know about Dean's child, let alone the fact that she had been named Fleur. So what was going on? What was she up to?

'Another glass of wine?'

Startled, Julia turned and found herself looking straight into Dean Sylvester's dark expressive eyes. She gave a little gasp of shock. It was the same likeness that had caught her attention on the night of her own New Year party. Joanna must have seen it too. But she could only be guessing at the girl's identity of course – wildly guessing. There was no way she could know. None at all.

'More wine?' the girl repeated, holding out her tray.

Julia shook her head, staring at the girl. Was it actually *possible* that she was . . . Suddenly the room began to spin around her and a feeling of stark panic made her heart thump dizzyingly fast against her ribs. She put her empty glass down on the tray and looked around frantically for an escape route.

'Are you all right?' The girl was looking at her now with concern. 'If you're not feeling well, I could get you a glass of water or . . .'

'It's all right,' Julia said, putting out a hand as though to hold her at bay. '*I'm all right.* I just need – need to get some air.'

'Come with me.' Fleur turned and made her way out into the hall, Julia following. At the foot of the stairs she said, 'I wouldn't go outside if I were you. It's quite a cold evening. You could catch a chill.'

'Where's the bathroom?' Julia asked, her face ashen.

'At the top of the stairs. Do you want me to find your husband – to tell someone?'

Desperate not to faint and make a scene, Julia was already halfway up the stairs. '*No!*' She looked down at the girl's upturned face. 'Please don't say anything – I don't want any fuss.'

Fleur watched her go thoughtfully then went into the kitchen and closed the door, putting her tray down on the worktop. 'Sally, one of the guests is feeling ill,' she said. 'She doesn't want anyone told. I think she's afraid of making a fuss, but I don't think she should be alone. Can you take over while I go up to her?'

'Of course.' Sally was already taking off her apron. 'Off you go. Take her a brandy. I'll see to everything here. Let me know if you need any help.'

Joanna's sumptuous green and ivory bathroom was stiflingly hot. Julia opened the window and drew in several deep draughts of the cool night air. After a moment her heartbeat began to steady and the sickly faint feeling started to subside. Surely she must be imagining it? The girl couldn't possibly have traced her here. How would she even know Julia's name, let alone where she lived? Her name probably wasn't Sylvester at all. This was just the kind of trick Joanna would play to catch her out. There was no way she could possibly know of her child's existence. There was nothing to worry about. All she had to do was take control of the situation and play it cool. A soft tap on the door made her spin round.

'Who is it?'

'Are you all right, Mrs Grant?'

Julia's heart quickened again as she recognised the girl's voice. 'I'm fine, thank you.'

'May I come in? I've brought you something.'

Julia hesitated. Something made her want to look at the girl again – just to reassure herself. Maybe she was older then she'd thought. Perhaps if she talked to her there would be some hint, some clue that would put her mind at rest. She stepped up to the door, turned the key, opened it and looked out. 'I told you, I'm quite all right. See for yourself.'

Fleur held out the glass of brandy. 'I've brought you this,' she said, 'It will help to make you feel better.'

Julia took the glass, but she was looking at the girl. Suddenly something deep inside told her that there was no mistake. This tall girl with beautiful eyes and a honey complexion was Dean's daughter – *her* daughter. She knew it with an instinctive certainty that took her breath away. And now, looking into the girl's eyes, she saw that Fleur knew it too.

Julia tossed back the brandy in one gulp. It made her gasp a little but at least it steadied her trembling. 'You're Fleur,' she said. 'You are, aren't you?'

'Yes.'

'And you know who I am. You've tracked me down. Well, what do you want now that you've found me?'

Fleur frowned. '*Want?*'

'Yes. Don't look at me like that. You must want something or you wouldn't be here. Why don't you just say? Come on. How – how much?'

'How much *what?*' Fleur took a step towards her. It was a strange, almost bizarre experience, standing face to face with her natural mother at last. A thousand times, late at night when she couldn't sleep, in her secret heart of hearts, she had allowed herself to fantasise about this meeting. Now it wasn't in the least how she had imagined it would be. Never in her wildest fantasies had she imagined she would be accused of demanding money. She was shocked and hurt.

'I'm here because I'm doing my job,' she said.

'I meant, what are you doing in Elvemere?' Julia asked, her voice sharp with tension. 'I warn you, if you think you can blackmail me you're on dangerous ground. How much is your silence going to cost me?'

Anger burned Fleur's breast. She closed the bathroom door and stepped closer to Julia. She was slightly the taller of the two and Julia took an involuntary step backwards, suddenly intimidated by the angry gleam in the girl's eyes.

'I'm here because I promised Dolly, my grandmother, just before she died that I'd come and find you. That's the only reason. I found out who and where you were a long time ago. But I never intended to speak or to make myself known to you. If you want to hear the truth, I've never felt the need or the wish to know you. In my book, a woman who can walk out on her baby isn't worth the name of mother. And as for *blackmailing* you . . .'

'Please . . .' Julia winced and held out her hand. 'I'm sorry I said that. It was just that seeing you like this – finding out who you are – has been a shock. I couldn't think of any other reason, but . . .' She bit her lip. 'Look – there's an awful lot here that I don't understand. I didn't mean to insult you. I wish I could make you understand what happened all those years ago. There's – oh, God, there's so much I wish you could know.'

'Don't bother!' Fleur told her bitterly, turning on her heel. 'As far as I'm concerned you're a stranger. And you always will be.' At the door she turned. 'If you're feeling better I'll go and get on with the work I'm paid for.'

Julia reached out and made a desperate grab at the hand that was about to turn the door handle. 'Please, don't go. We can't just leave it at that. We have to talk. Fleur. You must know that neither of us can walk away from this situation. Not now.' She moistened her dry lips. 'Look, can we meet somewhere?'

Fleur looked at the floor. Half of her wanted to escape, never to see or speak to this despicable woman again. Standing up in public for the rights of single mothers after the way she had behaved! But there was a small part of her that was curious to know Julia's side of the story – that needed to know that at some time in the distant past her mother had loved and wanted her. Despising herself for this weakness, she lifted her head. 'I don't really think there's anything to be gained, do you?'

'*Yes*. Yes, I do! There are things I want you to know; things I need you to tell me too. Please say you'll see me, Fleur? Even if it's just the once.'

For a long moment the two women looked at each other, then Fleur gave in. 'All right,' she said. 'Where? And when?'

Julia let out her breath in a sigh of relief. 'There's a little pub called The Millstone in a village called Eastbridge. It's about two miles the other side of Merifield on the main Newmarket road. I'll meet you there tomorrow evening – if that's convenient?'

'Yes, all right.'

'About eight?'

'Yes.'

'Do you have transport?'

'I can borrow some, I think.'

'Right. If you can't make it, just ring the pub. They'll give me a message.'

Joanna walked out into the hall just as Fleur was coming down the stairs. She looked up at her inquiringly.

'Everything all right?'

'Yes, thank you.'

Joanna looked past her towards the top of the stairs. 'Is Mrs Grant up there?'

Fleur hesitated. 'I don't know. I've just been to get my handkerchief.' Joanna was staring pointedly at the empty brandy glass in her hand and she added quickly, 'Oh – I found this on the landing. Someone must have put it down.'

Unconvinced, Joanna nodded. 'Well, you'd better get back to the kitchen,' she said. 'I'll be wanting to serve the buffet in about ten minutes.' As Fleur closed the kitchen door she heard the bathroom door open and saw Julia quietly step out on to the landing. Smiling smugly to herself, Joanna turned back towards the chatter of her guests. So she had been right! So far, so good.

As she went into the room Charlie hailed her. 'Ah – there you are, lass! Lovely do. I think everyone is enjoying themselves.' He slipped an over-familiar arm around her waist. 'What was that you were saying earlier about finding a way to persuade Julia to change her mind about this doss house she's planning?'

Joanna smiled at him. 'I think you can leave that to me, Charlie,' she said mysteriously. 'I don't believe in counting my chickens, but I think I can safely say it's in the bag.'

'Good girl!' Charlie, mellow with whisky, hugged her painfully and bent to kiss her cheek. 'By heck, girl, I don't know what you're up to but you're a lass after my own heart!'

222

On the other side of the room Louise watched out of the corner of her eye. Was history repeating itself? Was she going to have to get rid of that woman again? Clearly this time it would be much more difficult. Joanna would not be intimidated by threats or tempted by money this time. She was also now a partner in the firm, which was regrettable, because Louise had the strongest feeling that if someone didn't do something to get rid of her, Joanna Hanson would be the ruin of them all.

Julia sat in the morning-room at Gresham House, having coffee with her parents. She'd understood and approved of their failure to put in an appearance at the party last night and after her encounter with Fleur everything else had gone out of her head. She'd got through the rest of the evening as best she could, concentrating on behaving perfectly normally, determined that Joanna should see nothing amiss. So, she'd been slightly surprised when her mother had telephoned this morning with an urgent request that she join them for coffee.

'There's something your father wants to talk to you about,' May said. 'It's quite important, dear, so we'd be grateful if you could make the time for us.'

When Julia arrived she'd been relieved to see that her father looked much better than the last time she had seen him. The doctor had put him on a mild tranquilliser and insisted that he get as much rest as possible. Already he looked more relaxed, the lines of strain around his mouth and eyes less deeply etched.

'We've booked a Caribbean cruise,' May told her excitedly as she carried in the tray of coffee. 'We leave the first week in April. That's only a few weeks away. There's so much I have to do before then. I was wondering if you and I might go up to town on a shopping spree?'

'Is that what you wanted to ask me?' Julia smiled, pleased to see her mother looking happier.

'No.' It was Harry who spoke. 'It's something much more serious than that, Julia. Your mother and I have talked things through very carefully and I've decided not to retire.'

Julia looked at him in dismay. 'Oh, Daddy! Are you sure about this?'

'I'm not going to be an active partner,' Harry told her. 'What I have in mind will need your cooperation. That's what I wanted to speak to you about this morning. What I'd like to do is to transfer my shares in the firm to you.'

'*To me*?' Julia felt a twinge of alarm. 'But why? I've never had anything to do with the business.'

'I think it's time you did. You'd be entitled to attend board meetings and vote on my behalf.' Harry looked at her dismayed expression. 'Well, you want your own way over the women's refuge, don't you? This could be a way of getting it. I intend to exercise my right to call an extraordinary general meeting to discuss this Victoria Gardens project.'

But Julia was shaking her head. 'But I'd only be outvoted, just as you were. Surely you can see that?'

Harry leaned forward. 'But you won't only have my shares. There'll be yours and your mother's proxy vote as well.'

'Even with those, it only brings it to evens.'

'You're forgetting Charlotte.'

'Her shares are in trust.'

'But as her mother you have control – I made sure that it was written into the agreement. In the matter of a decision as vital as this all shareholders have the right to vote. Charlie knows that only too well.'

'But what about Vernon's mother's shares?'

Harry smiled. 'You know what an old chauvinist Charlie is. She doesn't actually hold any shares in her own right. Theirs is a joint holding so she doesn't get a vote.'

Julia was shaking her head doubtfully. 'Wait a minute, Dad. I'm not sure I want to get into all this.'

Harry leaned forward, anxiety creasing his brow. 'Listen, Julia, Charlie Grant is going to wreck the firm with his crazy ideas. Nothing's surer than that. Think of it as saving GPC. You'll be doing it for Charlotte in the long run.'

'I'm still not sure.' For Julia the thought of sitting in at board meetings and voting against her father-in-law and Joanna – let alone Vernon – was anathema. 'They'll think I'm only doing it because of the house I've earmarked for the refuge,' she argued, looking from one to the other.

'Your motives aren't important. What is important is to stop this Victoria Gardnes madness from getting off the ground. Or at least to delay it.'

Julia sighed. 'I don't think you realise what you're asking. Vernon is my husband and you're asking me to vote against him. Can you imagine what that will do to our marriage?'

There was silence as her parents exchanged looks, then May said painfully, 'Julia, darling, there's somthing we feel you should know.'

'What? What is it?'

May glanced at her husband who nodded for her to continue. 'Charlotte came to see us last week. The child was very upset. It seems that she had seen Vernon with that woman – that Mrs Hanson. It was clear even to her that they were having some sort of – well – close relationship.'

'An affair, you mean?'

May winced. 'Not to put too fine a point on it, yes.'

'That's no more than I'd already suspected,' Julia said bitterly.

May's colour rose. 'I can't think how you can sit there and be so apathetic about it,' she said, her eyes blazing. 'He's been doing this to you for years, yet you choose to let him get away with it. Well, now it's affecting Charlotte, Julia, and it's time he stopped. If you don't care, we do, especially when we can see what it's doing to our only granddaughter!'

'And you're offering me a way of getting even. Or am I to use my vote as a threat, to bring him into line, is that it?'

'No, *no!*' Harry leaned across the table and laid a hand on his daughter's arm. 'It might look that way, love, but Charlotte will inherit the firm one day, remember. I'd like to think it will still be there for her to inherit.' He squeezed her hand. 'Julia, it's not revenge I'm after, believe me. I'm afraid that if Charlie gets his way it will be the end for all of us; the finish of GPC. I could just let them buy me out and be done with it – escape the disaster that's coming. What I'm doing is trying to avert it.'

Julia nodded. 'All right, how?'

'The property boom has been wonderful for us. Meadowlands is the jewel in our crown. If we get on with it and sell all the properties within the next few months it could bring us in enough to sustain us over the recession that I feel is inevitable. But if Charlie goes ahead with this Victoria Gardens plan – even with the help of Mrs Hanson's cash input – it could ruin us. Someone has to stop him. I'm asking you to be the one. Will you do it, for all our sakes?'

Julia felt trapped. She tried to visualise herself sitting in at a board meeting, facing Julia's feral eyes and the hostile faces of Charlie and Vernon as she dropped this bombshell her father was insisting on arming her with. The mere thought of it made her stomach churn. All the same, if what her father said were really true how could she refuse? 'Can I have some time to think it over?' she asked.

'Of course. But don't take too long,' Harry advised. 'Once they have my decision and my formal objection they'll have to call a meeting. That'll be your chance to exercise your voting power.'

Fleur had concocted a story in order to borrow the van for the evening. She hated lying to Sally but could hardly tell her the truth. She wanted to drive over to Eastbridge Garden Centre to buy some plants for her balcony. That was her story, and she meant to legitimise it by stopping off on the way and doing just that.

She had first tried to borrow Tom's car, but, as she had suspected he might, he was working and needed it.

'Where are you going?' he asked. 'Maybe I could drop you off and pick you up afterwards.'

Again she had been forced to fabricate a story. 'I said I'd meet Charlotte for a meal,' she said, hating to lie to him. 'I'd rather have my own transport. I don't know how long I'll be.'

'Okay.' He gave her a trusting grin and dropped a kiss on her forehead. 'Lucky you, having a slap-up nosh when I have to work. Bring me a doggy-bag, eh?'

'Sure, a doggy-bag.' She promised herself that if everything worked out he would be the first person she would tell.

She found the village without any problems. The Millstone stood at the end of the street. As she was early the car park at the side was almost empty. The pub was small and thatched. Daffodils were budding in tubs and window boxes and a brightly painted pub sign swung creakily at the top of its wooden pole. The millstone that gave the place its name was depicted on the sign hanging round the neck of a dyspeptic-looking female in medieval peasant costume. Looking up at it as she went in, Fleur shuddered, wondering if it was some sort of omen.

She went in through the low doorway and found herself immediately in the bar. A round-faced woman looked up from polishing glasses.

'Evening, love. There's a nice fire in the snug. There's a lady in there, waiting for you, I reckon. She asked me to tell you to join her there. What can I get you?'

'Oh, a tomato juice, please.'

Fleur took her drink and pushed open the door the woman indicated. The snug was a small cosy room with exposed beams. It was furnished with two or three dark oak tables and wheel-back chairs whose cushions matched the chintz curtains. Julia was sitting by the open log fire, a glass of what looked like gin and tonic on the table before her. She half rose as Fleur came.

'You came then. You managed to borrow a car?'

Fleur nodded. 'The van.' She sat down opposite and put her glass on the table. 'I had to lie to get it. I don't like lying, so I hope this is going to be worth it.'

Julia smiled wryly. 'You believe in speaking your mind, don't you?' She looked at Fleur for a long moment, searching for something of herself in the girl and failing to find it. 'There's so much you and I don't know about one another, Fleur,' she said sadly.

'Maybe we never will. Maybe it doesn't even matter any more.'

Julia took a sip of her drink. 'I was very young when you were born, you know. Much younger than you are now. Scarcely out of school.'

'I know, Grandma told me.'

'I fell desperately in love with Dean – your father.' She took a sip of her drink.' It was the first time I'd fallen in love and sometimes I wonder if the man I thought he was ever existed or if I made him up out of my own romantic dreams. If I'd been older and more experienced I'd have seen that it was doomed to failure from the first.'

'Lots of people make mistakes,' Fleur said dispassionately.

Julia smiled. 'What you're saying is that they stick with them – see them through and take the consequences.'

'Some have no choice.'

'You're right, of course. And you're entitled to your opinion. But perhaps one day you'll meet a man who tears your heart to pieces then lets you down. I hope for your sake that you don't.'

Fleur was silent, wondering if Julia knew that her husband was cheating on her. It seemed she hadn't had much luck in her relationships. She watched as Julia took another drink from her glass then looked at her.

'I'd had a sheltered, perhaps even a pampered, upbringing. Life in that little flat in Hackney was hard for me. When Dean told me he wasn't coming back to face his responsibilities, I panicked.'

'And you ran away. I know. Maybe that was understandable.' Fleur met her eyes for the first time. 'But you could have taken me with you.'

'Yes. That must seem unforgivably cowardly to you,' Julia admitted. 'But you can see for yourself what life in a small town like Elvemere is like. It was even worse twenty years ago. I couldn't face the thought of bringing disgrace on my parents – and myself. Of being talked about, gloated over.'

'Because you'd got an illegitimate baby?' Fleur held Julia's eyes. 'Or because of the colour of the baby's skin?'

'Both! I have to admit that it was both.' Julia leaned forward, her eyes earnest. 'We're here to be truthful with each other. Fleur. To lay our cards on the table, and I admit that to you now freely. I'm not proud of it and the guilt is something I'll carry with me for the rest of my days, though naturally I don't expect that to be any comfort to you.'

'Is that why you're campaigning for single mothers – because you feel guilty?'

'If you like. Yes, I suppose it is.' Fleur was silent and after a moment Julia went on, 'I did write and try to get you back, you know. Did Dolly ever tell you that?' Fleur's eyes swung upwards, meeting Julia's in surprise. 'Ah – I see that she didn't. She replied to my letter telling me that I was too late.'

'Too late.' Fleur frowned. 'What did she mean?'

'She said that you'd been adopted. In her letter she explained that she'd tried to manage on her own but that it was too much for her. She'd given you up for adoption and you'd gone to a childless couple who would give you a good home.'

Fleur shook her head. 'Why would she say a thing like that!'

'Maybe she'd grown too attached to you to give you up. She probably thought I didn't deserve to have you back – that I'd only leave you again. I don't know. It was months before I found out that she would have needed my permission to have you adopted. I wrote to her again, but she replied saying it had been an informal arrangement and that the couple had taken you abroad.' She took another sip of her drink. 'She said you would never know my name or anything about me. You were theirs now and it would be best for me to forget you.' She looked at Fleur, eyes dark with remembered pain. 'It was terrible. Such a brutal punishment. It was as though I'd never had a child. I wonder if you can imagine how it felt? I had nothing to remember you by, not even a snapshot. Only the aching memory of your trusting little face and your arms around my neck. The thought of the way I'd betrayed you broke my heart. It haunted me.' She bit her lip. 'God help me, it still does.'

Fleur was silent, trying to digest what Julia had just told her. Her initial reaction had been disbelief, but Julia had been honest with her about everything else, so why should she lie about that, especially after all this time? Dolly had been almost desperate in extracting her promise to seek her mother out. Could this be why? Had she felt guilty all these years for the lie she'd told in order to keep her grandchild with her? Fleur looked at Julia warily, still only half believing in her anguish.

'But can you honestly say you weren't relieved when Grandma said I'd been adopted?' she challenged. 'She must have known that you could have come and taken my any time you wanted to. I was your child. It was your right. She was just throwing you a lifebelt, that's all. And you grabbed it.'

'*No!*' Julia's voice was firm. 'I'd thought it through and I was prepared to face the music. I really wanted you back, Fleur. I wish I could make you believe that. I just wish it had been possible. Life would have been so different for us all.'

'Why didn't you come back and see for yourself?'

'I believed Dolly. She'd never struck me as a liar.'

Fleur could not argue that what Dolly had done was certainly out of character. 'All Grandma told me was that you'd left a note with your address,' she said slowly. 'But she never let me forget that I'd had a mother. She always spoke kindly and sympathetically about you.'

'That's something, I suppose. Probably more than I deserved at that.' Julia sighed. 'Were they good to you? Did you have a happy childhood?'

'They were very special people,' Fleur told her. 'It's only since I grew up that I've realised the sacrifices they made for me. I loved them both very much.'

'What about Maurice? Is he still alive?'

Fleur shook her head. 'No. Grandpa was killed in an accident at work when I was twelve. I had to give school and my "A" levels up when Grandma got ill. But whatever happened we always had each other and we were happy.'

'I'm glad.'

Fleur's dark eyes flashed. 'Oh? does that make you feel better?'

'Of course it does.'

'It doesn't bother you that your child grew up in near poverty while you were enjoying a luxurious life with your new husband and baby daughter?'

'You sound so bitter.'

'How would you feel? Grandpa and Grandma could have had an easier time if they hadn't had me to bring up. I could have stayed on at school and taken my "A" levels – maybe even gone to university. Who knows? Instead I had to leave and take a job in a fish and chip shop when Grandma's heart gave out. After she died I tried to live on alone at the flat in Brightman Lane. Perhaps you remember the place? Hardly a palace, was it? But I grew up there and it was the only home I'd ever known. But when I was left on my own I had a real struggle to afford the rent. Then, soon after that, I was attacked by a vicous thug late one night on my way home from work. That was when I decided I'd have to leave London.'

'To come and find me – as you promised Dolly?'

'Not really. It was just that I'd never been out of London before except on a day trip. Elvemere was the only place I counld think of to run to. The only place I had any kind of connection with. I told you, I never intended to have anything to do with you.' Fleur was into her stride now. The desire to hit back hard was strong, fuelled by the resentment stored up inside her. 'I suppose you could say that I ran away too. But the difference was that I had no one to run to. Although I had my mother's name and address, I couldn't expect any help from *her*. There was no comfortable home and loving welcome waiting for me!' She looked at Julia, her dark eyes defiant. 'But I survived. I got a room and a good job – eventually a nice flat. I've done without a mother for twenty years and I've coped okay. I can't see any reason why I should want or need one now. Can you?'

'Put like that, I suppose not.' Julia swallowed the last of her drink and looked long and hard at Fleur. 'I don't blame you for feeling the way you do, Fleur. And at the risk of sounding patronising, I want to say that I like the way you've grown up. You're strong and brave. You have principles and integrity.'

'If I have, I got them from my grandparents!'

'Yes.' Julia swallowed painfully. 'I deserved that. But you're right. Those things weren't inherited from me – and certainly not from your father. I've never had that kind of strength. They must have been very proud of you, the Sylvesters. What can I say, Fleur, except that I did try? I promise you that I did regret what I did and I really wanted to have you back.' She reached across the table to cover Fleur's hand with her own. 'I wish with all my heart that things could have been – could *be* – different. I wish I could tell everyone about you. Come out into the open.' She looked into Fleur's eyes. 'But you can see how impossible it would be now, can't you?'

She withdrew her hand. 'Yes, of course.'

'It happened because I fell foolishly in love with the wrong man,' Julia went on. 'I'm not trying to shift the blame to him. I chose him. It was my judgement that was at fault. But I do know that things would have been different if he hadn't let me down.' She looked at Fleur. 'Will you let me help you – do something for you, to make up for it all? If there's anything you need . . . money . . .'

'*No!*' Fleur stiffened. 'You accused me of blackmail the other night.'

Julia winced. 'I know and I'm sorry. I was in a panic. I didn't know what I was saying. Please try to forget I said that, won't you?'

'Okay, if you say so. But I meant it when I said I didn't need anything – or any*body*. And it was by accident that we met in the end. I would never have approached you.'

230

There was a moment of silence between, then Fleur got up from the table. 'Well, I've kept my promise to Grandma. I've found you. And now I've even spoken to you, which is more than I meant to do. But I think it's best for us both that this is where it ends. Right?'

Julia rose to face her. 'Isn't there some way we can see each other? I don't want you to go out of my life again. I'd like so much to get to know you, Fleur.'

She shook her head. 'There have been too many mistakes made to risk another. Maybe I'd disappoint you. Maybe we'd disappoint each other.'

'At least think about it,' Julia said. 'You know where I am. Any time you want to see me, or just, ring. I hope you will.'

'Yes. Well, I'll think about it.' Fleur walked away, but as she reached the door she looked back. 'Goodbye. It was nice meeting you.'

Julia sat for some time after she had gone, thinking about this girl who was her daughter. She had grown up with a strong character, but so bitter and full of mistrust. Had she done that to Fleur? It seemed that Julia's life was full of failures and regrets. She'd failed at being a mother, both to Fleur and to Charlotte, and it looked as though she must be a pretty unsatisfactory wife too. Was she about to lose her husband to Joanna? But would the breakdown of her marriage mean any more to her than humiliation? she asked herself. Love for Vernon had been short-lived and disappointing anyway.

She turned her mind towards what her father had asked her to do. He strongly believed it to be the right thing, and by doing it she could further her own aims too. Suddenly making up her mind, she got up from the table and walked out into the car park. She would do it. It was time she took her courage in both hands and fought for something worthwhile. Maybe it still wasn't too late to redeem herself.

Driving back to Elvemere Fleur went over the conversation she and Julia had had. One sentence had found its mark as surely as an arrow. *Perhaps one day you'll meet a man who tears your heart to pieces and then lets you down.* She thought of Peter and their ill-fated affair. Would he have deserted her in the same way if she had become pregnant? And if he had – who could know what might have happened? The thought sobered her, shaking her long-held belief in Julia's heartlessness. Everyone was vulnerable when it came to love. Could anyone really be sure of how they would behave, driven by misery and despair?

Then another, more immediate thought struck her. Maybe she should have confessed to Julia that she'd let slip to Joanna Hanson that Dean Sylvester was her father. She dismissed the thought at once. Joanna could prove nothing. There was no way she could use the information to harm anyone.

Chapter 12

'You *can't!*' Vernon stared at his father-in-law in shocked disbelief.

'I think you know perfectly well that I can.' Harry's expression was calm. 'I'm perfectly within my rights to demand an extraordinary meeting, just as I am entitled to transfer my shares to my own daughter. And I trust in her judgment in acting for me when it comes to voting. I shall be making my proposal known to your father later this morning. I'm only telling you in advance as a courtesy.'

'Very good of you, I'm sure,' Vernon said bitterly. 'And you haven't the slightest idea how she'll vote, of course! You haven't discussed it with her by any chance?'

'Of course I've discussed it with her. Julia and I are in complete agreement as regards your father's newest proposal.'

'Julia hasn't the slightest interest in, let alone any knowledge of, the business. All she wants is to gain herself some recognition as a councillor.'

'I think you underestimate Julia,' Harry said. 'You always have, Vernon, if you don't mind my saying so. It could turn out to be your downfall.'

'I'm her husband. I could forbid her to do as you say,' Vernon blustered, his face red with alarm.

'I wouldn't try if I were you.' Harry's mild blue eyes grew cold and grey behind his spectacles. 'You see, she knows about your affair with Joanna Hanson. And what is worse, so does Charlotte. The child came to me in deep distress. She saw the two of you together – in a situation that apparently made your relationship only too obvious. The poor girl didn't know what to do, whether to tell her mother or not.'

'And you told her to tell Julia?'

'No. I told her to try and forget what she'd seen. Then *I* told

Julia,' Harry said. 'This is one affair too many for my liking, Vernon. You've cheated on Julia ever since you married her. Now it seems you're not above flaunting your adultery for anyone to see, even your own daughter. This time you've gone too far and you're not going to get away with it. So unless you want the whole thing to blow up in your face, I'd go along with things quietly for a while.'

'*Charlotte* came to you?' Vernon was shaking his head. 'I don't believe it!' He was seriously taken aback by Harry's revelation. 'How could she have seen us? Where – and when?'

'Coming out of Mrs Hanson's house. It seems her aunt was driving her home, taking a short cut down Hazel Grove.'

'Kath!' Vernon muttered under his breath. 'I might have known she was at the bottom of this! So, I was coming out of her house. What does that prove?'

'Apparently your brazen behaviour said the rest,' Harry said grimly.

'All right,' Vernon challenged. 'Let Julia vote in your place. Let her try and defeat Dad's plan. She won't win. How can she?'

'With my shares and her mother's, plus her own,' Harry said. 'Then there are the shares I bought and placed in trust for Charlotte. Julia is entitled to vote on behalf of her daughter too. I think you're going to find yourself out-manoeuvred, Vernon.' Harry was unable to keep the smile off his face.

Vernon left Gresham House hurriedly, his mind in turmoil. When Harry had telephoned asking him to call and see him this morning on his way to the office he had wondered what he could possible have to say. He'd half expected to receive his father-in-law's resignation personally. He'd almost looked forward to the interview. But never in his wildest nightmares had he envisaged anything like this.

Jumping into his car he drove straight round to Joanna's house. He arrived just in time to see her coming out of the front door. Running up the drive, he grasped her arm and propelled her back towards the house.

'Inside,' he barked. 'We have to talk.'

'Wait a minute,' she protested. 'What do you think you're doing? I wanted to be at the office early. I've got a lot to do and . . .'

'*Shut up*! It can wait. This can't!'

'Don't speak to me like that!' She shook her arm free and glared at him indignantly for a moment. Then, seeing the distraught look on his face, she took out her key and reluctantly unlocked the front door. 'This had better be worth it,' she said as she held the door open.

Inside the hall Vernon slammed the door and turned to her. 'Harry Philips rang me this morning. He asked me to go round there urgently. He's not resigning after all.'

She shrugged. 'So—?'

'So – he's transferring his shares to Julia.'

She laughed. 'And the best of British luck!'

'Not only *his* shares but May's and Charlotte's too.'

'I didn't know Charlotte was a shareholder?'

'They're in trust for her.' Vernon shook his head impatiently. 'Don't you see, that gives Julia a majority vote! And it goes without saying how she'll use it.'

'Talk her out of it,' she said abruptly. 'For heaven's sake, Vernon, you're her husband. Surely it's in her interest to vote with you?'

He raked a hand through his hair and sat down heavily on the stairs. 'She knows, Jo – about us. It seems everyone knows. My sister was driving Charlotte home from the stables and they came this way. Apparently they saw me leaving here – saw you seeing me off.' He waved one arm in the direction of the front door. 'Out there.' He groaned and lowered his head into his hands. 'Oh, Christ, what a mess! It's going to ruin everything. And I'll be the one taking the flak.'

'Oh, pull yourself together, Vernon,' Joanna snapped. 'Letting yourself go to pieces isn't going to get us anywhere.' She chewed her lip thoughtfully. 'Look, – just leave this to me. I think I can get us out of it.'

He sprang to his feet and looked hopefully into her eyes. 'How? What can you do?'

'Never mind how or what. Just trust me.'

'Whatever you're planning it's going to have to be quick,' he told her. 'Harry's getting in touch with Dad later this morning. He's demanding an extraordinary meeting and telling him about the transfer of shares to Julia. The minute Dad gets that phone call there's going to be blood all over the carpet. *My* blood!'

She grasped him by the arms and shook him gently. 'Stop panicking! Just tell him calmly that you have everything in hand. Tell him *you'll* handle Julia. Be positive for once. It'll do wonders for your image.'

He put his hands on her shoulders. 'Oh, God, Jo, are you really sure you can pull this off?'

'Ninety percent sure,' she said. 'I'd better get on to it at once though, as you say. Can you manage without me for this morning?'

'Of course.' He was relieved. If his father was going to start bawling him out he'd rather Joanna wasn't around to witness his

235

humiliation anyway. 'Look, Jo, maybe we should let things cool off? Stop seeing each other outside office hours for a bit. Just for now, of course. Till this furore dies down. What do you say?'

She shrugged. 'Perhaps you're right. Now you'd better get moving. And remember what I said: be positive. Stand your ground with Charlie. Make him believe you're in charge for once.'

It was almost an hour later that Joanna stood on the porch awaiting Julia's answer to her ring at the bell. After Vernon had left she'd sat down to make her plan, thinking out carefully what she would say and how to approach the subject. No point in rushing into this without giving it plenty of thought, allowing for every possible eventuality. When everything was clear in her mind she'd gone upstairs and changed out of her office suit into a pair of well-cut trousers, a cashmere sweater and tweed jacket. Better to go casually dressed. It wouldn't do to appear intimidating.

To her surprise a thin young girl with blonde hair answered the door.

'Is Mrs Grant at home?' Joanna asked.

'Yes. Who shall I say wants to see her?' Tracey asked.

Joanna stepped over the threshold. 'Just tell her it's Joanna,' she said with a confident smile. 'We're old friends.'

'If you'd just like to wait . . .' The girl showed her into the sitting room. 'I'll tell her you're here.'

Joanna looked around her. The room was furnished tastefully, but in a provincial style. Pastel green walls and floral pictures; moss green carpet and matching velvet curtains. Twin settees with oatmeal linen upholstery were placed to either side of the Adam-style fireplace, and an onyx-topped coffee table stood between them. Joanna glanced at the magazines on it. Current copies of *Harper's* and *Vogue*. She smiled. She'd have taken bets on it. In one corner an antique glass-fronted cabinet displayed a collection of delicate porcelain figurines, Dresden or Meissen, Joanna wasn't sure which. She smiled to herself. It was all so predictable, restful but bland. It lacked style, like Julia herself. No wonder poor Vernon craved excitement.

When Julia came into the room she looked surprised and not altogether pleased. 'Joanna! What can I do for you?'

She came to the point at once. 'I've just heard about your father transferring his shares to you. And I thought it only fair to warn you that if you have any plans for outvoting the rest of us, you do it at your peril!'

'My peril?' Julia raised one eyebrow. 'Really? I'm surprised to

236

hear you make a melodramatic remark like that. And what am I supposed to be in peril of?'

'Of having a small episode from your past revealed.' Joanna had the satisfaction of seeing the confidence melt from Julia's face.

'If you're talking about something that happened when I was in my teens, long before Vernon and I even met . . .'

'Oh, yes, I *am*.'

'And you think the threat of revealing that twenty years ago I had a brief affair with a pop musician is going to make headlines, do you?'

'Maybe not – if that were all.' Joanna stepped closer to her. 'I'm surprised that you seem so unconcerned. Tell me, Julia, just between ourselves, what is your daughter doing here in Elvemere?'

Julia felt her blood chill. 'Charlotte?'

'Not Charlotte. You know perfectly well who I mean, Julia. *Fleur*. She is your daughter, isn't she? Your little flower child?'

'Fleur?' Julia fought down the panic that gripped her. 'I – do you mean . . .'

'The girl from the caterer's. Sally Arden's assistant. Yes. Don't pretend you don't know who I mean, Julia. *I know!*'

'You know nothing. How could you know?'

'From her own lips. That's how!'

She couldn't. Surely she wouldn't! Julia swallowed hard and took a deep breath, trying not to show the consternation she felt. Looking up at Joanna, she asked, 'Exactly what did she say?'

'Enough. Plenty in fact. It came out in conversation that Dean Sylvester was her father; that she'd never actually met him because her parents parted before she was born. It didn't take a genius to work it out. It all fits, Julia. She's just the right age. You spun your parents some tale and ran off with him. You were away from home for long enough to make it possible. It's true, isn't it? Don't deny it. I saw your shocked reaction to her the other night at the party.'

'This is all guesswork on your part,' Julia said. 'You can't prove anything.'

'Oh, I'm sure I could if I tried. And if you do compel me to start digging into the past, Julia, I shan't do it quietly, I assure you.'

'There's a law against what you're suggesting. There is such a thing as libel.'

Joanna smiled. 'True, but do you really want to get into anything as public as that? Not going to look too good for you as a councillor, is it? Not going to give this new philanthropic image of yours a lot of credibility. And what about your family – your parents, Charlotte and Vernon? Not to mention Charlie and Louise. Do they know?'

Julia's stunned silence told Joanna that she had scored. Her guess-work had paid off.

Julia looked down at the hands that lay clenched in her lap. She was sure that Fleur would never have volunteered the information that Dean was her father. Why should she? Joanna must have tricked it out of her. She was good at that.

'All right,' she said at last. 'What is it you want me to do?'

'Not much really. Just vote with us, that's all. It's important to Charlie that he gets his way over this Victoria Gardens plan.'

'My father thinks it could ruin the firm,' Julia told her. 'His motives for wanting to sink the plan are not malicious. He's thinking about the future of the business. That's in your interest too now that you have money invested.'

'Your father lacks vision, if you don't mind my saying so,' Joanna said brutally. 'He's like a lot of old men, he's living in the past – afraid to take risks, plodding along in the slow lane. Vote with us, Julia, and all will be well. Your little secret will be safe and the firm will flourish in the way it deserves to. You can trust me on that, I promise.'

A thought occurred to Julia. 'There's always the chance the council won't pass the plans. I'm only one voice there, you know.'

Joanna smiled. 'Seeing that Charlie is planning to do what the council was about to do anyway, I doubt if they'll raise any objections.'

Julia looked at her for a long moment. 'And if I do as you say, will you end your affair with Vernon?' she asked at last.

'Ah. Charlotte has been talking.' Joanna shook her head. 'You don't really believe the highly coloured ramblings of a resentful teenager, do you?'

'You're denying it?'

Joanna sighed. 'Charlotte has always disliked me for some reason. She's just trying to make trouble.'

'You haven't answered my question. Are you denying it?'

'Vernon and I had a teenage fling years ago. Before you met him. We're old friends, that's all. I've grown up quite a lot since then, Julia, unlike some of the petty-minded people I've met since I came back. Anyway, I don't know what you're worrying about. You and he are inextricably tied together by the business.'

'But you have been seeing each other?'

Joanna shrugged. 'Of course. How could we not? We work together, don't we? And occasionally an out-of-hours meeting has been necessary.'

'You've been using him, haven't you – just to get what you want? You always were greedy and devious, Joanna. Now you're . . .'

A tap on the door prevented her from finishing the sentence and Tracey came in with a tray. 'Excuse me, Mrs Grant, but I thought you might like some coffee,' she said.

Julia stared stonily at Joanna. 'I'm afraid Mrs Hanson hasn't time,' she said pointedly. 'She has to rush off to the office. It was good of you to call, Joanna,' she said, standing up. 'I'll see you at the meeting. Goodbye.'

She left Tracey to show Joanna out, sinking back into her chair with a stifled groan. What a mess. What a horrendous mess!

Tracey came back into the room and looked with concern at Julia's troubled face. 'I hope I did right, asking her in, Mrs Grant. Should I have asked you first?'

Julia shook her head. 'No, it's all right, Tracey.'

'I hope it wasn't bad news.'

Julia looked at the girl's kindly face and smiled. 'Nothing I can't handle.'

'Only you've been so good to me and Damie. If there was ever anything I could do for you, I'd be only too glad.'

'Sit down and have some coffee with me,' Julia invited. 'You've brought two cups and I'm sure you're ready for a break. There's something I need to talk to you about.' She poured two cups of coffee and handed one to the girl. 'We haven't had a chat for some time. Tell me how things are with you. Do you see anything of Rick these days?'

Tracey sipped her coffee thoughtfully. 'Now and again,' she said guardedly.

'He's not still demanding money, I hope?'

'No. He's been working. Only some casual labouring, but at least he's earning.'

'Is he still using that awful stuff?'

Tracey shook her head. 'I don't think so. I'm keeping my fingers crossed that he's off it for good.' She didn't tell Julia that Rick had found out where she was working; that he'd taken to watching until everyone had gone out, then calling round at the back door, insisting on seeing his baby son. There didn't seem any harm in it. In fact Rick had seemed almost like his old self lately. He seemed to be making the effort to pull himself together at last. Tracey looked at her employer and realised to her relief that she had only asked the question out of politeness and obviously wasn't going to press her for further information. Noticing Julia's strained look, she asked, 'Is there anything wrong, Mrs Grant? You said there was something

239

you wanted to talk about. Was it something to do with that Mrs Hanson?'

'In a way.' Julia forced a smile. 'She's someone I knew a long time ago, but she's no friend of mine now.'

'I thought there was something. I wish I hadn't let her in now. If I'd known she was going to upset you . . .'

'I'd have had to see her anyway.' Julia looked into the girl's open face. 'Tracey, I'm afraid we're going to have to wait a bit longer for our women's refuge.'

'Oh, no! But I though it was all set.'

'It was, but there's a hitch. We can't have the house in Victoria Gardens after all. It's only a setback though. We'll just have to look round for another empty property.' She paused. It would be such a relief to confide in someone – someone who would be on her side – totally outside her immediate circle. On a sudden impulse she said, 'Tracey – if I tell you something, will you promise to keep it to yourself?'

'Of course. You know I will.'

'Once, many years ago, when I was as young as you are now but not nearly as grown-up and sensible, I fell in love. I ran away with a young man – a pop musician. The affair was destined to end disastrously and if I hadn't been so immature I'd have seen that. But before I realised my mistake, I found I was expecting his child.'

'Oh, Mrs Grant.' Tracey's eyes were round. 'What happened? Did you have the baby?'

'Yes, a little girl. But her father wasn't interested. He only saw her the once, just after she was born, when he came home to tell me it was all over between us.'

'What did you do?'

'Something I've been ashamed of ever since. I was terribly home-sick and one day I just walked out and came home. I left my baby with her grandmother who adored her. No one ever knew about it. I started again – made a new life and thought it was all over and forgotten. Till now.'

'And now – that Mrs Hanson – she knows?'

Julia nodded. 'She was a close friend at the time, the only person who knew about the relationship. Now, somehow, she's found out about the child. And she's threatening to tell my family.'

Tracey gasped. 'But that's blackmail! You could go to the police.'

Julia smiled ruefully. 'Hardly.'

'No, I suppose not. And does this have something to do with why we can't have the refuge?'

'Partly. It's too complicated for me to explain properly, but unfortunately it means letting my mother and father down very badly in order to keep my past from them.'

Tracey frowned. 'Why don't you just tell them about the baby?' she said. 'Surely that would be better? People don't bother so much about things like that nowadays.'

Julia shook her head. 'I'm afraid they'd still be dreadfully upset. But it isn't just them, you see. There's my in-laws, Charlotte and my husband. Not to mention what it would do to my present position as councillor.'

Tracey nodded. 'Yeah, I see.' She looked at Julia sympathetically. 'Oh, what a shame, Mrs Grant, after you've worked so hard and everything. You're just like us, aren't you? You know how it feels, being left with a baby. Did you keep in touch with your baby's grandma?'

'No. I tried later to get my daughter back, but I was told she'd been adopted.'

Tracey frowned. 'That must've been awful. I don't know what I'd do if I lost Damie. So – what will you do, Mrs Grant?'

Julia sighed. 'I'm afraid I don't have much choice, Tracey. I'm just going to have to do what Mrs Hanson says.'

Fleur sang as she worked in Sally's pleasant little office. The sun was shining and this morning she'd had a letter from Bobby to say that she was getting engaged. She'd met Jeff at college and they'd decided to marry as soon as they both qualified. Bobby had mentioned him before in her letters, but this was the first inkling she'd given that the relationship was serious. Fleur reflected that the news might once have made her sad. A few short months ago it would have felt like the end of the closeness she and Bobby had shared all their lives. When she had first arrived in Elvemere she had missed her friend so much. But now her lack of sadness and her delight in Bobby's obvious happiness made her realise how firmly she had settled here.

Sally had gone up to London that morning, intending to spend the day shopping for her coming trip to Switzerland, including choosing her wedding outfit. The date of Peter's marriage drew closer with each day, but the thought of his betrayal no longer disturbed Fleur.

During Sally's absence she planned to work in the office during the morning, catching up with the paperwork, then spend the afternoon in the kitchen checking stocks and filling the freezer up with canapes and quiches for their next function. The work was pleasant, leaving her mind free to remember the happy weekend she and

Tom had spent painting the balcony. He had insisted they do it that weekend as he had a free Saturday for once. Besides, as he'd reminded her, he'd be moving out in a few days' time.

'I might need a favour from you then,' he told her. 'Packing's never been my strong point. You can have a look at my new place at the same time – advise me about furnishing and decorating.'

'You plan to make it permanent then?'

'As permanent as it can be. I'm planning to stay on at least until a better job turns up.' He grinned. 'Of course, if I'm asked to take over as editor of the *Clarion* I might stay longer.'

They worked steadily and companionably together. By Saturday evening the wrought iron railings had been thoroughly rubbed down and a coat of rust inhibiter and undercoat had been applied. Fleur had prepared a casserole, which had been simmering away slowly all afternoon. They tucked into it ravenously after cleaning their brushes and scrubbing their hands clean of paint splashes.

'You've been in a light-hearted mood all day,' Tom remarked as he looked at her across the table. 'Has something nice happened?'

She hesitated, wondering whether or not to confide in him, then, unable to keep it to herself any longer she said, 'I do have something to tell you, as a matter of fact.'

'I thought there was something.' He laid down his knife and fork and looked at her apprehensively. 'It's nothing to do with Arden, is it?'

'Nothing at all. That's over, Tom, I told you.' She paused. 'No – it's about my mother. I've met and talked to her.'

'Hey! Good for you. How did it go?'

'It was okay. Better than I thought, Tom. I got a lot of things off my chest. We both did. It made me realise that it wasn't as simple as I've always thought.'

'There are always two sides to every question.'

'I know. I always knew that. Grandma was always making excuses for her. It's just that hearing it from her made me understand her reasons for doing what she did at the time – how she felt, and why. She told me that she did once try to get me back. I never knew about that. It seems my grandmother told her I'd been adopted.'

'Well, at least you know she tried.'

'And I believe she really did suffer for what she did. She tried to make me understand how hard it was for her, especially when she couldn't tell anyone. It made quite a lot of difference to how I feel about her.'

'You've stopped being so angry with her then?'

'Well – yes.'

'And you liked her?'

Fleur nodded thoughtfully. 'Yes. More than I expected to. She was honest – didn't try to make excuses for herself. My father let her down badly and – well, I do know how that feels, don't I? But the most important thing is that now I've met her, I can think of her as a real person and not just the faceless woman who walked out on me when I was a baby.'

'That's great! So are you going to see each other again?'

'No.' Fleur shook her head regretfully. 'I don't want to make life difficult for her.'

'But surely you could still meet – see each other as friends?'

'She did suggest that, but I said no. I don't want to have some kind of hole in the corner relationship with her. I said it would be best if we just left it at that.'

'That's a pity. She won't come right out and acknowledge you then?'

'She can't. And I do see why. She's married with another daughter and a public image, I suppose you'd call it, to uphold. No one knows about me, you see, not even her parents. Admitting now that she had a child in her teens could be damaging for her.'

'Are you sure? There's a lot more tolerance and understanding about things like that nowadays.'

'I'm not so sure there would be in her case.'

'So, are you disappointed?'

'No. I've done without a mother all these years. Anyway, I've got good friends – and you.'

'What does that mean? That I'm more than a friend?' His eyes held hers for a moment, then she laughed.

'Stop fishing. Of course you're a friend. A very special one. Tell you what, when you're settled in at Park Row, I'll help you give a flat-warming party. I'll do a buffet like we do at Arden Catering. All the trimmings.'

'That'll be great.' He paused for a moment. 'Fleur . . .' He looked at her. 'Your mother – she's Julia Grant, isn't she?' He regretted his words the moment he'd said them. He saw her expression close up and her eyes cloud. She got up from the table.

'Look at the time! If we're going to get any more done to the balcony we'd better make a start. It's getting dark already.'

He rose quickly to face her. 'Fleur!' Putting his hands on her shoulders he looked down at her. 'You know there's no way we can do any more tonight. Look, I'm sorry I sprang it on you. Forget it. Put it down to journalist's curiosity.'

She looked at him. 'You knew before, didn't you?'

243

'I've had my suspicions for some time,' he admitted. 'But it was no more than an educated guess really. You don't have to worry. I'm not going to say a word about it to anyone.' He held her away from him to look into her eyes. 'You don't think I'd risk losing your trust now, do you, Fleur?'

'No, of course not.'

'And I'm really glad you did speak to her. It was what you needed, if only to lay a ghost.'

She relaxed, leaning against him for a moment. 'Thank you, Tom. You're the only person who's ever really cared about me. Apart from my grandparents, I mean.'

He held her close, dropping a kiss on the top of her head. 'Well, that's easy,' he said awkwardly. 'Seeing that you're you and I'm me. You do know that you're pretty special to me, don't you?'

'Yes, I know, Tom,' she said, her words muffled against his chest. When she looked up at him again he saw to his relief that her anxiety had gone. Her eyes were clear and shining again. 'So if we can't do any more work on the balcony, what shall we do with the rest of the evening – apart from the washing up, I mean?'

He grinned and pulled her close. 'Oh, I daresay we'll think of something,' he said.

Fleur sat staring at the flickering computer screen as she remembered the evening they had spent together. Tomorrow she would be helping him move out. It had been so cosy and convenient, having Tom under the same roof. She would miss him. She examined her feelings for him. He made her happy. She enjoyed his company – looked forward to being with him – being close. But was that love? Once she had thought that the heady excitement she had known with Peter was love, but that had proved to be an illusion. Was she really such a poor judge? All she knew was that if she were to lose Tom life would never be quite the same again. She sighed. If only she could be sure . . .

When Vernon got to the office he stopped by his father's secretary's desk.

'Is my father in yet, Phyllis?'

She looked up. 'No, Mr Vernon. He had some outside appointments this morning. Won't be in until this afternoon.'

He stifled a sigh of relief. 'Right. Did Mr Philips ring?'

'Yes. He's ringing back later.'

'I see. Give me ten minutes to go through the post then send

244

Charlotte in to me, will you? And make sure we're not disturbed until I tell you.'

In his office he hung up his coat and sat down at the desk to scan quickly through the pile of correspondence. Nothing there that couldn't wait. Just as well. He was going to have a few things to say to that daughter of his and wanted to have them quite clear in his mind before she appeared.

When she knocked and put her head round the door he was ready for her. 'Come in and close the door,' he said grimly.

She did as he said, then sat down in the chair opposite, her eyes bright and her mouth set in a defiant line. 'What am I supposed to have done now?' she asked defensively.

'I think you know very well what you've done,' he said, glowering at her. 'Going to your grandfather with mischievous tales. I hope you know the trouble you've caused.'

'I was worried,' she muttered. 'I needed to talk to someone. Would you rather I'd told Mum?'

He slapped his hand down hard on the desk, making her jump. 'You had no right to talk to anyone! Why didn't you come to me? I could have told that you were making a mistake. But no! You interpret something you see as an illicit assignation and go running to your grandfather screaming adultery!'

Charlotte blushed and looked down at her hands. 'What was I supposed to think? Anyone would have thought the same.' She looked up at him again, her eyes accusing. 'She was wearing a dressing gown!'

'As it happened, I had to drop something off on my way home,' he said. 'Joanna was about to have a bath. That's why she was wearing her dressing gown. Not that I owe you any explanations.'

'You were kissing.'

'For heaven's sake, girl, grow up! If we were really having an affair, do you think we would conduct it on the doorstep?' He leaned forward to glare at her. 'Well – *do you*?'

'How would I know?'

'Exactly! How *would* you know? You're a very silly, naive girl, yet you jump to conclusions and start spreading rumours, causing absolute mayhem. I hope you realise that because of you this firm may lose the chance to pull off its biggest deal ever!'

'I don't see how . . .'

'You don't see a lot of things!' he shouted. 'And those you do see, you get wrong. I should send you home – suspend you. But unfortunately you happen to be my daughter and I have certain obligations to you. Instead I want you to go round to your grand-

245

parents' house after work this evening and tell them you made a terrible mistake and that you're sorry for all the trouble you've caused. I'm going to insist that you apologise to Joanna too. Heaven knows what she must think of you.'

'I won't!'

'You'll bloody well do as I say, girl!' he thundered.

Charlotte stared at him, eyes blazing with bitter resentment and mouth trembling. She got up from her chair. 'Is that all? Can I go now?'

'Just one more thing, Charlotte. From now on I absolutely forbid you to go to your aunt's stables.'

Her eyes flew open in horror. '*Dad!* No, please.'

'You heard what I said. Your aunt and I have never seen eye to eye. She'd do anything to discredit me and I can see her hand at the bottom of this mess.'

'It's not like that. *Really* it isn't. She just happened to be with me at the time. Look, I'll apologise to Mrs Hanson, anything you say, but . . .'

'That's *enough*, Charlotte. You heard what I said. I don't want to hear any more arguments. I won't change my mind.'

'But I can't just not turn up. I'll have to go and tell her – explain.'

'I'll do any explaining that's necessary,' Vernon said. 'I'll ring her now.' He looked up as she hovered by the door. 'That's all. You can go now, Charlotte. I've said all I have to say and I don't want to hear any more about it.'

The extraordinary meeting of GPC shareholders took place a week later and went without a hitch. Later in his office Charlie Grant closed the door and took his bottle of malt whisky out of the filing cabinet, pouring a celebratory glass for himself and another for his son.

'Got to hand it to you, lad,' he said, handing Vernon the glass. 'When Harry Philips told me what he'd done, I thought we were up the creek without a paddle. How did you pull it off, eh? How did you bring Julia into line?'

Vernon took a grateful gulp of the whisky. 'Just put my foot down, that's all. You've always known how to do it, so why not me? Chip off the old block.'

'Well, I have to admit, I didn't know you had it in you.' Charlie threw himself into a chair and took out his pipe and tobacco. 'Looked more subdued than I've seen her in years. I thought this council business was going to her head. Quite snotty with me on the phone over that stupid women's refuge business, she was.' He applied a match to the pipe and sucked thoughtfully. 'Still, you seem to have knocked all that rubbish out of her, thank God. In my opinion there's nowt worse than an arrogant, over-confident woman, 'specially when she happens to be your wife! Now...' He leaned forward across the desk. 'The next thing is to get on to the negotiations. First off we have to find out who Victoria Gardens belongs to. I do know that one person owns all the properties, the whole shebang, which makes it easier. The question is, who?'

'There's an agent handling it, isn't there?' Vernon said. 'That seems to indicate the owner doesn't live locally, so we'll be going through him.'

Charlie drew hard on his pipe and blew out a cloud of smoke. 'Not if we can get to know who the owner is. Agents push for the last penny, lad. Now – if the owner is some old biddy, she'll likely be glad to get the responsibility off her hands for a lot less than the agent would press for. And if it means making a trip up to Scotland or somewhere then I reckon it'll be worth it.'

'But how do we find out?'

Charlie's eyes narrowed. 'Better leave it with me for now, lad,' he said. 'I've got one or two favours owed me, from several people I can think of. I'll get to know before the week's out, don't you fret.' He got up from the desk and downed the rest of his whisky. 'In fact, I think I'll make one call now – start eliminating folk.'

Eleanor was busy with her housework when the doorbell rang. Switching off the vacuum cleaner, she went to open the front door and was surprised to see who her visitor was.

'Charlie! To what do I owe this unexpected pleasure?'

He stepped inside with a grin. 'Glad you think of it like that, Lena lass. There's something I need to know and I reckon you might be able to help me.'

Eleanor turned to close the door, a wry smile on her lips. Knowing Charlie Grant she might have guessed he'd be wanting something. She smiled at him. 'I see. It's not just the pleasure of my sparkling company you're after then. Like a coffee? I was just about to make some.'

'Why not? I've got an appointment at the bank, but I can spare half an hour.' Charlie followed her through to the living room and made himself comfortable in her armchair, watching as she went about the business of putting the kettle on and setting out cups. Eventually they sat facing one another.

'So...' Eleanor passed him a plate of biscuits. 'What is it you want to know this time, Charlie?'

He shook his head at her. 'Oh, come on, lass. Don't make it sound as if I'm always on the nose.'

'Well, aren't you?' she said with a husky laugh.

'Go on, you're pulling my leg again. Always were a tease.'

'So what is it?'

He took a sip of his coffee. 'Nowt much really. Look, what I'm going to tell you is strictly between ourselves, Lena.'

'Of course. That goes without saying.'

'Well, since the council gave up the idea of redeveloping Victoria Gardens, I've been thinking. I've put it to my directors and we've decided to buy the Gardens up and carry out the redevelopment ourselves.'

'Really?' Eleanor looked surprised. 'Well, the best of luck, of course, but I don't quite see where I come in.'

'I understand that the whole street is owned by one person.'

'That's right. When the council was thinking of buying it things were being handled by the agent who handles the letting. I can give you his name if that's what you want?'

'No.' Charlie shook his head. 'I know that, but I don't want to mess around with one of those fellers. I'd rather deal direct with the owner. Do you know who it is?'

Eleanor hesitated. 'There has to be a good reason why an agent is handling it, Charlie,' she said.

'I know all that. I'm not planning some kind of swindle if that's what you're thinking. I'll make a fair offer for the properties.'

'I daresay the owner would prefer to have an expert handling her affairs.'

Charlie leaned forward. 'Ah! So it's a woman then?'

Eleanor bridled. 'That seems to encourage you, Charlie. I wonder why? Perhaps you think a woman will be a pushover.'

'Not at all. Oh, come on, Lena, don't mess me about with all that equality claptrap. What's this woman's name? Is it someone I know? Does she live here or away somewhere?'

'She lives here. As a matter of fact, she lives in Victoria Gardens, but I'm still not sure about this, Charlie. You're putting me in a very awkward position.'

'No one will know it was you who told me, Lena.' Charlie was growing impatient. 'Look, I'll be really grateful if you'll give me the name.' He glanced at her slyly. 'Tell you what, suppose I arrange a little commission for you? By way of thanks. How does that sound?'

'It sounds revolting!' Eleanor stood up, her face flushed. 'What

248

you're suggesting is very insulting, Charlie,' she told him. 'Do you know what you're saying?'

He waved his hands at her. 'Don't get upset. I want nowt to do with what you're thinking. Corruption never entered my head. Just a little present, between friends. For old time's sake. That's all.'

'I don't want your present, Charlie, and I think you'd better leave.'

'So you won't tell me?'

'No. I won't.'

She showed Charlie out in silence and closed the door sharply on his portly retreating figure. In the car he swore loudly, thumping the steering wheel with frustration. How could he have been such a fool as to try to bribe her? He might have known that Lena would come over all whiter-than-white on him. He drew a deep breath and tried to channel his thoughts in a positive direction. The conversation hadn't been entirely unproductive. He knew now that the owner was a woman and that she lived in the Gardens. That was something. And if this woman owned the whole street it meant that everyone else living there was a tenant. A triumphant smile spread across his face. Once he'd made sure of the loan it was in the bag!

After the meeting Julia drove herself home feeling chastened and depressed. She made herself a sandwich and a cup of coffee but she had no appetite for either. This morning when she'd got up she'd made up her mind to speak to Charlotte before she left the house. But the girl was still morose and uncommunicative. It was almost as though she blamed Julia for Vernon's conduct. Since the initial row she and Vernon had avoided each other as much as possible and Charlotte spent most of her time locked in her room. Over breakfast this morning the atmosphere had crackled with tension. Julia had found it impossible to concentrate on anything but the coming meeting. The three of them sat silently avoiding one another's eyes and Julia was relieved when it was over and they had each gone their separate ways. Once again there had been no opportunity to speak to Charlotte.

Now it was over. She had caved in and voted with the others. Try as she would, she could not erase the feeling of self-disgust or the memory of Joanna's triumphant smile from her mind. And now she was faced with the task she dreaded the most – that of explaining her action to her father. But at least she would not have to cross that bridge until he came back from his cruise.

The house felt empty and silent as she wandered restlessly from room to room trying to decide what she would say to her parents.

They were going to see it as a betrayal whatever she said. Finally, unable to bear the menacing silence any longer, she put on her coat and went out to the car again. She had no idea where she was going, but when she reached the end of the road she decided. Turning in the direction of Eleanor Maitland's house.

The older woman was not surprised to see her. Ever since Charlie's visit she had been expecting a call from Julia.

'Come in, my dear,' she said welcomingly. 'I had your father-in-law round here earlier. This seems to be my day for entertaining members of the Grant family.' She peered closely at Julia as she took her coat. 'You look as though you could do with a stiff drink. What's wrong?'

'Everything!' Julia dropped gratefully into the chair by the fireside. 'I hardly know where to begin.'

Eleanor settled herself in the chair opposite. 'How about the beginning? That's as good a place as any.'

Julia shook her head. 'Far too long a story to bore you with. The main problem is that we're going to have to shelve the women's refuge for the time being.'

'Oh, that's a shame, but it's hardly surprising. As a matter of fact Charlie was telling me about his plans when he was here,' she said. 'I saw at once that it was going to throw a spanner in the works.'

Julia nodded. 'Yes. And I can't even protest. My father has transferred his shares in GPC to me. He wanted me to vote against the proposal, but when it came to the crunch – I couldn't.'

'Of course you couldn't,' Eleanor said sympathetically. 'It was wrong of him to ask it of you.'

Julia was silent. If only she could tell Eleanor the full story. 'It looks as though my name is going to be mud,' she said gloomily. 'With the people I'm going to have to let down as well as with my parents.'

Eleanor looked thoughtful. 'There's not much I can do about your parents,' she said. 'But I do know of another empty property we might get. It doesn't have such a central position and of course it would mean going back for planning permission again, which means a delay.'

'Oh, Eleanor!' Julia's spirits rose. 'That would be marvellous. Can we go and look at it now?'

'Of course, if you like. I'll go and get my coat.'

By the time Fleur and Tom had carried down the last of his boxes the little car was loaded to the roof.

'I'd no idea I'd accumulated so much stuff,' he said as he climbed

250

into the driving seat. 'I just hope there'll be room for it all at Park Row.'

'You've got twice as much space,' Fleur laughed. 'So there should be.'

Sally had given Fleur the day off to help Tom. They had spent almost all of it packing and loading the car and now it was late afternoon. They made the short drive to Park Row in a matter of minutes and as they began unpacking the various boxes, suitcases and carrier bags, the front door of the little terraced house opened and Sadie came out to meet them.

'Hi, guys!' she called cheerfully. 'Want a hand with anything?'

Tom straightened up and introduced the two girls. 'Sadie, this is Fleur Sylvester. Fleur – Sadie.'

The girls smiled at each other and Fleur took in the tall, well-built girl, noting that Tom's description of her had been accurate. She wore jeans and an oversized man's shirt which reached to her knees. Her dark hair was cut very short and her face was innocent of make-up. It was clear that she was a young women well able to take care of herself; in total charge of her life.

Sadie's sharp eyes swept appraisingly over Fleur. 'I'd have known you anywhere,' she said. 'Tom talks about you *non-stop*! I've heard all about that balcony of yours and the fabulous garden you're going to create out there. If what he says is true you're going to have to open it to the public this summer!' She laughed and led the way into the house. 'Welcome to Park Row. I won't offer to help with the unpacking but feel free to bang on my door and demand a cup of coffee when you've finished.'

'Thanks, we might just do that,' Tom said over a mound of boxes as she disappeared upstairs.

The two rooms he was to occupy on the ground floor were small but comfortable. Fleur looked round admiringly at the slick new white paintwork and attractive wallpaper. She'd already peered into the smart little kitchen and looked enviously at the smooth tiled work surfaces and pine cupboards.

'You really are lucky, Tom,' she said. 'You've fallen on your feet here.' She put a hand on one of the radiators. 'Central heating too. What a luxury.'

He hung the armful of clothes he was carrying in the wardrobe and turned to look at her. 'It could be yours too, you know,' he told her. 'There's plenty of room for two here.'

She smiled and shook her head. 'When I made you a similar offer, I seem to remember being turned down.'

'That wasn't intended as a similar offer.' He put his hands on her

251

shoulders. 'And I didn't turn you down. Far from it. What I said was that I wanted you to be absolutely sure. I don't want you making an impulsive gesture you might regret. But if you wanted, you could move in here tomorrow – independently, I mean. We could have a room each. There are two. Sadie even has another small room upstairs that she wants to let.'

'I know. And I do appreciate your offer, Tom. It's just . . .'

'Just that you've realised now that I was right?' He slapped his forehead with a palm of his hand in a dramatic gesture. 'God! Why do I always have to be so damned *saintly*? Can you tell me? I must be mad!'

'That's not what I meant.' She laughed and hugged him. 'I like you just the way you are, so don't you dare change. Anyway, moving just when I'm about to get my very own balcony garden isn't on the cards, is it? Besides, if I lived here you'd have nowhere to come and have candlelit suppers, would you? Which reminds me – come back to the flat when we've unpacked and I'll feed you. Call it a farewell present.'

'Not on your life.' Tom shook his head. 'I've booked us a table somewhere special. It was meant to be a surprise. Anyway I don't like the sound of *farewell* present. I hope you weren't planning to get rid of me because I warn you, it won't be that easy.'

'I should hope not!' Fleur looked round at the stacked boxes. 'Now – are we going to get this lot sorted out tonight, or aren't we?'

Charlie Grant stood at the window of Ivy Franks's basement kitchen and watched as the two young people went to and from the front door to the small car parked at the kerb, already laden with boxes.

'Looks like a mass exodus,' he remarked. 'Losing some of your tenants, are you?'

Ivy joined him at the window and craned her neck upwards. 'Oh, just one of my young fellers moving out,' she said. 'But these rooms don't stay empty for long. Soon re-let that, don't you worry.'

'No need if you were to sell,' he said.

Ivy sat down and regarded her visitor solemnly. She hadn't yet decided just what his little game was and she certainly wasn't going to be rushed. 'Which property were you thinking of, Mr Grant?' she asked cagily.

'Which *one*?' Charlie repeated. 'I thought I'd just made that clear. All of them, of course.'

'And how did you know that I owned Victoria Gardens?'

'Never mind that. Let's just say it was a process of elimination.

252

In other words, I worked it out for myself. Come to that, why does it have to be such a well-kept secret?'

Ivy shook her head. 'My old auntie left me these houses when she died. My hubby and I rented this house from her for years and it was a big shock to me, I can tell you, suddenly finding that I owned the street. I reckon she was hoping it'd give me security, seein' I was a widow. But nowadays a woman on her own can't be too careful.' Let people get the idea you're a woman of property and they think you're made of money.

'Then there's the risk of burglary. If anyone thinks I'm well off they've got another think coming. Nothing worth pinchin' here, I can tell you. The rent from these places is my only income and I'm sure I don't have to tell you, Mr Grant, what old places like these cost in upkeep and repairs. Then there's the rates – er poll-tax. Cripplin' that is.' She shook her head. 'Not worth the candle any more. Hardly break even, I don't.'

'So – if you got the chance to sell, you'd think favourably?'

Ivy paused. 'An agent handles the letting for me. Same agent who's handled it for years. He takes his cut, of course, but it's worth it to save me collectin' the rents. There's some would take advantage of a defenceless woman on her own, you know,' she told him with a knowing look. 'A while ago he did have an enquiry from the council, but that seems to have fallen through.'

Charlie swallowed his impatience. 'You were willing to sell to them then?'

'I didn't say that.' Ivy folded her arms and drew her mouth into a thin line. 'Never got round to talkin' money, so I don't know if it'd have been worth my while, do I?'

'And what would you say to a firm offer now?'

'An offer of what? And who from?'

'From me, of course. From Grant Philips Construction.'

She narrowed her eyes at him. 'Plannin' to pull 'em all down, are you? Put up one of them what-d'ya-call-'ems – shopping mawls?'

'No. Victoria Gardens would be as they were always meant to be,' he told her. 'They'd be refurbished and let as offices and flats. Maybe a couple of public buildings too.'

'Pubs, you mean?' She wrinkled her nose.

'No. A health centre and maybe a library was what we had in mind.'

'I see.' She considered for what seemed to Charlie an eternity. 'Mmm. So – how much were you thinkin' of offering?'

'What would you say it's worth, Mrs Franks?' Charlie held his breath. In his experience old girls like this usually lived in the past. Their values bore no relation to present day prices.

'Well, now . . .' She took a cigarette from the packet that lay open on the chenille-covered table and lit it slowly, drawing thoughtfully, then shaking out the match. 'I reckon it must be worth – ooh . . .' She exhaled a stream of smoke. 'Goin' on for a couple of million, I'd say. Wouldn't you?'

'*What*?' Charlie almost fell off his chair. 'You must be joking, Mrs Franks.' He waved an arm around. 'Even in good repair old places like this fetch no more than forty thousand a piece at the very most. I'd be prepared to offer you that.' He did a rapid sum in his head. 'Five hundred and twenty thousand pounds. There you are. That's a fair price. After all, I'm going to have to rip them apart, you know. It's almost a rebuilding job. God only knows what problems I'll uncover. It'll cost me a packet.'

Ivy shook her head. 'That's your problem, Mr Grant. Not mine. You must think it's worth it, mustn't you? Daresay you've worked out that you stand to make a packet. I need enough money to live on. I'd have to buy somewhere to live, remember. That'd take a sizeable sum out of it for a start, 'specially at today's prices.'

Charlie stared at her. The old crone must be getting on for seventy. How did she think she was ever going to spend that kind of money? It was sheer greed! He swallowed his irritation and considered for a moment. You had to hand it to her. She was a far tougher businesswoman than he'd given her credit for. No flies on her!

'Look. I could let you have a nice little bungalow for what it cost me to build them.' Encouraged by the gleam of interest in her eyes he went on. 'Lovely little places. Two bedrooms, central heating, fitted kitchen and coloured bathroom suite. Nice little utility room for your washing machine. Very warm and labour-saving. What do you say, Mrs Franks? You wouldn't know yourself after this draughty old place.'

She drew hard on her cigarette, shaking her head doubtfully. 'Well – I dunno.'

'Just think about it. If you invested the rest of your money you'd be set up for life. Holidays abroad. Winter in the sunshine. Live like a lady on the interest and still have your capital.'

Her fishlike gaze was unimpressed. 'Where is this bungalow then?'

'A new estate out Merifield way. There's just the one left. Clean country air – no pollution.'

But Ivy was shaking her head, mouth pulled down at the corners.

254

'Never could abide estates. Full o' them yuppies. All toffee-noses and hor-pair gels. Don't like the country either,' she added gloomily. 'No shops for a start. And folks can't mind their own business in the country.'

Exasperated, Charlie got to his feet. 'Well, I hope you don't live to regret it, Mrs Franks. That's my last offer: five hundred thousand pounds and the bungalow. And I think that's very handsome.'

'Twenty thousand!' she said, staring at him aghast. 'You're tryin' to tell me it costs you twenty thousand to build one of them *rabbit hutches*? You gotta be jokin'!'

Red in the face, Charlie strode to the door. 'In that case, Mrs Franks, I'll bid you good day.'

It was dark as Charlotte rode up the winding drive to the stables and parked her bicycle against the garage door. Across the yard she could see that the stables had been closed for the night, the horses obviously bedded down, but there was a light on in her aunt's kitchen window. As she stood outside the back door she shifted the heavy sports bag she had brought with her from one hand to the other. She could hear the radio playing and Kath singing along to it as she prepared her evening meal. The sound reassured her.

Things at home had been unbearably uncomfortable over the past couple of weeks. Her parents weren't speaking, either to each other or to her. It was as though they both blamed her for their trouble. Her mother seemed too distant and preoccupied to approach, and as for Dad – she knew now that he was a liar as well as a cheat. Did he really think she'd swallowed that fairy story he'd told her?

It made something inside her curl up when she remembered the humiliation of apologising to Joanna. The condescending acceptance and that smile of triumph would stay in her memory for a very long time. And the feeble explanation she'd given her grandparents had been received with obvious disbelief.

Her only consolation was the belief that after carrying out her father's wishes he would relent over his ban on her visits to the stables. But he had stuck rigidly to his decision. She was still barred from visiting the one person who cared about her – as a cruel unjust punishment because she'd caught him out. It was more than she could bear.

Kath opened the door to her knock and stood staring at her in surprise. 'Charlotte! What are you doing here?'

'Can I come in, Auntie Kath?'

'Of course, child. But you shouldn't be here, should you?'

'Dad's been in touch with you then?'

Kath sighed, remembering the vitriolic telephone call she'd had from Vernon. '*In touch* is hardly the word for it. He telephoned to tell me what a bad influence I am on you and informed me that he'd forbidden you to see me again.'

'He can't stop me coming here if I want to though, can he?' Charlotte said truculently.

'He can make life pretty unbearable for you if you persist in disobeying him,' Kath said. 'For both of us.'

'What can he do to you?'

'He can put me out of business.'

'How can he?'

'The stables are on land I lease from GPC. The lease is up for renewal next September. If they decide they want to use the land for building . . .'

'Oh.' Charlotte's lower lip trembled. 'I *hate* him, Auntie Kath!' she said, her voice shaking. 'He's ruining my life! Anyway, I'm leaving home. I've made up my mind.'

Kath put her arms round the sobbing girl. 'You can't, darling. You're much too young. You must face the fact that you still need your home and your parents. I'm afraid you'll just have to do as your father says for the time being. It won't be forever.'

'It *will*! They've got me working in that rotten office, right under their noses all the time. I can't move without them knowing. I can't bear it. I *won't*! Other girls leave home and so can I.'

'Come and sit down,' Kath said kindly. 'You're all upset and you need to talk this through. I'll make you a hot drink.'

She watched her niece as she sat on the rug in front of the fire, both hands round the mug of Ovaltine. She looked so young with her fair hair loose around her pale face. But there were dark rings of strain under her eyes. She looked more stressed than any sixteen year old had a right to look. Her heart went out to the child.

'What happened to bring all this about?' Kath asked. 'You didn't say anything, did you – about what we saw the other night?'

Charlotte looked apprehensively at her over the rim of the mug. 'I told Grandpa,' she whispered.

Kath gasped. 'Oh, Charlotte!'

'I know. I wish I hadn't now, but I had to tell someone. I could hardly tell Mum, could I?'

'No wonder there was trouble. What did he say?'

'He told me to try and forget it. But he was angry, really angry, I could see that. And next morning Grandpa rang Dad. I heard them talking on the phone. Grandpa must have told him what I said because Dad had me into his office later and really blew me up about it. That was when he banned me from coming here.' Her lip trembled. 'He made me apologise to that woman. Can you imagine? If you'd seen the look on her face!'

'Oh, Charlotte.' Kath reached out to pat her hand.

'Everything at home has been really horrible ever since.'

'I'm not surprised,' Kath muttered. 'I wish you'd talked this through with me first.'

'You think I should have kept quiet about it then – let him get away with it?' Charlotte's eyes were bright with righteous indignation.

'Not entirely, but the way you've handled it has only made things ten times worse, hasn't it?'

Charlotte nodded. 'For you too. I'm sorry.'

'Don't be sorry. The thing is for you not to do anything else you might regret.'

'I meant it when I said I wanted to leave home,' Charlotte told her defiantly. 'Why am I being made to feel that I'm the one in the wrong? No one's talking to anyone in our house and I feel it's all my fault when it *isn't*. It's not fair.' She looked hopefully at Kath. 'I thought I might come and live here with you. Can I – please?'

Kath sighed regretfully. 'Oh, darling, you know you can't. Your father would be furious. I'd be thrown out and then where would either of us be?'

'Are you saying that I've got to do what he says and not visit you any more?' Charlotte's eyes were brimming with tears. 'Does it mean I won't be able to see the horses or ride or – or help you?' She broke off, choked by the hiccuping sobs that shook her shoulders.

Kath slid down on to the floor and drew her close. 'Hush, darling. Don't cry. I'll have a word with your father. We'll wait a couple of weeks till things have cooled down. He'll come round.'

'He won't. He's a pig!'

'Shh. You mustn't say such things. It will all come right in the end. You see if it doesn't.' Kath rocked the sobbing girl in her arms, wishing she could believe in her own assurance. She felt powerless to help the niece she loved so much. It seemed there was nothing she could do. Vernon was the one with all the power and he had made sure she knew just what would happen if she went against his wishes. After all, the stables were her livelihood.

Fleur slipped the key quietly into the door of her flat and opened it. 'Come in,' she whispered to Tom. 'But don't make a noise We don't want Poison Ivy up here reading us the riot act, do we?'

Stifling their giggles like children they crept into the flat and closed the door. Tom's treat had been a great success. After all their hard work they had relaxed over the meal, enjoying the food and consuming a bottle of wine between them as well as liqueurs to accompany their coffee. The evening had been fun and neither of them wanted it to end, which was why Fleur had invited him up for a nightcap.

'Coffee?' she asked. 'Or there might still be some of that sherry left over from Christmas.'

Tom pulled a face. 'I think coffee would be more appropriate after what we've already drunk.' He stood behind her and slipped his arms round her waist as she plugged in the kettle. 'Thanks for this evening, Fleur,' he said, resting his cheek on the top of her head. 'I've enjoyed it so much.'

She turned in the circle of his arms to look into his eyes. 'No, thank you. It was your treat and a wonderful surprise.' She put her arms round his neck. 'And I can't think of anyone I'd rather be with.'

'Do you mean that?' His eyes searched hers. '*Really* mean it? He kissed her and sighed deeply. 'Oh, Fleur, I love you so much. Ever since you first came here – since the day we first met – I've known. You could almost say it was love at first sight except that it's grown and grown ever since and what I feel now is . . .' He broke off to look down at her ruefully. 'You'd better listen to this. I suspect I can only say it because I'm ever so slightly pissed. I'd never have the courage otherwise. I want – want to spend the rest of my life with you, Fleur. I'm asking you to marry me.' For a moment they looked at each other, then he said, 'The trouble is that you don't feel as deeply as I do – do you?'

Fleur shook her head. 'It's not that. I do love you, Tom. I meant it when I said that there is no one I'd rather be with. It's just . . .'

'Just what?' He looked at her. 'Go on, tell me.'

'I can't tell you because I don't know.'

'If you loved me you'd know,' he said unhappily. 'If you loved me unreservedly there'd be no doubt in your mind.'

'Is it possible to love anyone that way?'

'Yes! I happen to think it is.'

The kettle boiled and she turned back to attend to it. 'So many marriages end in divorce nowadays,' she said. 'Even so-called permanent relationships seem to fizzle out after a few months. Happy-ever-after gets shorter all the time. It just makes me wonder what happens to all that love that people believed was so strong.'

'It dies because they take it for granted,' Tom said earnestly. 'They don't see that they have to work to keep it alive. People aren't prepared to make sacrifices. Anything worth having is worth working at.'

She turned and handed him the mug of coffee. 'Perhaps you're right. But who knows? Who really *knows*?'

'What you're saying is that you don't trust me,' he said exasperatedly. 'I'm not Peter Arden, you know. What do I have to do to prove it to you, for Christ's sake?'

'Nothing! I don't know. If it comes to that, what makes you so sure you can trust *me* after what happened?' She sighed. 'Oh, Tom, don't let's quarrel over it. We've had such a super evening.'

He put down his mug and pulled her into his arms again. 'No. You're right. As for trusting you, Fleur – if you ask me to, I will. It's as simple as that.'

She winced. 'You make me feel so guilty.' She took her coffee and sat down on the settee.

'Guilty! Hell, that's the last thing I want you to feel.'

'I think it's wrong to tie people down,' she said. 'Look what happens. Look what happened to me – a father who didn't want to know and a mother who walked out on me when I was a baby.'

'But they weren't married.'

She looked at him. 'If they had been, do you think it would have made any difference? I don't. The only kind of commitment that really works is the one that makes up your mind for you. When you stay with someone because you can't bear to be parted from them, not just because some legal bit of paper says you've signed a contract and you're stuck with it. Feelings have to stand the test of time.'

He sat down beside her and slipped an arm around her. 'So shall we take it from there then? Take our time and see if we still feel the same, say, six months from now?'

She turned her head and kissed him gently. 'That's what I'd like, Tom. It was what I had in mind when I asked you to stay with me that night. Just as long as . . .'

'Well?' He tipped up her chin, making her look at him. 'As long as what?'

'As long as we both face the fact that it may not be real after all. One of us might still be hurt. It might be me.'

He drew her close. 'I'm willing to risk it if you are.' He kissed her. 'I want you so much, Fleur – in every way. For always.'

The eyes that looked down at her were filled with longing and as his hands caressed her Fleur suddenly knew a desire that was infinitely deeper, more passionate, than anything she had experienced with Peter. Suddenly she understood the bewildering difference between love and lust.

Neither of them heard the soft tap on the door until it was repeated, louder. Fleur's eyes opened and her muscles tensed as she looked at Tom.

'Listen! There's someone on the landing.'

He groaned. 'What's the betting it's Ivy?'

'Surely not.'

As they lay quite still and listened, the knock came again. Whoever the visitor was he or she had no intention of giving up. Fleur swung her legs to the floor and pulled on her dressing gown.

'I'd better see who it is.' She smiled at Tom ruefully. 'It might be as well to put something on before I open the door.'

He swore softly under his breath as he scrambled into his clothes.

At the door Fleur asked, 'Who is it?'

'It's me – Charlotte.'

Fleur unlocked the door and opened it, shocked to see the girl standing on the landing, looking lost and forlorn, a large sports bag clutched in her hand. 'Charlotte! What on earth's the matter? What are you doing here at this time of night?'

'I – I've left home!' The girls' teeth were chattering slightly. She looked cold and miserable.

Fleur reached out to take her arm and draw her inside. 'Come in. You're cold.'

'I'm sorry to disturb you,' Charlotte said, 'but I couldn't think of anywhere else to go. I tried the door downstairs and it was open, so I just – just came up. I've chained my bike to the railing downstairs. It'll be okay, won't it? I couldn't ...' Suddenly she caught sight of Tom and stopped in mid-sentence. 'Oh! Oh, dear – I didn't realise. I'll go ...'

Fleur grasped her arm. 'Don't be silly. You can't go back out there at this time of night.' She shot a look of appeal at Tom who looked at his watch and said hurriedly, 'Heavens, I didn't realise it was that late. I really must be going.'

'Are you sure?' Charlotte looked from one to the other. 'I mean, I haven't – I don't want ...'

'You're not,' Tom said. 'Time I was leaving anyway.'

'I'll come down with you.' Fleur looked over her shoulder at Charlotte. 'Make yourself at home. I won't be a minute.'

Downstairs in the hall Tom turned to her. 'Who is she?'

'Charlotte. The girl I met on the computer course.'

'But what's she doing here? It's a bit much, isn't it, dropping in on you in the middle of the night?'

'I don't know, but I can hardly turn her out into the street, can I?' She put her arms round his neck. 'Sorry, love.'

'It's okay, I suppose.' He kissed her and tried to stifle his resentment. 'What about her parents, though? She looks pretty young to me.'

'She's sixteen.' Fleur gave him a gentle push towards the front door. 'Leave her to me, Tom. If you don't go we'll have Ivy here demanding to know what's going on.'

'All right. I'm going.'

She pulled him back and stood on tiptoe to kiss him. 'That's for being sweet. I love you, Tom.'

He hugged her briefly. 'Love you too.'

'And I'm really sorry about tonight.'

'No more than I am,' he told her wryly. 'Still, never mind. We've all the time in the world, eh?'

'Yes. All the time in the world.'

He kissed her again and was gone.

Upstairs in the flat Fleur made Charlotte a hot drink and a sandwich, then made up a makeshift bed for her on the settee.

'Is there a problem at home?' she asked as she worked. 'Have you had a row?'

'They all hate me,' Charlotte said dramatically. 'I spilled the beans about Dad and the Hanson women.'

'Oh my God!' Fleur bit her lip.

'It's caused ructions.'

'I can imagine. But your mother is bound to have missed you by now. She'll be worried about you. Shouldn't you ring her?'

Charlotte shook her head miserably. 'She won't even have noticed I'm not there,' she said bitterly.

As it happened she was right.

Chapter 13

'Isn't Charlotte up yet?'

Julia looked up from her breakfast to see Vernon looking at her over his newspaper. 'She should be. I tapped on her door about half an hour ago.'

He frowned at his watch. 'She's going to be late for work at this rate. It sets such a bad example to the other girls. Give her another shout, will you?'

'Vernon, I've been meaning to speak to you about Charlotte. She's been looking so unhappy. I think you were wrong to forbid her to go to Kath's . . .'

He rustled his paper angrily. 'I don't want to discuss it with you, Julia. You've always been far too soft with the girl. This time she's got to learn that she can't make trouble and get away with it.'

'She was upset by what she saw,' Julia said quietly. 'You're having an affair, Vernon, and you're annoyed at being caught out by your own daughter. Why bother to deny it?'

'I *do* deny it! I absolutely deny that Joanna and I are anything but working colleagues,' he said. 'If Charlotte had come to me with what she *imagined* she'd seen it might have been excusable, but to go to your father!'

Julia sighed. It was old ground. They'd been over and over it, and it was obviously an argument that was going nowhere. She rose from the table and went into the hall where Tracey was busy vacuuming.

'Tracey, go up and give Charlotte another call, would you?' she said above the roar of the machine. 'She's going to be late for work and I don't want her going off again without any breakfast.'

Tracey switched off the cleaner and looked at her employer. 'I thought she'd already gone,' she said. 'I've done her room. The bed was made and everything.'

262

Julia stared at her. 'Gone? Of course she hasn't gone. I've been up since seven and I haven't seen her.' Closely followed by Tracey, she ran up the stairs and pushed open the door of Charlotte's room. As Tracey had already said, the bed was neatly made and everything was unusually tidy. 'She couldn't have gone out without my seeing her,' Julia said, her heart beginning to thud with alarm. 'It looks as though she didn't sleep here at all last night. Where on earth can she be?'

'At one of her friend's perhaps,' Tracey suggested. 'Could you ring round and see?'

Julia sat down heavily on the bed. 'Most of her schoolfriends have gone off to college,' she said. 'And I don't think she's made any friends at the office.' Silently she admitted to herself that she had no idea what social life, if any, her daughter had. She'd never made friends easily. Always been rather a lonely child. Why hadn't Julia tried to find out the reason for this before?

'Is there anything I can do?' Tracey asked.

'No. I daresay there's some simple explanation,' she said without conviction. When Tracey had left to continue her work Julia got up and went to look in the wardrobe. Several items of clothing, including Charlotte's dressing gown, had gone and in the bathroom she found her toothbrush missing. Her heart sank like a stone.

Downstairs Vernon had already left for work. Going across the hall into his study Julia closed the door against the sound of the hoover and dialled Kath's number, hoping that her sister-in-law hadn't gone off on some equestrian errand or other. To her relief Kath answered almost immediately.

'Kath. It's Julia.'

'Hello. Lucky to have caught me. I was just on my way out.'

'Kath, is Charlotte with you?'

'No, why?'

'She's not here. I don't think her bed has even been slept in and some of her clothes are missing.'

'Oh, no! She did come to see me last night. She was very upset – wanted to stay here. But I sent her away.'

'But why, for heaven's sake? Where can she be, Kath? Whatever possessed you to turn her away?'

'Vernon rang me yesterday, threatening not to renew my lease if I had anything more to do with his daughter. I didn't want any more trouble for either of us. I made her a hot drink, sat her down and tried to talk some sense into her. I advised her to go home. When she left here she seemed much calmer and I thought she'd do just that. Oh, God, Julia, I'm so sorry.'

'Have you any idea at all where she might have gone?'

'Not off hand.' Kath paused, wondering whether she should say what was in her mind. 'I suppose you do realise how unhappy the child is over this business with Vernon?'

'I do *now*, of course!' Julia snapped. She was silent for a moment. She had to admit she was partly to blame. Her own problems had dimmed her awareness of others'. 'I'm sorry, Kath,' she said. 'I didn't mean to snap your head off. It's just that I'm so worried. She could be anywhere. One hears of such awful things happening to young girls who run away from home. Why couldn't she have come to *me* if she was so miserable?'

'Perhaps because she's seen you bury your head in the sand about matters like this so many times in the past,' Kath said bluntly. 'I'm sorry. I shouldn't have said that.'

'No, you're right,' Julia admitted. 'I just wish Charlotte and I were closer. Since she left school and started at the office I don't seem to have been able to get through to her. I've been meaning to do something about it – make time to sit down and talk. It's just that life has been so difficult over the past few months. Vernon has always criticised the way I've brought Charlotte up. Sometimes I feel that I can't seem to do right by one without hurting the other. But this isn't finding her. Look, Kath, could you just think? Has she mentioned any new friends to you? Is there any place you can think of where she might have spent last night? I *have* to find her.'

'Okay. Just a minute, let me think.' There was a long pause, then Kath said, 'There was the girl she met on that computer course. She's mentioned her quite a lot. She seemed to get along well with her. But she left after one term so I don't know if she still sees her.'

Julia clutched the receiver. 'Never mind. It's a start. Do you remember her name?'

'Oh, God, now what was it? It was an unusual name – Flora – Florence? No, *Fleur*! That was it, Fleur. Charlotte said she worked for a catering firm – Arden's.'

Julia's heart almost stopped beating. 'Are you sure about that?' she whispered.

'Quite sure. Look, Julia, do you want me to come over there? I was going over to Newmarket to look at a new brood mare but I could ring and postpone.'

'No, no. You go. I'll be all right. I'll try this girl first, then I'll get back to you to let you know what happens.'

'Yes, please do that.'

Julia put the phone down and sat for a moment trying to put her thoughts in order. So Charlotte and Fleur actually knew each other!

264

Had Fleur told Charlotte anything? She had to know. It could explain a lot. She opened the telephone directory and looked up the number of Arden Catering and dialled. She recognised the voice that replied instantly.

'Fleur. Is that you?'

'Speaking. Who is it?'

'This is Julia Grant. Fleur, you haven't seen anything of Charlotte, my daughter, have you?'

'Yes, I have. She came to my flat late last night. She was upset, said she'd left home. I put her up for the night. I hope that was all right? I did try to get her to ring you but she wouldn't.'

Julia felt faint with relief. 'Where is she now?'

'She went to work. I've been trying to ring you myself. I knew you'd be worried, but the number was engaged.'

'I know. It doesn't matter. Nothing matters just as long as she's safe. Look, Fleur, I think we should talk. Are you free at lunchtime?'

'Well, yes.'

'Would it be possible for you to drive out to The Millstone again and meet me?'

'I think so.'

'Good. I'll see you there then – about one?'

Charlie climbed up the area steps of thirteen Victoria Gardens and got back into the car. Damn that Franks woman! She would have to be out this morning. He looked at the street in all its decaying grandeur. If she hadn't been so stubborn it would be his by now. He could have presented his plans in time for this month's planning meeting and had things well under way by now. He could make this place look wonderful given half a chance.

Half closing his eyes he visualised the grimy Victorian façades sand-blasted to their original rose pink, the woodwork sparkling white with new paint. The rusting railings would be burnished and the road outside cobbled as it would have been when the street was first built. In the centre, replacing the railed-off patch of rubbish-strewn mud, would be manicured grass like green velvet, dotted with brilliant flower beds and maybe a fountain playing in the centre, surrounded by comfortable seats. He could almost hear the tranquil sound of birdsong and tinkling water. And somewhere in a prominent position there would be a plaque honouring the name of Charles Grant the restorer, complete with the date for all to see in perpetuity.

He seethed with frustration at the dream held just out of his reach by a greedy old woman.

When he'd told Vernon the price Ivy Franks had asked he'd laughed derisively. 'She must be off her trolley!' he'd said. 'Might as well forget it.'

But Charlie wasn't ready to forget it. He'd really set his heart on this project. Once achieved, he and the firm would be made. Of course two million was ridiculous, but he could go higher now, thanks to the security of Joanna's input. The bank would probably stretch his loan a bit further too if he played his cards right. More than half the houses on the point of completion on Meadowlands Park had been reserved so they were sure of their money there.

He lit his pipe thoughtfully, wondering what the old bat would accept. No point in offering over the odds if all she had in mind was another couple of thousand. He'd have to box a bit clever.

He saw her as soon as she rounded the corner, loaded down with supermarket carrier bags. She wore a motheaten fur coat that had seen better days and a scarf tied round her head. From the corner of her mouth dangled the inevitable cigarette whose smoke spiralled upwards into her hennaed hair. He tried to imagine her as a million-airess and failed. What the hell would a woman like that do with that kind of money? It was ludicrous!

Pocketing his pipe and composing his features into a genial smile he got out of the car. 'Mrs Franks! How nice to see you. And looking so well.'

Eyeing him suspiciously, Ivy put her bags of shopping down on the pavement while she fumbled in her handbag for her keys. 'What can I do for you then, Mr Grant?'

'Well, I was in the area and I suddenly thought about you,' he said. 'I was wondering if we might have another little chat?'

Finding her keys, Ivy picked up the assorted carrier bags and started down the area steps. 'S'pose you'd better come in then, hadn't you?'

Charlie followed her down the steps where she thrust the shopping into his arms while she unlocked the door. Inside she relieved him of the shopping and took it through to the scullery, then began to take off her coat, still eyeing her visitor balefully.

'Sit down then,' she said brusquely. 'No need to stand about. I suppose you want a cup of tea or something?'

'That won't be necessary,' he said. 'I don't want to put you to any trouble. I just wondered if you'd given any more thought to what we discussed the other day?'

'Not a lot,' Ivy said. 'Reckon I'm happy enough where I am. This

266

old place has been good enough all these years so I can't see why I shouldn't finish my days here. Movin' house is a big upheaval at my time of life. Not sure I want to go through it.'

Ivy's friend Mrs Jennings, who 'did' for the Grants on a daily basis, had told her often enough about their opulent lifestyle. In Ivy's view Grant Philips Construction was taking a dead liberty. They could easily afford to pay her more and she'd made up her mind that if they didn't make it well worth her while she wasn't budging.

Charlie sighed. 'That's a great pity,' he said. 'Especially as I was about to make you a better offer.'

Ivy's eyes gleamed and she reached for another cigarette from the packet on the mantelpiece. 'How much better?' she asked without looking at him.

'Shall we say another five hundred?'

'I wouldn't bother wastin' your breath if I was you.' She threw away the match and shot him a sharp look. 'Probably cost me that to move me furniture.'

'A thousand then?'

Ivy drew the corners of her mouth down and shook her head. 'Like I said, Mr Grant, it's not worth uprootin' myself for.'

Charlie struggled to contain his irritation. 'What *would* make it worth your while, Mrs Franks?' he asked. 'And let's be realistic about this.'

She glared at him indignantly. '*You're* the one not bein' realistic!' She sucked hard on the cigarette and exhaled explosively. 'I reckon if you was to double your first offer I *might* just change my mind. You know as well as I do, Mr Grant, that this street is worth that.' She leaned forward to jab the air with a nicotine-stained finger. 'An' I only said I *might* change my mind, remember.'

Charlie considered for a long moment. It was more – far more – than he'd intended to pay, but he could see that she wouldn't let him have it for less. Surely Meadowlands Park would finance the project – see them through until completion? 'I'll have to give that a lot of thought, Mrs Franks,' he said. 'But I don't want to waste time going to my fellow directors with your suggestion if you're only going to change your mind again. So am I to take that as a figure you'd definitely accept?'

Slightly taken aback by his sudden capitulation, she nodded. 'All right then. Yes.'

'Right.' Charlie stood up. 'I'll get back to you as soon as I've consulted my partners. Perhaps you could give me the name of your solicitor? It would save time when it comes to having contracts drawn up.'

'Heskith and Trowbridge, 5 Albemarle Terrace,' Ivy said briskly. She didn't add that she'd already contacted them about the likelihood of a sale.

Julia arrived at The Millstone early, bought herself a glass of white wine and went through to sit in the small snug where she and Fleur had first met. The pub was busier this time, but most of the customers were in the bar and once again she had the snug almost to herself.

These days she was becoming increasingly isolated. As well as the family rift, she had had to face the displeasure of some of her fellow councillors since she had won the vote over the women's refuge. And she'd been taken to task by the Town Clerk over the photographs that had appeared in the press too. She had been unaware that she should have asked permission to be photographed in the council chamber. And she still had to face her parents with the news that she had voted along with Vernon, his father and Joanna over the Victoria Gardens project, something she looked forward to with increasing dread.

She saw Fleur arrive in the big white Arden Catering van and watched as she got out and locked the door. It was so hard to realise that this tall, striking girl was her daughter; the little dark-eyed baby she had given birth to in such mental and physical anguish all those years ago. She looked so much like Dean. It was no wonder that Joanna had so easily put two and two together as soon as she discovered that her name was Sylvester.

A moment later Fleur put her head round the door. 'Hello. I thought you'd be in here.'

Julia stood up. 'I'm so glad you were able to come, Fleur. Can I get you a drink? Maybe something to eat? I know this is your lunch hour.'

'No, thanks. I can't stay long.' Fleur sat down in the chair opposite. 'I'm glad you rang me. I didn't know what to do when I couldn't get through to you. Charlotte begged me not to tell you she was with me, but I wouldn't promise. I wasn't comfortable with that.'

'First I want to thank you for putting her up,' Julia said. 'Heaven knows what might have happened to her if you hadn't. I didn't even miss her until this morning.' She sighed. 'I feel so guilty about that. I stopped checking on her at bedtime months ago. Anyway, she's taken to locking her door at nights.'

'I couldn't have turned her away,' Fleur said. 'She was obviously upset. What I don't understand is why you thought of ringing me?'

'I called her aunt first. She said Charlotte had talked of you quite a lot.' Julia looked at her. 'You didn't tell me that you and she knew each other?'

'No.' The unspoken question hung between them. 'We met quite by accident when we both taking the same evening class,' Fleur said. 'And before you ask, she hasn't a clue who I really am. Obviously I knew you wouldn't want her to know about me.'

'I see. Thanks.' Julia took a sip of her drink, trying not to show the relief she felt. 'I should have spotted that she was bottling things up. She must have been very unhappy to want to run away.'

Fleur looked at her hesitantly. 'I think I should tell you that she came to me with a family problem a few weeks ago.'

'I can guess – it was to do with her father?'

'Yes. She didn't know what to do about it. I'm afraid I wasn't much help. I didn't feel I could advise her, so I told her to leave things to sort themselves out.'

'Thank you for that anyway. And you say she went to the office this morning? That's a good sign.'

'I don't think her courage quite stretched to not showing up for work. Besides, she hasn't any money and she won't get paid till the end of the month. She seems a bit scared of her father, if you don't mind my saying so,' Fleur said. 'I don't know both sides, of course, but he does seem very hard on her.'

'I know.'

Fleur waited for Julia to explain further. When she remained silent she said, 'So – if she comes back this evening, what do you want me to do?'

'I rather think it will be a question of what *she* wants to do. If you like, you could tell her that you've seen me and that I'd like her to come home.'

'I'll try.' Fleur had a sudden thought. 'Look, it's only an idea, but maybe it would do Charlotte good to be by herself for a while? You know – stand on her own feet and have a taste of independence. I know someone who has a room to let. It's only a house in Park Row but it's been modernised and it's a nice little room. Maybe if she had some space she'd sort herself out.'

'Do you think she'd want that?'

'I think she might. I could tell her you said it was okay. That might make it easier for her to decide.'

'I wouldn't want her to feel we didn't want her,' Julia said doubtfully. 'She's so terribly young to be on her own.'

'I was a lot younger when you left *me*!' The words were out before Fleur had time to weigh them. Seeing the stricken look on Julia's face, she said quickly, 'Sorry. I didn't mean that as a reproach.'

Julia shook her head. 'If you did, it's no more than I deserve. You really think she'd be all right on her own, do you?'

'I think she'd be fine. A friend of mine lives there and we could both keep an eye on her – see that she's okay. I could keep you posted if you'd like me to. And she'll know that if she gets homesick you're not far away.'

'Well, I suppose it's better than having her run away to heaven knows where.' She smiled at Fleur. 'Thanks. It might be an idea. Try her anyway.'

'I'll try to get her to ring you and let you know what she decides,' she said. 'But if she won't then I will.'

Julia reached out to touch her hand. 'You've been very good over this, Fleur. And I do see that letting go a little is better than laying down rules.'

'Look, I'm sorry for what I said just now.'

Julia paused, wondering if this was the right time for the question she couldn't bring herself to ask at their first meeting. 'Fleur, I've been wondering – did your – did Dean ever come back?'

'No. He died soon after Grandpa Maurice was killed, when I was about twelve. It was in America and so it was months before they traced us. A priest came to tell us.'

Julia felt numb. 'Poor Dolly,' she said quietly.

'Yes. It was awful for her so soon after losing Grandpa, specially when she hadn't seen Dean for so long.'

Julia looked up. 'What happened? Did they say?'

'It seems he'd been out of work for some time. Grandma never told me all the details, perhaps she didn't really know, but I think he'd taken an overdose or something.'

Julia nodded. It fitted. Like so many others Dean had always thought he was indestructible. Grab everything life had to offer, that was his motto. Nothing could harm him as long as he had his music and the golden dream of fame and fortune to sustain him. Failure would have been a bitter blow. 'That's sad,' she said. 'He was talented, you know. But so were so many other young musicians. If he'd had the right kind of luck. Maybe if he hadn't met me . . .'

'You can't blame yourself for that,' Fleur said. 'You shouldn't keep putting yourself down. You seem to take the blame for everything that goes wrong and it can't all be your fault.'

Julia smiled wryly. 'I suppose it's force of habit. I've had years of practice at getting things wrong.'

Fleur hesitated. Maybe it was time she confessed to her own indiscretion. 'Look, Julia – there's something I think you should know. When I went round to Mrs Hanson's to arrange about her party she remarked that she'd once known Dean Sylvester. I was really surprised to hear the name mentioned and without thinking I'm afraid I . . .'

'Let slip that he was your father?' Julia finished for her.

'You know?'

'Yes. I know.'

Again Julia did not clarify just how she knew and after a pause Fleur went on, 'I've been worrying about it ever since. I hope it didn't cause you any trouble?'

'No. Mrs Hanson and I were once close friends. She won't say anything.' Julia paused. Why burden the girl with her own family problems? After all, it needn't affect her in any way.

'Good. That's a relief.' Fleur realised that Julia couldn't know that Charlotte had told her who her father's mistress was. She was silent for a moment, glancing at Julia and puzzling as to how she could feel so assured that her secret was safe with the woman her husband was having an affair with. She looked at her watch and got up from the table. 'Well, I'd better be getting back,' she said. 'Sally is off to Switzerland soon and we're trying to get as far ahead as we can in advance.'

'Thanks for coming, Fleur. And for all your help.' Julia stood at the window, watching as she crossed the forecourt and sprang into the driving seat of the van. She looked so self-assured and full of vitality. Far more mature and adult than Julia had been at the same age. If only she had been as sound and well-balanced. With a pang of regret she thought about the prospect of having Charlotte move out of the family home. It was true of course that all children grew up and wanted their independence, but all the same she couldn't help feeling that Charlotte had been driven out. Soon she would be as distant from Julia as she was from Fleur. Both of them grown to womanhood and a maturity for which she could claim no credit. Was it any wonder she was haunted by guilt and regrets?

'I don't believe I'm hearing this, Dad!' Vernon raked a hand through his hair. 'I'm supposed to carry out all the financial negotiations for this firm. What on earth were you thinking of to make an offer like this without even consulting me?'

'Now you just listen to me.' Charlie glowered at his son. 'I was doing this job when you were still in rompers, so don't start getting on your high horse with me, lad!' he said. 'Believe me,' he thumped the table, 'we have to have that street! A million's nowt but peanuts to what we'd have to pay if this were one of the big cities.'

'But it *isn't* one of the big cities. That's just the point,' Vernon shouted. 'When it's completed we won't be able to charge big city rents, but we'll still have to pay the same price for materials and wages.'

'You don't know how tough that old bird is,' Charlie blustered. 'I defy anyone to get her down any lower.'

'Then we should have gone through the agent. And when she pressed for such a large sum, abandoned the project. Maybe we still should, after all, there's nothing in writing to commit us.' He looked at his father. 'That's why you didn't want me along, isn't it? Because you knew I'd advise you to drop it. We just can't afford it, Dad. Not even with Joanna's investment.'

'You have to have vision in this business,' Charlie insisted. 'You have to speculate to accumulate.'

'I *agree*.' Joanna, who had been silent so far, leaned forward. 'I think Charlie is right. There has never been a better time for expansion and this redevelopment project of his is so good. Have you seen the plans, Vernon?'

'Yes, I've seen them. All I know is, it's going to cost an arm and a leg.'

'And that's all you *can* see!' She turned to Charlie with a smile. 'Accountants only ever see money going out, don't they, Charlie?' She clicked her tongue maddeningly. 'They have no imagination. No creativity. No soul.'

'I am *not* an accountant!' Vernon shouted, his face red. 'I'm as creative as the next man, but I can recognise bloody lunacy when I see it.' He paused to take a deep breath. They were going to get nowhere by yelling at each other. Besides, with Joanna on Charlie's side he was outnumbered. 'Look, Dad, why don't you leave the negotiations to me? We'll start afresh. I'll get in touch with the agent handling the property and we'll deal with him as we should have done in the first place.'

Charlie glowered at him. 'I started this and I intend to finish it. I shouldn't need to remind you that this is *my* business, Vernon, so pay me the courtesy of admitting I'm right for once, will you? You young 'uns think you know the lot, but you're not always right, even if you think you are.'

Seething with impotent anger, he got up from the table and gathered his papers into his briefcase. 'Right. If that's the way you want it, Dad, on your own head be it!'

When Charlotte came home from work Fleur was waiting for her.

'I've been to see your mother,' she said at once.

Charlotte stopped in the act of taking off her coat to stare at her. 'You *haven't!* Bloody hell, Fleur, how could you? You promised!'

'No, I didn't. She had to be told you were safe, Charlotte. She'd been frantic with worry.'

Charlotte threw herself into a chair. 'You're joking,' she said moodily. 'I bet she didn't give a damn. Probably glad to be rid of me.'

'That's not true at all and you know it. Your mum cares a lot about you.'

'Is that what she told you? Huh!' Charlotte snorted and hunched her shoulders. 'So, like a good little grass, I suppose you promised to deliver me home to them then? All tied up in bows and gift-wrapped.'

'No.' Fleur sat down opposite the girl. 'Look, we talked and I suggested something. It's an option for you to think about. And your mum is prepared to let you try it.'

'Try what – *cyanide*?'

'You're behaving like a spoilt kid, Charlotte. I'm beginning to wonder why I bothered. Now – do you want to hear this idea or don't you?'

'Okay, go on.'

'I know where there's a very nice bed-sit. How would you like to try living on your own for a bit?'

Charlotte sat up straight and stared at Fleur. 'You're kidding! Are you saying they'd actually let me do that?' she asked incredulously.

'On certain terms, yes.'

'Ah! I knew there'd have to be a snag. What is it?'

'Only that we keep in close touch. A friend of mine has just moved into a flat in the same house. Tom. You met him here last night. We'd both keep in regular touch with you.'

'And report back?' Charlotte said suspiciously.

'Only if we thought you weren't coping. And of course you'd have to keep your promise not to see your aunt.'

Charlotte slumped again, remembering her father's veto. 'No chance of that anyway. He's threatened Auntie Kath with eviction if she lets me go round there.'

Fleur reached out to touch the girl's hand. 'I'm sorry about that, Charlotte. But maybe when your dad sees how grow up and responsible you are, he'll change his mind? What do you say? Shall we go round and have a look at the room?'

They were ringing the front door bell at ten Park Row when Sadie rode up on her motorbike. She roared to a halt and dismounted.

'Hi! What can I do for you?'

Fleur explained that she'd brought a prospective tenant to view the vacant room.

'Great! Look, I've only come to pick up some spare films,' she told them, taking off her crash helmet. 'I've just got wind of a demo on the site of the new bypass and I'm on my way to take some shots and get the full story.' She grinned. 'If I'm quick off the mark I might be able to sell to one of the nationals. But I can show you the room quickly.' She led the way inside and up the stairs, her leathers squeaking protestingly at every step. 'I only need the other two rooms for myself,' she said as they reached the landing. 'This one's a bit small and I haven't furnished it apart from the carpet and curtains so you'd have to bring your own furniture.' She opened the door. 'Most people want a furnished room which is why it hasn't been let yet, but we could adjust the rent if you like it. Kitchen and bathroom are shared, of course. Cleaning on a rota.'

Charlotte looked round the empty room. It faced south and the sun streamed in at the window. On the floor was a green carpet with matching leaf-patterned curtains at the window. She looked at Fleur with shining eyes. 'I expect Mum would let me bring the stuff from my bedroom at home,' she said excitedly. 'I'd like to take it, please.'

Fleur laughed. 'You haven't even asked what the rent is,' she said. 'And you'll be paying for it out of your wages, remember. You'll have to start budgeting if you're going to be a bachelor girl.'

Charlotte's smile slipped a little. 'Oh, yes. Er – how much is it, Miss Freeman?'

Sadie named a figure which caused Fleur to gasp. It was less than she had paid for the miserable attic room she had started out with in Victoria Gardens. She nodded her approval at Charlotte. 'That's very reasonable.'

'I'll take it.' Charlotte smiled at Sadie. 'Can I move in tomorrow?'

Sadie laughed. ''Course. Any time you like. Now if you don't mind, I've got to go.'

Back at thirteen Victoria Gardens half an hour later Charlotte spoke to her mother on the telephone. 'It's such a sweet little room, but it isn't furnished. So can I move my bed and things over there?'

'If you're sure this is what you really want?'

'I am, Mum. But are you sure Dad won't do something to stop me having it?'

'Leave him to me,' Julia said. 'Give me the address and I'll hire a van. We'll get your things moved tomorrow.' She paused. 'Are you coming home tonight?' Into the pause that followed she said, 'I think you should speak to Dad yourself. It would come much better from you. But I'll back you up, of course.'

Charlotte looked at Fleur and covered the mouthpiece with her hand. 'She wants me to go home tonight,' she whispered. Fleur nodded her agreement.

'You won't let him try to talk me out of it?' Charlotte asked.

'No,' Julia promised. 'But it would be nice if we could all three have a talk.'

'Okay then. See you later.'

Tracey finished wiping down the worktops in the kitchen. She loved working in Julia Grant's kitchen with its cool green-tiled work surfaces and silky wood-faced cupboards. One day, she promised herself, she would have a kitchen just like it. Damian sat in the highchair Julia had lent her, playing contentedly. The chair had been Charlotte's and it had a row of coloured balls attached to the tray, which he never grew tired of. He chuckled contentedly, watching his mother and listening as she sang along to the radio. As usual she had it tuned in to Radio 1 and Chris DeBurgh was singing her favourite, 'Diamond in the Dark'. As it came to an end a tap on the back door made her look up.

'Who can that be, Damie?' she said. Switching off the radio, she crossed the kitchen to answer it.

Outside the door Rick stood leaning against the wall. He wore work-stained jeans and a tattered anorak. 'Hi,' he said hopefully. 'On my way home from work an' I thought I'd give you and the boy a look in.'

'I'm working,' Tracey said shortly. 'I've told you before, Rick. You can't just call here whenever the mood takes you.'

'Go on, you're entitled to a tea break,' he said. 'And Lady Muck's gone out. I saw her drive off with me own eyes.'

It was true that Julia was out. She'd gone to a committee meeting.

'Come on,' Rick wheedled. 'I got a right to see me own son, haven't I?'

'You've got no rights at all, Rick Kendle. You gave them up when you did what you did to me.'

He pulled a face. 'Oh, don't start on that again, Trace. How many times do I have to say sorry, eh? Look, I won't stop long.'

'No.' She tried to shut the door but his foot was in the way.

'I been workin' since eight this morning on that buildin' site and I've only had a bar of chocolate. I'm nearly passin' out with hunger.'

'Oh, come on in then,' Tracey sighed and held the door open for him. 'And take them filthy boots off. I've just done this floor.' She went to put the kettle on while Rick made a bee line for Damian.

'Hey, he's gettin' a big boy,' he said, lifting him out of his chair and sitting down with him on his knee.

Tracey looked round. 'He's got another tooth through. That's eight.'

'Soon be walkin', I reckon.' Rick put Damian on the floor and watched him crawl towards his mother. 'I wish I could see more of him Trace. You too. Why won't you let me move into your place?'

'It wouldn't work,' she said, her lips tight. 'I haven't forgotten the way you treated me before. I'm not having Damie grow up with a violent man like you.' She picked the baby up and put him back into his chair. 'You threatened me. And him – a helpless little baby. Mrs Grant wanted me to go to the police.'

'What did she want to go stickin' 'er nose in for?' he said angrily. 'None of 'er bloody business!'

'Good job I had someone on my side,' she told him hotly. 'You scared the livin' daylights out of me, Rick Kendle, them things you said you'd do to Damie an' me.'

'I didn't know what I was doin'. I was clean out of my tree at the time.' He sidled up to her. 'Oh, look, that was ages ago, Trace. I'm not violent. You got to admit it was just the once. I never hit you before, did I? It was that stuff I was on, that's all. It changes you something horrible. But I'm okay now. I'm off it. I got a job an' everything and I'm really tryin' hard.' He gave her a reproachful look. 'Not that I'm gettin' much encouragement from you.'

He went across to where she stood making the tea. 'You oughta see the room I'm in, Trace. A proper rat 'ole, it is, honest. An' there's you with a whole house all to yourself.'

Tracey poured the tea without comment and pushed the biscuit tin towards him. 'Knew I shouldn't have let you in,' she said. 'Look, have your tea and biscuits then go, Rick. I don't want to hear no more.'

He took a biscuit, peering at it disconsolately. 'Got any chocolate ones?'

'No.'

'There's nowhere to cook in that place I'm in,' he said. 'I get sick an' tired of fish an' chips and takeaways. You got anything you could make me a sandwich of? Bit of cold meat? Cheese?'

'No.'

He dunked the biscuit resignedly into his tea and munched. 'Just look at this place,' he said, his mouth full. 'Concealed lightin';

276

ceramic tiles. I know what these things cost and this must've cost an arm and a leg. What you wanna work here for anyway? Givin' up your benefit money so's you can skivvy for toffee-nosed gits like them.'

'I haven't given anything up,' Tracey said.

He stopped chewing to stare at her. 'What d'you mean? You don't work for nuthin', do you?'

Instantly realising she had slipped up, Tracey tried to cover her mistake. 'I work for Mrs Grant because she's been a good friend to me,' she said.

He gave a snort. 'What you mean is, she takes advantage of you?'

'No. She pays me low, but she gives me a present now and again.'

'You mean she pays you when she remembers to? That's not a very good arrangement, is it?'

'It's none of your business, Rick Kendle.'

'Well, I hope you help yourself to the larder,' he said. 'I hope you make sure that you and the kid get well fed for your trouble.' He swigged the last of his tea and passed his cup for more. 'Anyway, how do you mean, she's been a good friend to you?' His eyes narrowed. 'Given you any money, has she?'

'No.'

He laughed. 'Thought not. Them do-gooders never do. Hands you her old cast off clothes, I expect. Big deal! I read about her in the paper. I expect she's been generous with her advice, is that it? Warned you off nasty rough yobs like me. Her and her women's refuge. Wants to keep her nose out of other people's business, interferin old bag.'

'Don't you talk that way about her. She isn't like that!' As he stepped up behind her and slipped his arms around her waist she tried to push him away. 'Leave off, Rick. I told you . . .'

'Oh, look, I know I've treated you a bit rough, Trace,' he murmured, pressing his lips close to her ear. 'But I always thought you liked it that way. And it don't mean I don't care about you. You were the first person I looked up when I got out of stir.'

'The first soft touch, you mean.'

'Don't be like that. I got into bad habits inside, an' when I first come out things was hard. But I've sorted meself out now. Straight up, Trace, I want us to get back together again. Set up home. Just you and me and little Damie – just like what we planned.' His voice took on a wheedling tone. 'You shouldn't be doin' a job like this, you know. You're worth somethin' better, a girl like you. You're a good hairdresser. I hate this job I'm doing. I'm not like you, see, with a trade to my name. I get all the rotten jobs to do. At everybody's beck an' call all day, I am. Now – if I moved in with you, I could look after the kid and you could go back to your proper job, full-time. What do you say, eh?'

'I couldn't do that, Rick. Mrs Grant gave me this job when I really needed it. I couldn't let her down now.'

'Not even for me?' He pulled her round to face him and fixed her with the persuasive brown eyes that had always been her undoing. He drew her towards him, kissing her hard. At first she stiffened, resisting him, but as he persisted he had the satisfaction of feeling her body begin to relax in his arms.

'Oh, Trace, I miss you,' he whispered into her hair. 'I lie awake in that dump they call a room and think of you alone in your bed, an' sometimes I feel like I'm goin' round the twist.' He pushed her back against the worktop and pressed close to her. 'I could always go an' look for some other girl, you know. There's plenty of 'em around. All of 'em willing. But you've spoilt me for anyone else, Trace. It's you I love and I want you so bad it hurts.'

Damian, feeling left out of things, chose that moment to emit a piercing shriek, drumming his little fists on the tray of his chair. Rick glanced round at him. 'Doesn't he have a sleep in the afternoons?'

'Yes.'

He pressed his mouth to hers again, parting her lips hungrily and pulling her so close she could scarcely breathe. She could feel his arousal pressing against her thigh and her heart began to beat faster. Reaching up, she tangled her fingers in his thick curly hair.

'Oh, Rick,' she murmured. But the words were lost in the moist heat of his kiss and she felt her excitement mounting, scattering her resolve like leaves in the wind.

'See to him now.' His voice was urgent and persuasive in her ear. 'Then you an' me can go upstairs.'

'No! We couldn't.'

'Yes, we could. No one'll know. Oh, come on, Trace. Please don't chuck me out again.'

'Mrs Grant – she might come back,' Tracey said breathlessly in a final, half-hearted attempt at resistance. But he was shaking his head at her, chuckling softly.

'Come off it. You know she won't, don't you? I saw her go and she had her briefcase with her. Some meetin' or other. They take hours.'

'Well . . .'

Damian was already half asleep when she put him into his pram and wheeled him out into the garden. Back in the kitchen Rick was waiting impatiently by the door, his hand held out to her invitingly.

278

In Charlotte's room only one single bed remained, the rest of the furniture having been removed to Park Row. Rick closed the door but Tracey opened it again.

'In case anyone comes back,' she said in a whisper. 'We wouldn't hear with the door closed.'

'You're always so scared,' Rick said as he sank on to the bed and pulled her towards him, his hands cupping her buttocks. 'You're like a little rabbit. You got rights the same as anyone else, Trace. We're not doin' any harm.'

He began to undress her, his hands roughly caressing her naked skin. Tracey began to shiver, all the promises she'd made to herself forgotten. She'd always known that if she once let Rick make love to her again she would be lost. She'd been fighting against it for weeks but now all she could think of was the clamouring need of her body for his.

He pulled her down beside him on the bed and slipped off her bra. His hand cupped one breast and he bent his head to nibble at the soft flesh, drawing the nipple deep into his mouth. She shuddered convulsively, sinking back against the pillow. His breath was warm in her ear and his lips on hers were like fire. It was too late to resist now. Much too late.

As his body pressed close to hers in the narrow confines of the single bed all thoughts of what was wise and prudent dissolved. And as he began to make love to her in the demanding, insistent way that had always thrilled her so, she felt her heart pound with feverish desire. She closed her eyes and heard the blood sing in her ears as she enclosed him with her limbs, matching her rhythm to his. It was so good, making love with Rick again. It had been so long. She wanted it to go on forever.

'So – what do you say then, Trace. Can I move in?'

Finally sated with their lovemaking she lay with her head on Rick's chest, her eyes half closed and her body bathed in a warm, rosy after-glow. 'I don't know,' she said dreamily.

He wound a strand of her hair around his fingers. 'Why not?'

''Cause Mrs Grant wouldn't like it.'

'What the hell has it got to do with her?' He gave her hair a tug to emphasise his resentment. 'She don't own you! Oh, come on, Trace. Just think, we could sleep together every night, all private in our own place. We could have it like this whenever we felt like it. No more snatchin' a crafty half hour in someone else's gaff. I could give up this poxy job on the buildin' site an' you could go back to your hairdressin'.'

'I'm not letting Mrs Grant down,' she said stubbornly. 'I told you, I can't leave. Not now.'

Rick shifted his position to look down at her. 'Don't kid yourself, Trace. If she decided she didn't need you no more, d'you reckon she'd keep you on out of the goodness of her heart? Would she 'ell! Why do you set so much store by her?'

'I told you, she's been a good friend. She's worked really hard to try and do something for single mums like me.'

'Well, you're not goin' to be a single mum no more, so she should be pleased for you. Anyway, what does *she* know about single mums?' he sneered.

'More'n you think,' she said enigmatically.

'How could she? A woman like her – pampered and spoilt, never been short of money in her life. How can *she* know what it's like?'

'Well, she does. Take my word for it.'

He raised himself and pinned her down, a hand on each shoulder. 'You believe anything anyone tells you, don't you? You'd believe the devil 'imself if he smiled at you. Time I was lookin' after you again, if you ask me.'

'It's true. I'm not stupid,' she protested. 'It's not just some story she made up. No one'd make up a thing like that.'

'A thing like what?'

'I can't tell you.'

'No, because there's nothing to tell. You're makin' it up just to let her off the hook.'

'No, I'm not!'

'Tell me then.'

She paused. Suddenly he seized her face in both hands and kissed her long and hard. Then he began to stroke her again in the way she always found irresistible, his fingers teasing the velvet soft skin of her inner thigh, breathing softly in her ear as his hand moved higher.

'Rick! Leave off,' she protested, trying to push his hand away. 'Time must be getting on. We can't risk gettin' caught.'

'Tell me then.'

'I told you, I can't.'

'Right.' He moved on top of her, pinning her down with his weight. 'Once more then. And afterwards I'm gonna have a bath in that ritzy bathroom next door.'

'*No!*' She struggled frantically. 'We've been up here for hours. Damie'll be awake by now and Mrs Grant must be due home any minute.'

But he held her fast, his knee holding her thighs apart, one hand

280

grasping her breast, squeezing till he heard her gasp with pain. '*Tell me then! How* come Lady Muck knows so much about bein' a single mum?'

'Because she had a baby herself before she married Mr Grant.' She twisted her head this way and that. 'You're hurting, Rick. Stop it and let me get up, can't you?'

He stopped his rough caressing and raised himself up to stare down at her, his eyes wide and incredulous. 'No *kidding*? Well, who'd have thought it? Just shows you, don't it? No better than anyone else for all their airs and graces. To some other guy, you mean?'

'Yes. And no one else knows. She told me in confidence, so don't you go shootin' your mouth off about it, Rick Kendle.'

''Course not.' He rolled over, releasing her abruptly. 'Go on then, *chicken*. I'll let you off – this time. Get up if you must.' As she got off the bed he gave her bottom a resounding slap. 'What do you say then, Trace? Can I move in or not?'

'No! Not after what you just did,' she said, close to tears as she pulled on her clothes. 'You always have to spoil things, Rick. You always did.' She looked down resentfully at him, lying on the bed with his hands behind his head, grinning impudently up at her. 'Are you gonna get up then, or what?'

'Okay, in a minute. But I'm still havin' that bath, *no* danger!' He grinned at her wickedly. 'An' if Lady Muck comes home you can just send her up to scrub my back! Give the poor cow a treat for once in her life.'

'So, I've been volunteered as baby-sitter in general, have I?'

Tom took the last of the planted hanging baskets from Fleur and hung it on its hook. 'There – what do you think then?'

Fleur beamed with pleasure. 'Trailing fuchsias, petunias and lobelia. It's all going to look wonderful when the flowers come into bloom. Thanks for helping, Tom.' She threw her arms around his neck and gave him a resounding kiss. 'What was that you said about baby-sitting?'

'This little Charlotte what's-her-name? I'm supposed to keep an eye on her, am I?'

'Only from a distance. I feel a bit responsible for her. You see, it was my suggestion that she should leave home and try living on her own.'

'What did you say her name is again?'

'I didn't.' She gave him a rueful look. 'But it happens to be Grant.'

He stared at her. 'Oh my God! She's not one of *those* Grants, is she?'

'Afraid so.'

'Does she know – about you?'

'No.'

'Why get involved then? Are you mad? Isn't life complicated enough for you? I thought you were keeping your distance.'

'I was. But you saw what happened the other night. I couldn't just turf her out into the night, could I? Look, when I first met Charlotte at night school I had no idea who she was. She doesn't seem to have any real friends and she's been having a rough time at home. Problems with her parents.'

'She's confiding all that to you?' He groaned. 'It gets worse!'

She took his hand and drew him back inside the flat. 'Never mind all that. Let's eat now.' She laughed. 'You know, you spend more time here now than when you lived here.'

'Don't change the subject, Fleur. You're playing with fire, do you know that? Next thing you know you'll be expected to take sides. Fancy letting yourself get sucked in to the Grants' family problems.'

'I don't see what else I could have done. Once Charlotte's had a taste of coping alone, and when things have had time to cool down, she'll probably go home again anyway.'

'Well, I hope you're right.'

They prepared their meal together in companionable silence. Outside spring was beginning to bloom in earnest. The sun still shone and a solitary blackbird was singing in the dusty branches of the fir tree at the bottom of the garden. They left the doors to the balcony open, enjoying the balmy air and the last of the evening sunshine.

'When does Sally leave for Switzerland?' Tom asked.

'In a couple of weeks' time.'

He ate in silence for a moment, glancing across at her surreptitiously. 'Does it bother you?'

'No. I'm looking forward to managing on my own. There's an eighteenth birthday party booked for the Tuesday of that week and Beardsley Engineering is having a social evening on the Friday.'

'That's not what I meant, and I think you know it.'

'Oh. The wedding, you mean. I've told you, Tom. Whatever I felt for Peter is over and done with.'

'And the thought of him marrying someone else doesn't hurt?'

'Why should it?'

He nodded. 'Just wanted to know.' He got up and began to clear the table, but Fleur stood up and took the dishes from him, putting them back on the table.

'Leave that for now.' She took his hand and drew him towards the settee. 'Tom, what do I have to do to convince you?' She sat and pulled him down beside her. 'I allowed myself to be taken in. I was made a fool of and I want to forget it. I wish you'd let me.'

'Sorry.' He sighed and leaned back, his arm around her shoulders. 'Call it vanity if you like but I hate the thought of being second best.'

She turned her head to look up at him. 'You could never be that, Tom,' she said softly, 'Especially to someone like Peter Arden.'

For a moment her eyes held his, then he said, 'Its just that I love you, Fleur. Okay, I know I'm not supposed to say it and I don't expect you to respond, but it's nice to get it off my chest.'

She reached up to kiss him. 'You're the nicest person in the world.' Her dark eyes twinkled at him. 'By the way, did you remember to bring your toothbrush?'

He smiled. 'Funny you should ask.' He kissed her and for a while they sat wrapped in each other's arms, contentedly silent. Then he asked, 'You don't regret not being able to be a part of your mother's life, do you, Fleur?'

'No. I always knew she'd have a new life and family,' she said. 'I never really expected her to want to acknowledge me.' She rubbed her cheek against his. 'Besides, look at all I've got. I've got the flat almost the way I want it. I've got a super job that I enjoy. And best of all I've got you. Sometimes I wonder what I've done to be so lucky. I think that coming to Elvemere was the best thing I ever did.'

Fleur wakened during the night. The moon was full. Shining in through the windows, it bathed the room in silver light and made everything, even the threadbare carpet, look brand new. That was how she felt. Last night, her first with Tom, had been like a revelation. He had made love to her so reverently and gently. Yet his lovemaking had been no less exciting for that.

Now I know, she told herself with a little shiver of satisfaction. Now I know what love really is. And now that I know everything suddenly makes sense, like the last piece of a puzzle falling into place. She raised herself on one elbow to look down at Tom's sleeping face. In repose he looked so young and defenceless and a surge of love swept through her as she bent to kiss him. He stirred and opened his eyes.

'Hello,' he mumbled drowsily.

'Hi. Can I tell you something?' She snuggled down close beside him, her eyes intent on his face.

He yawned. 'Can it wait till morning?'

'No. It can't. It can't wait a second longer.'

'Okay then, what?'

'It's just that I love you,' she whispered, her lips close to his. 'Really love you, I mean. In other words, I think we've passed the test.'

His arms closed around her and he smiled in blissful content. 'That's wonderful,' he murmured sleepily. 'Now, can we get some sleep? I'll give you your certificate in the morning.'

Chapter 14

Sally was packed and ready to go. Her suitcases were in the car and she stood giving final instructions to Fleur on the front doorstep.

'I think you'll manage all right with two helpers for the birthday party, but for the social at Beardsley's you might need four,' she said.

Fleur laughed. 'It's all laid on, Sally. I did it yesterday. Betty and Paula are helping me with the party and I've booked Mrs Thompson and her daughter Doris to team up with them on Friday.'

'Of course.' Sally smiled apologetically, but halfway through the door she stopped again. 'The birthday cake. They asked for it to have a floral decoration. You'll have to get on to Harvey's the florist's. Freesias, I think. Ask them to make you a spray with . . .'

'Ordered yesterday,' Fleur told her. 'Stop worrying, Sally. Go and enjoy yourself.'

Sally sighed. 'I know I shouldn't keep reminding you. It's natural, I suppose. This is the first time I've ever left the business in anyone else's hands.'

'I know. You told me – several times.'

'Am I being a frightful fuss-pot?' Sally took both of Fleur's hands in hers. 'Thank you, Fleur. Without you I might not have been able to go to Peter's wedding. These two functions were booked months ago. I couldn't have cancelled them.'

'Of course not. Don't worry, Everything will be fine.'

'Of course. I know it will. Now – have you any messages for Peter?'

'Messages?' Fleur was startled for a moment.

'Yes. You two did become quite good friends when he was here last, didn't you?'

'Oh.' Fleur made herself laugh. 'Of course. Just wish him every happiness from me.'

285

Sally kissed her cheek. 'I will, my dear.' She began to pull on her gloves. 'And I'll ring, of course, the minute I get there.'

'If you ever do get there!' Fleur gave her a little push. 'Go *on*. You'll miss the plane.'

She followed Sally, still fussing, out on to the drive. 'Maybe I should have gone up last night,' she said as she seated herself behind the wheel. 'By train – stayed in one of the airport hotels overnight. That would have meant taking another day though. I just hope the traffic isn't too heavy on the motorway.' She started the engine and slipped the car into gear. 'Well, here I go.' Bye then!' She waved as the car moved forward. 'See you in a week's time.'

'See you. Have a lovely time! And don't worry!' Fleur waved until the car was out of sight, then went back indoors and closed the door with a sigh of relief.

Sally had done nothing but worry and fret for the past week. She had even suggested that Fleur should move into the house whilst she was away, but Fleur had managed to talk her out of that idea. Now that the days were getting warmer she had been able to have the balcony windows open so she could see her plants growing. It was so exciting watching the buds grow fatter and burst into bloom. Not long now before she'd be able to have breakfast outside in the morning sunshine. She planned to share the experience for the first time with Tom, on the very first warm morning. It was something special to look forward to.

As she went through the morning routine, dealing with the mail and attending to orders and accounts, she thought of Charlotte. The girl seemed to have settled in well at Park Row. Sadie reported that she took her turn diligently along with herself and Tom when it came to the chores. She was quiet and clean. 'In fact, I'd hardly know she was there,' she said. Fleur worried slightly about this. Charlotte had been a bright, outgoing girl when she first met her. Now she seemed to have lost touch with most of her schoolfriends and become withdrawn and solitary.

Fleur had left the younger girl to settle for a week before popping round to Park Row to see her one evening. She found her in the kitchen, happily preparing her evening meal, a businesslike apron over the skirt and blouse she wore for the office, and Fleur was pleased to see her looking happy and relaxed.

'I never knew that cooking could be such fun,' Charlotte said, looking up from the pan she was stirring. 'I got fed up with those supermarket ready-meals so I bought myself this little book. It's got recipes for meals for one person. It's really good.'

'Why don't you ask a friend round?' Fleur suggested. 'To show off your cooking.'

Charlotte looked doubtful. 'I don't think anyone I knew at school would be interested,' she said.

'Don't you see them any more?' Fleur asked. 'Don't you go out – to discos or the cinema?'

Charlotte shook her head. 'Not really. Most of the people I used to be friendly with have gone to college.'

'Surely they aren't all away at college? Why not look up some of them now that you're here?' Fleur suggested. 'I bet they'd be impressed no end to know you had your own pad.'

The younger girl shrugged. 'I'm happy on my own.'

'My best friend has gone to college but I haven't lost touch with her,' Fleur said. 'We write to each other. I'd hate to think of us drifting apart after all the years we've been friends.'

'Maybe you've still got things in common,' Charlotte said. 'Anyway I never really had a best friend.'

'Well then, why not ask your mum?' Fleur suggested. 'I know she must be dying to see your room and she won't come unless you invite her, you know.'

'I don't know that I'm ready for that yet.' Charlotte stirred her pan, eyes downcast. 'She'd probably just say she was too busy anyway.'

'Not for you. I'm sure she'd love to come.'

'If I did ask her, would you come too? It would help to have you here.'

Fleur hesitated. 'I'm sure she'd rather it was just the two of you,' she said. 'But whatever you decide, you don't have to be lonely.'

'I know.'

'Tom and I aren't far away.'

'I *know*. You don't have to baby me.' Charlotte looked up. 'If you've come to see him, he's not in yet.'

'It was you I came to see, not Tom.' Fleur looked at her. 'Charlotte – you are happy here, aren't you? I mean, you're not just sticking it out to prove a point?'

'No! This is the best thing I ever did. Even work doesn't seem so bad now that I have my own place to come home to.'

'Have you been back to see them?'

'Mum and Dad?' Charlotte shook her head. 'If I went there'd only be a row. Anyway I see enough of Dad at the office and he's in a rotten mood most of the time.'

'Look, it's just a suggestion, but if you're at a loose end you could always come and give us a hand at Arden's if you felt like it? Earn yourself a bit of extra pocket money.'

Charlotte's face brightened. 'Could I really? That might be good fun.'

'Come and help me while Sally's away,' Fleur suggested. 'There's a birthday party on the Wednesday. I'll come and pick you up – around six okay?'

'Yes, fine.' Charlotte hesitated, then said confidentially, 'To tell the truth, Fleur, I've been out to the stables a couple of times on the quiet to see Auntie Kath. I hate doing it behind Dad's back and I'm scared that if he found out she would get into trouble.' Charlotte sighed. 'But when he plays the heavy father the way he does, he leaves me no alternative.' She turned back to her cooking. 'Sometimes I think that Dad doesn't really know me at all. He just knows what he wants me to be like. I hate lies and deception,' she said unhappily. 'There have been too many lies in our family already.'

Too many lies. Fleur was silent. Charlotte was unaware of just how many lies and secrets there really were. Or the enormity of them. Maybe it was just as well. She watched as the younger girl began to dish up her meal, tipping the drained spaghetti on to her plate and heaping the Bolognese sauce she had prepared on top. She turned to look at Fleur, her eyes shining.

'Can you keep another secret, Fleur?'

'Of course. If you're sure you want to tell me.'

'I do. Auntie Kath has taken this boy on. Well, he's a man really. He's nineteen! His name's James Parker and he's hoping to become a show jumper. He's a terrific rider and absolutely marvellous with the horses. His dad is an ophthalmic surgeon and James works in an accountant's office in the daytime and helps out at the stables in the evenings and weekends.'

Fleur smiled. 'I see. Is he good-looking?'

'Not bad,' Charlotte said, blushing.

'And you and he get along well, do you?'

Charlotte smiled as she put her plate on a tray along with a knife and fork. 'Yes. It's amazing how much we've got in common. His dad wants him to drop the horses and concentrate on exams, but James is determined to have a career with horses if he possible can – like me.' She picked up her tray and looked at Fleur inquiringly. 'Are you coming up with me?'

'No. I'd better go now – let you eat your meal in peace. Don't forget where I live, will you? Come and see my balcony soon. The spring flowers are coming out and it's going to look lovely.'

288

As she went about the morning routine Fleur thought about Charlotte. She seemed to be much more like her old self since she'd moved into her little bed-sit and met this James of hers. And she really didn't seem to mind being on her own.

As for her own life, she could hardly believe how much things had changed in one short year. Tom still wanted her to move in with him, but Fleur was adamant. Spending their free time together, having him stay for the occasional night, was as much as she wanted for the moment. She was so afraid that their relationship might burn out if they took things too hurriedly. She knew now that she loved and trusted him. She looked forward to being with him whenever they were both free. But although she couldn't tell him as much, she still wasn't completely convinced that she wanted to devote her whole life to him, or to any one person if it came to that. Her new independence was valuable to her and for the moment what she and Tom had was enough. Sometimes he grew frustrated and impatient when she refused to budge, but she stood her ground, believing that if their feelings were strong enough they would stand the test of time.

When she had finished dealing with the mail she rang the client whose party was next on her list and discussed details and checked times. Then she rang Beardsley Engineering and asked to be put through to Anne Roberts, the personnel manager, who was arranging the social evening. There was quite a lengthy wait before she came to the phone. When she did she sounded harassed and put out.

'I'm sorry to keep you waiting,' she said. 'We've had rather a traumatic morning here.'

'Really? Is anything wrong?'

'You could say that.'

'Anything I should know about?'

'Not really but the news will be public pretty soon so I might as well tell you. I've just been informed that the firm is going into liquidation.'

'Oh, no!'

'Afraid it's true. And I've got the thankless job of handing out all the redundancy notices. You can guess how I feel.'

Fleur's heart sank. 'Oh, dear. So are you saying that you want to cancel the social evening on Friday?'

'Looks like it. I'd have got round to ringing you later in the day.'

'Well, I understand of course, under the circumstances.'

'I can't see anyone enjoying themselves, even if they turn up. I'm sorry about that.'

289

'I'm sorry too,' Fleur said. 'But it can't be helped.'

'Thanks. It's good of you to be so understanding. I'm afraid we won't be the last firm in Elvemere to feel the pinch,' Anne said. 'From what I hear everyone's orders seem to have been dropping off over the past months.'

Back in the kitchen, as Fleur sliced wafer thin bread for sandwiches, she wondered how the closing of Beardsley's would affect the town. It was the largest factory in Elvemere and employed a lot of people. It would certainly swell the number of unemployed in the area and was bound to have a knock-on affect on all other businesses in the town too, including Arden Catering. She wondered if Tom had heard the news.

Wiping her hands, she went to the telephone and dialled the number of the *Clarion*. She asked for the news desk in the hope that he was in. Luckily he was.

'Fleur? Is something wrong?'

'No, I'm fine. I wouldn't have rung you at work but I wondered if you'd heard that Beardsley's is going out of business.'

'No! Are you sure?'

'Positive. I've just been talking to Mrs Roberts, the personnel manager. She was pretty choked about it. They've cancelled their social evening on Friday.'

'Well, thanks for tipping me off. I'll get round there right away.'

'You won't say Mrs Roberts told me, will you?' she asked. 'She probably wishes by now that she'd kept quiet about it.'

'A journalist never reveals his sources, don't you know that?' Tom told her. 'Have to go now, love. See you.'

Fleur hung up and paused to think about Sally. It was a good thing she had already left for Switzerland. She'd worried enough about leaving as it was. If she'd heard this news before she went she'd have worried even more.

Louise paid off the taxi and walked up the drive of the house in Hazel Grove. Joanna's little red sports car stood on the drive so Louise knew she was home. She hoped Joanna was alone. She'd thought carefully about what she'd come to say and it was for Joanna's ears only.

Louise had dressed very carefully for her visit, putting on the one classic navy blue suit in her wardrobe. Some instinct told her that she was going to need every shred of dignity she could summon for the coming interview. Nevertheless, when she stood looking at herself in the full-length mirror in her bedroom she couldn't help feeling how stark and plain she looked in the dark suit and white blouse. Opening her jewel case she put on her anniversary pearls and matching earrings, and, after a moment's consideration, added the large diamond and ruby brooch Charlie had given her last Christmas. Jewellery always gave her confidence. Without it she felt naked and vulnerable. The opulent pieces in place, she smiled at her reflection with satisfaction. Yes. That was better.

She paused outside the front door of Joanna's house, then extended one gloved finger and rang the bell.

When Joanna opened the door, her eyebrows rose in surprise. 'Oh! It's Mrs Grant, isn't it?'

'I think you know very well it is,' Louise said between gritted teeth. 'Unless my memory is better than yours.'

'What can I do for you?'

'You can ask me in for a start,' Louise told her bluntly. 'Unless you want your neighbours to hear every word I say.'

'Of course.' Joanna held the door open. 'Do come in, Mrs Grant. Can I get you something? A cup of tea perhaps?'

'No, thanks.'

'Well, come through anyway.' Joanna led the way to her sitting room and invited her to take a chair. She looked at Louise inquiringly. 'Now – is there something I can help you with?' she asked pleasantly.

'There certainly is! I want you to withdraw your investment from GPC and go back where you came from,' Louise said bluntly.

Joanna's smile remained though her eyebrows rose a fraction. 'I'm sure you know that isn't possible, Mrs Grant,' she said patronisingly. 'I'm a partner now. And I think the money I put into the firm is already committed.'

'That's just the point. My husband is overstretching the firm. You've given him big ideas with all your talk about your big business in American – what-d'you-call-it? – *real* estate! Vernon and I are right worried about it, I can tell you. But we'd just about manage if you were to pull out now . . .'

'But I'm not *going* to pull out.' Joanna's smile turned frosty. 'Did Vernon send you?'

'Of course he didn't! No one knows I'm here. I'm asking you to leave. Your influence is going to wreck everything my husband and son have worked for, so if you've got any kind of a conscience at all you'll do as I say.'

Joanna reached into the box on the coffee table for a cigarette and lit it slowly. 'Why is it I'm getting such a strong feeling of déjà vu?' she asked, exhaling smoke. 'I seem to remember our having a very similar conversation once before. In fact, when I come to think of it, you used the very same words that time.'

'Oh, so your memory's come back, has it?' Louise folded her arms and met Joanna's gave levelly. 'That time you saw the sense of what I was asking,' she said. 'I'm asking you to see sense again now, before it's too late.'

'It rather depends on your idea of what good sense is, doesn't it? Last time you bribed me to leave your son alone. If I remember correctly I don't think you saw me as quite suitable. I was young and as it happened I needed the money you tempted me with.' She shook her head mockingly. 'Oh, you were *seriously* interested in getting rid of me that time, weren't you, Mrs Grant? But this time the situation is rather different. We've all moved on in life. I don't know what incentive you were thinking of offering this time, but I can tell you that whatever you have in mind, it won't work. I'm here to stay because it suits me, and there's nothing you can do about it, I'm afraid.'

'I've got money invested in the firm too, you know.'

'Ah, but only in a joint holding with Charlie,' Joanna said. 'You have no vote, have you? No actual say in what happens. That rather surprises me, Mrs Grant, for a strong-minded woman like you, if you don't mind my saying so.'

Louise seethed inwardly. 'That's none of your damned business.' Her eyes narrowed. 'Come to that, why have you come back here anyway? Vernon tells me you did pretty well in America. You got a good divorce settlement. Why come back when you could spend your life enjoying yourself – do anything you wanted?'

'Because I want to do this,' Joanna said simply. 'This is what I enjoy.'

Louise was silent for a moment, wishing she could see into the mind of this complex woman; figure out what was really going on in that devious mind of hers. 'Is it *him* – Vernon – you want?' she said at last. 'Because you won't get him. If you insist on staying I might find it necessary to tell him how readily you dropped him before, for cash in hand. I don't think he'd find it very flattering, do you?'

'Maybe not.' Joanna shrugged. 'But if that's what you feel you must do, then tell him by all means,' she said. 'I think Vernon is mature enough now to appreciate his mother's motives for getting rid of girls she disapproved of. How many more were there, Mrs Grant, before you found a girl who was stupid and gullible enough to be manipulated into fuelling your greed?'

'How dare you! It was nothing of the sort!' Louise's self-control was running out fast. She got to her feet, her colour heightening. 'How could I let him ruin his life with a little trollop like you? she said. 'Everyone in town knew you'd sleep with anything in trousers – married or single. You even squeezed extra money out of me by conning me into thinking you were pregnant. You weren't having our Vernie's child at all, were you? It was just a trick to get more cash out of me.'

Joanna smiled. 'How perceptive of you, Mrs Grant. How could I *ever* have hoped to pull the wool over your eyes? But you seem to forget that this was all a very long time ago. Even money loses its potency in the end. I'm sure we've all learned the cruel lessons nature teaches us by now.' She stubbed out her cigarette. 'I'm afraid that, whether you like it or not, I am part of GPC now and there isn't one single thing you can do to alter the fact.' She walked to the door and held it open. 'I'm afraid I'll have to ask you to leave now. Shall I ring for a taxi for you?'

'*No!*' Louise pushed past her into the hall. 'I'll walk down to the phone box and ring for one myself. I'm not stopping in this house a minute longer than I have to.'

'Just as you wish.' Joanna opened the front door and saw with some satisfaction that it was beginning to rain. 'In that case, I'll say goodbye. Thank you so much for calling, Mrs Grant,' she called to Louise's broad, indignant back. 'Please feel free to call again – any time you're passing.'

She closed the door and leaned against it, a smile of triumph on her face. The telephone kiosk was about half a mile away. By the time Louise had trekked down to it she'd be soaked through. Joanne began to laugh. She'd dreamed of such a scene for years. It had been well worth waiting for.

Charlie had just finished dictating the last of his letters when Vernon burst into his office.

'Have you heard the news?'

Charlie nodded to his secretary. 'Thanks, Phyllis. I'd like those to go off as soon as possible.' He looked up at Vernon as the door closed behind her. 'I wish you wouldn't come bursting in like that,' he said. 'I could have had anyone with me – might have had old Phyllis on my knee, – been at what you might call a delicate state of negotiations.' He chuckled up into Vernon's anxious face.

'This is a delicate state all right,' he said. 'I've just heard the local news on the car radio. Beardsley's is going into receivership.'

The grin vanished from Charlie's face and he stared at his son in disbelief. 'Can't be. That can't be right! I saw Jim Beardsley only the other night at the Lodge meeting. He never dropped s'much as a hint.'

'Well, he wouldn't, would he? But it's true! They'd hardly have put it out over the radio if it wasn't.' Vernon dropped into the chair that Phyllis had vacated. 'You know what this means, don't you? Nearly all the houses that have been completed on the Meadowlands Park Estate have been reserved by executives and senior employees of Beardsley's.'

Charlie waved a dismissive hand at him. 'So what? We'll soon resell them. Houses like those are always in demand.'

'At the price we're asking? When there's such insecurity about? What we have to ask ourselves is, if Beardsley's have gone bust, who's going to be next? You know as well as I do that they were the key industry in Elvemere. Dad, look, I'm serious . . .' Vernon leaned forward earnestly. 'I think we should drop the Victoria Gardens project – now, before it's too late.'

'It's already too late. I signed the contract with old mother Franks yesterday. The plans have been passed. We've got the go-ahead. We can't pull out now.'

Vernon's colour drained. 'It's sheer madness. Did you get a survey done?'

'What for? We're going to have to gut the places anyway. Oh, don't be such an old woman, Vern. You're getting as bad as Harry. Look, if Meadowlands is going to take a bit longer to get off the ground, all the more reason for us to have another iron on the fire. We'll drop the price of the Meadowlands houses if necessary. Get them off our hands.'

'We're working on a low profit margin now,' Vernon argued.

'Well, we'll put cheaper fittings in those we haven't finished.'

'The fittings have already been bought. They're sitting in the store now, waiting.'

'Leave out the jacuzzis and the swimming pools then. Oh, don't worry about it, Vern. Everything's going to be fine. I'm seeing Bill Watts at the bank this afternoon. I'll ask him to extend our overdraft. He'll understand.'

Vernon sighed. 'I hope to God you're right.'

Charlie looked at his watch and began to get up from the desk. 'Damn you, Vern. Look at the time! I'll be hard pressed to be on time for my appointment now. You and your mitherin'.'

'Look, maybe I'd better come with you?'

'No!' Charlie was pulling on his coat. 'Bill and I go back a long way. We understand each other. You go sticking your panicky four penn'orth in and you'll only go and mess things up.'

294

Fleur was halfway up the stairs to her flat that evening when the telephone began to ring in the hall. She paused. It was probably for Ivy or one of the other tenants. But when no one else answered it she retraced her steps and walked down the hall to pick it up.

'Hello. Thirteen Victoria Gardens. Who are you calling?'

'Can I speak to a Miss Sylvester, please? Miss Fleur Sylvester?'

'Yes – speaking.' Fleur was surprised. She didn't recognise the voice. 'Who is it?'

'Sergeant Stanbridge of Hertfordshire Constabulary. I'm speaking from the police station, Miss Sylvester. Are you a friend of a Mrs Sarah Arden of twenty-two Fairfield Drive, Elvemere?'

'Yes, I work for her. I'm her assistant. Why – is something wrong?'

'I'm sorry to have to tell you that Mrs Arden was involved in an accident on the M1 several hours ago. We've only just recovered her handbag from the wreckage of her car. We found your name and number in it.'

The wreckage of her car! Fleur's heart froze. Out of the corner of her eye she was aware of Ivy's presence. She was standing at the top of the basement stairs, watching and listening, but Fleur was too preoccupied to be irritated.

'Where is she now?' she asked.

'She's in the intensive care unit at St Elspeth's Hospital, Miss Sylvester. I'm ringing to ask if you know who her next-of-kin would be?'

'Her son. But he's in Switzerland. She was on her way to his – his wedding!' Her throat constricted. Oh, God, poor Sally! All afternoon Fleur had been picturing her happy excitement at landing in Switzerland and meeting Peter, when all the time she had been lying in hospital.

'I'll ring him at once,' she said. 'I've got his number, but I've no idea how long it will take him to get here. How is Sally? Can I drive down there and see her?'

'She's unconscious, I'm afraid.'

Fleur's blood ran cold. 'How – how bad?'

At the other end of the line the policeman cleared his throat. 'I can only tell you that she has severe injuries, miss. They'll be able to tell you more at the hospital.'

Fleur's hand clutched at the receiver convulsively. It sounded so ominous. 'But – she'll get better, won't she?'

'I'm very sorry, miss, but I can't tell you any more.' Again he cleared his throat. 'If you could let her son know as soon as possible? We can notify him if you wish but I think if you know him . . .'

'Yes, of course. I'll do it now.'

'Not bad news, I hope?' Ivy was standing at her side now, her eyes bright with morbid curiosity.

'Yes. Yes it was. I have to make a call.' Fleur's hands shook as she rummaged in her bag for coins then leafed through her diary for the number of Peter's future father-in-law's hotel, the contact number that Sally had given her only this morning. She found it and turned to Ivy who was still standing there. 'Please – if you don't mind, it's private.'

Ivy bridled. 'Well, pardon me I'm sure! I was only trying to help. The last thing I ever do is pry into other folks' business!' She began to turn, then paused. 'While I think of it, I've been meaning to speak to you. P'raps you'll come down when you've got a minute?'

'Yes, all right,' Fleur said abstractedly as she began to dial.

Snorting indignantly, Ivy turned and stumped down the basement stairs, closing the door with a bang at the bottom.

Fleur finished dialling the number, then stood biting her lip anxiously as she waited. To her relief it was Peter's voice that answered. She could not have coped with someone who didn't speak English.

'Peter, it's Fleur. I'm afraid I've got some very bad news for you.'

'Mother? Something's wrong? I've been waiting for hours at the airport and there are no more flights today. I've only just got in.'

She told him as gently as she could, trying hard to keep her voice from breaking. 'I'm going to drive down there now to be with her,' she told him. 'Can you get a flight, do you think?'

'Of course. It may not be until tomorrow, but I'll be there.' He paused, then added, 'Fleur – how bad is she? Have they said?'

'I only spoke to the policeman. All he said was that she had severe injuries. I don't know any more than that. Shall I ring you again from the hospital when I've seen her?'

'No, I'll get on to the airport at once and see if I can get a night flight.'

Fleur was halfway up the stairs again when she remembered that Ivy had asked to see her. It was probably just an excuse to pump her for information about Sally, but if she was going to have to drive down to Hertfordshire this evening she had better get it over with. She turned and made her way down to the basement. Ivy was in her small scullery, frying fish for her tea. Fleur tapped on the door.

'You said you wanted to see me.'

Ivy removed the cigarette from the corner of her mouth. 'After tea would have done,' she said tetchily.

'I have to go out right away,' Fleur said. 'I have to drive down to Hertfordshire this evening.'

With a resigned sigh Ivy put her half-smoked cigarette down on the corner of the draining board and turned off the gas under the frying pan. 'Well, since you ask, I'm afraid I've got to give you notice to quit,' she said abruptly.

Fleur stared at her. '*Notice*? But why?'

Ivy folded her arms. 'I told you when you first come that I wasn't keen on girl tenants and now you've proved me right.'

'I – don't know what you mean. How have I proved you right?'

'You been havin' men up in your room,' Ivy said accusingly. '*All night!*'

'Men. Do you mean Tom?'

'He's a man, isn't he?'

'Yes, but it isn't the way you make it sound,' Fleur argued. 'Tom and I, we're . . .'

'You're not *married*, are you? Nor yet engaged either – not as far as I know. In my book that amounts to loose morals and I don't allow it. Not under my roof.'

Fleur bit her lip. She was going to lose the flat that she'd worked so hard on. Her beloved home. And her balcony garden. Just when it was coming into bloom. A lump thickened her throat. 'Please, Ivy, I'm sure we can work this one out,' she said. 'If you don't want Tom to stay then he won't, but don't make me leave. I've worked so hard to make the flat nice.' It felt like grovelling but she didn't care. Coming on top of the news about Sally it was too much to handle.

'I'm sorry but I got me principles,' Ivy said self-righteously. 'And even if I hadn't, I'd still have to ask you to leave. I've sold this place, y'see.'

Fleur stared at her. 'Sold it? Who to?' Her shattered hopes rose. 'What about the new people – will they let the rooms?'

'Gonna pull it to bits,' Ivy said, her eyes glinting with vindictive triumph. 'Turn it into a block of offices.'

Fleur's heart sank. 'How long?' she asked resignedly. 'When do you need me to get out?'

'A month's notice is what I have to give,' she said. 'But if you take my advice you'll go as soon as you can find somewhere else. If you find a place before your time is up, we'll come to some arrangement about the rent.'

Fleur was stunned into silence. It was as though history was repeating itself. Last time she'd been given notice it came at a traumatic time. 'I can't do anything right now,' she said. 'I have to go out. I may not be back at all tonight.'

297

'Oh? Goin' off on some jaunt with '*im* then, are you?' Ivy said nastily.

Fleur turned, her dark eyes flashing dangerously. 'As a matter of fact, Mrs Arden, my employer, has been seriously injured in a car accident. I'm on my way to the hospital in Hertforshire to see her!' Banging the door on Ivy's indignant expression she ran up the stairs, her eyes stinging with tears. In the hall she picked up the telephone and dialled. Charlotte answered.

'Hello?'

'Charlotte, it's me, Fleur. Is Tom there?'

'No. He rushed in and grabbed something to eat about half an hour ago – said he had to go out on some assignment or other.'

'Oh, no!' Fleur bit her lip. Just when she needed him so badly. 'Can I give him a message? Can he ring you back?'

'No. Look, Charlotte, will you tell him that I have to go down to Hertfordshire tonight? Mrs Arden has been involved in a serious road accident.'

'Oh, Fleur, how awful! Can I do anything to help?'

'No. Just tell Tom.'

'I'll leave a note for him on the board in the kitchen,' Charlotte said. 'That's what we do. He'll be sure to see it there.'

'Are you all right, Charlotte?'

'I'm fine. Mum was going to come round this evening but she rang to say there was some kind of crisis. I think she and Dad have had another row.'

'I'll call you when I get back. 'Bye for now.'

Upstairs Fleur pushed a change of underclothes and her toothbrush into a bag and checked to see that she had enough money for food and perhaps an overnight room. The fact that she was about to lose her flat was only just sinking in. She stood in the middle of the room and looked around her. Everything she had was between these four walls. Her space and privacy, her independence. It was her achievement; the vital proof to herself that she could stand alone. She'd had it for such a short time and now she was about to lose it again. She went to the window and looked out on to the sunlit balcony. The tubs of daffodils, crocuses and grape hyacinths were in flower now and the bulging green tulip buds were magically changing colour, a little each day, scarlet and pink and gold. Soon the little balcony would be a riot of sumptuous colour. But before that happened she'd be gone – who knew where? She swallowed hard at the lump in her throat and turned quickly away, ashamed of her selfishness. How could she stand here feeling sorry for herself when Sally lay unconscious and gravely hurt?

Since the afternoon of reckless abandonment Tracey had enjoyed with Rick at the Grants' house she had been filled with fear and trepidation. Remembering that afternoon still made her go hot and cold at the thought of what might have happened. It was a miracle they'd got away with it.

After she came downstairs that afternoon she'd gone through torture, knowing that Rick was still upstairs taking a leisurely bath in the Grants' en-suite bathroom when Julia might walk in at any minute.

She had remained in the hall, eyes glancing anxiously upwards as she strained her ears for the sound of Julia's car on the drive outside. Every muscle in her body was tense until at last Rick had come swaggering downstairs trailing a cloud of Vernon's aftershave in which he had obviously drenched himself. He wore a smile of smug defiance on his face.

'That was ace!' he announced. 'I could get used to living in a place like this.'

With a shrill admonishment she had grasped him by the arm and bundled him hastily out through the back door, telling him not to come back if he knew what was good for him. Locking the door firmly, she had rushed upstairs to eradicate every trace of him. Flinging the window open to let out the tell-tale steam, she had cleaned the tidemark off the bath and picked up the sodden towels from the floor where he had dropped them. Fetching the hoover, she had swept up the spilled talcum from the carpet and put the top back on the big bottle of Givenchy bath essence. As she worked she cursed herself for the fool she had been. She had known all the time they were making love that she was storing up trouble for herself. Why was she so weak when it came to sex? Why couldn't she have just said no and told him to sling his hook?

For a couple of weeks she thought she had got away with it. But now to her horror it was catching up with her in more ways than one. Rick had obviously taken more than just a bath that afternoon.

Two days ago she had frozen with dismay when she overheard Vernon asking his wife if she had seen his gold cufflinks. Then this morning he had missed the Rolex watch he'd been given for his twenty-first birthday. As she lingered over dusting the stairs this morning she had heard herself accused of theft as Vernon ranted at Julia over breakfast.

'It must be her. Who else could it possibly be? I told you at the time it was madness to employ someone with no references when we're both out so much. Why are you so easily taken in when it comes to these people? You're incredibly naive and stupid! You're so obsessed by all your do-gooding that you can't see that you're being taken for a ride. Soon we'll have every villain in the county round here, robbing us blind!'

'You don't know that you've been robbed,' Julia protested weakly.

'Can't you see that these wretched inadequate so-called battered women of yours probably deserve all they get?' he said. 'Well, you do what you like, but I'm not having them in this house, helping themselves to whatever takes their fancy. Get rid of her, Julia. Do it today.'

'I know Tracey wouldn't do a thing like that,' Julia insisted. She's honest, I'd stake my life on it. I once offered to pay her electricity bill when she'd been cut off and she wouldn't take the money.'

'You did *what*? You fool, Julia. Can't you see what kind of message that sent out? It was worth her while to refuse the money then, wasn't it? A sprat to catch a mackerel! The girl obviously thinks you're a soft touch.'

'I don't believe for one minute that your watch has been stolen,' Julia said firmly. 'You can't have looked properly. 'You're always putting things down somewhere and mislaying them.'

'It's gone, I tell you. The watch *and* the cufflinks. They were both in the top drawer of my bedside table. For heaven's sake, Julia! As if I hadn't enough to worry about, what with my only daughter cast out to live among drop-outs and getting up to God knows what.'

'Charlotte is *not* living among dropouts, and if you took the trouble to go round to see the house where she's living, you'd know that. Anyway, it was you who drove her out with your bullying and lies.'

Vernon snorted impatiently. 'As if I've got time to worry about things like that when Dad's doing his level best to ruin the business. You're the girl's mother. That kind of thing is down to you – along with the domestic arrangements. Surely you can do that! I want you to sack that thieving girl! Do you hear what I'm saying? That's one worry I *can* eliminate. I don't want her in the house any more after today. And if she's here when I get home, I'll kick her out myself!'

'Before you ask me to start accusing innocent people of stealing, perhaps you should ask Joanna if you left your watch and cufflinks there last time you slept with her!' Julia said.

'Listen to you!' Vernon's voice was scathing. 'You're even beginning to think and talk like them!' From where she stood on the stairs, Tracey heard his exasperated snort and the scraping sound his chair made on the ceramic floor tiles in the kitchen. She hurried to the landing and kept out of sight behind the banisters until she heard the front door slam, then she crept down to the kitchen and put her head round the door.

'Mrs Grant.'

'Oh, Tracey, have you finished upstairs?' As Julia turned with a start from the sink where she was washing up the breakfast things, Tracey was dismayed to see tears on her cheeks.

'Not quite. I came down because I couldn't help overhearing Mr Grant just now. There's something I think you ought to know.'

Julia dried her hands and indicated a chair. 'Sit down, Tracey. I'll make us some coffee.'

'No, I'll make it in a minute. I want to tell you first – get it off my chest.' She sat down opposite Julia. 'Rick's been coming round here. I never asked him to and I tried not to let him in but there was one afternoon a few weeks ago when he wouldn't take no for an answer.' She took a deep breath. 'He talked me round. Said he was sorry about that other time – that he'd turned over a new leaf. He said . . .' She glanced anxiously at Julia. 'Said he still loved me. I know it was wrong and – and silly of me, but I let him . . .' Unable to find the words to confess her weakness, she raised her eyes to Julia in mute appeal.

'Are you saying you let him make love to you? Here, in this house?' Julia saw beyond the audacity of the situation to the implications of what Tracey was trying to tell her. Suddenly her confidence evaporated. Had Vernon been right when he said she was a soft touch, to be taken for a ride by every villain in the county?

'Did you leave him alone upstairs at any time?'

Tracey nodded unhappily. 'But I can't believe he'd do a thing like this to me, Mrs Grant,' she said tearfully. 'He made me believe he meant it when he said he'd turned over a new leaf. He promised me all sorts that afternoon, he did. For a little while I was so . . .' She swallowed. 'So *happy.*' She fumbled in her apron pocket for a handkerchief. 'I thought everything was going to be all right again.'

Julia sighed. Why were women so easily taken in by a few flattering words and easily made promises? She remembered Dean suddenly: the soft husky voice, the lips and the hands that could lift her to the skies and beyond. She remembered too the misery that had resulted. The repercussions that were still resounding – even yet.

'Are you still seeing him?' she asked.

Tracey blew her nose. 'He's been round a few times but I sent him packin',' she said. 'I think he's been to the house too. He wants to move back in with us, you see. But I never open the door after dark these days.' She sighed. 'I should have known he'd take advantage as soon as he got what he wanted. That afternoon – soon as I said I wouldn't have him back to live with me and Damie, he got nasty.'

'He didn't hit you again?'

'Oh, no, nothing like that.' With a sudden cold feeling Tracey remembered what Rick had forced her into telling him that afternoon in bed. That was one thing she couldn't confess to. 'He got a bit rough,' she said. 'And just – just sort of turned off. You know how they do.'

'Oh, yes.' Julia nodded ruefully. 'I know.'

'Now it looks like he found another way to get even too.'

'The watch and cufflinks, you mean?'

Tracey nodded unhappily. 'Mr Grant wants you to sack me, doesn't he?'

'I'm sorry, Tracey. I know you didn't take the things. You wouldn't do a thing like that, but I can't convince him unless the things can be found.'

'If I can get Rick to give them back, I will. But I reckon if he did take them they'll have been sold on by now. Oh, I could *kill* him for muckin' things up for me! I've loved working here for you.'

'Maybe I could get you another job if I asked around.'

'No, you won't be able to. It's like Mr Grant said, I've got no references.'

'I'll give you a reference.'

'It won't be any good. No one'll want me with Damie, will they? He's getting bigger now. Soon he'll be walking and then what? Get into everything, don't they, at that age? No. I'll just have to manage on the benefit money.'

'Can't Rick give you anything? You said he was working.'

'That labouring job won't last long. He hates it. That why he wants to move in with us. So that he can give up his job and I can go back to the hairdressing,' Tracey said. 'Maybe it's something I should look at.'

'You can't really want that? Not after the threats he made.'

'He swears he never meant them – that he's off that stuff now. And he is Damie's dad,' she said. 'Anyway, I might not have much choice.' She looked up at Julia despairingly. 'You see, I think I might be pregnant again.'

'Oh, Tracey, no!'

The girl gave her a wistful look. 'Well, I'm only a few days late so I'm keeping my fingers crossed, but I got this feeling. You know how you do?'

302

Julia sighed. She was far from happy about the girl's decision but, like Tracey, she had little choice in the matter.

It was dark by the time Fleur arrived at the hospital but she was infinitely relieved to get there. She'd never driven on the motorway before. It had seemed so long and so monotonous. Even then she'd missed the turn off and had to drive on to the next roundabout and find her way back. Then she'd had difficulty in finding the hospital. But at last she saw it looming ahead of her, lit up like a huge ship sailing through the night. With a grateful sigh she drove into the car park and found a space.

Inside the entrance hall the reception desk was closed for the night, but looking on the direction board she saw that the intensive care unit was on the fourth floor. She made her way to the lift.

The unit was dim and hushed but the sound of bleeping monitors reached her ears as soon as she slipped inside the doors. At the nurses' station the night sister sat quietly working on some charts by the light of a desk lamp. She looked up.

'Can I help you?'

'I've come to see Sally – er – Mrs Sarah Arden.'

'Are you her next-of-kin?'

'No. That's her son. He's on his way over from Switzerland. He might not be able to get here till morning so I said I'd come. I'm Fleur Sylvester, her assistant.'

'Oh, yes, the policeman said he'd contacted you.'

'How is she?'

The sister glanced towards the drawn curtains of a cubicle. 'The doctor is with her now. Perhaps he'll have a word with you before he goes.'

Fleur waited until the curtains parted and a grey-haired doctor emerged. The sister looked up and said, 'This is Miss Sylvester, Mr Farrar. She's a close friend of Mrs Arden's.'

Fleur looked at the doctor. 'How is she?' she asked, holding her breath. 'Is she badly injured?'

His face was grave. 'I'm afraid so. She suffered multiple injuries in the accident. She has a fractured skull and there's some internal bleeding too.'

'Is there anything . . . can't you operate?'

He shook his head. 'We've done what we can for the moment. We'll see how things go.' He glanced at the sister. 'Her next-of-kin?'

'On his way,' Sister said briefly.

'Can I see her?' Fleur asked.

303

'She's unconscious.' The doctor hesitated then nodded. 'All right then, just for a few minutes.'

Fleur was appalled and frightened by the sight of so many tubes and the array of bleeping monitors surrounding the bed. Sally's head and one arm was swathed in bandages and her face was bruised almost beyond recognition, but one hand lay on top of the covers. Fleur touched it gently. She'd read somewhere that unconscious people could sometimes hear if you spoke to them or played music. She bent closer.

'Sally,' she said quietly, 'it's me, Fleur. Peter is coming. He's on his way and you're not to worry. You're going to be fine.'

For several minutes she sat there talking to Sally, urging her to recover, telling her that everything was going to be all right, until the curtains parted and the sister touched her on the shoulder.

'I must ask you to leave now, Miss Sylvester,' she said. As they moved away from the bed she asked, 'Have you made any arrangements for the night?'

Fleur shook her head. Finding somewhere to sleep had completely slipped her mind. 'No. Do you know of any place I could get a room?'

'You won't find anything now, dear. It's after midnight. But I'm sure we can find you a room here in the hospital under the circumstances. There's usually one vacant in the private wing.'

In the small impersonal room Fleur sat on the high bed and stared numbly at the wall. A kindly nurse had brought her a tray of tea and a sandwich. She'd drunk the tea but the sandwich seemed to turn to ashes in her mouth and in the end she had to abandon it.

She couldn't get the sight of Sally out of her mind. She had looked so dreadful. Was it a bad sign that they weren't going to operate? And if the unthinkable happened and Sally were to die – what then? At last, out of sheer exhaustion, she lay down on top of the bed and closed her eyes. But behind her closed lids she could still see the swollen, bruised face and the body that lay there, so still and lifeless, and although she was exhausted, sleep seemed out of the question. At last, just as the sky was beginning to lighten, she fell into a fitful, restless sleep, but it was full of haunting images and deep, dark fears.

She was awakened by a nurse coming into the room. 'Good morning,' she said breezily. 'It's eight o'clock and I've brought you some tea. If you'd like some breakfast you can get some in the staff canteen.'

'Oh – thank you.' Fleur sat up, rubbing her eyes. Her mouth was dry and her head ached as she stared bemusedly round the strange

304

room. Then the events of the previous day slowly filtered back into her mind and she remembered where she was – and why. 'Can you tell me how Mrs Arden is?' she asked anxiously.

The nurse shook her head. 'I'm sorry, I don't know, but I do know that her son arrived about half an hour ago. He's up in ICU. Sister rang down to ask me to let you know.'

As Fleur turned the corner of the corridor she saw Peter come out through the swing doors of the intensive care unit with the doctor she had seen the previous night. They stood together for a moment outside the doors, heads bowed, faces grave. Fleur stopped. Something about the way Peter stood, the set of his shoulders, filled her with a cold feeling of dread. After a moment the doctor touched him on the shoulder in a gesture of sympathy, then walked away in the opposite direction.

Peter turned slowly and their eyes met. In that instant she knew that Sally had lost her battle for life.

Chapter 15

Peter drove the van back to Elvemere. Both of them were in such a state of shock that afterwards Fleur hardly remembered the journey at all. They spoke of immediate mundane things, blocking out the suddenness and horror of their loss. Peter asked if Fleur would carry out the catering engagements already booked and she agreed, knowing that Sally would have wanted that.

At the house he parked the van in the drive and they went indoors together. In the office Fleur attended to the answering machine, relieved when there were no pressing messages needing attention. So far she was in no fit state to break the news to people.

In the kitchen she made a snack meal for them both while Peter took his case upstairs to his old room. When he reappeared he had showered and shaved and looked refreshed. Sitting opposite each other at the kitchen table, they tried to eat.

'She was looking forward to the wedding so much,' Fleur said. 'When she left here she was so excited. It's hard to believe it was only yesterday morning.'

Peter laid down his knife and fork. 'We should have had the wedding here,' he said. 'It was what she wanted. She wanted to do the catering herself, but I . . .' He broke off. 'Oh, my God. If only . . .'

'Don't.' She reached out to touch his hand. 'Nothing can make any difference now.' She looked at him. 'Have you telephoned your fiancée yet?'

'Lorraine?' He shook his head. 'No. I'll have to tell her to postpone the wedding. There'll be an inquest, of course. God, I'm not looking forward to it.'

Fleur glanced at his ravaged face. He looked terrible; his eyes were bloodshot and his skin had a greenish pallor. She imagined she must look as bad. Both of them were still reeling from shock and lack of sleep. 'You'll stay on then?' she said. 'Till it's all over?'

'Of course. I must. There'll be so much to arrange. Even after the funeral. There's the business, the house – all her things. I can't begin to think.'

'Yes, I know.' She glanced at him. 'What can I do to help?'

'I'll need a hand with her personal belongings, if you wouldn't mind?' He took a deep breath and straightened his shoulders. 'I know she made a Will, but I don't know what her wishes were. I always thought it would be years and years before . . .' He looked at her. 'For the time being, will you carry on with the business?'

'Of course. I said I would, didn't I?'

'I don't mean just this week. I'd like you to take over Arden Catering for me permanently. I'd like to keep it going if possible, but being abroad I'll need someone I can trust. What do you think?'

'Well . . .' Fleur swallowed hard. 'I might need some help, part-time perhaps, but I can do most of it myself. Luckily we were well stocked up.'

'Good. Get in anyone you think you need, of course. We'll work out the financial details later. I expect we'll need some kind of contract drawing up.' He looked up at her. 'Do you think you could move into the house too? This is the business premises in a manner of speaking and I think it might be a good idea for security reasons. After I've gone back, of course,' he added quickly.

'I'll move my things over. I was going to have to leave my flat anyway.' She looked at him. 'How long do you think you'll be staying?'

'As long as it takes.' He pushed his plate away, barely touched. 'Sorry, Fleur. I'm not hungry. You've been marvellous over all this, but . . .' He looked at her. 'Look, I think we should clear the air. There's something that has to be said.'

'No. There's no need.'

'Yes, there is. I'm sorry about the way I treated you – really sorry. It was unforgivable. I suppose you . . .' He looked at her sheepishly. 'Did Mother know?'

'Of course she didn't.' Acutely embarrassed, she got up from the table and began to clear the used dishes, scraping the uneaten food into the waste bin. 'Your mother thought the world of you. I could never have done anything to hurt her.'

'I'm grateful to you for that. But . . .'

'Please, Peter. It's all in the past. I'd rather forget all that if you don't mind, especially now.'

'Yes, of course. But thanks anyway.'

She stacked the dishes into the dishwasher and switched it on. 'I'd better go home,' she said. 'My number is in your mother's desk

307

diary if you need me. I'll come in tomorrow and work in the office – deal with anything that crops up. And there's an engagement tomorrow evening. A birthday party. I was going to do that on my own anyway.'

He smiled. 'Looks as though you've got everything buttoned up.'

'If you need my help with anything, just ring.'

'I'll remember.'

'There's plenty of food in the fridge. And your room is ready. Your mother always kept the bed aired in case you . . .' Her voice trembled. 'I'd better go.'

'*Fleur*. Oh, damn it, come here.' He reached out and grasped her shoulders, drawing him towards him, and for a moment they clung to each other, drawing comfort from the closeness of their shared grief.

'Thanks for all you've done,' Peter said huskily. 'She was very fond of you, you know.'

'And I thought a lot of her too,' Fleur said. 'I owed her so much. It seems so cruel. I still can't . . .' She swallowed painfully. 'I can't believe . . .'

'Neither can I. It's going to take a hell of a lot of getting used to.' He looked down at her and wiped the tears from her cheeks with his thumbs. Then he bent and kissed her lightly. 'Come on, I'll drive you home.'

'There's no need, really. I can get the bus.'

'I wouldn't hear of it. You look tired out. You should try and get some sleep.'

In the flat that had become so dear and familiar Fleur opened the windows and stood for a moment on the balcony, breathing in the fresh spring air. Since this time yesterday her whole world had been turned upside down. She looked around her at the tubs and baskets she had planted, inhaling the honeyed scent of the spring flowers, her heart heavy with the knowledge that she must soon leave before she had enjoyed even one summer. It was cruelly ironic that she would be moving into Sally's house just now when she most needed somewhere to live. Sally would have offered her a home anyway. She'd been a kind friend as well as employer. It was impossible to believe Fleur would see her no more. It was hard to believe that so much could have happened in just twenty-four hours. She went inside and closed the windows, then, too weary even to undress, she lay down on the bed and was almost instantly asleep.

Tom had been turning his car into Victoria Gardens when he saw the distinctive white Arden Catering van drawing up outside

308

number thirteen. He'd got in very late the previous evening and gone straight to bed. He'd decided to drive round to the gardens on his way to work on the off-chance of catching Fleur before she left, but she must have been out before him.

But before he could drive up behind her he was surprised and puzzled to see Fleur getting out of the passenger side. She seemed to be talking to someone in the van and did not glance in his direction. He pulled into the kerb as a man got out of the driver's side of the van and escorted her to the front door. Tom watched as they exchanged a few words, then the man bent and kissed her cheek, pressing one of her hands in both of his.

Tom sat in the car, trying to control the surge of jealousy and resentment that overwhelmed him. As he sat there trying to decide what to do the white van turned and drove past him, giving him a glimpse of the man at the wheel. Dark and smooth-looking. He'd seen him once before – passed him on the stairs when he lived at Victoria Gardens. It was that bastard Peter Arden! What the hell was going on? He was supposed to be in Switzerland, getting married but now it seemed he was back in England instead. Back in Fleur's life again, after all she had said and in spite of what he had done to her.

The first thing May Philips did on the morning after she and Harry returned from their cruise was to telephone her daughter.

'Darling, we're home. Our plane was late getting in, but we drove straight back – didn't get in till about eleven o'clock last night. I can't tell you what a wonderful time we've had! Your father looks so much better – tanned and relaxed. I wish I'd been able to persuade him to take a holiday like that years ago. Now, when are you coming round to see us? I've brought presents for you and Charlotte, and of course Daddy is longing to hear all the news from GPC.'

Julia's heart sank. She had been dreading the coming interview. 'You must both be dreadfully jet-lagged. Why don't I leave it until tomorrow?' she offered hopefully.

'No. We've had a good night's sleep and we both feel fine. Do come, darling. We're both longing to see you.'

Julia sighed resignedly. There was obviously no hope of post-poning the interview. 'Well, I've got two meetings this afternoon,' she said. 'But I could come this morning if you're not too busy unpacking?'

'Of course. Come for coffee. And if I'm busy with all my little chores, I can leave you and Daddy talking. I'm sure you two will have a lot to talk about.'

Julia sighed. She doubted it. Once she'd told him she'd let him down he probably wouldn't want to speak to her again. 'Right. See you about half-past ten then,' she said with an enthusiasm she didn't feel. She had planned to visit the women's refuge this morning. Now that things were well and truly under way she made regular trips round to Alexandra House and enjoyed watching her project taking shape.

The empty property that Eleanor had found was a rambling Edwardian house in the maze of rather rundown streets between the park and the railway. The owner had died eight years before, leaving the house to a nephew who lived in Yorkshire. But it was in such a sad state of repair and so lacking in mod-cons that he had little hope of selling it. In the end, thanks to Eleanor, he'd been happy to agree to rent it to the local council for use as a women's refuge. There were three storeys to Alexandra House and eight bedrooms. The ones on the first floor were large enough for four beds with space for cots too. On the ground floor there were four reception rooms and a kitchen large enough to be used as a communal dining room. Two of the ground-floor rooms were to be turned into a small flat for a caretaker, yet to be appointed.

The structural repair work was being carried out by a local builder and the decorating by a team of volunteers whose lack of skill was made up for by their enthusiasm. Furniture, carpets and curtains had been generously provided by donations and charity shops and the house was beginning to look bright and welcoming already. The opening, which was now only weeks away, was to be covered by the press and, somewhat to her surprise, Julia had been asked to perform the opening ceremony.

She tried to visit the refuge at least twice a week to encourage the volunteers and supervise the progress. It gave her battered self-esteem encouragement to know that at least one thing she was doing was promising to be successful.

As she parked the car on the drive of Gresham House her stomach began to churn with apprehension. May, who had seen her arrival from the window, came out on to the front porch to greet her, arms outstretched in welcome.

'Darling! I've missed you all so much.' She kissed her daughter warmly then held her at arm's length to look at her critically. 'Oh, you're looking very tired, darling. I hope you're not overdoing things, what with your council work and everything?'

'I'm fine, Mum, honestly.'

'How is the refuge coming along?'

'Wonderfully well. Everyone is working really hard, though it's a bit nerve-racking, wondering if everything will be done in time for the opening?'

May looked at her searchingly. 'And Vernon?'

'As far as I know he is fine,' Julia said, fielding her mother's unasked question about his relationship with Joanna. 'Preoccupied with work, of course, but that's par for the course.'

May looked at her daughter's closed expression and knew better than to pursue the subject. Sometimes she wished Julia would confide in her more. She had always been the same. Could she have gone wrong somewhere? She made herself smile. 'I see. Well, shall we go through? Daddy's in the garden. Everything out there has just gone mad since we left. There's always a lot of work to do in the spring but what with having been away for so long . . .' She smiled. 'Still, now that he has more time, I'm sure he'll enjoy it.' She led the way through to the sunny little morning room at the back of the house. Opening the window, she called to Harry whom Julia could see pottering away with his secateurs in the rose beds, battered old gardening hat perched on his head.

'Harry! Julia's here. Come in now and have some coffee.' May picked up two brightly wrapped parcels from the coffee table. 'These are for you and Charlotte. I do hope you like them. There's a carved fruit bowl for you and a silk shawl for Charlotte.' She turned as Harry came in at the door. 'Are, there you are, dear. I'll go and make the coffee now and you two can have a chat.'

He kissed his daughter's cheek. 'Good to see you, love.'

'And you, Dad. You look so well. I hear you had a wonderful time.'

'We certainly did.' Harry nodded and sat down in the wing chair near the window. 'Pity about the garden, though. Going to take me weeks to get it round again in time for planting.' He looked at her. 'Sit down, love, and tell me how things are going. How did the meeting go? I must admit I thought you might have cabled to let me know the outcome.'

'Well, I would have but . . .' Julia sat down and took a deep breath. 'I might as well come clean right away, Dad. I couldn't do as you wanted. I had to vote along with the others when it came to the crunch.'

Harry's jaw dropped. 'My God, you're not serious?'

'I'm afraid I am.'

'Oh, Julia.' He shook his head in disappointment. 'But why?'

She had given a lot of thought to what she would say in reply to

311

the inevitable question. Obviously she couldn't tell him the truth. 'Try to see it my way, Dad. It would have meant ending my marriage right there and then in the boardroom.'

'But what about Vernon's affair with that Hanson woman? Do I take it you've forgiven him for that?'

'He swears there was nothing in it.' She avoided her father's reproachful eyes. 'Don't you see, Dad? Having me wield power over him and his father would only have inflamed the situation. It would have made things so difficult. And if we had separated, it would have been impossible for me to remain as a director anyway.'

'Ah – I suppose you're right.' Harry slumped in his chair. 'If I'd known you were determined to remain loyal to Vernon, no matter what, I would never have put you in such an impossible position.' He sighed. 'You've been looking so unhappy, Julia. I have to admit that your mother and I hoped . . .'

'Leave it, Dad.' She shook her head. 'Let's just leave it, shall we?'

'Of course. If you say so.' Harry paused and cleared his throat. 'So – Charlie is getting his own way after all, then? He's going ahead with this crazy Victoria Gardens scheme in spite of everything?'

'Yes, I'm afraid so. But it isn't all plain sailing. To begin with I think he had to pay over the odds for the Gardens and now there are other complications too. Things have moved fast since you left. Beardsley's has gone into liquidation, which means most of the prospective buyers of the Meadowlands houses have pulled out. Vernon doesn't say much but I think he's very worried.'

Harry looked startled. 'Beardsley's? My God, that's a blow!' He was quiet for a moment. 'This looks extremely serious, Julia,' he said. 'With Beardsley's gone it's inevitable that others will follow. Under the circumstances, I feel I should resign formally. Sell out.'

She looked at him. 'GPC is stretched to the limit, Dad. I doubt if they can afford to buy you out. If you insist it could be the last straw.'

'Not necessarily. Perhaps there are too many eggs in the family basket. Selling my shares would spread the load.'

'Another new partner, you mean. Who, though?'

'Would you be prepared to sell your shares too?' he asked.

'Yes. Vernon has never liked my taking any part in the business anyway.'

'Never mind what Vernon wants for a moment. Is it what *you* want? In fact, I think it's high time you started asking yourself that question about a good many things.'

'Yes, Dad. It is what I want. I'd be only too happy to sell my shares.'

'Right.' Harry fell silent as he gave the idea some consideration.

Julia watched him for a moment, unsure what was in his mind. At last she asked, 'Who would buy them under the present circumstances, Dad? Things are beginning to look bad for a lot of the town's business people already. I really can't see anyone taking on new commitments.' She sighed. 'I'm really sorry. I feel I've let you down badly after you trusted me enough to transfer your shares to me.'

'Don't be sorry,' he said. 'We might come out of this better off in the long run, as you say.'

May came in with the coffee tray, but the bright smile on her face faded as she looked from one to the other. 'Oh, dear, you do look serious. Don't tell me you two have been falling out?' she said as she put the tray down.

'We've been talking about the possibility of selling our shares in GPC,' Julia told her.

May looked relieved. 'Well, if you ask me, I think that's an excellent idea,' she said. 'Charlie Grant has always wanted to prove to everyone how clever he is. Always wanted to be the local rags-to-riches success story and cock a snook at everyone. He's let it run away with him and this time he's gone too far.' She shook her head. 'You know, there's a lot of truth in the old saying: "Pride goeth before a fall." '

Julia glanced at her father as he sat there in his chair, eyes glinting. She knew that look of old. Harry Philips was a mild man but once he had the bit between his teeth there was no stopping him. 'Have you got an idea, Dad?' she asked.

He nodded. 'I might have, but I don't want to say anything at the moment. Just bear with me for the time being.'

May smiled confidently as she poured the coffee and handed them each a cup. 'Now,' she said, sitting down, 'tell us how Charlotte is? What's she been up to? I want to hear all about her.'

Julia took a long drink of her coffee. She had successfully negotiated one hurdle. Now she had to tell her parents that their only granddaughter had left home to live in a bed-sit!

When Fleur went round to Park Row to pick Charlotte up on her way to the birthday party the following evening, she found Tom's door firmly closed. When she knocked there was no reply.

As they drove to the party venue she asked Charlotte if she'd seen him? The younger girl shook her head.

'I left a message on the board in the kitchen when you called and it wasn't there next morning so he must have found it,' she said. She looked at Fleur. 'It's terrible about Mrs Arden. What will you do now?'

'I'm going to run Arden Catering for her son Peter,' Fleur told her. 'He's going to get everything legally worked out. I'm going to move into the house.'

'Will you like that?' Charlotte glanced at her doubtfully. 'What about your lovely little flat?'

Fleur sighed. 'I had notice to leave anyway. Mrs Franks has sold the house.'

'Sold it? Oh!' Charlotte's face cleared. 'Of course! Victoria Gardens. GPC has bought the whole street. It's going to be redeveloped. Granddad is really excited about it.' She looked sympathetically at Fleur. 'I'm sorry, Fleur. It's rotten for you when you like the place so much.'

'I might have been homeless for all Ivy cared,' she said. 'And she had the cheek to pretend that she was giving me notice because I've had Tom there once or twice.'

'Did you know she owned the whole street?' Charlotte asked.

'*All* of it?' Fleur stared at her in amazement. '*Every house*?'

'That's right. I don't know for sure, but they're saying that Granddad has paid her a cool million for the deal.'

Fleur gasped. 'Ivy – a millionairess? I can't believe it!'

The party went well. The news about Sally Arden's death wasn't public yet and few people knew though the hostess had heard. She took Fleur aside halfway through the evening.

'My dear, I just wanted to say how grateful I am to you for carrying on as though nothing had happened,' she said. 'I only heard the news this afternoon.'

Fleur shook her head. 'Sally would have wanted everything to go on as normal,' she said. 'I'd have felt it was letting her down to cancel a booking.'

It was late when she dropped Charlotte off at Park Row. As they drew up outside the house the girl looked at her.

'Thanks for asking me along this evening, Fleur. I've really enjoyed it. Are you coming in for a last coffee?'

Fleur was about to refuse. In spite of what she had said to the party hostess earlier, putting on a brave face all evening had been a strain and she was tired. Then she noticed a light in Tom's window at the front of the house. 'All right then. Just a quick one. I can say hello to Tom as well. I haven't seen him for days.'

314

She tapped on his door while Charlotte went through to the kitchen. He opened it at once.

'Hi! I thought I'd drop in and see you as you haven't been in touch,' Fleur said. Then, seeing his grim expression, she asked, 'What is it? What's wrong?'

'I'm surprised you have to ask!'

'*Tom*! What is it?'

'I came round to see you on my way to work yesterday morning.'

'Did you?'

'Yes, I did,' he said angrily. 'But you were too busy to notice me.'

'Busy?' She shook her head him, bemused.

'Yes, busy. As a matter of interest, it *was* Peter Arden who was kissing you, wasn't it?' Without waiting for her reply he went on, 'How could you, Fleur, after the way he treated you? After all the things you said! Anyway, I thought he was supposed to be in Switzerland, getting married.'

'He was. You obviously don't know. He came over because . . .'

'I don't want to *hear* any more. It seems to me there's a hell of a lot I don't know about you, Fleur. And if you ask me, I think I'm better off *not* knowing!'

As the door was closed in her face, she stood there, too stunned to react. She raised her hand to knock again. Obviously he didn't know what had happened to Sally – hadn't received the message she had left for him. It was all a misunderstanding. Then suddenly angry resentment flared up inside her. She didn't deserve – didn't *need* – this. Why should she beg him to listen to her explanation? He didn't trust her, thought her a liar. Seeing Peter and her together, he'd jumped to the first conclusion that came into his head. Turning away towards the front door, she blinked hard at the stinging tears that sprang to her eyes. She had no reason to apologise or to beg him to listen to her. And she'd be damned if she'd give him the satisfaction of seeing her cry!

'I won't stay for coffee after all, Charlotte,' she called. 'Goodnight! Thanks for your help.'

After he had heard the van drive away Tom went through to the kitchen and found Charlotte there making coffee. 'Hi,' he said moodily.

'Why didn't Fleur stay?' she asked him. 'You haven't had a row, have you?'

'Nothing you need concern yourself with,' he said rudely.

She looked at him. 'You did get the message Fleur asked me to give you, didn't you? The one I left for you the day before yesterday?'

He turned a blank face towards her. 'Message?'

'She rang to speak to you but you were out. She wanted you to know that she had to drive down to Hertfordshire. The police had rung to say that Mrs Arden had been injured in a car crash on the motorway.'

Tom's jaw dropped. 'Oh, bloody hell! No, I didn't get any message. Where did you leave it?'

'On the board – I couldn't find a pin so I stuck it behind...' Charlotte reached out and moved the row of storage canisters on the worktop. The slip of paper was behind them. 'Oh! It must have fallen down. The draught from the front door is...'

'Let me see that.' Tom snatched it from her hand and read it. 'Oh, God! Is Mrs Arden badly hurt?'

Charlotte stared at him. 'You mean you haven't heard? I'd have thought – with you working on the *Clarion* and everything...'

'Heard what?'

'She died, Tom. Mrs Arden died in hospital later the same night – of her injuries. It was awful.'

'I see.' He stood there, crumpling the note in his clenched fist as he tried to decide what he could do to repair the damage he had caused, then he turned on his heel and flung out of the kitchen, slamming the door behind him.

'I've missed you,' Vernon sat in the conservatory at Joanna's house. It was warm from the day's sunshine and the scent of flowers drifted in through the open French doors. He felt pleasantly relaxed from the double brandy she had poured him.

'How can you have missed me when we've seen each other every day?' She said as she tucked her feet under her in the chair opposite.

'You know damned well what I mean.'

She raised an eyebrow as she took a sip of her Campari and soda. 'As I remember, it was you who said we should cool it.'

'Haven't you missed me at all?'

'Have I missed sleeping with you, you mean?' she said bluntly. 'The answer to that is yes. But why should you care about my feelings?'

'I do care, Jo. And it isn't just the sex. You know how I feel about you – how I've always felt. It was just that things were beginning to get out of hand.'

'So why are you here now, Vernon?'

'Because I couldn't stand it any longer. I need you, Jo. I want to be with you.'

'Then ask Julia for a divorce and marry me.'

He stared at her. '*Marry*...?'

'Why look so shocked? Am I not the sort of woman a man marries?' she said. 'Am I just the eternal *bit on the side*?' She stood up, her green eyes flashing. 'Well, if you think you can just walk in here whenever you feel like it, Vernon, you'd better think again.' She took a cigarette from the box on the table and lit it. 'Maybe I made a mistake when I put money into the firm. Maybe I should get the hell out of Elvemere and away from you.'

He was on his feet, his hands on her shoulders. 'Jo! Don't talk like that. You know I love you. It's just – well, not that easy.'

She stood very still and looked into his eyes. 'Nothing worth having is ever easy, Vernon. I know that. But if you really want it, you'll find a way. I did.'

'Are you saying that you came back to Elvemere just – just for me?'

'What do you think?' She pushed him away. 'But I can just as easily go away and start over. I'm tough, Vernon. I've had to be, the kind of life I've had. But if I go I take my money with me. Business partners don't make good mistresses. So it's up to you.'

He paused, moistening his lips as he tried to think. 'It might take time. It's not the kind of thing you can fix overnight. There's more than just the three of us to consider.'

She shrugged. 'Who else? You don't have old man Philips to consider any more, do you? I'd have thought it'd be fairly straight forward.'

Vernon frowned. 'Julia has her parents' shares, remember, as well as her own, and voting power on Charlotte's.'

'That's something you're going to have to resolve yourself,' Joanna said. 'But knowing Julia I'd say she'd probably be happy to take the house in place of the shares as settlement. She's never seemed quite comfortable in the boardroom, has she?' She crushed out her half-smoked cigarette. 'Can I leave it to you then, darling? Can we trust each other?'

'Of course we can. Oh, Joanna, you know I'd do anything for you.' He moved towards her and drew her into his arms, kissing her hungrily. 'I'll talk to Julia tonight, or at least as soon as I can. Our marriage has been dead for years and, as you said, Harry Philips is out of the frame. Even Charlotte has left home now, so there's nothing to stay for.'

'Nothing to lose and everything to gain.' As she hid her face against his shoulder Joanna was smiling.

There was a strong smell of frying bacon coming from the basement kitchen of thirteen Victoria Gardens as Tom stood waiting for Ivy to answer the door. Finally she opened it a couple of inches and squinted out at him suspiciously.

'Oh, it's you!'

'I'm sorry to bother you, Ivy but I've been up to Fleur's flat and she doesn't seem to be in.'

'No and she won't be neither,' Ivy interrupted with some satisfaction. 'She's left – *gorn*.'

'Gone?' Tom's eyes opened wide. 'Where to?'

'Well now, I'm surprised *you* don't know.' Ivy smirked at him mockingly. 'You two had a row then, 'ave you?'

Tom wanted to tell the old witch to mind her own business but he swallowed his irritation and forced himself to smile. 'I've been away,' he said lamely. 'So if you can tell me if she left a forwarding address.'

Ivy cackled derisively. 'Oh, she done that all right. It's twenty-two Fairfield Drive. Very posh. Moved in with her *other* fancy man, 'asn't she?' She clicked her tongue disapprovingly. 'And 'is poor mum hardly cold. Disgustin', I call it! I expect he stands to inherit a few bob and that's what the attraction is.' She looked him up and down. 'But there. That's 'ow you young people carry on nowadays, isn't it? You've 'ad your chance. Now it's 'is turn. But there, you can 'ardly complain, can you? No more'n you deserve if you ask me!' And with that final parting shot she shut the door in his face.

As he climbed up the area steps Tom's head spun with angry bewilderment. How could Fleur coolly move out of the flat she loved so much and into her late employer's house the minute Peter Arden invited her to? By the time he reached the car he was shaking with hurt and rage. She might at least have had the decency to tell him. If that was all he meant to her – if she was really that shallow, he was well rid of her!

Charlie sat in his study at Queen's Lodge, the desk before him covered in papers. He'd had a heavy afternoon with the firm's accountant. At tomorrow's board meeting he would have the uncomfortable task of presenting the surveyor's report on Victoria Gardens and telling Vernon and Joanna that the bank had refused to extend their loan. He was still reeling from the shock.

The survey had come as a blow. Charlie hadn't expected any problems apart from the odd bit of dry rot or perhaps a little rising damp. In his experience the Victorians had built houses to last. How could he or anyone else living possibly have known that this particular development had been built directly over an ancient chalk pit, as the searches had proved?

When he'd received the report he'd gone straight round to the firm of surveyors he'd employed and demanded an immediate interview. The houses had stood for a hundred and twenty years, he'd argued. So why not another hundred and twenty? But the surveyor had pointed out that as long as the houses remained as they were there wasn't much to worry about. It was only when structural work was begun that things could go badly wrong.

'But if we find ways of doing it?' Charlie had said. 'Locating this old chalkpit and filling it in, for instance.'

The surveyor shook his head. 'That could prove to be a very costly business, Mr Grant,' he said. 'Extremely costly and there's no guarantee it would be effective either.'

'But damn it all, the council itself was prepared to do this work,' Charlie blustered, his fist hitting the desk. 'Surely they must have looked into it.'

The surveyor smiled wryly. 'Has it ever occurred to you that maybe they knew what they were doing when they abandoned the idea?' As Charlie digested this unpalatable thought the man leaned forward. 'What I would suggest, Mr Grant, is that you change your plan for something that requires less structural alteration. A tasteful restoration of the properties perhaps, with sympathetic modernisation. It could be very attractive. Victoriana is coming into vogue.'

Just remembering the interview made Charlie groan. All that cash! And all his plans for civic eminence, gone out of the window in a puff of smoke – or chalk! He dropped his head into his hands. Surely if the council was already in possession of this devastating knowledge someone could have told him. When he thought of all the favours he'd done for that bunch in the past! He'd have no alternative but to cut his losses by doing as the surveyor had suggested.

There was a tap on the door and Louise came in with a glass in her hand. 'I've brought you a whisky,' she said. 'And I think it's about time you stopped poring over those old papers and came and had something to eat.'

Charlie took the glass from her and downed the contents in one gulp. His wife looked at him.

'What's up, Charlie?'

'Oh, just a snag we've hit.' He sighed deeply. 'I've rung Vernon and asked him to drop round after supper. I need to talk to him.'

'I wish you'd said. You could have asked him to supper. I daresay

Julia is out again, or too busy to cook a proper meal for him – as per usual!'

'As a matter of fact he wasn't at home.'

She frowned. 'How could you speak to him then?'

He hesitated. 'I took a chance and rang Joanna's. He was there.'

'*Was* he now?' Louise's cheeks coloured. 'Does he spend a lot of time round at her place?'

'I don't think so. But if he does you can hardly blame him. Julia being out so much.'

Louise's lips tightened. *Damn* the woman. She was probably trying to get her claws into Vernie just to get back at her. Well, she'd see about that. She looked at her husband's worried face. 'What's wrong, chuck? Is it anything I can help with?'

He shook his head. 'No. Like I said, just a hitch with the surveyor's report. Nothing for you to worry about.'

'Well, I'll get back to the kitchen. Supper in about ten minutes, right? And don't go shutting yourself in the lav the minute it's on the table!'

Vernon had been extremely irritated by his father's phone call. He and Joanna had been in bed when the telephone rang. It had taken him an hour to convince her that what he felt for her was all-consuming passion and not just sexual attraction. By the time they reached the bedroom his need had become desperate and they'd undressed frenziedly – only to have the phone ring the moment they fell on to the bed together.

He'd tried to persuade Joanna to ignore it, but by the time it had shrilled persistently in their ears for several minutes their passion had evaporated somewhat. At last Joanna had rolled over and reached for the receiver with a resigned sigh.

'Hello. Joanna Hanson.'

'It's me, Joanna – Charlie Grant. Vernon wouldn't happen to be there, would he?'

She hesitated. 'As a matter of fact he is. He dropped in on his way home. Hold on.' Her hand over the mouthpiece she whispered, 'It's your father.'

Vernon swore softly and took the phone from her. 'Hello, Dad. What is it?'

'I need to see you, Vern.'

'You will see me, Dad. First thing in the morning.'

'No, I mean now. I wouldn't ask if it wasn't important.'

Vernon sighed. 'What on earth can be so urgent that it can't wait till morning?'

'Can't talk about it over the phone. Get yourself round here as soon as you can.'

And to Vernon's extreme annoyance he hung up.

Charlie opened the door to his ring and ushered him into the study straight away. 'I'll come straight to the point,' he said. 'I couldn't get the bank to extend our loan.'

'Why?'

'Mainly because of this.' Charlie pushed the surveyor's report across the desk. 'Though the fact that several local businesses are going bust didn't exactly help.'

'You'd think the banks would be keen to look after the ones that are solvent, wouldn't y . . .' Vernon broke off as he got to the crucial paragraph. '*Christ*! I see what you mean.' He looked up at his father, his face flushed. 'I told you not to touch Victoria Gardens. Why in God's name wouldn't you listen to me?'

Charlie waved the pipe he was in the process of lighting. 'Don't get on your high horse with me. You couldn't have foreseen this any more than I did.'

'That doesn't make it any better. It's still a disaster! We've got most of the Meadowlands houses back on our hands now too. What the bloody hell are we going to do?'

'Well, all I can say is, thank God for Joanna.'

'You're *joking*!' Vernon stared at him. 'You can't ask her to throw good money after bad. What do you propose to do with this white elephant you've landed us with?'

'The surveyor suggested a tasteful restoration,' Charlie said, carefully employing the man's exact phrase. 'With sympathetic modernisations. That would mean we wouldn't have to hack them about too much. And Victoriana is coming into vogue, or so I'm told.'

'And then what?'

'We'll sell them.'

'Oh, we'll sell them will we – just like that? More houses on the market that no one wants to buy. Another lot of plans to have drawn up at enormous expense! Besides, anyone intending to buy will have a survey done the same as you did. Once they know about this bloody chalkpit you won't see their heels for dust. What's more the word will spread.'

'Stop panicking. If we can't sell we can turn the places into luxury flats and rent them out lucratively.' Charlie leaned back in his chair. 'Suppose we ask Joanna what she thinks?'

Vernon gave a derisive snort. 'Ask her if you like – as long as

321

you don't mind her telling you! I dread to imagine what she'll say when she knows how you've wasted her investment. She'll probably demand her money back and book herself on the first flight to the States!'

'It's not wasted.' Charlie looked at his son speculatively. 'Look, there is another alternative.'

'Yes? Come on then, let's hear it.'

Charlie lit his pipe with a painstaking precision that made Vernon want to scream. At last he looked up through a cloud of exhaled smoke. 'We could mortgage the houses.'

Vernon stared at him. 'What houses?'

'Yours and mine of course. Charlie puffed on his pipe with an attempt at nonchalant bravado. 'We'd get a tidy sum for the both of them. Enough to tide us over.'

Vernon's expression was one of incredulity. 'You *are* joking, I take it?'

'Course I'm not joking. That what property's for – investment. If we can't realise a bit of ready cash on our own bricks and mortar it's a poor do. For God's sake, Vern, don't look at me like that. We'll get our money back in the end. This is just a bit of a cash flow problem. Luckily we've got the means to deal with it.'

'I only wish I had your confidence, Dad.' Vernon's head was reeling. He was thinking about Joanna's remark earlier, that Julia would probably be happy to take the house as a settlement in a divorce. It looked as though that would be out of the question now. At least for the time being.

Louise tapped on the door and put her head round it. 'Come and have some coffee, you two,' she said. 'You've been shut away in here too long. Vernie, come out into the kitchen and talk to me while I make it. It's weeks since I saw you to talk to properly.'

Glad to remove himself from his father's presence for a while, Vernon followed his mother through to the kitchen and sat on one of the breakfast bar stools while she spooned coffee into the filter machine. She glanced at him sideways.

'I hear your father caught you round at Joanna Hanson's.'

He looked up, suddenly defensive. 'How do you mean, *caught me*?'

'Just that. You want to stay away from her out of office hours, Vernie. She might have money but as a women she's bad news.'

'Don't be ridiculous, Ma. I've known Joanna ever since we were kids.'

'You knew her when you were kids. That's not quite the same thing,' she said meaningfully. 'You and her had a red hot affair

322

when you were very young.' She shook her head at him. 'Oh, I knew what was going on, don't worry. I wasn't born yesterday and I could see the way things were going. I can read her sort like a book.'

'A teenage fling. That's all it was.'

'Mmm, to you, maybe,' Louise said. 'Take it from me, that one had other ideas.'

'How do you mean?'

'Oh, Vernie, how can you be so naive? She knew your dad's firm was doing well. She was after a lady's life. An easy time with plenty of money. She was a slut and she'd have led you a right merry dance if you'd married her.'

'Rubbish!'

Louise swung round, stung by his abrupt dismissal of the truth. 'Rubbish, is it? If that's so, why did she accept money to leave you alone then?'

For a moment he stared at her, his mouth agape in astonishment. '*Money*! Who from?'

'From me.'

'You – you paid her to – to . . .'

'To go as far away as she could and leave you alone. And it didn't take her long to find a Yank with plenty of cash to chuck about, did it?' Louise retorted. 'I dangled the bait and she swallowed it without a single qualm. No, I tell a lie. She pushed my offer up by pretending she was pregnant.'

'She what?'

'You heard. She said she was expecting. I couldn't prove otherwise so I had to take her word for it and give her the money for an abortion. I told you she was a scheming slut.'

Vernon was on his feet now, his face dark with anger. 'You gave her money to get rid of my child?'

'There was no child,' Louise said scathingly. 'She more or less admitted as much later. But I couldn't risk calling her bluff, could I? She threatened to make it all public if I didn't pay her.' She slapped her hand down on the worktop. 'That's the kind of woman she was then. And she still is, Vern, only twice as cunning. Take my advice and drop her before she ruins your life again!'

Fleur had moved all her belongings over from Victoria Gardens single handed, using the van. When the flat was empty she'd stood for a long time at the open French windows, looking out at the now bare balcony. All her pots, tubs and hanging baskets had been removed to Sally's house. There was a large patio there which easily accommodated them. But it wasn't the same. The house was lovely, but it didn't feel like home. Everywhere she looked there were reminders of Sally. It was too large for her too. She had never been used to so much space and felt more lonely than when she had first arrived in Elvemere.

She'd kept busy since Peter's departure for Switzerland after the sad business of tying up Sally's affairs. She had helped all she could and Peter had promised to return after his honeymoon to attend to the legalities of her new job as manager of Arden Catering.

Meantime there was plenty to do. There were scores of letters to reply to in Peter's absence. Over the years Sally had made a good many friends among her clientele. At first Fleur had worried about whether Sally's clients would trust her with their future business, but to her relief, once people knew that she was to stay and carry on, the bookings began to resume as briskly as ever. Bookings for summer barbecues, weddings and garden parties were being made now and Fleur could see that it was about to be a busy season in spite of the recession that was beginning to stamp its mark on the town.

In the daytime she was too busy to think much about her own emotions, but when she was alone in bed at night they would rush in on her like an overwhelming tide, almost suffocating in their intensity. Why had Tom been so unyielding in his accusations? He must know by now about her reasons for meeting Peter. He would have heard from Charlotte about her move from Victoria Gardens too. Yet she'd had no word from him. Why was it that everyone in her life – apart from her grandparents eventually rejected her? Sometimes she wondered whether it could be the old racist thing that she seen so many people fight. Her skin was pale it was true, but she was and always had been aware that she looked different. Perhaps if she were truly black like Bobby she would be more acceptable. And perhaps it was nothing to do with any of that. Perhaps it was she herself who was somehow lacking.

It was about a week after her move that she received an unexpected telephone call in the office one morning.

'Arden Catering. Fleur Sylvester speaking. Can I help you?'

'Fleur, hello. It's Julia Grant.'

'Oh! – Hello.'

'I had to ring you to say how sorry I was to hear about Sally Arden,' Julia said. 'I was at the funeral service but I – didn't get a chance to speak to you.'

Fleur didn't reply for a moment, guessing that what Julia really meant was that she was afraid to be seen speaking to her, foolishly and guiltily terrified in case someone should speculate about their relationship. 'No,' she said. 'I did see you in the distance. The church was full.'

'Yes. Sally was a well liked woman.'

'She was very good to me,' Fleur said. 'I'm so proud to be taking over the business. A mother couldn't have done more for me than Sally did.' She bit her lip, wincing at her unintentional gaffe.

'Quite.'

Into the awkward silence that followed Julia said, 'I'd like to thank you for keeping an eye on Charlotte for me.'

'Oh, there's no need really. She's coping fine. Have you been round to see her room?'

'No. She rings occasionally, but I haven't been invited yet.'

'Maybe she's hoping you'll ask, or just turn up,' Fleur said. 'She's quite stubborn when it comes to making the first move, isn't she?'

'Don't I know it!' Julia said.

'I've moved myself. I'm living here at Sally's house now. It made sense from a security point of view, but I would have had to move anyway with Victoria Gardens being redeveloped.'

'Oh, of course. I'd forgotten you lived there.'

'There's no reason why you should remember, is there?' Fleur said with a hint of sharpness. 'By the way, I see from the *Clarion* that your women's refuge is coming along well.'

'Yes, everyone has worked really hard.' Julia paused. 'As a matter of fact, Fleur, I was planning to give a little luncheon, just for the press and councillors on the day of the opening. Would you be free to do it for me?'

'What date would that be?'

'The fifteenth of next month. There'll be room in the dining room at Alexandra House. I heard just this week that the local television and radio people will be there too, so better cater for about forty. Just a simple finger buffet will do nicely.'

As Fleur replaced the receiver she couldn't help feeling that Julia might easily have thought up the idea on the spur of the moment; or offered her the job as some kind of compensation. She wished now that she'd invented some prior booking. The last thing she wanted was Julia's patronage.

Charlotte hated the Saturday afternoons when she didn't go to the stables. She spent the mornings doing her washing and cleaning her room – doing the other household jobs on the rota when it was her turn. But the afternoons were a drag. Usually the house was empty. Both Sadie and Tom were usually busy with sports

325

events for the paper, and Saturday was Fleur's busiest day too. Everyone seemed to have something to do, except her. So when she heard the front doorbell ring soon after lunch that Saturday she went down to answer it with a sense of anticipation. Perhaps one of the friends who had deserted her had found out where she lived and come round to visit, though she didn't hold out much hope of that.

'Hello darling.' Julia stood on the doorstep, an overflowing shopping basket in one hand.

Charlotte stared in surprise at her mother. 'Mum!'

'Well, I got tired of waiting for an invitation,' Julia said. 'So I thought, if the mountain won't come to Mohammed . . .' She peered past Charlotte into the hall. 'It all looks very nice. Am I going to be asked in?'

'Oh! Yes, of course. I'm sorry.' Charlotte held the door open to admit her mother and led the way upstairs, feeling glad that she'd given the little bed-sit a good turn-out this morning. She opened the door with a flourish.

'Ta-raa! This is it,' she announced. 'My very own home.'

Julia looked round with a smile. 'Darling, it's charming. And you're keeping it so nice.'

Charlotte flushed with pride. 'There's no one else in at the moment. I'll show you the rest of the house if you like?'

Julia shook her head. 'No. It's you I've come to see.' She put the basket down. 'I brought you a few goodies. Some of those chocolate chip cookies you like and some of your other favourites. Nana and Granddad are home from their cruise and they sent you a present.' She unpacked the basket including May's brightly wrapped parcel. 'It gave me a good excuse to come and see you.' She looked at her daughter. 'I've missed you so much darling. You are all right, aren't you? You're happy?'

'Yes, Mum.'

'And eating properly?'

'Fine. I've discovered I like cooking.' Charlotte grinned cheekily. 'As a matter of fact I think I eat better than I did at home.'

Julia smiled apologetically. 'I was getting a bit slack about meals, wasn't I? I got fed up with neither you or Daddy ever being there to eat what I'd cooked.'

'I know. I see that now. Look, Mum, I would have asked you before but I didn't feel . . . I didn't know how I'd feel when I saw you again. It was important that I – gave it enough time. Do you see?'

'Of course.' Julia knew exactly what Charlotte meant. She'd suffered the pangs of home sickness herself. The difference was, she'd given in to it – hadn't given herself enough time to adapt.

The two of them looked at each other for a long moment, then Julia reached out and drew her daughter into her arms. 'Oh, come here. It's lovely to see you,' she said.

'And you, Mum.' Charlotte hugged her mother tightly, then said. 'Come down to the kitchen with me and we'll make some tea.'

Julia was impressed with the bright little kitchen, and with the new competent young woman her daughter had become. Fleur had been right to say she would benefit from being allowed to stand on her own feet.

'How are things going?' Charlotte asked as she set a tray with cups and saucers. 'The refuge must be almost ready for opening.'

'It is. You must come along to the opening on the fifteenth. Fleur is doing a buffet lunch for me.'

'Is she? Sounds great, but I doubt if I could get the time off.'

'It's going to be quite an occasion, photographs for the paper and there's a chance that the local television and radio people will be there too.'

'Wow! My mum on the telly! I can't wait to see you!'

Upstairs Charlotte opened her grandmother's present and shook out the brightly embroidered shawl with an expression of dismay. 'Oh God! When on earth would I wear a thing like this?'

Julia smiled. 'I have to admit that it wouldn't look quite right with jeans or a mini skirt, but it's very pretty. You could always drape it over the bed or perhaps here . . .' She draped the heavily fringed shawl over the headboard, bringing a splash of colour to the corner of the room. 'There. How's that?'

'Brilliant! Just the thing. Thank Nana for me when you see her.'

'Why not go round and thank her yourself? You're still part of the family, you know.'

'Am I?' The girl sighed. 'What about Dad?'

'You see him at the office every day. You tell me.'

'He treats me like any other member of the staff. And I still have to work under *her* of course. I just wish I could leave and do something else, but I have to eat.'

'Of course.'

'And whatever he says, Mum, I wasn't just trying to make trouble. I *did* see them that night. And it wasn't innocent like he said.'

'I know.'

'You do? Then why . . .' Charlotte paused, looking at her mother. 'Oh, Mum. It wasn't because of you that I ran away from home, you know. At least . . .'

'Tell me the truth,' Julia said quietly. 'It's time we talked to each other woman to woman. You're grown up now.'

'Well – it was the way you've always let Dad walk all over you,' Charlotte said. 'Ever since I was old enough to see what was going on I've wanted to yell at you to stand up for yourself. He's always been so patronising – treated you as though you were half-witted when I knew all the time that you were a damn sight more intelligent than he was. I've known since I was little that he was seeing other women, but you seemed to prefer to look the other way. It made me . . .'

'It made you despise me?'

'Not exactly, but . . .'

'I wouldn't have blamed you,' Julia said. 'I know now what a fool I've been all these years.'

'I was a selfish little kid though. When you did start to be your own person; when you got your seat on the council I should have been pleased – proud of you. Instead I felt resentful because I thought I was being neglected.' Charlotte smiled ruefully. 'I could easily have done what I do here; just got on with things and helped instead of moaning.'

Julia smiled gently. 'We all have to learn.' She reached for Charlotte's hand. 'So – what do you do in your free time these days?' she asked.

'I still go to Auntie Kath's occasionally,' she admitted. 'Mostly in the evenings when there's no chance of Dad driving by and catching me. I've been helping Fleur too, occasionally – for a bit of extra money.' She looked at her mother. 'Poor Fleur. Wasn't it awful about Mrs Arden?'

'Yes, terrible. You and she are good friends, aren't you?'

Charlotte nodded. 'I like her so much. She's been a good friend. She doesn't hassle me, that's what I like. She's there for me when I need her. She even tells me off if she thinks I'm being a prat, but she doesn't preach or push.' She looked at her mother with a wistful smile. 'She's almost like an older sister might be, though that's something I wouldn't know about.'

Julia was silent. If only she could tell Charlotte that Fleur was the closest she'd ever have to a real sister. If she just had the courage to stand up and tell the world about her. This new adult Charlotte would understand. She might even be pleased. For a moment she had a crazy impulse to tell her. She opened her mouth. 'Charlotte . . .'

'Yes?'

'Oh – nothing.' The urge – and the sudden burst of courage faded. 'I just wondered if there was any more tea in the pot.'

'I think so.' Charlotte refilled her mother's cup. 'There's something else, Mum,' she said. 'I've met this boy. He helps out at the stables in his free time and his name is James. He's really nice. I know you'd like him.'

Julia smiled, though deep inside she felt a pang of anxiety. Charlotte was so young and inexperienced. If she were to be hurt as Julia herself had been hurt. If she were to run off as she herself had done. . . . Yet what could she do to prevent it? What could any mother do?

'I'd like to meet him,' she said, forcing down her rising dread.

'I'm not bringing him home!' Charlotte said at once.

'Well, perhaps I could drop round sometime when he's here.' Julia looked at her daughter. 'He does come here, I take it?'

'He hasn't so far,' Charlotte said, her colour rising. 'And if you want to know if I'm sleeping with him, I'm not!'

In spite of herself Julia felt immense relief. She laughed to cover it. 'Darling! There's no need to be touchy. I remember what it was like being your age.'

'We're just friends,' Charlotte said defensively. 'We have a lot of things in common.' She glanced at her mother. 'Would you really like to meet him?'

'Of course I would.'

'Maybe I'll have a party,' Charlotte said with a sudden flash of inspiration. 'A flat warming.'

Julia smiled. 'That sounds fun. I'll look forward to it.'

'I'm really glad you came today, Mum,' Charlotte said. 'It was horrible feeling cut off from you.'

'You were never cut off darling. Not as far as I was concerned.' Julia looked at her watch and stood up. 'Time I was going. Can I come again?'

'Of course.'

'And will you at least think about coming home? Maybe for lunch next Sunday.'

Charlotte chewed her lip. 'Well . . .'

Julia hugged her. 'At least give the idea some thought. Ring me and tell me what you think.'

'Okay. I'll think about it.'

Rick turned up the volume on his radio as he slapped mortar onto the brickwork of the porch at Alexandra House. At least a bit of music drowned out the churning of his tortured mind. The job of pointing the brickwork was boring and he was already fed up.

When Tracey had first agreed to his moving in with her and the kid he was over the moon – A feeling that was to be short-lived once he discovered her reasons for giving in. It had been a bitter blow to learn that she was pregnant again. He really would have thought that the stupid little bitch would have taken care not to let it happen. To make matters worse, she'd lost her job at the Grants. Something for which she blamed him. He'd never have believed that people with all that money would be so mean over a pair of poxy cufflinks and a watch. If they left them lying around in unlocked drawers they deserved to have them nicked. What did they expect? To add insult to injury he'd had to get rid of them quick and he'd got nothing like what they were worth. Barely enough to pay off what he owed at the bookie's. Talk about out of the frying pan into the fire! Instead of being able to give up his job, have an easier time with Trace as the breadwinner and a roof over his head, it now looked as if he was going to have a council rent to pay and three mouths to feed. He felt well and truly lumbered.

'Do you think you could get out of the way, please?'

Rick looked round to see an elegant high-heeled shoe hovering delicately above the board that held his mortar. The shoe was on the end of a well-shaped leg in a sheer black stocking and, glancing up from where he crouched on the ground he glimpsed a pleasantly dimpled knee and the thigh above it, tantalisingly concealed under a slim skirt.

'Sorry darlin'.' He grinned cheekily, pushing his baseball cap onto the back of his head. 'Can't have you stepping in anything nasty, can we? Not with them sexy shoes on.'

She gave him a withering look and stepped over him to disappear into the house. He stared after her. Councillor Mrs Julia bloody Grant. Snotty cow! Looking down on him like he was dirt. All dressed to kill in her sharp suit, blonde hair all done up and nails varnished. He wouldn't mind betting she'd spent more money just on her hairdo than he earned in a week. And from what he'd heard about her from Trace she was no better than any of those women who'd be moving into this place when it was finished. That was well-off folks for you. Underneath they were no better than anyone else. But give them some cash, a posh house and fancy car and they treated everyone else like they was muck!

Swallowing his resentment, he carried on with his work only to be interrupted a few minutes later by another female voice.

'This is Alexandra House, isn't it?'

Looking up, he saw that the woman addressing him this time was very different. She wore motorbike leathers and sported a nose stud. And if he wasn't mistaken the classy machine parked by the gate was the one he'd heard roar up the road just now. He got to his feet and looked at her respectfully.

'That's right miss. There is a sign but I took it down in case it got splashed with the mortar.'

'Right. Thanks.' She swung off the heavy bag she carried on her shoulder and he saw that it was in fact a camera.

'Oh – you the press then, are you?' As a mark of respect, he pulled off his baseball cap to reveal his mass of curly hair.

Sadie nodded. '*Clarion.* I want to get some pictures of the final stages of the work, as a lead in to next week's big opening story.' She took out her camera, peered at him through the lens. 'How about a shot of one of the handsome building workers in action?' she asked with a lift of one eyebrow.

'Okay then. Anything to oblige a lady.' Rick grinned, his eyes glinting mischievously. 'Want me with the shirt on or off? How about a touch of the old Chippendales, eh?'

Sadie laughed. 'What's your name?'

'Rick,' he told her. 'Rick Kendle.'

'Go on then, Rick. The sun's shining, why not?' She took several shots of him from various angles, then thanked him and disappeared into the house.

Rick pulled on his shirt thoughtfully and prodded the hardening mortar with his trowel. Photo's in the paper, eh? No telling what a thing like that could lead to. He was a good looking guy – that photographer bird had seen that all right. He might be seen by some big London photographer and taken up by a modelling agent. He dabbed abstractedly at the brickwork, his eyes far away as he dreamed of seeing himself in telly commercials and up there on the hoardings, his well muscled torso tanned and oiled and ten times as big as lifesize, advertising sports gear or hair gel. He thought of what he could do with the cash he'd earn, holidays in the Bahamas and Acapulco, the classy birds he'd pull and the cars he'd buy, and sighed with longing. Maybe it needn't just be dreams though. What if he were to chat up that photographer bird a bit? Not that she looked the kind to fall for his kind of line. Not exactly what you'd call a pushover. Not even his type, come to that. Nose studs were a dead turn off as far as he was concerned. But what was important was that she worked for a newspaper and looked as if she might have some clout behind her. If he could get some cash together he could get out before things got too heavy with Trace. The way things were heading he'd be in up to his neck before he was much older.

Julia came out of the house to find him sitting on the front step smoking a roll-up and leaning against the wall.

'Have you finished?' she asked briskly.

He squinted up at her. 'No.'

'Then don't you think you should get on? At this rate we'll never be ready for the opening next week. You're not paid to sit there listening to the radio.'

'All right, missis. No need to get your knickers in a knot,' he said. 'I'm entitled to me break, same as anyone!'

He had the satisfaction of seeing her blush as she turned away. 'Serve her right, cheeky cow. He could make her sneer on the other side of her snooty face, he comforted himself. If he were to let slip what he knew about her!'

He was working again when Sadie came out of the house. She grinned at him. 'Still hard at it?'

'You bet.' He dropped his cigarette stub on the ground and trod on it. 'You doin' anything tonight then?'

She looked surprised. 'Depends. What did you have in mind?'

Rick winked. 'You can show me your etchin's if you like. Or how about bringing them shots you took of me? Maybe they could make the two of us some cash.'

She laughed. 'How would they do that?'

He flexed his muscles. 'Always fancied a bit of modellin'. Reckon I got the body an' the looks for it. Don't you?'

Sadie laughed in a way that brought angry colour to his cheeks. 'Modesty isn't exactly one of your failings, is it? Modelling is more than just strutting about with your shirt off, you know.'

He gave her what he thought of as his Mel Gibson look. 'You think I don't know nothing, don't you? Well, you might learn a thing or two if you got to know me better. Right, are we on? The King's Head – eight o'clock. Okay?'

Sadie looked him in the eye. 'You've got to be joking! Give me one good reason why I should want to have a drink with you.'

Rick burned with indignation. Who the hell did she think she was? Her and her spiky hair! Wouldn't normally touch her with a barge pole! He glanced from side to side and pushed his face close to hers. 'I reckon we've both got something the other one could use.'

'No kidding! What would that be then?'

'How about if I've got a juicy bit of gossip?'

'So – how about it?'

'Real gossip, I mean. I know something that'd make your hair curl,' he said. 'Something about a certain woman on the town council.' He jerked his head in the direction of the house. 'Mentionin' no names, but not a million miles from here.' He watched her face carefully. 'It'd make a story any newspaper reporter would kill for. Topical too. Still – if you're not interested . . .' He shrugged and turned back to his pointing.

'Is this some kind of wind-up or are you on the level?'

He looked at her. 'Oh, I'm on the level all right. Not that I'm givin' it away, mind.'

'If it's as hot as you say, I'd pay.'

'How much?'

'Come on, Rick. I can't make wild promises until I know what it's worth.'

'I'll think about it,' he told her. 'Be in the pub at eight. If you're not there by ten past I'll ring up another paper.'

Chapter 16

When Joanna answered the door on Sunday evening she was surprised to find Vernon standing on the doorstep. But any pleasure she might have felt was to be short-lived.

'I can't stay,' he told her breathlessly. 'I've slipped out on the pretext of driving round to the office for something I left behind.'

'So why are you here?' she asked.

'I had to see you. Something has come up. I thought it only fair to put you in the picture as soon as I could.'

'In that case you'd better come in.' Joanna held the door open. Inside the hall she looked at him. ' "Only fair to put you in the picture at once" sounds ominous,' she said. 'Is something wrong?'

'Dad had the result of the survey on the Victoria Gardens properties.'

'Right. But I don't see . . .'

'Apparently there are old chalkpit workings running underneath. It looks as if we won't get the planning permission to re-structure after all. We're going to have to rethink the whole thing and it's likely to take longer, not to mention being considerably more expensive than we'd allowed for.'

'I see. That's bad news.'

Vernon ran a hand through his hair. 'I *told* him to leave it alone. If only he'd listened to me.'

'Vernon – have you come here just to tell me you were right all along?'

'Of course not.'

'Then why—?'

'Because it affects *us*, that's why. You and me. Our future.'

'How?'

'Dad has come up with the idea of mortgaging both our homes.

If I have to do that, there's no way I can afford to divorce Julia. At least, not for some time.'

'Then tell him you won't do it.'

'I can't.' He shook his head helplessly. 'You know Dad.'

Swallowing her exasperation, Joanna said, 'I thought I was supposed to be a partner in this firm. Why wasn't I consulted about this?'

'You mean, you'll help?' Vernon looked at her hopefully. 'You'll put more money into the firm – to tide us over?'

'I'm not made of money, Vernon. And if I'm not considered trustworthy enough to be consulted, why should I offer to bale the firm out?'

'But I thought . . .' he swallowed nervously. 'Look, I expect Dad felt he couldn't talk to you about any of this because it was more a family matter than business,' he offered.

'Oh, I see,' Joanna said icily. 'Well, until he treats me like a business partner and not just an endless source of cash handouts, until he takes me into his confidence in the way I deserve, there'll be no more money available.' She looked at him. 'Just as a matter of interest, Vernon, why did you really come round? Is it to tell me we should cool it again?'

He winced at her cold directness. 'Well – until we get over this blip I do think it might be best.' He reached out to touch her shoulder. 'Don't take it like this, Jo. We can still be together occasionally, can't we? We'll still be working together and there's no reason why we shouldn't stay – well, more or less as we are now. Just for the time being, of course,' he added with an attempt at a reassuring smile.

'*Just for the time being*? It seems to me that investing with GPC was the worst thing I could have done – for all concerned!' Joanna was seething. No one – no one – got away with treating her like this! Vernon had always been weak. There could never be any kind of future for her with a man this spineless. She must have been mad ever to think there could be. In that moment her mind was made up. She walked to the door and opened it.

'Goodnight, Vernon,' she said. 'Thank you for "putting me in the picture", as you put it. I think this might well be crunch time, don't you?'

He stared at her. 'Oh, come on, Joanna. It's only for a . . .'

'I mean it. *Goodbye*, Vernon!'

The look she gave him almost froze him to the spot. He opened his mouth to remonstrate, then closed it again. As he passed her he said, 'Don't do anything hasty that you might regret, Jo. What we have is worth waiting a little longer for, surely?'

'I think it's you who might be the one with regrets, Vernon,' she told him. 'I never regret anything. I've tried to overlook your weakness and your shortcomings, but this is the final straw.'

She stood in the hall and listened to his car backing out of the drive, her blood racing with anger. Just for a while she'd allowed her guard to slip with Vernon. She'd actually imagined that their relationship would make a real man of him. She'd even, God help her, been prepared to take on that vulgar old hag of a mother of his. She'd nurtured dreams of herself and Vernon running the firm in double harness – raising the name of Grant Hanson to national greatness like Wimpy or Barratt. She shook her head as if to rid herself of the ridiculous, fanciful notion. It would never have worked with a man as feeble as Vernon at its head. She would have had to push him every inch of the way; wring every decision out of him. Thank God she'd come to her senses in time. But she'd have the last laugh yet. She'd see the Grants grovelling at her feet before she'd done. Including Julia! The trump card was right there within a telephone call of her grasp. For the past few days, ever since she'd had the surprising and unexpected offer from Harry Philips, she had been tortured with indecision, but tonight Vernon had unwittingly pointed the way to her.

Lifting the receiver, she dialled carefully then sat down to wait. At the other end of the line a woman's voice answered: 'Elvemere 98736.'

'Good evening, Mrs Philips. It's Joanna Hanson speaking. Can I have a word with your husband, please? I think he'll be expecting my call.'

Among the letters on the mat when Fleur went downstairs on Monday morning she saw that two were addressed to her personally. The first was addressed in Bobby's round handwriting and the other was typewritten and had a Swiss postmark.

Sitting at the table in the kitchen as she waited for the kettle to boil, she tore open eagerly Bobby's letter. It contained an invitation to her engagement party, to be held at her mother's flat in Hackney the Saturday of the coming weekend. With it was a short letter from Bobby, who sounded happy and excited.

Bring this Tom of yours I've heard so much about. I wouldn't want you to go falling for any guy who didn't have my personal seal of approval!

336

P.S. Mum says to tell you she'll find room for you both if you want to stay over. Please, please, please come! It won't be the same without you.

Take Tom with her? Fleur sighed. Bobby knew nothing about the rift that had opened between them, of course. Tom had been constantly in her thoughts since their angry exchange at Park Row. Determined not to be the one to make the first move, she had waited for him to get in touch with her again. After all, he had been the one in the wrong. He had hurt her deeply with his wild assumptions, and at a time when she was already upset and needing him.

Eventually there had been a note from him. It arrived on the day before Sally's funeral, short and to the point. In it he said he was sorry about the misunderstanding – that he'd be covering the funeral for the *Clarion* and would be at the church if she wanted to speak to him afterwards. But in the absence of family or relatives she had been at Peter's side throughout the service and had been required to play hostess to the handful of guests at the house afterwards. Although she had seen Tom in the distance, exchanged glances with him across the churchyard as she and Peter were getting into the car, there had been no opportunity for her to speak to him. She hadn't heard from him since that day. As for asking him to go to Bobby's party with her . . .

She looked again at the invitation. It was to take place on the Saturday after the opening of the women's refuge and she knew that so far there were no bookings for that weekend. She made up her mind to keep it clear. Her best friend's engagement party was something she was determined not to miss, though she was pretty sure that she'd be going alone.

The kettle boiled and she made a pot of tea, then sat down again and opened the other letter. As she'd guessed, it was from Peter. She read it through once. Then, with a cold feeling in the pit of her stomach, she went back to the beginning and read it again, her heart sinking like a stone.

Dear Fleur
After careful consideration and a long discussion with Lorraine, my wife, I have come to the reluctant decision to put Arden Catering on the market. This of course will include the house and other effects integral to the business. We – that is Lorraine and myself – are eager to buy a hotel of our own over here in Geneva and for this we will need all the resources available to us.
The agent handling the sale is R.J. Matthews and Co. of 128

High Street, Elvemere. I shall not be coming back to England
until an acceptable figure is negotiated, at which time I shall be
required to sign the contract. I shall understand if you wish to
leave to take up alternative employment, but I would be grateful
if you would remain to honour any existing bookings. Also it
would be helpful if you were on hand to show prospective buyers
round and answer any queries regarding the books, etc.

With thanks in advance for your help.

Yours sincerely,

Peter

She laid the letter down on the table, her heart racing with anger and hurt. She'd been conned! Once again Peter Arden had used her. He had accepted her support; taken advantage of her fondness for his mother and her willingness to help. And now that she had fulfilled her purpose she was to be tossed aside without consideration or regard. But apparently not before she had carried out Peter Arden's wishes to the letter.

Her first impulse was to pack and get out right away; to write him a letter telling him what she thought of him, advising him to get over here and attend to the sale himself. He clearly had not the slightest qualm about depriving her of her job and her home. He even expected her to help sell the business! Not one word was mentioned about a reference for a future employer. With Sally gone she had nothing to show for all her hard work.

All that morning as she worked, the words of Peter's stiff, formal letter swam before her eyes, mocking her for the fool she had been. As she planned the week's work, the pleasure and enthusiasm she normally felt were gone. Luckily there was little preparation to be done for the two functions booked for that week. She had already seen to it that all the freezers were full which was just as well. She would have had little heart for the creative cooking she normally enjoyed so much.

If she were to walk away today, no one in Elvemere would miss her, she told herself bleakly. She had never been anything but an embarrassment to Julia. Only Charlotte had been anything like a friend.

By lunchtime she had decided. She would pocket her pride and go round to see Tom, show him Bobby's invitation and let him decide whether he wanted to go with her or not. After she had closed the office for the day she took the van and drove into Elvemere.

338

At Park Row Charlotte was just arriving home from work. She was delighted to see Fleur and invited her in.

'You'll never guess. Mum came to see me last Saturday,' she said as she dumped her bag on the hall table. 'She brought me this silk shawl that Nana lugged back from some Caribbean island or other.' She laughed. 'Wait till you see it. It's *ghastly*! Are you coming upstairs for a minute? I'll make us a coffee.'

'That'd be lovely,' Fleur said, glancing towards Tom's door. 'I'd like a word with Tom first though. You go on up. I'll join you in a few minutes.'

'Tom? Oh, he's not there,' Charlotte said.

'Not in yet, you mean?'

'No. He's away. The paper has sent him on an assignment somewhere in the Midlands. I think it's to do with the local football team. Some hunk they're buying – I don't know the details but he seemed quite chuffed about it. It's to be a two-page spread, whatever that is. With a by-line. Then he's got this interview.'

Fleur looked at her. 'What interview?'

'I'm not sure. Didn't he tell you? A job interview. Sports editor, I think. On some Northern paper.' Charlotte looked at Fleur's crestfallen face. 'Oh, I'm sorry. I thought you'd have heard.' She paused. 'You and Tom haven't been hitting it off too well lately, have you?'

Fleur lifted her shoulders in an effort to disguise the pain and disappointment that threatened to overwhelm her. It was such an anticlimax after she'd plucked up all her courage. 'He did write me a note on the day before the funeral, but I haven't had a chance to reply.' She opened her bag. 'This morning I had an invitation for both of us to go to an engagement party and I wanted to see if he'd like to go.'

Charlotte smiled. 'That's great! It might break the ice, get you two back together again.'

'I know but it's this coming Saturday, in London. I'll have to go up on Friday evening. Will he be back?'

'Oh! Probably not. I couldn't say.' Seeing Fleur's disappointment, Charlotte held out her hand. 'Look, give it to me. If he does get back before the weekend I'll make sure he gets it this time. I'll pin it to that board with a six-inch nail if I can find one.' She looked at Fleur sympathetically. 'You've had a really rough time lately, haven't you?' She reached out her arms shyly. 'Can I give you a hug?'

Touched, Fleur nodded and Charlotte hugged her warmly. 'There,' she said. 'I know a hug always helps me when I'm fed up. Come up and have that coffee. Stay for supper, if you like? I'm making lasagne and there's always too much for one.'

Over the meal Fleur showed Charlotte Peter's letter about the sale of Arden Catering. The girl was indignant.

'Of all the nerve! After all you've done too. What'll you do, Fleur?'

'I've more or less decided to leave Elvemere,' She said. 'I might even stay on in London, not just for the weekend but for good. Bobby's mother will put me up until I find a job and somewhere to live. There isn't anything here for me any more.'

Charlotte looked dismayed. 'Don't make any quick decisions, Fleur,' she said. 'Things will work out somehow. You could even move in here, especially if Tom's leaving. I'd really miss you if you left now.'

Fleur smiled at the younger girl. It was a comfort to know that at least there was one person who would miss her. 'Well, I'll see,' she said.

Sadie's meeting with Rick at The King Head had been well worthwhile. At first she had been sceptical about the 'juicy piece of gossip' he had dangled in front of her, suspecting it was an elaborate chat-up line. But he'd turned up at the pub looking as if he meant business, his curly hair shampooed and brushed and his cheeks shaved smooth. He'd tried hard with his appearance, wearing a rather flashy shell suit. She guessed he was still under the false impression that she could help him on to the first rung of the ladder to a modelling career, and until she had some inkling as to whether he was on the level about this story she was content to let him go on nursing it.

'Well,' she challenged as they sat over tall glasses of lager in the bar. 'Do I get to hear this amazing story of yours then?'

He grinned at her. 'Tell me what it's worth first.'

'You know I can't, Rick. Can you at least give me a clue?'

He sipped his beer thoughtfully. 'I told you already, it's about a woman councillor,' he said.

'Yes. And that she has something to do with the new women's refuge. I'd have to be a complete idiot not to realise who it is we're talking about, but that still isn't to say it's a story I could use.'

Rick stared into his glass for a moment. 'Ever asked yourself why she's so keen on this refuge place?'

'She's sympathetic? A bit of a feminist? Feels that in spite of the advances that have been made, women – especially single mothers

340

– still get a raw deal?' Sadie shrugged. 'All that has already been in the *Clarion*.'

'All that crap, yes.' He looked up and his eyes met hers. 'But not the *real* reason,' he said softly. 'Not many people know that she was once a single mum herself.'

Sadie looked up, her attention focused. 'You mean her daughter was born out of wedlock? That's hardly hot news nowadays, Rick.'

'Yeah. But I'm not talking about the daughter everyone here knows. This was another one, born and hushed up when she was a teenager. And only me and one other person knows about it.' He paused for effect. 'Not even her old man.'

Sadie's mouth dropped open for a second. 'I couldn't print that.'

'Why not?'

'My editor would never agree, not even if it were true,' she said. 'This is Elvemere, not London. The Grants have a lot of clout in the town. They'd probably sue the *Clarion* for every penny it owns for printing a story like that. Anyway, how would I ever prove it if no one else knows?'

'It *is* true,' Rick insisted. 'The person who told me got it from the lady in question. Straight from the horse's mouth.'

Sadie was silent. If it *was* true there could be a whale of a story here. She could see the headlines already. *Secret Love Child of Local Councillor. Champion of battered mums and wife of local businessman makes startling confession.* Not that Councillor Mrs Grant *would* confess, of course. The child would presumably have been adopted and proof of a thing like that would take some digging up after all these years. She sucked in her cheeks thoughtfully. Although there might be ways . . .

'Come on then.' Rick was looking at her. 'You gonna buy it or ain't you?'

'I don't know. I mean, that fact on its own isn't madly exciting, is it? How much more do you know?'

'Quite a lot. It's hot stuff too.' He rolled a cigarette deftly with one hand, peering at her as he flicked his tongue along the edge of the paper. 'You don't get no more though, not till you've made me a proper offer. I told you too much already.'

Earlier that day, after Damian was in bed and Tracey was too tired to withstand his determination, he'd wheedled the rest of the story from her. Using his not inconsiderable cajoling skills, he'd extracted from her the rest of what Julia had told her.

Sadie was eyeing him suspiciously. 'If you're winding me up, Rick . . .'

'I'm not. There's stacks more. Straight up.'

341

Sadie made up her mind. 'Okay then, providing it's worth it . . .' She named a figure that disappointed him.

'No deal,' he said, getting up. 'I thought you news hounds paid good money for stuff like this. Maybe some other paper – the *Eastern Chronicle.*'

'No, *wait!*' Sadie's appetite for the story was well and truly whetted now. If she had to pay him the rest out of her own pocket she was determined to have exclusive rights. 'You'll have to promise me not to sell it anywhere else though.'

'Okay, you're on. What do you reckon?'

She named a new sum and Rick sat down again. It wasn't a fortune but it would be enough to get him out of Elvemere. Going straight had got him nowhere, had it? If he didn't get out of here soon he could see himself being well and truly trapped. He'd made a couple of good contacts when he was inside – up in London. If he could get up there with enough over to keep him in food and a cheap room for a few days . . . Freedom beckoned seductively. 'Okay,' he said eagerly. 'You're on!' He leaned forward confidentially. 'It was in 1970. At a pop festival . . .'

Julia knocked on the door of Eleanor's little house and waited. She'd been intrigued by the mysterious phone call she'd received this morning. Eleanor had refused to tell her over the telephone why she wanted to see her, insisting that she call round at the house as soon as possible. And when the older woman opened the door Julia could see at once that she was pleased about something and eager to tell her about it.

'Julia! Come in, my dear.' Eleanor led the way through to her sunny little living room where coffee was already brewing. 'Forgive me for dragging you round here but as I have no transport of my own . . .'

'That's all right. I don't mind in the least. What is it, Eleanor? Has something exciting happened?'

'Well, yes, it has rather.' The other woman poured the coffee and sat down. 'I had a telephone call from the Town Clerk yesterday afternoon,' she said. 'It's off the record for the moment, but Philip Forsyth, the Deputy Mayor, is about to resign. It's something to do with his wife's health. He doesn't think she could stand the taxing round of engagements entailed in his being Mayor.'

'I see.' Julia was still wondering in what way the news could affect her when Eleanor said, 'So it seems they're about to ask me officially to take over from him.'

'Eleanor!' Julia smiled. 'Congratulations. No one deserves the honour more than you do.'

'I must admit that I am thrilled,' she said. 'Though I have a sneaking suspicion that as the longest standing member of the council I'm the only one who knows the drill well enough to take it on at short notice.' She paused to sip her coffee. 'Because, you see, it'll mean taking over as Mayor very soon. Next month, in fact, and the only snag is that as I no longer have a husband, I'm going to be short of a Mayoress.'

'Well, yes, but that shouldn't be a problem, should it? You must know plenty of nice men who would be only too happy to be your consort.'

'Yes, but I don't want any of them, Julia. I want you.'

Julia's eyes widened with surprise as she stared speechlessly at her friend and fellow councillor. '*Me?*'

'Who better? You have the necessary charm and grace. I don't want some old bald-headed deadbeat trailing round after me. I'll be needing all the glamour I can get.' She chuckled good-naturedly. 'After all, who's going to turn out to see what an old bag like me is wearing? Besides, you've already proved yourself a damned good councillor. You've tackled a controversial social issue many would have baulked at, and won.' She peered at Julia's stunned expression. 'Well, my dear, what do you say? Will you do it for me?'

'Well – I'd be honoured, of course.'

'Naturally you'll want to speak to Vernon about it before you commit yourself. It'll mean a bit of disruption to your domestic arrangements, so it'll be as well to have his cooperation and support.'

'Yes. I'll tell him what you've proposed tonight. I won't keep you in suspense, Eleanor. I'll get back to you as soon as I can.'

It wasn't difficult for Sadie to find out where Julia went to school. She only had to look in back numbers of the *Clarion* for her election details. The records showed that the headmistress at that time had been a Miss Treadgold, now retired and living in a cottage down at Ormsborgh on the Norfolk coast. On being told on the telephone that Sadie was researching the history of the school for a newspaper article the old lady had readily agreed to see her the following Sunday.

It turned out that Miss Treadgold had kept every copy of the school magazine between the years 1958 and 1980 when she had retired, and from them Sadie obtained a list of teachers and pupils, including Julia Philips, as she had been then.

Mrs Mary Griggs, who taught Form 5A at St Hilda's, had been a young newly qualified teacher in 1969 and Sadie discovered to her delight that she was still teaching at the school. On the same pretext she had used to see Miss Treadgold, Sadie got her to agree to see her in the lunch break.

'I married an Elvemere man soon after I came here,' Mrs Griggs told her. 'We made our home and brought up our family here, which is why I never moved on. I love the town and the school, and I'm so pleased you're going to write an article about the history of it.'

Sadie listened politely to what seemed an endless stream of reminiscences and anecdotes, wondering how she could lead the conversation around to what she really wanted to know. At last she said, 'Quite a lot of your girls have done well, haven't they, Mrs Griggs?'

'Oh, yes. There are several doctors and a barrister whom I remember well,' the teacher said proudly. 'One girl became an opera singer and . . .'

'And there's Councillor Mrs Grant, of course,' Sadie broke in. 'The councillor responsible for the new women's refuge that's about to be opened.'

'Yes.' Mrs Griggs looked doubtful. 'Yes, I remember Julia very well. Not academic, of course, but a pleasant enough girl – if only she hadn't been so easily influenced by the unsuitable friendship she formed.'

'Friendship? Who with?' Sadie was intrigued. Maybe at last she might be getting somewhere.

'A girl called Joanna Bloom,' Mrs Griggs said, drawing down the corners of her mouth. 'They were inseparable, unfortunately. I always wondered what they could possibly have in common. They seemed such opposites. Joanna's family was – not to put too fine a point on it – rather bohemian in outlook, whereas Julia came from a very nice family, highly respected. Her grandfather was the most popular doctor in the town in those days.' She sighed. 'I did my best to part them when they were in my form, but that just seemed to make matters worse.'

'What became of her?' Sadie asked.

'Joanna? She married an American serviceman at quite an early age and left the country.'

An American! Sadie's heart sank. Obviously if she'd been able to talk to this Bloom girl she might have uncovered a lot of useful information. 'I see. So she – this Joanna Bloom – lives in America? You don't happen to know . . .'

344

'Oh, she's not there any more,' Mrs Griggs interrupted. 'She must have come back here after her divorce. A few months ago I saw a photograph of her in your paper. There was a small article saying that she'd just become a partner in the building firm of Grant Philips. Her name is different now, of course. I can't remember what it is, but I would have recognised her anywhere. Obviously she and Julia must have remained in contact which is why she joined the firm. I daresay she has grown out of her wild ways by now. I certainly hope so!'

Back at the office Sadie returned to the *Clarion's* back numbers and found the article in question. It was quite a small piece with a photograph, just as Mrs Griggs had said, and reported that Joanna Hanson, ex-wife of an American real-estate tycoon, had become a partner in Grant Philips Construction last November. Sadie realised that it must have been just before she had joined the staff of the *Clarion.*

She sat back to think. If Joanna was a partner in Julia's family firm – if the two women had been close friends and, presumably, still were – it was hardly likely that Joanna would want to spill the beans on her pal's secret past. All the same, it was her only lead, and as such she couldn't afford to pass it up. Thumbing through the telephone book she found Joanna's address and made a note of it. She wouldn't ring first. She'd pay her a surprise visit later this evening. Taken off guard, she might open up. You never knew your luck!

Julia had waited until they'd finished eating that evening to break the news to Vernon. She wasn't sure how he'd take it. He'd never been keen on her being on the council and as for her being Mayoress . . . He'd been preoccupied over the past few days. Several times she thought he was about to tell her something, but so far he had held back on whatever it was. She looked up at him over her coffee cup.

'Eleanor asked me to go round and see her this morning.'

'Oh, yes?'

'I thought I might ask her to come and have a meal with us. I thought perhaps next Sunday. Charlotte is coming too.'

Vernon grunted a reply which could have been yes or no. Julia cleared her throat. 'Vernon, Eleanor . . .'

'Look, Julia,' he interrupted. He put down his cup and met her eyes across the table. 'There's something I think you'd better know.'

'What?'

'Dad has got himself into a bit of a bind about the Victoria

345

Gardens project. There's a problem with the survey and he thought – *we* thought – it might be a good idea to mortgage both houses.'

She stared at him. 'You mean, hand them over – to the bank?'

He groaned. 'It's merely a business arrangement, Julia. It won't affect you at all. This will still be your home. It's just to tide us over for a few months – as security.'

'I can't see anything secure about living in a house that belongs to the bank,' she said. 'What if the Victoria Gardens thing falls through? We could be homeless just like that.'

'Trust you to overdramatise it! Thousands of people have mortgages. It's perfectly normal.' He shook his head. 'This is the kind of reaction that stops me from telling you things about the business!'

'I'm not a fool, Vernon. With Beardsley's going under, the Meadowlands Estate is in jeopardy. Things look bad, don't they?'

He shook his head. 'You know nothing about it, Julia. Why don't you leave these things to people who do?'

'The people who *do* don't seem to be making much of a job of it, do they?' she said hotly. 'I think your father is playing with fire. He's contemplating taking our home from us without any guarantee we'll ever get it back.'

'I know that!' Vernon snapped. 'But as he bought it in the first place there isn't a lot I can say, is there?'

'It is in your name though,' she pointed out. 'You could refuse. You've always been against the buying of Victoria Gardens anyway.'

'He's my father. How can I leave him out on a limb, for God's sake? Besides I do have a pretty big interest in what happens to GPC.'

'Then why didn't you block his buying Victoria Gardens in the first place?'

Vernon shrugged impatiently. 'Joanna seemed to agree with Dad and I trust her judgement.' He glared at her. 'Damn it all, Julia, even *you* voted for it!'

She fell silent, unable to argue. 'Well, there's obviously nothing to be done about it, is there? All we can do is hope for the best.' She cleared her throat and made another attempt at breaking her own news. 'Vernon – I've been trying to tell you,' she said, 'Eleanor Maitland has been asked to be Mayor.'

He frowned. 'I thought Philip Forsyth was Deputy.'

'He's resigned because of his wife's health. The thing is, Vernon . . .' She glanced at him. 'Eleanor has asked me to be her Mayoress.'

For a moment he stared at her, then he threw back his head and began to laugh. 'You? *Mayoress*! Oh, my God! I can just see the two of you. Talk about Morecambe and Wise! I sincerely hope you told her where to go.'

'As a matter of fact, I said I'd be delighted,' Julia said coolly. 'I'm glad you see it as amusing. I take it you have no objections then?'

He stopped laughing to glare at her. 'If you think I'm going to come home to an empty house night after night, no meal waiting, no shirts ironed, you can bloody well think again, Julia! I think it's high time you came down to earth. This council business has gone to your head.'

She sprang to her feet. 'When are you ever here to eat a meal I've prepared?' she demanded. 'And if it's clean shirts you want, why don't you ask Joanna to wash and iron them for you? Most of your spare time seems to be spent with her anyway!'

He stood very still, looking at her with an expression of near loathing. 'As a matter of fact up till now it's only been my sympathy – my *pity* for you – that has prevented me from asking you for a divorce.'

'Your *pity*? Well, you can stop feeling sorry for me, Vernon. You can have your divorce any time you like.'

'Don't be ridiculous!' He looked at her incredulously. 'You couldn't possible manage on your own. What do you think you'd do for money? You haven't a clue. You need my support, Julia. Without me you'd fall apart.'

'I don't think so.' She stood up very straight and took a deep breath. She felt like a swimmer coming to the surface after being submerged for a long time; filling her lungs with the clean, sweet breath of life. 'I've got news for you, Vernon,' she told him. 'Dad sold our shares in GPC a few days ago. Mine and Charlotte's as well as his own and Mum's.'

'Sold . . .' The colour left Vernon's face and he turned a sickly white. 'Who – who to?' he whispered.

'To Joanna. I'm sure your father will be immensely relieved. And you will soon have a taste of what it's like to be in Joanna's pocket!' She pushed past him on her way to the door. 'That's what you wanted, isn't it? Well, I hope you find it cosy there, Vernon, because you'll never get out.' At the door she turned. 'And you can start divorce proceedings as soon as you like!'

Joanna opened the door and looked at the young woman standing on her doorstep with distaste. She loathed women who dressed like men. And as for the nose stud . . . 'Yes?' she said sharply.

'Mrs Hanson?'

'That's right. Who would you be?'

'My name is Sadie Freeman. I work for the *Clarion*.'

'I see. What do you want with me?'

'I wondered – could I have a word with you, Mrs Hanson?' Sadie paused. This woman was clearly a tough cookie. It wasn't going to be easy. If she really was a friend of Julia Grant's there was no way a woman like this would dish any dirt on her.

Sadie smiled and took a deep breath. 'I've been doing some research on St Hilda's School,' she said, 'and one or two of its more notable ex-pupils. Some rather interesting stories have emerged that I'd like verified. You know how things get twisted and exaggerated over the years. Someone said that you and Councillor Mrs Grant were once close friends and I thought . . .'

The expression on Joanna's face changed from hostility to one of delight. 'Julia?' Her green eyes shone. 'Oh, yes, we were as close as two peas in a pod at school. But that's going back a long time. What have you heard?'

'May I come in?' Sadie asked. 'It's a little confidential. I don't want to talk about it on the doorstep.'

'Of course. What must you think of me?' Joanna opened the door wide. 'Do come in and have a drink. I'll tell you anything I can.'

Half an hour later Sadie left the house in Hazel Grove almost punch drunk with what she had learned. Without the slightest hesitation Joanna Hanson had told her more then she could ever have dreamed about Julia Grant. It was an incredible story and she told it as though it was common knowledge. At seventeen Julia Philips had run away to live with a pop musician she'd met at a festival on the Isle of Wight. That much she'd already heard from Rick, though not that he was half-West Indian. Or that the daughter Julia had abandoned as a small baby was right here in Elvemere running a local catering firm. But the most stunning revelation of all was that the daughter in question was – *had* to be – Tom Markham's girlfriend. Yes, *Fleur*! There could be little doubt. It all fitted, her age, her looks, all of it.

But why had she come here? Sadie mused. That seemed to be something Joanna would like to know too. Was it merely a daughter's curiosity about her real mother, or did she have a deeper, darker motive? Revenge, perhaps. But one glaringly hard fact had emerged from her interview with Joanna Hanson. She was no friend of Julia Grant's! For some reason she wanted – intended – to do her as much harm as possible. And that intrigued Sadie most of all. One thing was for sure: there was more – far more – to be extracted from all this than a mere piece of small-town gossip!

On the morning of the opening of the women's refuge Julia was up early. Since their row Vernon had removed himself to the spare room. Each morning he rose early and left the house without breakfast. They had hardly made contact since that night. It was a miserable existence. She had thought he would move out to join Joanna but as he hadn't it looked as though it was up to Julia to find somewhere else to live.

In the silent kitchen she made herself some toast and coffee and tried to prepare herself for the coming day. Fleur had promised to be at Alexandra House early to lay out the buffet lunch and Julia had booked a nine o'clock hair appointment so that she could be there to help. Everything seemed to be satisfactorily organised. She was just about to go upstairs to get dressed when the back door bell rang.

With a small exclamation of annoyance, Julia went to answer it and found a distraught Tracey standing outside with Damian in his buggy.

'Oh, Mrs Grant, I'm sorry to trouble you. I know you must be busy but I had to come.'

'What on earth is wrong, Tracey?' Julia held the door open. 'Look, you'd better come in.'

'It's Rick,' she said as she manoeuvred the buggy through the door. 'He's gone. When I woke up this morning he'd just – just left.'

'Are you sure?'

'Yes. He left a note. He isn't coming back.'

'But where has he gone?'

'He didn't say.' The girl fumbled in her bag. 'Look . . .' She held out a crumpled scrap of paper that looked like part of an old envelope. Julia took it.

Deer Trace, Sory I got to go. Being a dad is no good for me. You are beter of without me. Love Rick.

Tracey burst into tears. 'What am I going to do, Mrs Grant?' she sobbed. 'I thought we were gonna to be okay. I thought he was as happy as me. Now this!'

Julia put down the letter and put her arms round the girl. 'Oh, Tracey, I'm sorry. I know it isn't helping you right now, but I do think Rick has a point. He wasn't very good father material, was he? He would have broken your heart in the end – may have even turned violent again. You really are better off without him. Maybe some day you'll meet someone else – someone kind and hard-working who'll take care of you.' She knew the words were banal and unlikely and wished there was something more constructive she could do for the girl.

'There's no way I'm going to be able to manage,' Tracey said desperately. 'Not with two kids. Rick took all the rent money with him too. I save it, see, in a jam jar on the top shelf of the kitchen cabinet. I looked before I came out. It's gone – every penny of it. They'll chuck me out if I can't pay again this month.'

'Well, that's one thing we can do something about.' Julia went to her bag and opened it but Tracey held up her hand. 'No! Rick took them things from Mr Grant. I still owe you for them. I couldn't take any more from you. No, *really*.' She took a handkerchief from her sleeve and blew her nose. 'If I could just get a job. Maybe a housekeeper's job where I could live in. But with one kid and another on the way, who'd take me on?'

'I do see what you mean . . .' Suddenly the idea hit Julia. 'Of course! Why didn't I think of it before?' she muttered. 'Tracey – how would you like to be caretaker of the women's refuge?'

Tracey's brimming eyes opened wide with hope. 'Oh! Oh, Mrs Grant, do you really think I could do it?'

'I don't see why you shouldn't apply. I can vouch for the fact that you're honest and a good worker. There's a little flat with the job. Only two small rooms but it's on the ground floor so it would be handy for you with the children. And the rule at the refuge is to be that the women will be responsible for their own rooms, so you wouldn't be expected to keep the whole place clean. Just supervise and be there to take charge. What do you think?'

The relief on the girl's face was touching. 'I'd be ever so grateful, if you'd put in a word for me Mrs Grant. It's like the answer to a prayer.'

'Look, Tracey, I've got to go to the hairdresser's now but why don't you come along to the opening?' Julia suggested. 'I can introduce you to the social worker who'll be in charge of Alexandra House and you can have a chat with her.'

Sadie arrived at Alexandra House just as Fleur was putting the finishing touches to the buffet table. She unstrapped her camera and equipment from the bike and dumped them in a corner of the kitchen, eyeing Fleur as she did so.

'You're early,' Fleur remarked.

'Yes. As a matter of fact, I was hoping to have a quiet word with you.'

Fleur smiled. 'Well, here I am. What can I do for you?'

350

'It's awkward. Look, there's a rumour that you are Julia Grant's daughter. Is it true?'

Fleur was stunned. 'I've heard no such rumour. Where did you hear it?'

'I can't tell you that. I just want to know if there's any truth in it?'

'Why?' Fleur asked suspiciously.

Sadie shrugged. 'I hate uncertainties. Besides, you have to admit that it's a damned good story.'

Fleur turned away to hide the flush that she could feel warming her cheeks. 'I've heard no rumours,' she said non-commitally. 'I can't think who could be spreading a story like that.'

'So – there's nothing in it?'

'Do you think I wouldn't know if there was?' She stalled.

'It's possible you wouldn't.' Sadie looked at her. 'Tell me – were you an adopted child?'

'No,' Fleur said firmly. 'And now, if you'll excuse me, I have to get on.'

She escaped to the dining room and stood for a long moment looking out over the back garden, her mind in a whirl. Where had Sadie's information come from? As far as she knew Tom was the only other person who knew. Was it possible he had told Sadie? She shrank from the thought. Surely he would never betray her confidence, however angry he was with her. Would Sadie publish the story in the paper? Not without solid proof, surely? It could do untold harm to Julia. Somehow she must warn her before Sadie sprang her startling accusation. It could ruin the whole day.

She saw Julia arrive, but she was accompanied by a social worker. Then a girl with a baby in a push chair claimed her attention and the three of them were engaged in earnest conversation. Soon a party of councillors arrived, then the TV and local radio people began milling around, setting up their equipment. Finally it was almost twelve o'clock and time for the Mayor to arrive and perform the opening ceremony. If she didn't get Julia's attention now it might be too late. Fleur seized the opportunity of a small lull to edge through the crowd to Julia's side.

'Can I have a quick word?'

'Of course. Is there a problem with the buffet?'

'No. It's a bit more worrying than that,' Fleur said, taking her arm and drawing her to one side. 'One of the journalists – the girl in the motorbike gear – has been asking me if, well, if there's any truth in the rumour that I'm your daughter.'

The colour drained from Julia's face. 'Oh, God! Where did she get hold of that?'

'I've no idea. It wasn't from me.'

'What did you tell her?'

'That I'd heard no rumours myself. She asked me if I was an adopted child. I said no, but I don't think she was convinced.'

One name was in Julia's mind. *Joanna.* She glanced anxiously at her watch. 'I've a pretty good idea who's responsible for this,' she said. 'But I haven't time to worry about it now. Thank you for warning me, Fleur. Don't worry, I'll think of something.'

There was a sudden flurry of activity as a limousine pulled up in the street outside. Julia said, 'I think that will be the Mayor arriving. It will have to wait for the time being.'

Fleur watched as the Mayor, resplendent in his scarlet robes and chain, cut the ribbon strung symbolically across the doorway and declared the refuge open. Cameras flashed and for the half-hour that followed Julia was surrounded by reporters, either wanting to record statements for the radio, TV or for the papers. Sadie waited, biding her time until last. Fleur watched her but, frustratingly, the other girl had still made no move towards Julia when she received the signal to begin serving the buffet.

'Mrs Grant, can I have a few words from you for the paper?' Sadie placed herself squarely in front of Julia, her pencil poised. 'I know you've made statements for the other papers, radio and so on, but I thought there might be something more personal you could say. Your own intimate view of all this as a local woman and – er – mother?' She was watching Julia's face intently. 'For instance, there's a rumour going round that you yourself might have had occasion to use a refuge like this some years ago.'

'I can truthfully say that I have never experienced domestic violence, I'm glad to say,' Julia said carefully. 'But that doesn't mean that I can't empathise with the plight of women who have.'

'I was talking about being a single mother,' Sadie said daringly. 'Rumour has it that you had a child prior to your present marriage. A daughter. And that she actually lives and works here in Elvemere.'

Julia's expression did not change. 'Really? Is that how rumour has it? How interesting.'

'So – will you deny that?'

'I really don't see why I should deny or confirm anything. I'm not on trial, am I? I think my personal life, especially something that allegedly happened so long ago, is entirely my own business.'

352

'Some people might not think so, Mrs Grant,' Sadie said. 'I'm sorry, *Councillor* Mrs Grant, I mean,' she added pointedly. 'There is also a rumour that you're being tipped as the town's next Mayoress.'

'So many rumours. And all in one day!' For a long moment Julia stared at the reporter, suddenly aware that she was fighting a losing battle. She was facing a turning point in her life. In the next few minutes her life – her whole future – would be in jeopardy. Now it was all down to her. The next hour was make or break time. She could give in and watch her life crumble round her, or she could stand with her back to the wall and fight. Gathering every ounce of her courage, she said firmly, 'After lunch I shall be making a speech. If you'd like to stay until then you can print everything I have to say. In fact . . .' She took a deep breath. 'In fact, I'm relying on you to do just that!'

During lunch, trying not to think of her coming ordeal, Julia made sure she spoke personally to everyone and thanked them for coming. Afterwards, the guests mellowed by wine and good food and the atmosphere more relaxed, Julia decided that the time had come. Her heart drumming with apprehension, she clapped her hands for silence.

'If I could just have your attention for a moment or two, ladies and gentlemen, I'd like to say a few words,' she said. 'As many of you know, this refuge has been the dream of local underprivileged and abused women for some time and I am very proud to be able to say that it was I who finally managed to bring the scheme to fruition. I hope that it will prove to be a haven for all the women and children who need respite and sanctuary, either for a few days or for longer. My hope is that it will prove to be a quiet place where they can pick up the threads of a broken life, heal their damaged self-esteem and make a new start.' She paused, trying to calm her nervousness. 'I would also like to take this opportunity of telling you my own story so that you will understand why this place is so close to my heart.'

She saw that she had the attention of everyone in the room and had to pause again to gather all her strength and wait for her heartbeat to steady. 'Most of the women who will take shelter in this refuge will do so because they have made a very basic but devastating mistake,' she began. 'I have good reason to know that no one, however clever or wise, from whatever walk of life, is ever immune from that folly. My own mistake was a familiar one. I fell in love too young, and with the wrong man. Too naive to realise the heartache I was causing, I ran away with him. But that wasn't my worst mistake. I'm ashamed to say that I later followed it with an even worse one: that of not facing up to the havoc I had caused, of failing to see it through.'

Suddenly aware of the deep silence that had fallen on the room, she looked at the faces turned towards her. All eyes were upon her – waiting intently. She had passed the point of no return. There was no going back. She cleared her throat and went on.

'I was seventeen when my first child was born, and by that time her father had already left me. But I was too unhappy, too homesick, to see how lovely my baby daughter was; too immature to realise how trusting, how totally dependent on me she was. When she was a few months old I could bear it no longer. I took the easy way out – left her behind with her grandmother and ran away again. I ran away from my responsibilities, but I couldn't run away from the consequences. I didn't see that because of my cowardice I was sacrificing the love of my child. I didn't foresee the pain of not being there to see her take her first steps or hear her first words. And because no one knew my secret, I had to suffer the heartbreak alone. The fact that I never saw my child grow up and blossom into the beautiful young woman she is today is something I shall regret for the rest of my life.'

Julia suddenly caught sight of Eleanor, standing on the fringes of the crowd. The older woman was watching her, eyes misty with compassion. Strengthened by her sympathetic support, Julia turned towards the back of the room where Fleur stood.

'This afternoon, for the first time, I would like to introduce you publicly to my elder daughter,' she said boldly. 'Although she has not been in Elvemere long, many of you already know her. In the few months that she has been here she has made her mark as the late Sally Arden's very capable assistant: Fleur Sylvester.' She held out her hand. 'Fleur – will you come and join me, please?'

All eyes turned to look at her, and after a moment's hesitation Fleur moved forward to stand beside Julia as cameras flashed from all sides of the room.

'May I introduce you to my daughter?' Julia said. She reached for her glass and held it up. 'Please will you join me in drinking to the future of Alexandra House Women's Refuge, coupled with a toast to my daughter, Fleur!'

There was a pause as everyone drank. Then a burst of enthusiastic applause.

'I wish you'd warned me, Julia,' Fleur whispered. 'It was very brave, but if I'd known what you were going to do . . .'

'I should have done it years ago.' Julia reached out and squeezed her hand. 'Don't worry, neither of us has anything to be ashamed

354

of,' she said. 'Later we must talk, but first there's something I have to do. You won't go away, will you?'

'No, of course not.'

Julia smiled. 'Right. I'll see you later.'

She walked across to where Eleanor was waiting. 'I'm sorry, Eleanor,' she said. 'All that happened on the spur of the moment. If I'd planned it I would have prepared you. It's a long story. I'll explain everything to you in detail some time. I'll be resigning my seat on the council, of course. And naturally I won't hold you to your offer to appoint me your Mayoress.'

'Stuff and rubbish! If you won't be Mayoress, I won't be Mayor!' Eleanor said stoutly.

Julia laughed and bent to kiss the older woman's cheek. 'Bless you for that, but you must accept. You know that.'

'And so must you, whether you're on the council or not. I mean it!'

'Well, we'll see.'

Sadie paused at Julia's elbow. 'Excuse me. Did you mean what you said about going public, Mrs Grant?'

'Of course. I want you to print every word,' Julia said firmly. 'Just make sure you spell the names right, that's all?'

Sadie laughed. 'I'll do my best!'

The media people moved in after that. Julia gave a brief interview to both radio and TV reporters and more photographs were taken. The rest of the guests drifted away in groups until at last Fleur and Julia were left alone.

'It's been quite a day,' Julia said.

Fleur nodded. 'Tomorrow will be difficult for you.'

'When the papers come out?' Julia sighed. 'Maybe radio and TV will be even quicker with the story.' She gathered her coat and handbag together. 'I think my first priority is to get round to my parents' house. It's vital that I break this news to them before they see or hear it from some other source. I'll go round and see Charlotte when she gets home from the office. She must be told too.' She looked at Fleur. 'Will you come with me?'

Fleur shook her head. 'I think it's probably a bit too late for that, don't you?' she said. 'There isn't much point anyway. I shan't be around for much longer.'

'You're surely not leaving?'

'I'm afraid I'll have to. Sally's son is selling Arden Catering, complete with the house and everything that goes with it. When it's sold I'll be out of a job and a home. I'm going up to London tomorrow for a friend's engagement party. I'm thinking seriously of moving back there once everything is tied up here. After all, it's where my roots are.'

'I suppose it is.' Julia smiled wistfully. 'So – unlike me, you won't be around to catch the fall-out when the local paper hits the street!'

'No.' Fleur opened her handbag and took out a tattered brown envelope. 'You might like to have these,' she said. 'It's just a few old photographs. There are some of me as a baby and a couple of Dean – all I ever knew of him.'

Tears sprang to Julia's eyes as she took out the snapshots and looked at them. Her heart contracted painfully as she looked at the fading images she had carried in her memory. 'But they're yours,' she said.

Fleur shook her head. 'Take them. I know them by heart. Maybe your parents might like to see them.' She looked at Julia. 'I don't need reminding of the past any more now. You laid all those ghosts for me when you made your speech. I have to concentrate on the future now.'

Julia put them into her bag, looking at Fleur with regret. 'I'd have liked that future to have included me. It's such a shame you're leaving just when we've found each other.'

Fleur wanted to correct her, to say, 'Just when I've finally been forced to acknowledge you, you mean'. But she reminded herself that what Julia had done that afternoon had taken courage and instead she shook her head and said, 'Let's face it, I daresay I'd only be an embarrassment to you if I stayed. After all, there's your husband to think of, isn't there? I don't suppose the prospect of running into me round every corner would please him much.'

'None of this will concern Vernon,' Julia said. 'It isn't public knowledge yet but we're about to start divorce proceedings.'

'Oh. I'm sorry.'

'Don't be. It's for the best.' Julia looked at her. 'I wish things had been different, Fleur. I meant everything I said, you know. I wasn't just looking for cheap publicity when I made that speech this afternoon. Leaving you the way I did was the worst thing I ever did. It has been the greatest regret of my life and if I could turn back the clock and do it differently, I would. All this means that I'm going to have to resign my seat on the council, but I know now that it isn't important. For the first time in my life I feel like a complete person. I feel strong enough to face the future.'

Chapter 17

Julia was packing. The past few hours had been traumatic and once tomorrow's paper came out she would be obliged to move out. She decided that she might as well go now, before Vernon came home from work. *If* he came home, that was.

After the opening of the refuge the previous day she had gone straight round to Gresham House, anxious to get the ordeal of telling her parents over as soon as possible. A surprised May had opened the door to her.

'Julia! What a nice surprise, dear. I thought you were going to be tied up all day and too busy to . . .' The look of pleasure on her face faded when she saw Julia's expression. 'Darling, whatever is the matter? You look as if you've seen a ghost.'

'I need to talk to you and Daddy right away,' she said.

'Of course. Come into the morning room. We've just come in from the garden and I've made some tea.'

Harry looked up with a smile as his daughter came into the room. 'Hello, Julia. Just in time for tea. I always . . .'

'Julia has something she wants to talk to us about,' May interrupted him. She pulled out a chair. 'Sit down, darling, and take your time. I'm sure that whatever it is, it can't be as bad as you think. And Daddy and I will be able to help.'

'To begin with, Vernon and I have agreed to divorce,' Julia said. 'That will come as no surprise to you. He told me that Charlie wants to mortgage both houses to tide the business over financially. It seems he's had some kind of setback over the houses in Victoria Gardens. That brought things to a head but . . .' She paused to take a deep breath. 'But when tomorrow's *Clarion* comes out, I think he'll probably feel that he has good grounds for divorcing me.'

'Julia!' May looked alarmed. 'Whatever do you mean?'

'Someone – Joanna, I suspect – told a reporter from the *Clarion* about something that happened a long time ago; something I did.'

Harry glanced at his wife's distressed face and cleared his throat. 'I think you'd better come to the point, Julia. What has Joanna said?'

'You remember the time when I lived in London – before Vernon and I met?'

May frowned. 'When you had that secretarial job and shared a flat with that girl – what was her name?'

'There was no job, Mum. No flat either. I went to a pop festival with Joanna on the Isle of Wight that weekend, not on a school trip as I led you believe. I met someone there – a musician called Dean Sylvester. I fell wildly in love with him and when he asked me to stay with him, I couldn't resist.'

A little cry of dismay escaped May's lips. 'Oh, Julia!'

Harry frowned at his wife. 'Let Julia finish the story,' he said. 'What happened?'

'It didn't work. If I'd been older, more mature, I'd have known it was destined for failure. When I became pregnant he took me to his parents' home in East London and left me there. I saw him a few times after that, but eventually he told me it was over between us.'

'So you had an – an abortion. Is that what you're trying to tell us?'

'No, Mum.' Julia looked at her mother. 'I had a baby daughter. I called her Fleur. Dean's parents were very kind to me. They were disappointed in their son but they adored the baby. They were quite happy for me to stay there with them. But I couldn't settle. As time went by it grew worse. I was so unhappy and homesick that I couldn't see things straight. In the end, when Fleur was just a few months old, I left her with them and I – came home.' She looked at the faces of her mother and father.

'I knew it. I knew there was something wrong.' May's eyes were brimming with tears. She was remembering all the little things that had puzzled her at the time; the muffled sounds of sobbing, heard through the bedroom wall late at night, the wraith-like thinness and the haunted look in the girl's eyes.

Harry looked hurt and angry. 'How could you do that to us, Julia?' he said. 'Didn't you trust us enough to know that we would have forgiven you? We would have been hurt, of course; disappointed maybe. But to leave your child – to keep this secret from us all these years.' He shook his head, trying to come to terms with

358

this new facet of the daughter he thought he knew so well. 'What did you think we were – monsters?'

'I can't help feeling that we must have failed you somewhere,' May said sadly. 'But I think I can understand how you must have felt.'

'I did try to get Fleur back,' Julia told them. 'I hadn't realised how much I'd miss her. I wanted her so desperately that I thought my heart would break. I wrote to Dean's mother, but she wrote back saying that Fleur had been adopted and that it wouldn't be possible to get her back.'

'And all through this you never said a word,' May said, shaking her head. 'You suffered all of it alone.'

'Soon after that I met Vernon,' Julia went on. 'It seemed to please you both so much when we were married. Then Charlotte was born and having another baby in my arms helped take away the pain.'

'Vernon – does he know about this?' Harry asked. 'Did you tell him?'

'No.' Julia turned to look at her father. 'That's what I meant when I said he'd have grounds to divorce me. You see, all this came out at the opening of the refuge today. One of the journalists asked me about it point blank. It was obvious that it was going to be exposed so I decided my only course was to spike their guns. I stood up and told them about it. The story is bound to be in tomorrow's paper.'

May began to weep quietly into her handkerchief and Julia reached out to touch her shoulder.

'Oh, Mum, I'm so sorry. I thought after all these years I'd saved you the pain of this.'

'It's not for me I'm upset,' May said. 'It's for you. All this time without seeing your child and now you're to be made to suffer for it all over again.'

'You never found out what became of her?' Harry asked.

'Yes, I did. You haven't heard everything yet. Fleur came to find me,' Julia told them. 'She was never adopted at all. Dean's mother must have felt guilty about lying to me about it. She made Fleur promise to come and find me, and last year, after her grandmother died, Fleur kept her promise and came to Elvemere to look for me.'

'So you've met her?'

'Yes, we've met. At first she was bitter. She didn't know I'd tried to get her back, and somehow we never managed to find any common ground. There was no way we could make our relationship public so there seemed to be no future for us. I'd have liked us to be friends and remain in touch, but she wouldn't agree to that and now I'm afraid she's going back to London. Perhaps she could never quite bring herself to forgive or trust me. And who can blame her?'

'You mean she's going away again without our having had a chance to meet her?' May said. 'Our own granddaughter?'

'I'm afraid so.' Julia opened her handbag and took the envelope out. 'I've got some photographs though. Fleur herself gave me these today.' She passed the faded snapshots to her mother. 'The young man is Dean, Fleur's father. She never actually knew him. He died in America when she was a little girl. The others are of her when she was little.'

May looked for a long time at the photographs, then at her daughter. 'Dean – he was black?'

'Yes. Half-West Indian on his father's side. I loved him very much, Mum,' Julia told her. 'He was very talented and so – so beautiful. For a little while we were very happy. It was entirely my fault that things fell apart. I was too immature. I thought life was going to be some wonderful idyllic dream and when it wasn't I complained – all the time. I must have been a real pain.'

May studied the photographs carefully, then passed them to Harry. 'This was the real reason you didn't bring the baby home, wasn't it?' she said quietly. 'Little Fleur looks so sweet. Oh, Julia, if only you'd brought her home with you all those years ago.'

'How could I, Mum?'

May frowned. 'Are you trying to tell us that you were ashamed of her?'

'No!' Julia said hotly. 'Not of Fleur – of the fact that I hadn't married her father, perhaps; ashamed that he'd abandoned me. I thought you might be embarrassed; that you'd think I'd let you down. I was thinking of your friends and your social life. Elvemere always was a narrow little place. In many ways it still is.'

'What would any of that have mattered?' May said angrily. 'We would have stood by you and your child, Julia. We would have made sure she had everything she deserved – a good upbringing and education. None of this was her fault, bless her. If you'd brought her home with you, you might never have married Vernon. It hasn't been a happy marriage for you, has it? And now, to know that we have a granddaughter of – what? – twenty years old, that we will never know . . . might never see!'

'You have seen her actually,' Julia told them. 'Her name is Fleur Sylvester and she is – rather was – Sally Arden's' assistant.'

May frowned, biting her lip as she tried to remember. 'At your

360

New Year party? The tall attractive girl with the long dark hair? Do you mean you knew then?'

'No, not then. It was later.'

'Julia.' Harry was looking thoughtful. 'You say Joanna knew all this. Is that why you voted with her and the others?'

'Yes, Dad.'

'So she's been blackmailing you? Of course, so much is clear now.' He shook his head. 'If only you'd told us.'

Julia left Gresham House feeling chastened. Her parents' reaction was not what she had expected. She should have known them better than to think they would have set more store by public opinion and their social life than the future of their daughter and granddaughter. If only she had confided in them back in those far-off days, so much misery might have been avoided.

The house was empty when she arrived home. She worked quickly, packing as many of her belongings as she could into a large suitcase. Eleanor would put her up for a few nights until she could begin to sort out something more permanent for herself. She wrote Vernon a letter, explaining as much as she could, preparing him for tomorrow's revelation in the *Clarion* and agreeing to a no fault divorce.

It was a bitter irony that after all the years of infidelity it would finally be Vernon who could claim to be the injured party.

As an afterthought, she added Eleanor's telephone number to the letter so that he could contact her if he needed to, sealed the envelope and propped it up on the hall table, where he would see it as soon as he came in.

Outside she pulled the front door firmly behind her and stood looking up at the house. It had been her home for the past eighteen years and although she had never liked the house, she felt oddly bereft at leaving it. Now she must go and see Charlotte. The sooner she told her about Fleur, the better.

Fleur did not open her copy of the *Clarion* until she was on the train the following afternoon. It was all there – a centre-page spread complete with photographs. Sadie had really gone to town. There was a picture of the Mayor performing the opening ceremony; one of Julia and Councillor Eleanor Maitland; even one of the waif-like Tracey Brownlow, in line for appointment as the refuge's resident caretaker, pictured with her small son, Damian. Fleur read it through very carefully but there was no word of Julia's personal revelation until right at the end when the reader was instructed to: *Turn to page eight for the heart-tugging personal secret of one of*

Elvemere's women councillors – as told to our reporter, Sadie Freeman.

Fleur quickly turned to page eight and there it all was – Julia's speech almost verbatim, along with another photograph, this time of Julia and herself together. She'd never forget the way she had felt when Julia made that speech. In front of everyone, including the press, she had revealed the secret she had kept all these years. It had taken courage, Fleur had to admit that. But Julia seemed to have no understanding of what the revelation would do to her daughter. It would have been nice to have had some kind of warning. Julia's speech had made Fleur feel so vulnerable; the fact of her illegitimacy and rejection laid bare for all to see had been humiliating. Julia clearly had not given a thought to her feelings on the matter.

But her mother had still to face the hardest part – telling those closest to her how she had deceived them. That would not be easy, and it was something she must do alone. Their situation was reversed. Ironically, this time it was Fleur who was running out on Julia at a time when she needed her most. She supposed she should be feeling that justice had been done. But strangely, she could feel no triumph, only a sad nostalgia.

When it came to leaving Elvemere she had felt surprisingly emotional. She would have to return after her weekend visit. During the next two weeks there were functions booked that she would have to fulfil and there would be the rest of her packing to do. But it was today that she felt she was symbolically saying goodbye to the town that had been her home for the past eight months.

She had wanted to go round to Park Row and say goodbye to Charlotte, but in the end she couldn't face the girl. Would Julia have told her by now of their blood relationship? And how would she have taken the news? Perhaps Charlotte would resent her. Fleur shrank from the thought, preferring to remember their friendship as it had been.

Tom had not been in touch. Each time the telephone rang, right up till the moment she had left the house, her heart had leaped in the hope that it might be him. In her mind she had worked out what she would say to him. But now she had to face the fact that he did not intend to see her again; had no wish to hear her explanations. And certainly had no intention of accepting her invitation to join her at Bobby's engagement party. Their relationship, it seemed, was at an end.

Till now she had been too busy to make any firm plans for her future. There had been a lot of work to do in the office. She had suspended all future bookings for Arden Catering, explaining to potential clients that the business was to be sold. She had written to Peter, saying that she intended to move back to London as soon as she could and that he should make other arrangements for showing prospective buyers round. Finally she had notified the estate agents that she would be away for a few days, recorded a new message for the answerphone and given the house a thorough clean in case any prospective buyers came while she was away.

Folding the newspaper and pushing it into her bag, she leaned back in her corner seat and looked out of the window. As the train gathered speed the outskirts of Elvemere gave way to the suburbs, the sports field with its football and cricket pitches flashing past; she could catch a glimpse of the roof of the Fairwoods Country Club, and the serried rows of cars in the car park. But dominating everything still were the great twin towers of the medieval cathedral, grey and majestic in the spring sunshine. Fleur swallowed hard, caught by a sudden and unexpected pang of nostalgia. Elvemere was a beautiful town. It had come to mean so much to her. There had been a time when it had felt like home, the place that held her future. But now there was nothing left for her here. She blinked back the tears that blurred her vision and turned her face away from the fast receding town. Her roots were in London. She should never have left it. Now she must forget the past months and look determinedly towards a new start.

Bobby was waiting to meet her train at King's Cross. Fleur saw her waiting at the barrier almost as soon as she stepped down from the train, her scarlet jacket making a splash of colour against the grey surroundings. Her eyes were bright with excitement as she scanned the faces of the disembarking passengers and Fleur felt her heart lift in anticipation as she waved. Bobby's face lit up in a broad smile of recognition as she caught sight of her and waved frantically back.

'*Fleur*! It seems like years since I saw you. You look marvellous! Here give me your case. Shall we go and have a coffee before we catch the tube?'

'Where's this Jeff I've heard so much about?' she asked, looking round.

'I left him at home,' Bobby told her. 'I wanted to come and meet you on my own.' She linked her arm through Fleur's. 'I want to tell you all about him and I can't do that with him listening, can I?' she laughed. 'Can't have him getting big-headed! Now, I want to hear all about you – *everything*. Wasn't it exciting, finding your mother like that?'

363

Fleur smiled wryly. 'It wasn't difficult. I knew where she was.'

'And how did you two get along together?'

Fleur shook her head. 'We got along all right. But it's far too late to form any kind of relationship, Bobby. I should never have tracked her down really.'

Bobby looked crestfallen. 'Oh, that's a shame. But going to Elvemere has obviously worked out. Tell me all about this balcony garden of yours and the flat, your job – and Tom, of course. *All* about Tom. He is coming to the party, isn't he? If he is he can share the spare room with Jeff.' She giggled. 'Mum has put you and me in together. I think it's to avoid what she calls hanky-panky. You know Mum!'

Fleur sighed. She hadn't written Bobby a proper letter since her world had started to fall apart. She was going to have a lot to tell her. Most of it difficult and painful.

To Fleur's surprise, Hackney looked exactly the same as when she had left it. Somehow, although she had been away only a few months, she had imagined that there would be changes, but apart from the fact that Bobby's mother had moved into a small modern flat in one of the high-rise blocks since Fleur left, everything was much the same. As they passed Wallace's Fish Bar Bobby nudged her.

'Remember when you hit that skinhead with the fish slice?' she said. 'I laughed so much when you wrote and told me about it. I'd have given anything to have been here and seen it.'

Fleur nodded with a smile. Maybe some day she'd tell Bobby about the savage revenge that skinhead had subjected her to. Or maybe not. It was something she preferred not to dwell on. There was a time when neither of them held anything back. In childhood and their early-teens the two girls had known everything about each other. Already that had changed. Bobby chattered happily about her life at college and friends whose names were unfamiliar to Fleur. Although they were still close friends their lives had taken separate courses. A small but unmistakable gulf had opened between them that would inevitably widen as the years went by. Nothing would ever be quite the same again.

As they walked down Brightman Lane, past the Smiths' shop, Fleur noticed that Ethel's daughter had acquired an off-licence and had opened a video library, advertised in the window by a lurid poster. There were different curtains at the windows of the flat too, but apart from that the building looked the same. She tried to

364

summon up a feeling of homecoming, but somehow the sense of belonging she had once known was missing.

Auntie Ada's iron grey hair was newly permed ready for the party and Fleur was comforted to find her the same as ever. She stood at the cooker in the neat little kitchen, her plump figure enveloped in a brightly coloured print overall as she prepared supper for them all. When she saw Fleur she held out her arms to her, enfolding her in a characteristic bear-like hug.

'Welcome home, love,' she said, kissing her soundly. 'We're so glad you could come. Now, off you go and freshen up. Supper in about ten minutes.'

Bobby took Fleur by the hand and led her into the living room. 'Come and meet Jeff first,' she said.

A young man sat watching the television. 'Jeff, this is my best friend Fleur,' Bobby said.

He stood up and held out his hand to her. 'Hi Fleur. I've heard a lot about you.'

Fleur saw a tall serious boy with gentle dark eyes. Bobby had already told her he was of mixed parentage. His skin was dark like hers and they looked so perfect together that the sight of them brought a lump to Fleur's throat. She shook the hand Jeff offered and smiled up at him. 'You're lucky. She's the best,' she told him. 'Even if she is a bit mad.'

Jeff slipped an arm round Bobby and grinned. 'Right,' he said. 'On both counts!'

Later, when the light was out in the room the two girls shared Bobby asked the inevitable question.

'You haven't said much about Tom. When are we going to meet him?'

'I'm afraid you aren't.' Fleur poured out the whole sorry tale, from the sale of Victoria Gardens and the loss of her flat to Sally's tragic death and the subsequent failure in communication between Tom and herself.

'Just when everything seemed to be going so well,' she said. 'Now it's all in ruins. There isn't a single thing that's worked out for me. I even feel guilty now about Julia's having to tell her story to the press. If I hadn't been in Elvemere I doubt if it would ever have happened. It's all my fault and it's going to make so much trouble for her.'

'I don't think I'd waste too many tears on her,' Bobby said. 'After all, she didn't give you too much consideration when she walked out on you, did she?'

'I don't know. She says she did – that she tried to get me back.'

Fleur sighed. 'I'm so mixed up about it all. Now that I've met Julia, got to know her, I can see that things weren't as simple as I'd thought.'

'And Tom?' Bobby asked.

'I think I've lost him,' Fleur said in a small voice. 'If he wanted to make it up he'd have done it by now. Anyway, he's been interviewed for a new job up North. I bet he'll get it. I'll probably never see him again.'

'I'm so sorry about it all, love,' Bobby said. 'I know from the letters you wrote how much it all meant to you, finding you-feet – making a new life. And your garden. You sounded so excited about it. You always did like growing things. Remember Dolly and her geraniums? The window sills were always full of them . . .' Bobby broke off. In the darkness she could hear Fleur quietly crying. 'Oh, Fleur, don't cry, love. Everything will be all right, you'll see. I bet when you go home . . .'

'I haven't got a home,' she said brokenly. 'Definitely not in Elvemere. I'm coming back to London as soon as I've got all the loose ends tied up. It didn't work, Bobby. I'm going to have to start all over again.'

Bobby threw back the covers and crossed the room to the other bed. Putting her arms round Fleur in the darkness, she held her close. 'Maybe it's for the best,' she whispered. 'At least you have friends here. No one here will let you down.'

Tom arrived back at Park Row soon after nine o'clock on Friday evening. As he let himself into the house the first person he saw was Sadie, on her way upstairs with a mug of coffee. She looked him over dispassionately.

'God! You look shattered.'

'I feel it. Had a terrible drive down from York. I've been on the road for hours and I feel filthy. First the fan belt went and then I had a puncture.' He pulled a face. 'Wouldn't you know it, the spare was knackered too. Been meaning to get it fixed for weeks. You know how it is.'

Sadie grinned. 'You should get yourself a good bike. A BMW or a Harley maybe.'

Tom groaned. 'You're joking!'

'So – was it all worth it?' she asked.

'Depends what you mean by worth it. I managed to interview this footballer, Graham Moxton, but he turned out to be an insufferable moron, arrogant and ignorant at the same time. More interested in boasting about how many birds he could pull than anything else.'

366

Sadie laughed. 'Tell me about it! I know the type all too well.'

'I did what I could with it. Tried to make him sound like a member of the human race, but it read like pretty routine stuff. I faxed the article last night, but it's hardly likely to win me Journalist of the Year.'

'Poor old you. You do sound depressed. And the job interview?'

He shrugged non-committally. 'You know the drill – don't ring us, we'll ring you. I'm not sure I'm bothered one way or the other.' He looked at her. 'Any messages for me?'

'No. Look, if you want to make yourself a coffee the kettle has boiled.' Halfway up the stairs she paused. 'Oh, by the way, there's a copy of the *Clarion* in the kitchen. Have a look at it when you've got a minute. I'm rather chuffed with myself. I think I might have pulled off quite a coup.'

Tom made himself a coffee and dithered over whether to cook some bacon and eggs. He decided against it. Maybe when he'd had his coffee and a look at the paper he'd pop out for a Chinese or some fish and chips.

When he opened the door of his sitting room he groaned. It looked as though a bomb had hit it. There had been no time to tidy up, and now he remembered that he hadn't even had time to make the bed before he left for York. He sighed and decided to forget it. Sitting down, he opened the paper and saw the article about the opening of the women's refuge. It had Sadie's by-line and he assumed that this must have been what she meant him to see. There were some nice photographs, including one of Fleur who, apparently, had done the buffet lunch. His thoughts lingered painfully on her. Obviously she hadn't tried to get in touch with him – probably didn't even know he was out of town. He still smarted when he remembered the way she'd clung to Peter Arden's side on the day of the funeral. It was almost as though she was flaunting her closeness to the creep, wanting Tom to see that she had no further interest in *him*. He read through the article, wondering why Sadie had thought it so special. Then he spotted the footnote and quickly turned to page eight.

Five minutes later he was taking the stairs two at a time and hammering furiously on her door.

'What the *hell* did you think you were playing at?' he demanded angrily when she opened the door. 'Do you have any idea what you've done?' He waved the paper under her nose.

Sadie's eyebrows rose. 'Keep your hair on. What's eating you, Tom? It's a damned good story.'

'Where did you get it?'

'A tip off, but I did a lot of work researching it thoroughly. There's nothing in there they can sue us for. It's all true. If you read it you'll see that she admitted everything.'

'Obviously she knew bloody well you'd blow the lid off if she didn't.'

Sadie shrugged. 'All's fair in love and journalism.'

'That's not the point! It's Fleur I'm thinking of. How do you think this made her feel? How did she react?'

'She didn't seem all that upset to me. What did you expect – hysterics?' Sadie shook her head at him. 'Look, Tom, I'm a journalist. I thought you were too. I know you and Fleur were an item and that you've had some kind of bust up, but if you're going to get emotionally involved with every story you write, you're going to get nowhere fast.'

'Don't tell me how to do my job!' he shouted. 'My relationship with Fleur has nothing to do with this. It's none of your business either! I might not be the greatest journalist in the world – as you obviously think *you* are! – but at least I don't grind people's faces into the dirt, screw up their lives.'

'Sometimes it's unavoidable, Tom,' she told him calmly. 'And what's more, you know it. You have to hold yourself back from all that angst, keep your personal feelings in check. If you can't do that then I'm afraid you're in the wrong job.'

'*Really*? Is that a fact? You'd know all about that, of course, wouldn't you? Well, for your information I've been offered the job of deputy editor of the *Clarion*, so not everyone can have your low opinion of my work, can they?' Fuming, he turned on his heel and ran back down the stairs.

His coffee was cold and suddenly he'd lost interest in food. He was too angry to relax now. What in God's name had made him blurt out the offer he'd had when it was supposed to be hush-hush? He'd probably blown his chance of that too now! Was everything he touched doomed to explode in his face? Maybe he'd go to the pub. If ever there was a night for getting drunk, this was it! He took his mug into the kitchen and poured the cold coffee down the sink, swilling the mug under the tap. It was as he turned to put it back on the worktop that he noticed the card on the notice board with Charlotte's message attached.

She called out 'Come in' to his tap on her door and he found her sitting on the bed with her feet tucked under her, wearing a blue wool dressing-gown that made her look about twelve. She was watching a play on her portable television.

368

'Sorry to disturb you,' Tom said, 'but I've just seen this card and the message you left for me on the board. When did you see Fleur?'

'A few days ago. She came round to see you but you'd already left. You saw the invitation for you both to her friend's engagement party in London?' She looked at him. 'I suppose it's too late now?'

'She's already gone?'

'Yes, this afternoon. The party's not till tomorrow though.'

Tom closed the door and sat down beside her on the bed. 'Charlotte, I've only just seen the paper – all this drama at the opening of the refuge.'

She nodded. 'I wasn't there but Mum came round and explained it all to me afterwards. It was a big surprise, I can tell you – took me a while to get my head round it, this business of Fleur's being my half-sister.'

'But you're pleased?'

'I would be if I thought we were going to be a family, but she's going back to London to live. We'll probably never see her again.'

'Back to London? Because of this, you mean?'

'Oh, no. She'd already decided before that.' She looked at him. 'She's been having a pretty rough time lately, Tom.'

'Has she?' He sighed. 'Yes, I suppose she has.'

'She showed me a letter she'd had from Peter Arden to say he was selling his mother's catering business. I think that was the last straw for her. I think he's a real rat after all that Fleur did for him. She really put herself out to support him when his mother was killed, you know. He just wrote her this really stuffy letter saying that he needed the money so that he and his new wife could buy a hotel. He even expected her to stick around and help sell the place for him. Cheek!'

Tom felt his heart sink. 'And you say she's decided to leave?'

'She says there's nothing to stay for so she might as well.' Charlotte sighed. 'You can't blame her, I suppose. I know I'm going to miss her though.' She glanced at him hesitantly. 'Maybe I shouldn't say this, Tom, but you haven't helped her much, have you?'

He was silent. It looked as though he'd made a prize fool of himself. 'Was it losing her job that upset her – or was it because Arden let her down?' he asked.

'Well, it's the same thing, isn't it? She was losing everything. She'd already lost her flat in Victoria Gardens.'

'*Lost* it? Moved out to be with him, you mean?'

'Mrs Franks had given her notice, didn't you know? She said it was because Fleur let you stay overnight but really it was because my grandfather had bought the place from her. Poor Fleur. It hit her very hard and . . .' Charlotte stopped as his words sank in. '*To be with him?* What, you mean you thought she – like *that*? Oh, Tom! How could you think she'd do that?'

To his embarrassment he felt himself colouring. 'Well, I don't own her! It's up to her who she . . . I just thought . . .' He looked at his watch. 'Oh, hell! Look, what time did you say she left? Would she be there by now?'

Charlotte looked doubtful. 'She might be.'

'I could ring her then.'

'You could, but I haven't got a phone number for her. I don't know her friend's surname either. There's just her Christian name and the address on the card.'

Tom grimaced. 'Oh, shit!'

When Joanna opened the door she was wearing her outdoor clothes and, seeing Vernon standing there, looked less than pleased.

'Oh, it's you!'

'Have you seen today's *Clarion*?' He held out his own copy of the paper. 'God what a shock! When I got home last night Julia had already moved out. It wasn't too much of a surprise. We've hardly spoken for days. But when I read the letter she'd left, explaining that all this would be in today's paper and offering not to contest a divorce, I had to come round at once.'

Joanna looked faintly irritated. 'Vernon, what does any of this have to do with me?'

'What does it have to do with *you*! It's what you wanted, isn't it?' Realising he had raised his voice he leaned forward. 'Look, can't we go inside, Jo? We can't talk about this on the doorstep.'

'I don't really think we need to talk about it at all.' She turned and picked up her car keys from the hall table. 'I'm sorry but I have to go, Vernon. My case is already in the car. I'm booked on the eleven-fifteen flight out of Heathrow tonight.' She looked at her watch. 'I'll have to go right now if I'm going to check in in time.'

He stared at her open-mouthed. 'Flight? Where to? Where are you going?'

'To the States,' she told him calmly. 'I've got some business to attend to.'

'How long will you be gone?'

'I don't know. Not more than a week or ten days at the most. I've told Charlie about it.'

'You've told *Dad*? Didn't it occur to you to tell me? We have to talk, Jo. It's important. Look, let me drive you to the airport then we can talk on the way.'

370

'There's no need, really.'

'Yes, there *is*.'

With a sigh she gave in. 'Oh, all right then, if you must. My case is in the boot. You'd better get it.'

After Vernon had negotiated the town traffic and they were on the motorway he looked at her. 'You haven't reacted to my news yet. Have you seen the *Clarion*? Julia actually stood up in front of everyone at the opening of that refuge place and confessed that she gave birth to a child after some mad teenage affair. It's bizarre but it solves everything, doesn't it? I mean, I can divorce her now without involving you! She hasn't got a leg to stand on. We can be married, Jo. It's good, isn't it?'

Joanna seemed unimpressed. 'I think you should make up your mind, Vernon. First you come and tell me we have to cool things because you can't afford to divorce Julia. Now, you're back with a different story. As far as I'm concerned nothing has changed. As I told you, I don't think marriage is on the cards for us.'

Vernon felt his blood chill. Ever since he had discovered that Joanna was now the major shareholder in GPC he'd felt as though he was walking a tightrope. 'Well, maybe not – not yet. But we certainly don't have to hide our feelings for each other any more. We can be together as much as we like from now on. It's what we've always wanted, isn't it?'

'I think that for the time being we should do as you said before and put our relationship on hold.'

'Jo . . .' He glanced at her. 'Ma said something when we were talking one evening recently. She said . . .' He cleared his throat nervously. 'Said that she'd paid you to get out of Elvemere. You know, all those years ago.'

She looked at him coolly. 'Really? She said that, did she?'

'Yes. She also said that you told her at the time you were pregnant with my child. Was it true, Jo?'

'Give me *some* credit, Vernon. I was never that kind of a fool, even then.'

'That's what I thought.'

'Your mother assumed that I was pregnant. She even offered me the money for an abortion, she was that keen to be rid of me.' Joanna shrugged. 'Having been grossly insulted, I figured I might as well let her pay for the privilege.'

'So there was no truth in it?'

'What do you think?'

He nodded. 'Jo, look, just one more thing. I've been wondering

371

– about that article: where did the press get all this stuff about Julia's past from?'

'I suppose it was from me – partly,' she said casually.

'But how was it that you knew and no one else did?'

'Simple. We were schoolfriends, remember? I didn't know the whole story though, not until recently when I found out some things about the Sylvester girl and began to put two and two together.' She looked at him. 'How did you think I was able to get Julia to vote with us over Victoria Gardens? Didn't you ever wonder?'

'No. I just thought that as you'd been friends ... You mean you threatened to spill the beans if she didn't toe the line?' Vernon fell silent as he digested this. He was beginning to see just how ruthless Joanna could be and reflected that it was going to be infinitely safer to have her with him than against him.

'But what made you decide to tell them now?' he asked. 'It came as a shock to me, I can tell you.'

'I daresay it did.' She looked faintly amused. 'On the other hand I daresay there are things about you that would probably come as a shock to Julia.'

He ignored the remark. 'I must say, you might have warned me before running to the press. It would have made me look pretty foolish if they had come asking me questions about it.'

'How was I to know that Julia had kept you in the dark about her past? After all, you are her husband. Anyway, I didn't run to the press. They already knew. Don't ask me how. Some reporter girl came round asking questions. She was remarkably knowledge-able about most of it, so someone else is obviously in the know. I figured that if she already knew that much I might as well fill in the blanks.'

'Why are you going to the States?' he asked. 'It's a pity you have to leave right now. If you'd asked me to go with you, I would have.'

'No need. It's just some loose ends I need to tie up. Besides, someone should be here to keep an eye on Charlie. He seems to be getting more and more manic these days. God knows what he might do if he were left to his own devices.'

Vernon opened his mouth to point out that up until now she had positively encouraged him in his excesses, but he thought better of it and bit back the retort.

At Heathrow Joanna wouldn't let him wait and see her off, insisting that he'd only have to hang around and that she'd rather be alone. It seemed to Vernon that there was an air of intrigue about this flying visit to the States. Did it have something to do with the business, and if so why hadn't she told him? He drove back to Elvemere feeling resentful and distinctly uneasy.

All Saturday afternoon Fleur and Bobby helped Ada with the preparations for the party. It was to be held in the large community room on the ground floor of the block and Jeff and two of Bobby's brothers were busy decorating it with streamers and balloons. All her family would be at the party as well as some of the girls' old schoolfriends. Jeff was from Notting Hill but his family and some of his friends would be there too. Bobby prattled away happily as they worked.

'Jeff is very talented,' she told Fleur. 'He's a year ahead of me at college and last year he won the Student of the Year award. He's hoping for a career in advertising.' She smiled proudly. 'His mother is American. Her family came from New Orleans, but she's been here for a long time, ever since she was a baby. Both her parents were musicians and she's a singer. She has the most beautiful voice. I'm hoping maybe she'll sing for us tonight.'

'And his father?' Fleur asked.

'His dad is a sergeant in the Metropolitan Police. He's from Yorkshire.' Bobby laughed. 'One of the biggest men I've ever seen and with a Yorkshire accent you could cut with a knife! Jeff says he couldn't be more of a mixture if he'd been born in a cement mixer.'

'Well, it must have worked well. He's gorgeous,' Fleur said.

Bobby smiled happily. 'Well, I think so, but then I just might be a little bit prejudiced.'

For most of the evening Fleur occupied herself with serving drinks and food. She was dismayed to find that she felt like a stranger. Most of her old acquaintances were engaged or married and all of them came with partners. They had other topics to discuss. When they weren't dancing they sat around in huddles discussing babies, husbands and their homes. Although they didn't mean to exclude her she felt left out, and without a partner of her own, awkward and out of place.

Jeff asked her to dance, but she suspected that he had been prompted by Bobby.

'I like your dress,' he said.

'Thank you.' Fleur looked down at the flame red dress she'd bought 'specially. There was a defiant quality about the colour she had chosen, but now that the evening had come she found that its gaiety didn't match her mood. She smiled up at Jeff in an effort to

373

be light-hearted and vivacious. The last thing she wanted to do was to spoil Bobby's engagement party with a gloomy expression.

Jeff's mother was persuaded to sing. She was an attractive woman with a beautiful soprano voice. She sang Gershwin's '*Summertime*' with a haunting poignancy that enchanted everyone. Fleur sat at the back of the room, grateful for the excuse not to have to talk and appear sociable.

At midnight Bobby and Jeff stood up and formally announced their engagement. As they stood side by side he put the ring on her finger and they kissed to delighted cheers and applause. The DJ had put on a romantic waltz and Fleur watched wistfully as they led the dancing. They looked so happy that she felt her eyes fill with tears. Soon Bobby will be married to Jeff, she reflected. She'll have a whole new life ahead of her and that will be the end of one more chapter of my life. Why are there only ends and no beginnings for me? she asked herself unhappily.

She busied herself clearing the remains of the food away and washing up in the kitchen until Ada came to find her.

'Fleur, love, why don't you go and have a dance before the party's over?' she said. 'You've done nothing but work all evening. Haven't you enjoyed yourself?'

Fleur smiled and hugged her. 'Of course I have, Auntie Ada. It's been a lovely party, something I wouldn't have missed for the world. I'm so happy for Bobby.'

'And what about you?' Ada asked, searching her face. 'I've been too busy to chat to you since you arrived.' She pulled out a chair. 'Come on, sit down. We'll have a glass of that wine and a chat.'

'But there's so much to do,' Fleur began weakly. Ada waved her protests away.

'You're supposed to be a guest. Besides, we've got all day tomorrow to finish what don't get done tonight,' she said. 'Bobby tells me things haven't worked out quite as you hoped and that you want to come back to Hackney?'

'That's right.'

'Are you sure it's a good idea?' Ada's kindly face was serious. 'This is no place for a young girl livin' on her own any more.' She peered into Fleur's eyes. 'You're not running away from something, are you?'

'No. There just doesn't seem to be anything for me in Elvemere any more.'

'Bobby says you found your real mother.'

Fleur looked down at her hands. 'Yes, I found her. I never really meant to, and none of it was as I imagined it would be. She isn't the selfish bitch I'd always imagined. She's quite nice actually. But even though she's acknowledged that I'm her daughter she still doesn't really want me around.'

'But do you really need her?' Ada asked. 'You're a person in your own right, love. Some day soon you'll have your own family. Wouldn't it be better to forget about Julia and get on with your own life?'

'She told me that she tried to get me back once but that Grandma told her I'd been adopted.'

'I know.' Ada nodded gravely. 'Poor Dolly always regretted telling that lie.'

'Its true then?'

'Oh, yes, it's true. She loved you so much, you see. She couldn't bear to part with you. But not only that, she didn't trust Julia not to leave you again. She never even told your granddad what she'd done and that troubled her conscience, bless her. That was why she was so anxious for you to go and find Julia for yourself after she'd gone.'

'Julia never told anyone that she'd had me,' Fleur said. 'I knew that the chances were she'd have married and had a family by this time, but I thought at least someone would know about me.'

'You must have come as a bit of a shock to her then,' Ada said. 'Turning up out of the blue after all those years.'

'I know, and I never expected a big welcome. But I wasn't prepared to be swept under the carpet like some shameful secret.'

'Maybe her worst mistake was making a secret of it in the first place. I daresay none of us gets through life without doing something we're ashamed of,' Ada said wisely. 'We have to learn to make the best of it. Try and turn the mistakes into blessings and hope that others can understand. But it's not always easy.' She was silent for a moment then asked, 'What about this young man of yours? Have you fallen out? Is that why he didn't come with you?' Fleur nodded. 'Not a race thing, is it, love?' Ada asked with a sigh. 'I know it's not easy for you kids from mixed marriages. That's why I'm so grateful my Bobby's found someone who has that in common with her.'

Fleur shook her head. 'No, it's nothing to do with that. Tom just . . . It just went wrong between us.'

'And that's why you've been looking so unhappy all evening.' Ada reached out to touch Fleur's hand. 'Poor baby. It's hard to be young. But it'll all come right in the end, you just see if it don't. That Tom of yours will be sure to make it up. And if he don't then he's a fool. He don't know what a good girl he's letting slip through his fingers.'

Fleur looked up at Ada and smiled. 'Oh, Auntie Ada, I do love you. You always make everything seem so simple.'

'Most things are, love,' Ada said with a smile. 'It's people make the complications.' She patted Fleur's hand. 'Now listen, if you're set on comin' back to Hackney you can come and stay with me for as long as you like. That goes without saying. I'd love to have you. I get lonely now they've all gone. But if you take my advice you'll go back to that Elvemere place and face all these problems. Kick 'em all into touch and stand on your own feet just to show folks you can do it, 'cause you can, you know. And if you're honest with yourself it's what you really want, deep in your heart.'

It was very late when they all got to bed and Ada let the girls sleep late the following morning. It was almost midday when they eventually sat round the kitchen table for breakfast. Ada put bacon and eggs in front of them and returned to the stove to make toast.

'Where's Jeff?' Bobby asked.

'Gone down the shop for a paper,' Ada told her. 'He should be back in a minute. I hope he is. His bacon's gonna get cold.'

Jeff came in a moment later and dropped an assortment of Sunday papers on the table. 'I found some guy wandering about downstairs,' he said.

'I hope you didn't try and talk to him,' Ada said. 'Sometimes we get some queer types hanging around down there, 'specially at weekends. Dropouts and winos, most of 'em. It's best to leave 'em be.'

'He wasn't like that,' Jeff said. 'He asked where this flat was. Said he was looking for a Miss Fleur Sylvester.'

Fleur looked up in surprise. 'For me?'

'That's right.'

'Well – where is he?' Bobby asked, looking from one to the other.

'Outside. He wouldn't come in.' Jeff was trying hard not to smile. 'I think he said his name was Markham or something. Tom Markham. Does that ring a bell?'

Bobby nudged Fleur excitedly. 'Hey, it's your Tom, isn't it? Well – what are you waiting for? He's come all this way to find you. Least you can do is ask him in for some breakfast.'

He was standing at the open front door, his back towards her, and Fleur felt her heart quicken. Closing the kitchen door carefully, she walked down the hall towards him.

'Tom. What are you doing here?'

He turned. 'I didn't get back till late Friday evening. I'd have

376

telephoned you but Charlotte didn't have a number. I thought at least I could come and take you home.'

'You needn't have bothered. I've got a return ticket.'

He looked wounded. 'Oh, well, I'm sorry I bothered. Do you want me to go away again?'

'No.' She bit her lip. 'I didn't mean to sound ungrateful. I . . .'

'I don't want your *gratitude*, Fleur. I thought you might be pleased to see me.'

'You missed the party,' she said lamely.

'I know.'

'It was a good party.'

'Good. I'm glad you enjoyed it.'

'I didn't enjoy it,' she told him angrily. 'I didn't enjoy it one bit without – on my own when everyone else was there with a partner.'

'Well, I'm sorry I couldn't have been there to provide you with one.'

Suddenly her eyes filled with tears. Here he was. Here they both were, speaking to each other again, yet it wasn't working. He was spiky and defensive, spoiling for an argument, and it was making her nervous.

'Oh, why did you come, Tom?' she said. 'Was it just to taunt me – to make me feel worse? If it was you won't succeed because I couldn't feel any more miserable than I already do!'

His hands shot out and grasped her shoulders. 'God, Fleur, you make me want to shake you!' he said. 'I'm trying to say I'm sorry, but you don't make it easy, do you? I know I've made a fool of myself but if it's any comfort to you, I've been miserable too. It was seeing you with Arden again.'

She shook him off impatiently. 'He was here for his mother's funeral, Tom,' she said. 'What was I supposed to do?'

'I know.' He ran a hand through his hair. 'I know, I'm sorry. Look, Charlotte told me about the letter he wrote you, saying that he was going to sell the business.'

'Did she? That must have given you a good laugh,' she said bitterly.

'*Fleur*! Of course it didn't!' He pulled her towards him. 'Look, I love you,' he said raggedly. 'If I didn't love you I wouldn't give a damn what you did or who you saw when you weren't with me. I thought we had something good going for us.'

'*So did I*!' She was close to tears now and blinked hard, not wanting him to see. 'So did I, Tom. That's why it hurt so much when you didn't trust me. I was only doing my job – and what I felt I owed to Sally.'

377

'I know. I know!' He pulled her close and kissed her. At first she resisted, trying to push him away, unwilling to give in in spite of the fact that she knew they were both to blame. But at last the pressure of his lips and his arms holding her close in the way she had missed so much were too much for her. She relaxed and responded. When they drew apart he looked down at her.

'Am I forgiven?'

She nodded.

'And can I take you home or are you going to insist on using that return ticket?'

She managed a smile. 'No. I'm glad you're here. I'll come with you.'

'We've got some talking to do on the way. Shall we make a start now?'

Before she could reply the kitchen door was flung open and Ada's voice rang out. 'Fleur Sylvester! Are you gonna keep that feller standin' on the doorstep all mornin', or are you gonna bring him in where we can all get a dekko at 'im?'

Fleur laughed. 'I think you'd better come and be introduced to Auntie Ada, Bobby and Jeff. If not I'm going to be in big trouble!'

An hour later they were on their way. It was a glorious morning and Fleur felt happiness and relief lighten her heart as they left London behind and headed north-east for Cambridgeshire and Elvemere.

'You're not seriously thinking of going back to London to live, are you?' Tom asked.

'Why not?'

He glanced at her. 'I don't think you really belong there any more.'

She sighed. 'The thing is, do I belong anywhere?'

'I think you do.'

She looked at him. 'Where, Tom?'

'Do I have to spell it out for you? Elvemere, of course – with me.'

'But you're leaving Elvemere too, aren't you?' she said accusingly. 'I hear you've applied for a job up North.'

'I only applied when I thought you and I were finished,' he said. 'I had an interview last week, but in the meantime my editor on the *Clarion* has offered me the job of deputy editor.'

'And—?'

'And I'd say that was largely up to you. If you stay then so will I.'

'I'll have to look for another job – and a home too. It'll mean starting over again. Back to square one.'

'There are worse places to start.' He looked at her. 'Look, you say that Arden Catering is for sale. Why don't you buy it? That way you'd be killing two birds with one stone and you'd be your own boss into the bargain.'

'*Buy* it!' She stared at him. 'Would you mind telling me with what?'

'Money. You get a loan – go and talk to the bank manager.'

Fleur shook her head. 'With the house and the van and all the other equipment it's going to cost a fortune. No one in their right mind would ever lend *me* that kind of money.'

'Why not? 'Course they would. That's what banks are for. I'd say you were a pretty good risk. You're young and healthy and you're good at the job.'

'But what would I do with a house that size?'

He shrugged. 'Take in lodgers. Or you could always marry me? It might come in handy if we ever got around to raising a family.'

'It wouldn't work, Tom.'

He pulled the car into a lay-by and stopped, turning to look at her. 'What wouldn't work? Marrying me or buying the business?'

'I meant buying the business, but since you ask . . .' She laughed but the expression on his face stopped the laughter in her throat. 'Tom? Oh, Tom – you're serious!'

'Of course I'm serious. Would I joke about a thing like that? I've never been more serious about anything in my life.'

For a long moment she was silent then she looked up and met his eyes. 'Auntie Ada was talking to me last night,' she said. 'She knew I was unhappy and asked me if it was the *race thing*, as she put it. If we were to marry, Tom, if we were to have that family you mentioned, our children might be – might take after their great-grandfather.'

His eyes held hers. 'They might be black, you mean?'

'Yes. We have to think about that, Tom. You're going to have to ask yourself how you feel about it.'

He reached out to touch her cheek. 'I want you, Fleur. No other girl – ever. I think I've known that since the first moment I set eyes on you. And anything you ever give me of yourself can only be wonderful as far as I'm concerned. Our children could never be anything but perfect.'

She swallowed hard at the lump in her throat. 'Oh, Tom,' she whispered.

'These last weeks without you have been hell. I felt I had no purpose, no direction any more. I don't intend to lose you again whatever happens.' He cupped her chin and looked into her eyes.

'So I think you'd better tell me right now how you feel about marrying me, because if the answer's no I'm going to take that job in York and get the hell out of it.'

Stunned, she looked into his eyes for a long moment. 'Tom! Oh, Tom, I don't know what to say. It's . . .'

He put his fingers across her lips. 'If you dare say, This is so sudden, I'll tip you out and drive off without you!' He pulled her close and kissed her hard. 'Tell you what,' he whispered, stroking her hair, 'come back to Park Row with me tonight and let me show you how much I need you.'

'Yes – yes, please.'

'I love you, Fleur.'

'I love you too.'

He kissed her again.

Julia's time was fully occupied. She was glad. Having no time to dwell on the happenings of the past few days was a distinct advantage. Since leaving Vernon and the home she had known for the past eighteen years she had felt disorientated. Eleanor had made her welcome, but her home was small and Julia felt it would be unfair to impose on her hospitality for too long. Besides, she felt the need to put down new roots. She had been married for so long that making major decisions and taking charge of her own life was uncharted territory and the business of finding herself a flat or a small house somewhere, furnishing it and making it her home was slightly daunting. She would need a job too – something to help augment her income. For although the money from her GPC shares would be adequate for her to live on, buying a house and furnishing it would take up a large chunk of it.

But quite apart from that she needed some kind of rewarding work with which to fill her time and occupy her mind. She already had a vague idea at the back of her mind. She had tried to telephone Fleur over the weekend and ask her advice. After all, it wasn't so long ago that she had started out on a totally new life herself. Julia had meant to talk to her after the opening of the refuge. They had had little time together and there was so much she wanted to say to her. It was only when she tried to reach her and heard the recorded message on the Arden Catering answerphone that she remembered Fleur's saying she would be away for a few days.

Having written and posted her letter of resignation to the Mayor via the Town Clerk Julia prepared herself for the coming council meeting with some trepidation. Everyone would have read about her public confession in the *Clarion* by now and although she was

380

quite prepared to be ostracised by her fellow councillors, she dreaded the ordeal. Only Eleanor remained firm and positive.

'I'm sure you underestimate them,' she said. 'Remember the old adage, "Let him who is without sin cast the first stone". There are very few on the council without sin, believe me, my dear! What happened to you was no crime, it was human error. One that is all too common. Besides, it happened so long ago. It would be a pretty bigoted person who would judge you by it after all these years.'

There was a meeting of the planning committee to follow the main council meeting scheduled for the same evening, and Julia saw from the agenda that Charlie's plans for Victoria Gardens were down for consideration. As she was no longer anything to do with the business, she wondered whether she should declare an interest or not. In the end she decided that she must. She had no wish to risk taking the blame should the plans be turned down.

As the council chamber filled she took her seat beside Eleanor, her heart quickening with nervousness. The Mayor arrived and took his seat as chairman and the Town Clerk tapped his gavel for silence.

The agenda that evening was not too lengthy. Julia calculated that her resignation would come up under the category of Any Other Business, right at the end of the meeting. Before that came the proposal that Councillor Mrs Eleanor Maitland should be next Town Mayor in place of Councillor Philip Forsyth. On a show of hands the motion was unanimously carried. Eleanor rose to her feet.

'I am honoured to be asked to be Town Mayor,' she said. 'And I would like to say thank you to all who voted for me. However, as you all know, as a widow I have no natural consort and shall need to appoint someone to support me in office.' She turned to glance at Julia. 'I have decided that there is no better person for the job than Councillor Mrs Grant. I know that Mrs Grant will only agree to do this with your approval, so I am asking you to support me in my choice.'

The Town Clerk asked for a show of hands from all in favour of the proposal and Julia held her breath, hardly daring to look as, one after another, all the hands in the council chamber rose. Then the Mayor himself got to his feet.

'In view of what Councillor Mrs Maitland has just proposed, I must tell you that I have received a letter from Councillor Mrs Grant offering her resignation from the council.' He glanced briefly across at Julia over the top of his spectacles and cleared his throat. 'I'm sure she will have no objection to my telling you that she gives her reason for resignation as the personal disclosure she recently

381

made on the opening of the Alexandra House Women's Refuge and its subsequent coverage in the press.' He removed his glasses and looked round at them. 'As this is a personal matter I have taken the liberty of speaking informally to my fellow councillors and everyone agrees with me that events that happened in the distant past can have no bearing at all on the good character of Councillor Mrs Grant as she is today. Therefore, I think I can safely say on behalf of all present that it is not the wish of this council to accept Councillor Grant's resignation on these grounds.' Smiling directly at Julia he concluded, 'So, Councillor Grant, we would ask you to reconsider your resignation and remain as the very valuable and hard-working councillor we have come to appreciate.' His eyes swept round the room. 'Can I please have your endorsement of that point?'

There was a unanimous show of hands, followed, to Julia's surprise and embarrassment, by applause.

Eleanor leaned over and patted her arm. 'What did I tell you?' she whispered. 'They're all on your side.'

When Charlie's plan came up for consideration at the planning meeting later, Julia declared an interest and left the council chamber. It was only after the meeting was over that she learned that the plan had been turned down. Philip Forsyth explained why to her when they were putting on their coats after the meeting.

'The whole place is likely to collapse. We discovered that for ourselves some months ago when the council had the idea of putting a compulsory purchase order on the street. Under the circumstances it's amazing the old places have stood up for so long. If Charlie Grant hadn't bought them the council would have had the job of demolishing them eventually.' He smiled wryly. 'Now he can have the pleasure himself.'

Julia's heart sank when she remembered the amount of money her father-in-law had invested in the property. 'Is there nothing that can be done with them?' she asked. 'Not even renovation?'

Philip shook his head. 'Afraid not. It'd be risky even replacing the windows. Looks like poor old Charlie has caught his toe badly this time!'

Chapter 18

Sadie paused in the hall outside the kitchen door. She knew that Fleur had spent the previous night with Tom and that they were washing up their breakfast dishes together. Normally she would have kept a discreet distance. Ever since the row she and Tom had had they'd been wary of each, each of them maintaining an excruciating politeness whenever they happened to meet. But this morning she needed to speak to him urgently and was glad that Fleur was there too. She opened the door and put her head round it.

'Hi, you two. I'd like a word, if you're not too rushed?'

Tom looked round. 'If you're about to give me notice . . .' he began defensively. Sadie held up her hand.

'No. Relax, it's nothing like that. Look, Tom, how about burying the hatchet – declaring a truce?'

'Okay with me if you say so.'

'I do. What I wanted to tell you was that I'll be moving on very shortly. I've just heard this morning, I've been offered a job on *Good Morning* magazine.'

'*Good Morning*, eh?' Tom whistled softly. 'Wow! Well done,' he said admiringly. 'How did you pull that off?'

Sadie had got the job on the strength of the piece she'd done about Julia Grant for the *Clarion*, but with Fleur there she could hardly say so. Instead she shrugged. 'Oh, you know, just my natural talent.'

Tom grinned. 'Plus all that reticence and modesty, I expect! From now on you'll be chasing the cream of society round Europe, looking for the latest scandal, eh? I hope they're paying you well for the privilege.'

Sadie grinned. 'Well enough, I'm happy to say.'

'Great! So – when do you start?'

'Next month, which brings me to what I wanted to speak to you about. It means I'll be putting the house on the market straight away, and in view of the fact that you two seem to be a fixture, I'd like to offer you first refusal. If I could count on a quick sale I'd let it go at below the market price.' She looked from one to the other with a grin. 'Well? I take it you two are together again on a permanent basis? I thought you might just be looking for something.'

Tom looked at Fleur. 'Well, we'll need a bit of time to think about it, Sadie, but thanks for the offer.'

'That's okay. I had a survey done before I bought it so you'd save money there too. It's the least I can do under the circumstances.' She glanced at Fleur. 'Maybe it'll go some way to making amends for – well, for what we fell out over, Tom.'

'Fell out? What's all this about?' Fleur asked.

Sadie smiled wryly. 'Oh, he hasn't told you then? Tom gave me one hell of a rocket over the article I wrote about your – er – about Mrs Grant.'

'But you're a journalist. You had every right to report the story.'

'That's not exactly how Tom saw it. At least, not at the time.'

'Let's forget about it,' he said quickly.

'Well, think about my offer and let me know by the weekend,' Sadie said. 'I don't want to rush you but time is short and I'll have to put the house on the market soon.'

As the door closed behind her Fleur said, 'You never told me you'd had a row with Sadie?'

Tom shrugged. 'It's water under the bridge. It made me angry, that's all, to think of her walking all over your life without even asking.'

'How did you know she didn't ask?'

He stared at her. 'You mean – she did?'

'She did try to confirm that what she'd found out was true. I suppose you could count that as a tip off. At least it enabled me to warn Julia and give her time to think what to do about it. If the whole thing had been sprung on her suddenly it could have been much worse.'

He sighed. 'And it did get us back together again, so it did some good. Put it down to my jumping in with both feet again.' He looked at her. 'So – what do you think? About buying the house, I mean?' He put his arms around her and drew her close. 'We were going to get married anyway. And you've already moved in – almost.'

'I know, but I think you're forgetting something.'

'What?'

'Suppose – just *suppose* – I were to get a loan to buy Arden Catering? Sally's house goes with it, remember?'

'Ah, I'd forgotten that.' Tom looked down at her. 'That means we can't take the next step until we know one way or the other.' He looked at her. 'It's make-up-your-mind time, Fleur. I think you should get along to the agent's right away and see what the asking price is.'

They went together, Fleur making a detour down the High Street on her way to catch the bus. They stood hand in hand in front of the window of Matthew's Estate Agents and looked at the properties for sale. Arden Catering was in the business section. There was a photograph of the house, but to Fleur's surprise and dismay there was a SOLD strip pasted across it. She looked at Tom.

'How can it be sold without my knowing?' she said. 'No one has been to view, or asked to see the books or anything.'

Tom shrugged. 'Maybe just an estate agent's trick to make people keener.'

'Why would they do a thing like that?'

Seeing her disappointment, he slipped an arm round her and hugged her close. 'Oh, I'm sorry, love. I know how much it meant to you. But you'll soon find another job.'

'Oh, yes? In a factory canteen maybe, or as a school dinner lady,' she said bitterly. 'Arden's is the only catering firm for miles around.' She was dismayed to discover that she was much more upset at losing the chance than she'd envisaged.

'At least we still have the option on Sadie's house,' he said, giving her a reassuring squeeze. 'Look, darling, I'll have to go now or I'll be late for work. Give me a ring at lunchtime and we'll talk, yes?'

'Yes. Yes, okay,' she said absently. After he'd gone she stood for a long time staring at the photograph with its SOLD sign, wondering how on earth it could have been sold without her knowledge. At last she made up her mind. Walking into the shop, she asked to see one of the sales staff.

'I was interested in making an offer for Arden Catering,' she said boldly. 'As a matter of fact I'm managing it at the moment for the owner. I see from the window that it seems to be sold, but as I'm the one in charge at the moment I thought there might be some mistake?'

'I see. No, there's no mistake,' the young man told her. 'It's a pity you didn't make an offer sooner. I had acceptance of the offer from the owner just before closing yesterday afternoon.'

'From Mr Peter Arden, you mean?'

'That's right. The buyer is eager to exchange contracts as soon as possible and that suits Mr Arden too. We hope to close the deal very quickly, all things being equal.'

Fleur was silent. Peter hadn't even contacted her to say he'd had an offer, let alone that he was going ahead with the sale. 'Who – who has bought it?' asked Fleur.

He shook his head, smiling apologetically. 'I'm sorry. I'm afraid I can't tell you that. We have to observe discretion about these things.'

'Yes, of course. I only thought...' Embarrassed, she backed towards the door. 'Well, if the sale should fall through for any reason, I'd be glad if you'd let me know.'

'It's very doubtful, but I will of course. And your name?'

'Sylvester. Fleur Sylvester. And for the moment you can contact me at Arden Catering.'

'Certainly, Miss Sylvester. Good morning.'

Fleur's shoulders drooped as she walked down the street. It had all been a crazy dream anyway. Tom had almost persuaded her to believe that she might have been granted a loan to buy the business. Now she'd never know.

The telephone was ringing when she let herself in. Without pausing to take off her coat she snatched up the receiver. 'Good morning, Arden Catering,' she said breathlessly. 'Can I help you?'

'Good morning, Miss Sylvester, this is Eleanor Maitland. Councillor Maitland. I'm ringing to ask if you're booked for Friday, May the twenty-eighth.'

'Just a moment.' Fleur quickly found the appointments diary and thumbed through to the relevant week. 'Yes, that date seems to be vacant at the moment, Mrs Maitland,' she said.

'Oh, good. I'm so glad. I'd like to book a buffet luncheon for my Mayor-Making reception,' Eleanor said. 'I thought that the lunch you provided for the opening of the women's refuge was excellent and I'd like something similar. It will be at the Town Hall, of course. Catering for about two hundred guests. What can you suggest?'

'We have several menus,' Fleur said. 'I think the best thing would be for me to come round and show them to you.'

'Well, if you could do that I'd appreciate it.' Eleanor gave her the address and Fleur arranged to go round that evening.

She replaced the receiver with a sigh. A lunch for the Mayor's reception at the Town Hall would be a feather in her cap. But, ironically, it looked as though it would most probably be the last job she ever did for Arden Catering.

Vernon was already tired of living alone. The house seemed so dreary and empty and he hated coming home to the prospect of making his own dinner and spending the evening alone. His mother, appalled and indignant that Julia should have walked out and left him, insisted on sending her own cleaning woman round for an hour each day to tidy up and make his bed. Vernon hated the thought of a strange woman invading his private space, poking her nose into his cupboards and drawers when he wasn't there, touching his clothes.

Once Julia had left he'd envisaged Joanna sharing his home with him but he hadn't heard from her since she had left for the States. She must be due back any day now but she hadn't been in touch. Not even so much as a postcard from her. He missed her. As far as he was concerned she couldn't come back soon enough.

Most evenings after work he either ate out or went round to Queen's Lodge to eat with his parents, but his mother's constant carping about Julia's deceitfulness and the shocking transgression she had recently disclosed was beginning to grate on his already raw nerves.

This evening was to be no exception. Vernon had arrived early, going on ahead of his father who had driven into town to see if he could gather any information about the result of that evening's planning meeting. Louise began almost before Vernon had time to take off his coat.

'There was always something about her I couldn't fathom, you know,' she said as she poured him a sherry. 'A slyness. Never could get to the bottom of her.'

'You mean, she wouldn't tell you all her business?' Vernon said, irritably.

Louise went on as though she hadn't heard him. 'And of course she always acted as though she thought herself a cut above us Grants. It just shows, doesn't it? No one in *my* family, or your father's either, ever went off the rails like that. Or lived a lie about it like she has. Just fancy – she had that child and never told a soul about it. Not even her poor mother. The deceit of it! If you ask me a woman who can do that is capable of anything!'

Vernon was relieved to hear the front door slam, heralding his father's arrival. A moment later Charlie came into the room and went straight to the drinks cabinet, pouring himself an enormous whisky.

'Oh, Charlie, really!' Louise admonished. 'You won't want your dinner, drinking all that whisky. I've made your favourite too. I've been . . .'

'Don't *start!*' Charlie shouted, his face red. 'I can't cope with any more tonight.' He looked up at Vernon with bloodshot eyes as he slumped into a chair. 'The bastards have scuppered us!'

387

Louise and Vernon both stared at him. 'The plans?' Vernon ventured. 'They've turned them down?'

'I can't understand it. They were going to buy Victoria Gardens and do what I planned to do. They must have known about the chalkpit workings all along. Why couldn't one of the devious buggers have had the decency to warn me?'

'Maybe if you'd asked . . .' Vernon ventured, but Charlie wasn't listening.

'They won't even let us restore the properties and recoup our money.' He looked up at his son despairingly. 'What the bloody hell are we going to do?'

'Well, I always said Victoria Gardens was a white elephant,' Vernon said. 'It's a good job we're mortgaging both houses. At least we can keep our heads above water for the time being. There will have to be some cut-backs. First we'll have to lay off some of our workforce, then tough it out and hope we can shift the Meadowlands houses.'

Louise spun round, her face colouring as she looked from one to the other, 'Mortgaging the houses! What houses?'

Charlie shot Vernon a savage look. 'Ours, love, Vernon's and Queen's Lodge,' he said, trying to sound nonchalant. 'We've had to, Lou. There was nothing else for it. I was going to tell you . . .'

'Going to *tell* me!' Louise's face was red. 'I think you must mean *ask* me! It was my money bought this house, Charlie Grant, even if it is in both our names. I think I was due a bit of consideration. This is *my* home, remember?'

'It can't be helped,' Charlie said. 'It's not a decision I took lightly. We've hit a rough patch and we're strapped for cash. These things happen in the best of businesses. It's only a bit of a blip.'

'*Bit of a blip*! I've heard that one before somewhere!' Louise stood looking at her husband and son, her arms folded. 'It's all that woman's doing,' she announced.

Vernon looked up. 'Julia?'

'No! Not Julia – Joanna Hanson,' she said. 'Ever since she joined the firm things have started to go down the pan. And where is she now, I ask you?' She shook her head as both men looked blank. 'She's gone, that's what. Buggered off. Left the sinking ship like the rat she is! You'll be lucky to see her again! She's taken both of you for the ride of your lives and you still can't see it!' She turned on Vernon. 'I told you to watch your step with her, didn't I? It was only down to me that she didn't land you in a right old stew years ago. Now what are you left with? A wife and daughter who've both left you and a mortgaged house!' She blew out her breath in an

388

explosive snort. '*Sex!*' she said scathingly. 'That's what it all comes down to in the end. You men are as weak as kittens when it comes to sex. One flash of a stocking top or a bit of cleavage and you're putty in any tart's hands. You make me bloody *sick*, the lot of you!'

She stormed out of the room, banging the door so hard behind her that the silver on the sideboard tinkled.

Charlie looked at his son. 'She'll calm down,' he said unconvincingly. 'I suppose I should've told her about the mortgage. Didn't want to worry her. You know how it is.'

Vernon sighed. 'Joanna – you don't happen to know when she's coming back?'

Charlie shrugged. 'Soon, I suppose. No reason to think different. Nothing in what your mother said. I mean, why would she clear out when she's got money tied up in the firm?'

'No. Of course not. Jo wouldn't do a thing like that.' Vernon looked at his father. 'I haven't heard from her since she left. Have you?'

'No.' Charlie cleared his throat. 'What did your mother mean about it was down to her that Joanna didn't land you in a right old stew years ago?'

'Nothing.' Vernon avoided his father's eyes. 'You know Ma. It was when Jo and I were in our teens. She didn't approve of our going out together.'

Charlie nodded. Heaving himself out of his chair, he said with a resigned sigh, 'Oh, well, I suppose I'd better try and make my peace with her or we'll get no dinner this side of breakfast!'

Fleur hadn't been able to get Tom on the phone at lunchtime. He'd been out on an assignment. She went round to Park Row after work, but arrived before him. She was just scribbling a note to leave for him when Charlotte appeared.

'Hi, Fleur. I saw you arrive and thought we might have a word.'

'Of course. Come in.'

'I take it you and Tom have made it up? I mean – well, I know you've been spending quite a lot of time here.'

Fleur smiled. 'You could say that.'

'I'm glad. I know how fed up you were. I've been hoping to see you.' She paused, tucking a stray strand of hair behind her ear. 'Look, Fleur, I've been trying to pluck up the courage to come and see you,' she said. 'You can probably guess how I felt when I found out that you and I were actually half-sisters.'

'I was afraid it might have been a shock. That's why I haven't been in touch. I wanted to leave it up to you.'

389

Charlotte looked surprised. 'It wasn't a shock. A surprise. A nice one. I thought you hadn't been to see me because you were mad at us all.' She smiled shyly. 'I've always wanted a sister and if I'd been able to choose, I'd have chosen someone just like you.'

'That's sweet, Charlotte. Thanks.'

'I mean it.' The younger girl bit her lip. 'I take it you already knew?'

'Yes. Before my grandmother died she gave me your grandparents' address and asked me to promise to come and find Julia. I kept my promise but I never meant to do anything to disrupt your lives.'

'You haven't.' Charlotte shook her head. 'To think you knew all along and never let on. I'm sure if it had been me I wouldn't have been able to keep quiet about it.' She bit her lip. 'Look, you probably haven't heard – Mum and Dad aren't living together any more. They're getting a divorce.'

Fleur nodded. 'I knew it was on the cards, but I didn't know Julia had actually left. Where is she? I feel I should go and see her.'

'She's staying with Mrs Maitland at the moment. I daresay she'd like to see you if you felt like it. She's looking for somewhere to live and says she's going to try and find a job,' Charlotte told her. 'It's not going to be easy for her after all these years. An enormous change. As far as I know she's never actually been out to work.'

'You'll have to try and support her as much as you can,' Fleur said. 'I'd like to help too – if that's what she wants, of course.'

'I thought I might go and live with her when she gets a new place,' Charlotte said. 'It might be nice, just Mum and me.' She looked at Fleur tentatively. 'I daresay you could come too if – well, you know.'

Fleur smiled. 'As a matter of fact, Tom and I are thinking of getting married.'

'Oh, Fleur! That's wonderful!' Charlotte hugged her warmly. 'If you want a bridesmaid, can I put my name down?'

'I daresay we'll be having something very simple,' she said. 'We're going to need all our money. Sadie's leaving, you see, and we might be buying this house from her. I've got to start looking for another job too. Tom wanted me to try and get a bank loan and buy Arden Catering but someone has beaten me to it.'

'Oh. That's a shame.'

'Yes, it is,' Fleur sighed. 'Arden Catering is a good business. Councillor Mrs Maitland rang today and booked me to do the lunch for the Mayor's reception.'

'That's great!' Charlotte's face lit up. 'Did you know that Mum is going to be Mayoress to her Mayor? I'll be taking time off to go along,' she said. 'Wouldn't miss that for anything. Auntie Kath and James are invited too. If Dad doesn't like it he can sack me. In fact, I hope he does!' She looked at Fleur. 'I'm sorry you didn't get the business, though.'

'Oh, well, it was probably a mad idea. I don't suppose anyone would have lent me the money anyway.'

When Tom arrived home he found Fleur in the kitchen preparing a meal.

'Sorry I couldn't ring you back, darling,' he said. 'I've been out all day. Any more news?'

'I went into the agent's after you'd gone. Sounds as though the sale is going through quite quickly. I've definitely lost it, Tom.'

'Poor love.' He kissed her. 'Never mind. Something else will turn up. You'll see.'

'I could have made a success of it, I know I could,' she told him. 'I was even booked today to do the lunch for the Mayor's reception. Why couldn't Peter at least have let me know?'

'Consideration is hardly his strong suit, is it? But having said that, he couldn't have known you wanted to make an offer yourself, could he?' He put his arms round her. 'Listen, I went to see the editor today. I accepted the job of deputy editor and start next month. It means a rise in salary. I saw Sadie at lunchtime and asked her what her lowest figure for the house was. And – guess what? I've worked it out and we could just about afford it.' He kissed her. 'So what do you say? Are we on?'

'Oh, Tom!' She slipped her arms around his neck. 'I want it to be something we do together. I want to make my contribution too. And I will too – when I get another job . . .'

'To begin with, what about accepting the job of being Mrs Markham?'

'Are you sure? We don't really have to rush. We're fine as we are.'

'Speak for yourself,' he said, giving her a little shake. 'I want to put a ring on your finger so that everyone can see you're mine. Besides . . .'

'Go on, besides what?' A wicked glint had come into his eyes and Fleur half guessed what was coming.

'Besides, you're not a bad cook. And you are quite good at keeping the place nice and clean. I never was much of a hand with a duster.'

'*Tom Markham*! For that you can get the rest of the meal by yourself!'

He grasped both her flailing arms and held her quite still. 'Who cares about the meal?' he said, looking deep into her eyes. 'I can think of much more interesting things we can do to celebrate.'

'*Joanna!*' Vernon stopped short as he walked into the office and saw her sitting at her desk. 'I'd no idea you were back. Why didn't you let me know?'

'It was very late last night when I got in,' she told him coolly. 'The small hours of this morning actually.'

'You must be jet-lagged. You should have stayed in bed this morning. Can I get you some coffee?' He fussed around her like a mother hen and Joanna shook her head impatiently.

'I'm fine, thank you, Vernon. I don't need anything and I don't feel sleepy at all. I daresay it'll hit me later. If it does I'll go home.'

'Dad is going to be pleased to see you,' he said, perching on a corner of her desk. 'Though the news isn't good. I'm afraid the plans for Victoria Gardens were turned down at the planning meeting last week.'

'Really? That's too bad.'

'Too bad? It's disastrous! I think we should have a meeting as soon as possible so we can work out a plan of action.'

'I agree. Suppose we schedule it for tomorrow morning?'

Vernon was slightly taken aback by her eagerness. 'Oh – well, of course. If you're sure you're going to be up to it that soon?'

'I'll be up to it. The sooner the better.'

'Right – if you say so.' He glanced over his shoulder to make sure they weren't overheard. 'Julia has finally left,' he said. 'If you wanted to you could move in with me – right away.'

'I don't think so, Vernon,' she said. 'Not right now.'

'Well, no. Maybe it wouldn't look too good at this particular moment in time,' he said. 'Would you like me to move in with you?'

'No, Vernon.'

'I've missed you, Jo,' he said, covering her hand with his. 'Shall we have lunch together? I could book us a table at the Fairwoods – and a room for afterwards if you . . .'

'*No, Vernon!*' She looked up at him, eyes glinting with something he hadn't seen before. The shock caused him to take an involuntary step backwards.

'Oh. Right then. I expect you'll need a couple of days to catch up. Well – I'll leave you to get on with it then.'

All morning he sat in his office unable to keep his mind on work.

Through the glass panel of his door he could see Joanna, her head bent in concentration. She made several telephone calls, her voice lowered and face earnest. He had the distinctly uncomfortable feeling that she was planning something. And that, whatever it was, he did not figure in it.

When Louise heard that there was to be a directors' meeting the following morning she insisted on attending.

'It's my right,' she told her husband and son. 'And if you ask me, this is something I should have done a long time ago. Maybe we wouldn't be in the mess we're in now if I'd been allowed to have my say.'

The meeting had been arranged for ten-thirty and she arrived at twenty past, wearing her dark suit and hardly any jewellery. Today she was determined to be taken seriously. After all, it had been her money that had started the company. She was responsible for the birth of GPC, and no mother gave up her child without a fight – with the possible exception of Julia, she reminded herself wryly.

Charlie's middle-aged secretary, Phyllis, greeted her warmly. 'Good morning, Mrs Grant. They're almost ready. Can I get you a coffee while you're waiting?'

'No, thank you.' Louise's face was a mask of determination as she settled herself stolidly on a chair by the door.

Ten minutes later, after a buzz on the office intercom, Phyllis ushered her into the boardroom where she took a seat beside Charlie. Her eyes were steely with the light of battle as she eyed Joanna across the table. Joanna herself looked calm and in control.

Examining the current situation they all agreed that at present things looked bleak for the firm. The Meadowlands Estate remained unfinished, with two houses still incomplete, and insufficient funds to continue building to the required specifications. Many of the buyers who had reserved houses had now withdrawn and the only two who had not were still trying to sell their present properties in a failing market.

'Then there is the problem with the Victoria Gardens project,' Charlie said reluctantly. 'Of course it's not the end of the road. We could always re-think our plans and present them again.'

'What could possibly be done with the place when there are chalkpit workings running underneath?' Joanna asked. 'Even if we demolished the houses there is no way we could ever rebuild on the site.'

'No. Well, um . . .' Charlie cleared his throat noisily. 'I thought perhaps an ornamental garden?' he suggested. 'For the public. We'd

393

build it and get the council to take it over – maintain it and so on. You know, children's corner with animals and birds, a paddling pool . . .'

'And have the kiddies vanish down a gaping hole some sunny afternoon?' Joanna challenged. 'Realistically, I can't see us even getting planning permission for that, can you? And I wouldn't put money on the prospect of persuading the council to take it over even if they sanctioned it.'

'So what would *your* proposal be, Mrs Hanson?' Louise put in. 'You're quick enough to pour cold water on everything. How about letting us hear your ideas.'

'My suggestion is that we write it off. Chalk it up to experience, if you'll forgive the pun.'

Vernon gave a nervous laugh which his mother silenced with a searing look.

'A million quids' worth of experience?' she cried. 'Hardly a matter to joke about!'

Joanna shrugged. 'Sometimes we have to pay a high price for our little mistakes.'

Louise puffed herself up like a balloon, her face turning puce. 'A high-priced little mistake, was it? More like a ruinous flaming *catastrophe*, if you ask me! Do you realise that us Grants – Charlie, Vernie and me – are in danger of losing our homes over this *little mistake*, as you call it?'

'I realise that and I'm sorry,' Joanna said, unmoved. 'However, I do have a suggestion to make, if you'll allow me?'

The other three waited with bated breath, watching as she scribbled some notes on her pad. At last she looked up at them. 'I have to admit to you that I did see this blow coming, which is why I went over to the States. I have brought someone back with me who would be interested in a joint takeover of GPC. If you are all in agreement I will personally underwrite the outstanding debts.' She looked at Louise. 'That would mean, of course, that you would not lose your home, Mrs Grant, and I would like to suggest that Charlie take this opportunity to retire so that you can enjoy it together.'

She paused while they all digested her recommendation. 'My partner and I would take over as joint managing directors.'

'In other words, you're offering to buy us out?' Vernon said.

Joanna turned to look at him. 'In effect, yes, although of course as I am already the major shareholder – and the only solvent one – no money will actually change hands.'

Three stunned faces stared speechlessly at her. Then Louise said, 'Would this mean that Queen's Lodge will belong to you?'

'If you want to look at it that way, yes,' Joanna said. 'But you'll be paying me back instead of the bank. I'll charge you a lower rate of interest, which has to be of benefit to you. Don't you agree?'

Vernon said, 'May I ask where I stand in all of this? Do I still have a job?'

She turned to him. 'If you want to stay on, of course, Vernon.'

'In what capacity?'

'I think we could offer you the position of sales manager or something of that kind.'

'Sales manager?' He stared at her. '*Sales manager* when I was joint MD with Dad?'

Joanna shrugged. 'Things alter, Vernon,' she told him coolly. 'As I said before, there is often a high price to pay for mistakes.'

'But it was you who egged Dad on to buy Victoria Gardens!' he said, his colour deepening.

'You voted for it too,' she reminded him. 'As I remember, you even asked me to go along and persuade your wife to vote with us when she had voiced her dissent. I agree that we all made the same mistake. All I'm doing is offering to get you out of the difficult situation you find yourselves in.'

Charlie, who had been sitting slumped dejectedly in his chair, suddenly sat up and asked, 'Who might this new partner of yours be when he's at home? Are we allowed to know?'

'Of course you are.' Joanna rose from her seat. 'His name is Vince Kendrick and, unless I'm very much mistaken, he'll have arrived in the building by now. With your permission I'd like to ask him to come in and meet you all.'

In response to their dazed affirmation she went to the door and slipped out. A moment later she reappeared accompanied by a tall young man with dark hair and horn-rimmed glasses, whom she led forward.

'I would like to introduce you all to Mr Vince Kendrick. Vince – Mr and Mrs Grant – Louise and Charlie. And this is Vernon, their son.' The young man shook hands gravely with each of them in turn.

'Happy to meet you all,' he said pleasantly. 'Mom has told me a lot about the company and all of you.'

Three pairs of shocked eyes opened wide as Joanna smiled coolly at them. 'Yes, it's true. Vince is my son,' she announced triumphantly. 'And I need hardly tell you that this is a very proud day for me. Having my son as my business partner is something of a dream come true, as I'm sure you will all understand.'

She pulled out a chair at the boardroom table for Vince. 'Sit down, darling. We have a lot to discuss.'

Joanna was in the cloakroom freshening up after the meeting when the door opened and Louise came in. She stood with her back against the door, face pink with suppressed fury and eyes glinting stonily.

'You *knew*, didn't you?' she demanded.

Joanna did not turn round. Putting the top back on her lipstick she glanced up at Louise through the mirror. 'I'm sorry – knew what?'

'You know what I'm talking about. Victoria Gardens. You knew it would finish us. I bet you even had your own searches done on the quiet, you devious bitch. You knew about the chalkpit and everything. You set this whole thing up. Admit it!'

Joanna's eyes narrowed. 'I don't think you'd better say any more in your present frame of mind, Mrs Grant,' she warned. 'You're on dangerous ground and unless you have positive proof of your allegations . . .'

'And another thing: that Vince of yours – he's our Vernon's boy, isn't he?'

The silence that hung in the air between them was almost tangible. Joanna broke it. 'That's nonsense,' she said, turning to face Louise. 'And you know it.'

'I know nothing of the sort,' she said. 'He's the living spit of our Vernie at that age – same build, same colouring. He's the right age too. You said you were pregnant before you went off and wed that Yank.'

'But you always knew I was lying, didn't you?' Joanna said carefully. 'You left me in no doubt about that. And even if I wasn't lying, don't you remember making me promise to have an abortion? Why, you even gave me the money for it. So how can you possibly claim that Vince is your grandson?'

At the word 'grandson' Louise blanched. 'He *is*. I know he is,' she insisted. 'There has to be some way of proving it. His birth certificate . . .'

'It has his father's name on it,' Joanna said. 'Jim Kendrick. My first husband.'

'The date . . . a blood test . . .' Louise blustered.

'Don't be ridiculous!' Joanna laughed. 'On what grounds could you possibly demand a blood test? Vince is twenty-one. He's a man in his own right. You'd have to get him to agree and I can tell you now that he wouldn't. What you're suggesting is bizarre in the extreme. You're clutching at straws, Mrs Grant.' She took a step towards Louise. 'You wanted me out of your lives all those years ago. Well, I got out. And now I'm getting out again. You should be thanking me for saving your husband's face; for saving your home for you. I could always change my mind, you know. Do you want the disgrace of bankruptcy? Do you want to move out of Queen's Lodge and into a council flat?' she added brutally.

Louise flinched, her plump face sagging in defeat. She was beaten and she knew it. Charlie and she had always wanted a grandson to inherit the business he had worked so hard to build. She had never been more convinced of anything than that Joanna's son was that grandson. But there was no business any more. It was all gone. Even their home wasn't truly theirs now. And there wasn't a single thing she could do about it.

Julia was preparing a meal for herself and Eleanor when the front doorbell rang. She dried her hands and went to answer it. To her surprise Vernon stood on the doorstep.

'Julia, I wondered – could we have a word?'

She held the door open reluctantly. 'You'd better come in. Eleanor is out at a committee meeting and I'm preparing a meal so if you don't mind coming through to the kitchen?'

'No, of course not. Anywhere.' He followed her through to the tiny kitchen at the back of the house and she pulled out a chair for him. 'I'd offer you a drink, but . . .'

'No.' He shook his head. 'No, it's all right.' He ignored the chair and stood awkwardly in the middle of the floor, looking at her.

'So – what can I do for you, Vernon?' she asked. 'Is it about the divorce? I told you, I won't contest . . .'

'No. Nothing to do with that. I wanted you to hear the news first-hand – before it has the chance to be garbled and exaggerated.'

'What news?'

'GPC has been taken over,' he said. 'It was either that or voluntary liquidation.'

She nodded, unsurprised. 'I see.'

'It's a bit worse than you might have thought. Dad had already mortgaged both our homes, so the house isn't mine any more. It will obviously affect any settlement I might be required to pay you.'

'That doesn't matter.'

'Both houses now belong to the new owner.'

'And that is?'

He swallowed painfully. 'Joanna Hanson.'

'I see.'

'Joanna – and her son.'

Julia's eyes widened. 'Her *son*?'

'Yes. He came back with her from the States. It was a surprise to us too. His name is Vince Kendrick, her first husband's child. Apparently his father left him pretty well provided for, so with that and Joanna's share of her second husband's real-estate business they're well able to pick up GPC's debts.' He cleared his throat. 'I don't figure in the new scheme of things at all. At least not in any kind of executive capacity.'

'I'm sorry to hear this, Vernon,' she said. 'I feel partly responsible. If Dad hadn't sold her our shares . . .'

He shook his head. 'It would have happened anyway. Looking back, I think this was always in her mind.' He smiled wryly. 'It might amuse you to know that she's offered me the job of sales manager.'

Julia tried to hide her shock. 'But I thought – thought that you and she were . . .'

'Apparently not. Not now that she's got what she wanted. I have the uncomfortable feeling that we've all been taken for a ride, but that's something none of us wants to face. I've decided to get out, Julia. I'll find a job down south somewhere.' He took a step towards her and reached out to touch her shoulder. 'I suppose you wouldn't consider – coming with me? We could forget about divorce – put the past behind us and start again. I wouldn't hold what you did, this public scandal thing, against you. We could forget it all and . . .'

'No, Vernon!' She heard her own voice, firm and strong. 'My big mistake was to try and forget it. I regret that more than anything I've ever done. Now I mean to acknowledge Fleur and try to make up for what I did.'

'Well, all right. You can still do that.'

'No, I can't. Even if I wanted to come back to you, I have commitments here, people I can't let down. For one thing I've promised to support Eleanor for the coming year; then there's Charlotte to consider. But in any case you know as well as I do that our marriage has been over for a long time. We really should have parted years ago. Now I think we should make a new start, each of us, while there's still time.'

He nodded his agreement. 'I thought you'd probably say that.' He shrugged. 'It was worth a try, though. You can't blame me for trying.' He gave her a crooked smile. 'It was good once though, wasn't it? At the beginning.'

Julia was silent, remembering only the numberless affairs she had turned a blind eye to, the hurt and the feeling of rejection that had lowered her self-esteem. The put-downs and humiliations he had subjected her to in order to boost his own ego. The past few weeks had been an eye opener. She was a whole, complete person now; someone who counted. She was discovering more about herself every day. It was like being reborn. But even now it wasn't in her to kick him when he was down.

'Yes,' she said quietly. 'It was good once – for a little while. Now it's over.'

'I'll be moving out of the house,' he said. 'I daresay Joanna and her son might move in. But in any event I'll try to get the furniture for you. You'd like it, I expect.'

'Thank you. Yes, I would.' She went with him to the door and watched him drive away, slightly surprised at the lack of regret she felt; the utter absence of remorse or pity. A chapter of her life was officially closed and new and exciting horizons were opening up for her.

On the morning of the Mayor-Making ceremony Fleur was up bright and early. She had arranged to pick up her regular band of helpers on her way to the Town Hall. The waiters she had hired from the agency would be arriving later. Charlotte was going along with her too at her own suggestion.

'If I come and help you, you'll be able to finish in time to watch the ceremony,' she said. 'It would be a pity for you to miss all the excitement.'

Cleaners were still busy when they arrived. As they carried in their boxes they could hear the sound of hoovering coming from the council chamber and the Mayor's parlour.

'Is Julia nervous?' Fleur asked.

Charlotte nodded. 'As the proverbial kitten! Wait till you see her outfit though. If that doesn't give her confidence, nothing will.'

They worked hard for the two hours that followed, spreading the long buffet tables with snowy cloths, then setting out the array of tempting dishes. The florist arrived with the table arrangements: blooms in delicate pastel shades, iris and delicate freesias, arranged simply in gilded baskets, their sweet perfume filling the air. The wine merchant came next and Fleur set Charlotte to work uncorking the red wine to allow it to 'breathe' whilst she packed the champagne and white wine in ice buckets to chill.

At half-past eleven the main protagonists began to arrive. First the Town Constable who was responsible for seeing that all procedures were carried out correctly. He bustled round making sure that the cleaners had done their work efficiently and that programmes were placed on every seat then disappeared into the Mayor's parlour to attend to the civic wardrobe which was also his responsibility. Then the Town Clerk arrived, closely followed by the outgoing Mayor and Mayoress, who would begin the ceremony robed and wearing their chains of office. They went straight through to the Mayor's parlour to change.

'Isn't it exciting?' Fleur whispered to Charlotte. The other girl nodded.

'Yes, but not half as exciting as my news. I leave CPC at the end of this week! Joanna the Hun has taken over the firm so I don't have to stay any more. I'm working full-time for Auntie Kath as from a week next Monday!'

'That's good news for you, Charlotte. But I imagine it isn't so good for your family.'

She shrugged. 'Looks like it lets them off the hook,' she said. 'No one ever tells me anything though from what I gather Granddad made a bad mistake money-wise and Joanna's buying him out, debts and all. She's even brought her son over from America to go in with her.' She pulled a face. 'Vince, his name is. *Vince!* I ask you! He looks a bit of a wally to me, but what do I care? I'm well out of it.'

Fleur laughed. 'Well, I'm glad it's worked out for you.'

When Fleur was satisfied that the tables were perfect and everything was ready she and Charlotte went along to the council chamber where guests were already beginning to take their seats. Standing by the door Charlotte pointed out her grandparents, May and Harry Philips, who had already taken their places. Next to them sat Kathleen Grant. 'They're all dying to meet you,' she said. 'Mrs Maitland asked me to tell you that she's had this seat reserved for you,' she said, pointing to a chair close to the door, 'so that you can slip out before everyone else at the end of the ceremony. My seat is over there with James, next to Auntie Kath. I'd better go down to the front entrance now. I said I'd wait for him there.'

When Charlotte had gone Fleur sat looking around her with interest. She had never been inside the council chamber before and she was impressed by the huge oak-panelled room with its circular benches of polished wood and leather. The walls were hung with portraits of past Mayors looking suitably dignified in their official scarlet robes. Charlotte reappeared after a few minutes with a young man Fleur assumed was James, but there was no time for introductions. As they took their seats the ancient clock in the tower above them struck twelve.

A hush settled over the assembly and a moment later the doors

400

to the Mayor's parlour opened and everyone stood as the procession entered. First the Town Constable, resplendent in his dark blue livery, carrying the mace, then the Mayor and his Mayoress, followed by the black-gowned Town Clerk. The councillors and aldermen followed, walking in pairs to take their seats on the council benches.

The Mayor made his outgoing speech after which the incoming Mayor was proposed and seconded and officially adopted by the council. Fleur listened as Councillor Eleanor Maitland's qualifications and achievements were read out by a senior alderman, followed by an appreciation of her character as a worthy citizen of Elvemere. Then the Mayor and his Mayoress were escorted back to the Mayor's parlour to pass over their robes and chains of office to the incoming Mayor and Mayoress. Fleur knew that Sadie would already be there with her camera to photograph this unseen part of the ceremony for the *Clarion*.

When they re-emerged it was Eleanor who wore the scarlet robe, white frothy jabot and heavy gold chain. It suited her. Her stout figure carried it with dignity. Fleur watched as she stepped proudly up on to the dias followed by Julia who looked beautiful in a cream wool suit, the slender chain of office gleaming against the pale material. To complete her outfit she wore a pale lemon straw hat trimmed with a single cream rose.

Eleanor made a good maiden speech, spiced with her characteristic pithy wit. It was clear that she was enjoying every minute, her eyes twinkling with delight as she looked around at the distinguished assembly.

Fleur seized the opportunity of the applause at the end to slip from her seat and cross the hall into the room where the reception was being held. Swiftly she checked everything, satisfying herself that nothing had been left undone. The wines were at the perfect temperature, the bread rolls were warm and fragrant and her helpers stood by, ready to serve and replenish the tables. The hired waiters looked immaculate as they waited with trays of wine to welcome the guests. The pianist was seated at the grand piano by the fireplace softly running through the music Eleanor had chosen. The doors were opened and guests began to crowd into the room. The social part of the morning had begun.

During lunch Fleur circulated among the guests, keeping her eye open for empty glasses and plates. She had seen Tom arrive, wearing his best suit, to report on the reception, but she had been too busy to speak to him.

Eventually Julia tracked her down. 'Eleanor wanted me to tell you how pleased she is with everything,' she said. 'It's all been so well organised, Fleur. And the food is delicious.'

'Thank you. I'm glad she's pleased,' Fleur said. 'I enjoyed watching the ceremony very much. It was fascinating. And you look lovely,' she added shyly.

Julia smiled. 'Thank you, Fleur. I can't tell you how glad I am that you decided not to leave Elvemere after all. Charlotte tells me you're engaged to the young man from the local paper?'

'Yes. I don't know when we'll be getting married though. I'll have to find a job first. I'd been hoping to get a loan and make an offer for Arden Catering but someone got there before me.'

Julia took her arm and drew her to one side. 'I've been meaning to speak to you about that, Fleur. I've bought Arden Catering.'

Fleur stared at her. '*You* have?'

'Yes. No one else knows yet. I wanted you to be the first. I needed a home now that Vernon and I have parted. I wanted somewhere large enough to have Charlotte with me, if she wants to come, and I'll also need to earn a living of course. I'd always liked Sally's house and when I saw that it was for sale along with the business it seemed the ideal solution. I'm sure I shall be very happy there.'

'Oh – yes. I'm sure you will,' Fleur said faintly.

'But I haven't a clue about the catering business,' Julia went on. 'And with this coming year promising to be so hectic with my work as Eleanor's Mayoress, I can't see that I'll have much chance of getting to learn it. Which is why I was hoping to persuade you to run the business for me.'

'*Me?*'

Julia laughed. 'Well, who better? After all, Sally herself taught you. I know you're popular with the clientele and you've certainly proved today that you're more than equal to the job.'

'Oh!' Fleur's heart was beating fast. 'I – I don't know what to say.'

'Do you want to think about it before deciding?' Julia asked.

Fleur shook her head. 'Oh, no! I'd love to stay on and run the business for you!'

'It will be permanent, of course,' Julia said. 'We'll talk about salary later but the fact that you'll be taking full responsibility will mean you will be paid more than you were as an assistant.' She smiled. 'And of course you're going to have to teach me a bit about the business eventually too. I'll ring you tomorrow and we'll have a long talk – think about drawing up some kind of working plan.'

Fleur's head was still reeling as Eleanor joined them. 'My dear, the lunch is perfect,' she said with a smile. 'Everyone is delighted.

402

I'm having a few close friends round to my house this evening for a celebratory drink. I'd like you to come – around eight. It's quite informal. And bring that young man of yours along too, of course.' She smiled. 'All your family will be there, so you'll be in good company.'

'Thank you, Mrs Maitland. I'd like that very much.' Fleur looked at Julia. The significance of Eleanor's phrase 'all your family' had escaped neither of them. Julia smiled.

'It's time you met your other grandparents,' she said. 'I know they're looking forward to getting to know you.'

Julia and Eleanor were just getting into the Mayoral car at the rear of the Town Hall when a raucous shout made them look up. A portly, red-faced figure was weaving its way towards them across the car park.

'Hey there, *Madam Mayor*! I want a word with you.'

Julia recognised Charlie Grant and her heart sank. He was clearly very drunk and obviously spoiling for a fight. 'Eleanor, I think you'd better get into the car quickly,' she said. 'He'll only make a scene.'

But Eleanor stood her ground. 'No,' she said. 'I've an idea what it is he wants to say. Let him get it off his chest.'

With great reluctance Julia waited until Charlie reeled up to them. He stood swaying in front of Eleanor.

'Fine friend you turned out to be, *Councillor*,' he said, his words slightly slurred and his eyes bloodshot. 'You could have told me what I was letting myself in for,' he said accusingly. 'You could've warned me off paying that greedy old cow good money for a crumbling heap of old crap. But *did* you? No, you bloody didn't!' He took a step towards her, standing close enough for her to get the full force of his whisky-laden breath. 'You stood by and let me walk right into it. And all the time . . .' he shook his finger at her ' . . . all the time *you knew* that Victoria Gardens were falling down a sodding great hole in the ground. And I – I was going to lose – lose my shirt!'

To Julia's horror the bleary eyes filled with tears which began to roll down his cheeks and drip on to his crumpled shirt-front. 'We were mates as kids, Lena,' he mumbled. '*Mates*! And you stood by and watched me slide down the pan without lifting a finger!'

Her face compassionate, Eleanor put out a hand to steady him. 'I told you to forget it, Charlie,' she said softly. 'I'm sorry about what's happened but I really did try to warn you. There wasn't any more I could say without breaking a confidence. Look, let us take you home. You're in no fit state to drive.'

But he shook off her hand angrily, almost losing his balance in the effort to regain his bruised dignity. 'Get off me! I might be ruined but I've still got my pride. I'm having no woman drive me home. I'll get a bloody taxi.' He drew himself up, turned and began to make his unsteady way across the car park. The two women looked at each other helplessly.

'Poor Charlie,' Eleanor said, shaking her head. 'Poor old devil.'

Fleur found Tom in the kitchen at Park Row. He was slicing onions for the spaghetti Bolognese he was making for supper. Without a word she went to him and threw her arms around him, hugging him tightly.

'*Hey*!' Taken off-guard, he stood with both his hands sticking out straight. 'I'd like to have warning of this kind of thing, if you don't mind,' he said. 'You never know what a shock like that might do to a fragile person like me. Besides, my hands are all oniony and I can't . . .' She stopped the rest of the sentence with a kiss.

'You'll never *guess*!' she told him excitedly. 'Oh, Tom, it's been the most wonderful day!'

He grinned at her. 'Well, whatever it is, I'm already in favour of it. Look, let me wash my hands, then I can respond properly.'

'Guess who's bought Arden Catering?' she demanded.

'Micky Mouse.'

'Come on, don't be silly.'

'Okay then, Margaret Thatcher? Terry Wogan?'

She grasped his shoulders and looked into his eyes. '*Julia Grant*, that's who! She and Charlotte are going to live in the house. And she wants *me* to run the business for her. Take sole responsibility – at an increased salary!'

'Well, why shouldn't she?' Tom's eyebrows rose. 'She knows when she's on to a good thing if you ask me!'

'Yes, but don't you see? That's just the point,' she told him. 'I never wanted Julia to do me any favours – to give me anything. I'd have hated the idea that she was trying to ease her conscience. This way we'll be helping each other – on an equal footing – a proper business footing. And I really believe she needs me. I wonder if you know what that means to me, Tom?' She hugged him again. 'And not only that: I'll be able to pay my share of the mortgage here. Oh, darling, I'm so happy, and so *excited!*'

He looked into her shining eyes and his face softened. 'You really are an independent lady, aren't you?'

She nodded. 'Independence means everything to me. Being my own person is so important after the way I began life.'

404

'I know it does, darling.' He kissed her. 'And I'll always respect that.'

'We have an invitation for tonight,' she told him. 'We are invited to the Mayor's house to have a celebratory drink with her and some friends.' She drew back her head to look at him. 'Do you know what she said to me, Tom? She said, "All your family will be there". Can you imagine that? All my life I've dreamed of what it would be like to be recognised as part of Julia's family. But the funny thing – the *magic* thing – was that quite suddenly when I heard Mrs Maitland say that I realised that it didn't really matter any more.' She hugged him close, her cheek pressed against his. 'And do you know why?'

'No, tell me?'

'Because *you're* the only person that matters to me now, Tom. You're the only family I'll ever want. You and the children we'll have some day, here in this house – our home.' She kissed him. 'Oh, Tom. I love you so much!'

He held her close. Now he knew she'd come home at last. She'd found herself and her own special place in the world. And his heart was filled with gratitude that that special place was with him.